Nyr

Praise for Patricia and
THE WORLD AROUND MIDNIGHT

"Griffith succeeds with grace and humor. . . . Reminiscent of Larry McMurtry and Dan Jenkins, *THE WORLD AROUND MIDNIGHT* gives us a rollicking view of Texas eccentricity."
—*Publishers Weekly*

"*THE WORLD AROUND MIDNIGHT* is a hilarious tale about what women get up to, or down to, with men. . . . Pati Griffith crafts a tale that makes Texans vulnerable, winsome and so dad-gummed folksy that she can hardly stand it. . . . Every page has a fragment any writer would be proud to lop off and claim for his/her own . . . [with] a very real character named Dinah . . . [who] happens to have the kind of brass and sass that makes the rest of us, deep down, wish we had more Texas in us."
—*Boston Sunday Globe*

"Prepare to laugh often, for the wry humor permeating this novel is infectious."
—*Library Journal*

"Patricia Browning Griffith is an accomplished storyteller with a great ear for dialogue and an irrepressible sense of humor. *THE WORLD AROUND MIDNIGHT* is riddled with tongue-in-cheek commentaries and one-liners that are a sheer delight, and the story moves along like brush fire."
—*Los Angeles Times Book Review*

Winner of an ALA Notable Book of the Year Award

"Patricia Browning Griffith has an unusual gift."
—Larry McMurtry, *The Washington Star*

"Fresh and appealing . . . Griffith's sense of place is strong. It's her characterization, though, that really carries the tale. From Dinah's mother, who cries at the drop of a hat; to her friend Cissy Sanders, into whose field of Swiss chard the airplane crashes; to her spunky grandmother Lilly, who falls in love in her 90s, the book is filled with memorable eccentrics who remind us of ourselves."
—*San Antonio Express News*

"Ms. Griffith manages to tell a lively, sometimes touching, often funny story and to provide some down-to-earth wisdom about life and love at the same time."
—*Winston-Salem Journal*

"Dinah struggles for balance with a delightful sense of humor, humanity and human foibles. Midnight is a quirky, sweet-spirited, winsome place that readers will come to care about."
—*ALA Booklist*

"This novel is a deep delight! I'm still hearing Dinah Reynolds, the wise and witty narrator, a woman for whom work and love don't cancel each other out, a woman strong enough to suffer and thrive all at once."
—Joyce Reiser Kornblatt, author of *Nothing to Do with Love*

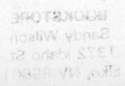

Also by the Author

The Future Is Not What It Used to Be
Tennessee Blue

THE WORLD AROUND MIDNIGHT

Patricia Browning Griffith

WASHINGTON SQUARE PRESS
PUBLISHED BY POCKET BOOKS
New York   London   Toronto   Sydney   Tokyo   Singapore

FOR MY PARENTS
WITH LOVE AND GRATITUDE

A Washington Square Press Publication of
POCKET BOOKS, a division of Simon & Schuster Inc.
1230 Avenue of the Americas, New York, NY 10020

Copyright © 1991 by Patricia Browning Griffith

Published by arrangement with G. P. Putnam's Sons,
a division of the Putnam Publishing Group.

Griffith, Patricia Browning.
   The world around midnight / Patricia Browning Griffith.
      p.   cm.
   ISBN 0-671-75950-7
   I. Title.
[PS3557.R4894W67   1992]
813'.54—dc20   91-37655
                                              CIP

First Washington Square Press trade paperback printing July 1992

10 9 8 7 6 5 4 3 2 1

WASHINGTON SQUARE PRESS and colophon are
registered trademarks of Simon & Schuster Inc.

Cover design by John Gall
Cover art by Pamela Patrick

Printed in the U.S.A.

"Training for the Apocalypse" appears by permission of Gloria Frym

Consider the will to love
as the decision to survive.
That's how the agents of Eros operate.
They sneak into your dreams
just before the world ends.

—GLORIA FRYM
"Training for the Apocalypse"

HALLEY'S comet had been a big disappointment the year before. A few times I might have seen it if I'd gotten up between one and three A.M., driven away from the Dallas lights, and gazed toward Waco. I kept thinking I might do that some night, but the weatherman reported day after day that you couldn't see it for the cloud cover anyway. I read that the only way to see Halley's comet really well was to go to Australia and camp in the outback. Of course I didn't know anyone who cared enough to do that. People around here are more interested in the flying saucers they think the government is trying to hide from us. For years literally thousands of people have gone to Marfa and seen strange objects regularly zooming across the horizon at incredible speeds.

What happened in Midnight, Texas, the year after Halley's comet was a plane crash with repercussions that have turned a lot of people's lives inside out. A slick little twin-engine Cessna 340 crashed right in the middle of what had been Claude Sanders's calf lot—back when he had calves, before the bottom fell out of the cattle market, as it has out of everything else in Texas, and he started raising Swiss chard and other designer vegetables. Cissy Sanders, drinking a Diet Pepsi and watching the news during her cocktail hour in her three-bedroom Williamsburg-style mobile home, said she heard the plane's engine chugging and gasping right overhead so close it shook her Texas Sesquicentennial Memorial Plate right off the wall. Cissy rushed to the window just in time to see the plane trim the tops off two of the tallest live oaks in the county and then slide into the Swiss chard and an instant later explode. Immediately Cissy phoned the sheriff, Lemuel Malone, commonly referred to as Easy, and then, since she, like everyone else in this day and age, is always looking for fame or at least publicity, she phoned me at the *Midnight Citizen*. Since this fit our possible news profile, I grabbed Daddy's old Rolleiflex and headed north.

It took me less than ten minutes to reach the scene, where a big black cloud of smoke was rising over the woods. Already the highway was clogged with two-thirds of the approximately three thousand inhabitants of Midnight, along with the ambulance from the Dunn Brothers' Funeral Home. It was around five o'clock on a Monday and people were just starting home from their jobs—most of them in Fort Worth or Dallas or the nearby suburbs that merge raggedly somewhere near the Cowboys' stadium in Irving. So a lot of people, bored or curious or a combination of both, or for whatever other weird reasons people seek out disasters, headed toward the billowing smoke. The last major high-concept event in Midnight was two years earlier, when there was a shoot-out inside the Tidy Washateria during which two Midnight residents shot each other and disabled themselves and three dryers.

By the time I got to the plane crash, a large crowd had already gathered and the volunteer fire truck was spraying the area with an aqueous white foam that looked like the artificial snow Mama used to whip up with Lux soap flakes for our Christmas trees when I was a kid. You can see a million pictures of a plane crash but they're nothing like the real thing. It is first of all an awful violence to the earth, and the burned and mangled remains of the plane are such that you sympathize with those people with perhaps superior imaginations who refuse to fly.

One of the passengers had been thrown clear of the plane. He lay near a woman's white spangled boot bizarrely standing upright just outside the fire, so we knew there had been at least one woman inside. The Dunn Brothers' ambulance had already arrived, and a Dunn brother and coworker were kneeling on either side of the survivor. Soon the Airlife helicopter out of Dallas appeared above us, darkening the sky like a

great, roaring horsefly, and settled on the road in front of
Cissy's house. As soon as it touched down, two paramedics
leaped out and rushed to the survivor, loaded him onto a
stretcher, and in only a few minutes the helicopter swung away
and lifted, leaving us with the beating sound of the rotary
blades and the stench of its fuel.

Meanwhile Easy Malone radioed for the highway patrol and
I walked around taking some pictures, but staying as far from
the heat of the burning plane as I could. It was then that I
noticed the first peculiar thing. There together stood Claude
and Cissy Sanders, who only recently had undergone one of
the most bitter divorces in the history of Dallas and Tarrant
counties. Claude, it seems, had been heading out to check his
Swiss chard, which he still worked part-time along with his
manager's job at the Radio Shack in Arlington. Cissy ran the
Pastel Beauty Studio and Exercise Center in Midnight, but
she was closed on Mondays, though she spent Monday mornings giving senior-citizen sets and perms at the Happy Acres
Nursing Center. But Claude had managed to convey some
concern for Cissy along with his Swiss chard, so by the time
I got there, Cissy, teary-eyed and holding Pattycake, her white
miniature poodle, was leaning against Claude and his Dallas
Hard Rock Cafe T-shirt, and Claude had his arm around Cissy's back, patting her shoulder. This, after only two weeks
earlier she'd marched into the *Midnight Citizen* saying she was
going to kill Claude Sanders with the pearl-handled Saturday-
night special she had in her purple Le Sportsac handbag and
she wanted me to know I'd have a hot story as soon as she
found him. Everyone tries to get his or her name in the paper,
no matter the reason, let me tell you.

The reason I was running this paper—it wasn't my idea—
I'll tell you later. The fact is, it's a weekly, with the slogan
"Midnight, the Town Where Texas Still Is." What we carry
are wedding announcements, obituaries, the Midnight High
School Owls Class AAA football news, sometimes an agricultural news release from the county agent, a few classifieds—
garage sales, good-as-new Cuisinarts, that kind of thing. Also
school board election reports and community news such as
the weekly garden club "Yard of the Week" winner, a weekly

Bible lesson, and who from out of town visited relatives on Sunday. Sometimes as a filler we might use a news-service story or a canned editorial. Around 1970 Daddy ran a canned editorial admitting that the Communists seemed to have taken firm control of the USSR and China. The word *perestroika* has yet to appear.

What we do not carry is the real news of the town—like when the bank went bust, or when the Methodist preacher got kicked out of town for adultery with a minor majorette, or when the insurance company discovered its Midnight agent had for years added to the number of roofs blown off after a tornado when sometimes there hadn't been any roofs blown off, thereby feathering his own brick-with-white-columns nest south of town. The real news we stay away from—or my father stayed away from, because it's his newspaper not mine, and I'm here only because he had prostate surgery and lost his marbles and passed away one Sunday night more or less in the arms of his night nurse in Baylor Hospital. At least, I tell Mama, he was spared deteriorating for years in the Happy Acres Nursing Center down the highway, where, Mama says, before long the majority of Midnight citizens will reside. (Just as, if we don't quit selling Texas real estate to foreigners, before long we'll be sitting here in Japan.) "After all," Mama says, "what sane, mobile person would linger in Midnight with the glittering skyscrapers of Dallas and Fort Worth beckoning like ladders to heaven on either side of us?"

Daddy, editor of the *Citizen* for forty-one years, was a crusader of a certain kind, embattled year after year and never willing, despite enormous obstacles, to admit defeat—defeat being the arrival of a Pizza Hut, McDonald's, Wal-Mart, or any other business franchise within the city limits of Midnight, Texas, population 3,604. "Templates for the mind" he called such businesses, claiming they diminished individual responsibility, squelched creativity, and ultimately led to championing the profit motive ahead of human concerns. Our forefathers, Daddy used to say, did not intend democracy to be overwhelmed by cutthroat capitalism. So he took his stand right there in Midnight, located just south of Dallas–Fort Worth, straddling Tarrant and Dallas counties, the first town outside "the Metroplex"—the term used by the news media in speaking of the combined metropolitan areas of Fort Worth and Dallas. As far as my father was concerned, the whole concept of the Metroplex was inimical to what Texas should be and had been and what Midnight would remain: a bastion of individualism, unsevered by an interstate highway, a town where people greeted even strangers they passed on the street, a town minus a single one-way street, a town without unisex anything, a town that he sometimes seriously considered should perhaps become a walled fortress like those in olden times, to keep out the hordes of newcomers and foreigners, who, he thought, were making Texas as dull and conventional, as vanilla, as, say, Connecticut.

Daddy was an intelligent man. He'd read tomes on World War II, most of Churchill, all of the so-called scholars' edition of the *Encyclopaedia Britannica, National Geographic,* and most of the books published on Texas history. It was simply that he did not adjust to change or accept modernity without a struggle if he felt it detrimental to the "quality of life"—a term he would not have used. He was a man who stopped his car to listen to the sweet mellow call of a bobwhite. He saw the garish, plastic spread of the Metroplex—its gray highways and concrete overpasses ever encroaching upon the landscape he loved—as leading to crime and impersonal human contacts, an invasion like that of the soldiers hidden behind uprooted bushes in *Macbeth.* Had he been a Catholic, he would have insisted on a Latin mass. As it was, he insisted on a flashlight in dim restaurants, despised foul language in movies and print, believed that one should be loyal to one's employer—a concept now nearly extinct—courteous, loving, and faithful to wife and mother. And he knew for certain that hell itself was right up there in abrasive New York City, with its clash of cultures and soul of acquisition—a way of life he saw as presenting to all America and especially Texas a clear and ever-present danger. The occasional excesses of the Texas rich that the eastern press so loved to flout Daddy explained as simply the result of an overflowing of energy and imagination. That he lost his marbles toward the end and fell in love with his night nurse was a cruel irony and one that only supports my theory that life truly is a game of spin the bottle.

On the day that Cissy came in to announce her prospective

Murder 1, I explained to her that I wouldn't report the event because my father, as a gentleman, made a point of not running stories about felonies unless the people involved were out-of-town minorities, so that there was no way even the distant relatives of our readers and advertisers could be involved. I don't know if that did it or not, but Cissy didn't use the pearl-handled Saturday-night special in her purple Le Sportsac on Claude after all, though they talked only over the phone and then through gritted teeth until the plane crash and only then about the travel plans of their eight-year-old daughter, Paisley Blue Sanders, who was on the Little Miss circuit. Then lo and behold, there were Cissy and Claude together, arm in arm, crowd center, around the smoldering plane, the stench of burning fuel violating the mild May evening and the spring fragrance of bridal wreath and climbing tea roses beside Cissy's mobile home and wafting into the windows of the scores of pickups and suburbans pulled up to witness what turned out to be, unfortunately, the end of the line for two travelers and, as I said, the beginning of numerous odd and startling events.

Of course strange and tragic things had been happening in Texas for several years, for instance, the price of oil had dropped to China—ten dollars a barrel, when it cost fifteen to pump it out of the ground. The whole population of Texas wore a sort of walkabout shell shock. Every other conversation was about hard times and the possibility of moving our economy into high technology or the wonders of agricultural genetics. The hard times changed lives everywhere. Ballerinas in tutus collected money in buckets from motorists along Turtle Creek Boulevard in Dallas. *Texas Monthly* reported that rich people in Houston were cutting back and no longer sending flowers when a friend's cat died. Unemployment was so high, whole teams of construction workers headed for the East Coast, where buildings were still rising. Competition among women selling beauty products to their friends and neighbors became so heated there were rumors of a pink-Cadillac shootout near Waxahachie. Millionaires of mythic proportion, men whose wealth had seemed as stalwart as Johnsongrass—even the most famous and handsome of former Texas governors—

were suddenly declaring bankruptcy. Rumors circulated about the ghosts of tycoons past haunting the corridors of new but empty skyscrapers in Dallas and Houston.

But it was more than a downswing in the economy, it was the death throes of a whole philosophy of life, because Texans grew up being told and believing that if you only had forty acres and a mule and believed in yourself and Jesus, *you too* could get rich. All you needed was determination and a willingness to work, maybe a self-help book or a Christian tape that told you how to get ahead with the Lord's help. And the quickest route to get ahead, we all knew, was to strike oil on those forty acres there beneath that mule. The possibility hung before us like a carrot and then quick as a flash it all changed, and it was an immense blow. From El Paso to Texarkana people felt they needed a shrink, a session on the couch, and they weren't just talking sex, though they talked that, too. Some University of Texas at Arlington Ph.D. candidate in sociology was conducting a survey on how the depressed economy was affecting people's sex lives. It seemed to be a cruel and horrible joke, as if Jesus himself had returned and said something like, "Sorry, partner, I was only kidding. What it all comes down to in the end is a few jalapeño peppers and a sandy land grave."

It was like the end of the world, Mama kept saying, when, according to her, the Bible predicts lots of strange things: wars and rumors of wars, earthquakes, the change in temperature patterns, and the return of the Jews to Jerusalem. Since such events seemed to be happening already, it made me nervous whenever she mentioned it.

But what began happening the day of the plane crash, or seemed to begin happening that Monday in May, was that people began to change partners as if we were all square dancing to a fiddle and the caller had sung, "Promenade left and do-si-do, change your partner and away you go. . . ."

I got home to Mama's a little late the evening of the plane crash, and there was my husband, Dude, waiting uneasily inside the doorway as if we were dating again. I said, "Dude, my Lord, honey, what brings you from Dallas on a Monday night?" I had no idea then that I didn't want to know what brought him over on a Monday night. "Let's have a drink," I said. "Where's Mama?"

"In the kitchen," he said, kind of funny. And I turned around and looked at him because I knew something bad had happened. But I thought maybe one of my cats had been run over by a careless neighbor. Something like that. "Nothing's wrong with Larry?" I asked, referring to our son, as I leaned up to give him a kiss.

Dude and I had been married twenty-two years. He was at that time an editor with a serious Dallas newspaper, the one always struggling to get ahead of the competition. When I gave him that kiss, I caught the faint, familiar aroma of Old Spice, and just for a moment, holding onto his firm arm, I felt stabilized in an uncertain world. Finally I said, "Well, sit down, honey," and I went into the kitchen and poured myself a glass of rosé, now called "blush" inside the Metroplex, and got Dude an ice-cold Pearl, which he prefers to drink from the can. Mama was on the deck absentmindedly picking the dry blossoms off her geraniums and not turning toward me, when I knew she could hear me. I said, "Hi, Mama. How're you, honey?"

She said fine, but from her voice I could tell her face was all pulled tight toward the middle like a string purse, the way it does when she's about to cry. (She cries a lot—watching Miss America contests, *Little House on the Prairie* reruns. She's been known to cry in musical comedies. Many fundamentalists are overemotional and it gets worse as they get older. By the time they get to Happy Acres, it's sometimes a steady drip.)

I took a deep breath and walked back to Dude. He was sitting on Daddy's big green Naugahyde recliner. I think recliners are repulsive, but men seem to love them, and I suppose, now that I think of it, they are rather male objects. I handed Dude the beer, sat on the foot of the chair, slipped my sandals off, and leaned on Dude's long lanky legs, touching my wineglass to his beer in a toast.

Dude and I live in North Dallas, and I myself wasn't supposed to be in Midnight at all. I was on leave from my very decent, sane, steady, and moderately lucrative job as an editor with a Dallas-based publisher that specializes in photo books of cowboys and memoirs of old settlers—Texana. (Texans will buy Texas because they're interested in their heritage.) I came back to Midnight to help out, as I said, after Daddy had to have an operation. We don't know exactly what happened, but he seemed to just go kind of crazy. The first inkling we had was when Mama went in to see him on a Sunday right after church and he told her he wanted to marry his night nurse. When I got there Mama was crying in the hall. I said, "Well, Mama, did you remind him he was already married?" She said no, she was embarrassed. She didn't want to be married to someone who wanted to marry his night nurse. She'd just give him a divorce. I said, "Mama, you don't just accept something like that! You fight back. Besides, he's out of his mind, he doesn't know what he's saying!" So we went in together and I introduced him to Mama as his wife, and Daddy told me he wanted to marry the night nurse, whose name was Audrey. I guess he'd had a stroke, because he wasn't talking right and his face had sunk down on one side. We called the doctor, very concerned, but it was Sunday and the doctor was off skiing somewhere in Colorado for the weekend. That night, with Mama asleep in the chair beside him, and Audrey, the night nurse, lurking nearby, Daddy died. And it was hard on Mama, his dying like that, not even remembering they were married.

Afterward I went home, and Mother ran the *Midnight Citizen* for a couple of months. But when Lilly, my grandmother and her mother, fell and broke her hip and had to go into Happy Acres and Mama came down with the shingles from all the stress, she had to quit the *Citizen* for a while. So, crying, she phoned me in Dallas and said would I come over and take care of the *Citizen* just till she could sell it. We couldn't close it, since she needed the income. For all Daddy's smarts, he wasn't what the late megabucks H. L. Hunt called a moneymaker. And we knew, too, that the whole town would dry up and blow away if that old Linotype machine and flatbed press didn't weight it down and the *Citizen* didn't remind them each Friday that they were living remnants of what Daddy considered a noble past. Besides, we had been promising Daddy for years that, whatever happened, the *Citizen* would live on to continue his crusade. But people were hocking their barbecue grills about then and nobody wanted to buy some old weekly newspaper that still set type. It was like walking into history itself, entering that old one-story office with photographs of assorted Texas disasters tacked all over the walls, with its dim overhead lighting, ineffective air-conditioning, and the walls aged a brownish ocher. Jud, Daddy's only full-time employee, who'd had a degenerative disease for the past ten years, was probably the last Linotype operator in the Western world.

So, regrettably, I took a few weeks' leave of absence and came to stay with Mama and take over the newspaper for a short while. But it had been more than a month of seeing Dude on occasional weekends when Mama was feeling well enough to stay alone, and worrying about whether or not my plants were being watered properly and my cats—Jerry Jeff and Bobby McGee—fed promptly at six o'clock, when one always climbs on the window ledge and the other hangs as if crucified from the back screen door.

Me, I'm a city person. I like tall buildings and strangers and their unexpected possibilities—at least I thought that then. I like speeding along the Woodall Rogers Freeway in traffic and passing so close to the glowing spires of the downtown that I feel I might brush the LTV Center with my shoulder. I like not having to smile at every person I pass, or speak to neighbors when I feel grouchy. Believe me, I lived in Midnight for nearly twenty suffocating years and I couldn't shake its dust from my feet fast enough. In fact, if my parents hadn't been there, I would never have darkened a one of its narrow doors.

So I was glad to see Dude, and he looked wonderful. He is a good man, Dude Reynolds, tall and straight, tough as a tree, a quiet man who hasn't gotten a beer gut like every man over thirty in Midnight. You line up any ten men in Midnight for a photo and it's like a belly tournament. But Dude looks better now than when we married, I think. His hair has a touch of gray, which gives him a dignified, seasoned look, I tell him. He's tan from playing tennis and his green eyes are warm and look at me with a kind of sweet humor as if he's forever expecting to enjoy our being together.

18

For a few minutes we talked about Larry, our twenty-year-old son, whom, unfortunately, the rest of Midnight calls "Little Dude," and his bride, Traci Dawn Love. They had just moved from an efficiency to what Traci called a "starter" apartment that they couldn't afford. Dude said he'd tried to explain to Traci over the phone that the term "starter" denoted ownership but he wasn't sure he'd gotten through to her. Dude also reported that Jerry Jeff, my gray tiger cat, had a swollen paw, and we had to laugh at that, since Jerry Jeff is so spoiled he always gets some ailment when I'm away. Dude said he'd take him to the vet that week if the paw didn't recover.

Then I watched Dude take a deep breath, and I saw the tips of his fingers strain against the forest-green Naugahyde until they were a bloodless white. I leaned on his knees and looked at him, waiting. He took a drink of beer, a couple of drinks of beer, and looked at me, and I said, "Yes-s-s-s—?" acting silly. But he stayed serious and then he took my hand.

"Dinah," he said, "I have to tell you . . ." and he looked right into my eyes the way an honorable man would tell you he'd just lopped off your outer extremities, and said, "only I don't know how to. Something's happened to change everything. I've met someone. . . ."

I pulled my hand away and grabbed for the arm of the chair, spilling rosé on the Naugahyde. I think I nearly fainted, and I've never in my life fainted, even when I pierced my own ears and my knees got so weak I had to sit on the floor. For a moment he looked alarmed. I pulled myself back from leaning against his knees, feeling silly to be leaning on a man's knees when he was telling me that he, the father of my only child, is about to erase me from the blackboard of our mutual lives after twenty-two semi-happy years.

I stood and walked around the room a minute. It was the living room I'd grown up with. Old couch of a style Mama called "Early Matrimony," matching easy chair, both of them slipcovered over and over, now in a small apricot print which hid their carved wooden feet. Daddy's chair pointed toward the twenty-five-inch console TV. Cheap reproductions of Rembrandt paintings with frames more expensive than the prints hung on the walls, and photographs of me and Dude and Larry sat on the lamp tables alongside pot plants of devil's ivy and fern on the round mahogany table in front of the draped picture window. Dude started telling me the details, sitting there in Daddy's chair, which seemed to give him an authority I resented. I didn't want the central events of my life to happen in this room. It wasn't mine and it didn't look the way I wanted to live. I couldn't hear what he was saying for all my rushing thoughts.

I looked at the framed photos and thought of Mama cutting Dude's face out of all the family photographs as my friend Marianne's mother had done after Marianne's divorce. There was page after page of the decapitated ex in the family album, even marriage photos with Marianne standing there in her wedding dress beside a headless man in a tuxedo.

I told Dude to hang on a minute, and I went into the kitchen and called Mama to come in, she didn't have to sit out there by herself and cry. I asked Dude if Mama already knew and he said of course not. But Mama was forever anticipating a catastrophe, so maybe she'd guessed.

"There's a casserole beside the microwave when you all are ready to eat," she called, her voice shaky at the end. I called, "Thank you, Mama," and we listened to her feet slowly pad down the hall to her bedroom, where we knew she would turn on the old black-and-white TV or study her Sunday-school lesson.

"She's always saying she's psychic," I said. "But she could be crying about the plane crash or her shingles. Who knows?"

Then I tried to listen to Dude's explanation, as if anything could make sense to me that moment. I heard the name "Marilyn." He sat there talking and shaking his beer can, glancing toward me occasionally, and told me he'd met her several months before, when her car broke down on the North Dallas toll road. He'd stopped to help. (I said he was a gentleman.) It had been a bad, rainy night.

"It's been dry lately," I inserted, and he paused a minute, waiting for me to continue and maybe make sense out of that statement. When I said nothing more, he went on the way people do when they've rehearsed a speech and don't want to be interrupted until they've reached the appointed ending. He said he'd given her a lift to an Exxon station and then driven her home, after which she'd asked him if he'd please drive the baby-sitter home. She'd asked him please to come back for a cup of coffee, after all he'd done to help her it was the least she could do. It had seemed rude to say no, so he went back and drank coffee and a week later she was broken down again on the toll road.

I said, "Come on, Dude!" I know design when I hear it. I could smell an entire campaign behind my back while I'd sat innocently, not to mention ignorantly, by.

"Cars do break down twice when something's wrong, Dinah."

I hated the sense of that notion as well as the looniness of random happenstance that can change lives in an instant. I drank my wine and watched him and asked a few questions. He pointed out in his defense that some people wait for opportunities like broken-down cars. I took that as his charging me with dreams and instability of passion, which was true. While he, he claimed, hadn't been looking or waiting for anyone. It was a random event like a tornado, an act of God.

Eventually I stood and began moving to the kitchen, my legs heavy as if I were wading in high floodwater. I managed to slide Mama's salmon casserole into the microwave, spread placemats on Mama's yellow dinette table, anchoring them with stainless on paper napkins, and pull out the jalapeño sauce and catsup Dude had the awful habit of using sometimes to disguise his food. "You want another beer or tea?" I asked him, acting on domestic automatic pilot.

"Tea," he answered.

I poured us two teas over ice and we sat down at the kitchen table. With trembling hands, I dished the salmon casserole beside the lettuce-with-tomato salad and passed him the Paul Newman salad dressing, though it didn't even cheer me up as it usually does when I think of putting Paul Newman on my grocery list. At that moment all the fun was gone out of everything.

"Is this serious? . . . Permanent? Forever?"

He didn't answer me, of course. He started with some circuitous lecture like one he might give Larry about rushing into hasty decisions and "regretting" and "planning" and "being careful," with all those constipating words that can quickly set about a person like concrete.

"Can't you just say yes or no?"

He couldn't because he'd studied philosophy in college. So he was never blunt, whereas I could sum up most of the world in a yes-or-no answer. He, however, always circled around a subject in thorough explanation, when usually I wanted one simple word I could bite into and chew.

Meanwhile, my taste buds had died. I couldn't taste a thing, so I finally stabbed my fork into my salmon casserole and left it protruding like a weapon.

"Maybe I'll lose weight," I said to myself, noting there was certainly nothing wrong with his appetite, though to be fair, Mama is a wonderful cook even if everything turns out a little sweet.

He was halfway through the casserole and two-thirds through his lettuce and tomato when I upended the jalapeño jar onto his plate. The little green slices heaped up like a bush while the fiery juice seeped into the casserole. Dude watched it a moment as if he were contemplating a rescue operation, then looked up at me and reached for his iced tea. We stared at one another for a whole minute over the damaged salmon.

"I could kill you for this," I said. Finally he shoved his chair back noisily and stood up.

In silence, we loaded the dishes into Mama's dishwasher. He rinsed while I stacked, because only I knew the particular way Mama has to have the dishes arranged—plates facing, like armies. Then I waded back into the living room, where we turned on the late TV news.

For many years I'd charged that Dude, as a newsman, would turn on the late news even if I were ten feet away being blown out the window by a tornado. And I suppose this proved my point. But it was on the late news that we found out the startling facts about the plane crash. The slick little Cessna had carried a religious pop singer, who was on his way from New Orleans to a performance in Dallas. When we found out who the singer was, we were stunned: it was our very own Calvin Troope.

Calvin Troope was the only celebrity ever born in Midnight. His folks had lived right down our street in a Sears bungalow. His cousin Bobby Joe had been my first love. Before Calvin became a semi-famous religious pop singer, he was already famous with us for being rumored to be the biggest baby ever born in Midnight. Watching the news, my hands gripping the chair as if it might rise and buck around the room, did manage to reconnect me to the world.

"I don't know how you can do this to me," I said to Dude during a commercial. I could see myself, one of those lonely middle-aged women who doesn't hold her stomach in or shave her legs, whose sexual experience is limited to reading *Cosmopolitan* and answering blind "in search of" ads in the back of local tabloids.

"I don't want to do this to you," he said, and his voice took on a note of wonder. "It just happened, Dinah. Like the plane crash."

"I don't believe that," I said, but that was a mistake because then he had to convince me. He turned back to the TV and squinted slightly in the way that made me tell him occasionally he should have his eyes checked.

"I didn't want it to happen, but now that it has I feel like I've been asleep for a long time and just woke up."

"Like Sleeping Beauty," I said, heading straight for the bitch track on which I was to settle for some time.

When the news was over, he stood to leave. I didn't know whether to sit and just let him leave or accompany him to the door or try to find a baseball bat and hit him on the head. Suddenly I realized that from then on, my every move would be debatable. Gone were the easy, familiar, unthinking paths I skipped along mindlessly in my summer sandals when my most pressing problem might be whether or not to paint my toenails, since nail polish irritated the one toe with the athlete's foot that I'd picked up from my athletic husband. He paused, looking back at me with concern, as if I were someone he'd just run over and he was waiting to see if there was still a spark of life in the body.

23

I rose woodenly and walked him to the front door like the obedient daughter of the Southwest that I am, who's been taught that courtesy and a smile get you halfway to heaven. At the door, he turned the knob but hesitated.

"I'm sorry, Dinah."

"I'm sorry, too," I said. It was maybe his last hesitation. And when I think back, it seems like the last moment we were married.

That night I lay in bed and cried. I cried and couldn't stop crying. After a while I began to wonder if there was a case in the annals of modern medicine of a person who'd never stopped crying. If not, I might be the first. I thought of the Indian woman who's supposed to have died of her sighs. I remembered that old country song about tears in my ears from lying on my back and crying over you. I'd always thought that was funny, but it wasn't anymore. It was obviously written by someone who'd felt like I did then.

I never did stop crying but I finally went to sleep. When I woke the next morning I lay conscious for maybe two seconds before it struck me with what seemed like the impact of the plane crash that Dude was in love with someone named Marilyn. I thought of how at home I'd sometimes stay in bed while he was shaving. He'd be standing just inside the adjoining bathroom with a towel wrapped around his waist just above his appendix scar and we'd talk as he shaved.

I had asked him the night before what she looked like. He'd said she was blondish. Medium height. Nice-looking.

"Bottle blonde?" I'd asked. He said he didn't know, which only proved he was in love.

"Is she thin?" Such a crucial question.

"So-so," he'd answered.

"I knew it," I'd said. "You *would* fall for a thin blonde." I'm about as black-haired as you can get and not be Asian, and no one but an obese liar would call me thin. "What does she do?"

He'd said she was a marketing director for a telecommunications firm. That fact I had to ponder. All I knew about telecommunications was that Cliff Robertson did AT&T commercials.

"I thought you were supposed to fall for someone who looked a lot like me." Second wives, I'd reminded him, usually resemble first wives, according to folklore, *Ladies' Home Journal,* and other such meaty resource materials. "Don't you remember that Mama had a cousin married to a man who still carried his first wife's picture in his wallet because she looked just like his second wife?" Somehow Dude had forgotten that tale.

"How old is she?" These details seemed excruciatingly important. Thirty-three, he'd said. That meant she was more than ten years younger than I was. Another generation. That was a complicated thing to consider. She'd know different songs, dress differently, probably wear pin-striped suits with female ties. Being in telecommunications, she probably read *The Wall Street Journal* and *Business Week.* She doubtless had a quick, tantalizing mind and watched only public broadcasting. She probably had capped teeth and fresh opinions, while Dude and I agreed about most things and sometimes sat for lengthy periods at a time without speaking. Doubtless, being in telecommunications, she'd always have something pithy to say about everything. She also had an eight-year-old daughter. Finally Dude would have a daughter. At eight o'clock in the morning I was taking it for granted the whole thing was a fait accompli.

"Does she have a good sense of humor?" I'd asked him.

"Okay," he'd said. I couldn't imagine Dude with someone with only an okay sense of humor. He was probably just trying to make me feel better. She was probably another Bette Midler, only thin, blonde, and gentile.

Suddenly the aroma of Mama's instant coffee made its way to me and I could hear her scraping her toast. I felt like pulling the sheet up over my head the way I used to as a kid when I didn't want to go to school. Well, I thought to myself, it's going to be a lot harder getting out of bed for the next forty years.

In the kitchen, Mama kindly said little, only sniffed as she drank her instant coffee and ate her scraped toast while flipping between TV channels to catch news about the plane crash.

"This would have been a big story for your daddy," she said once.

Of course Midnight was crackling with the news about Calvin Troope and what turned out to be his fiancée. Officials from the Federal Aviation Administration and other assorted agents of authority and bureaucracy had arrived to investigate the crash and had strung yellow plastic tape around the site to keep people away. That meant the curious had to make a second trip to see the area cordoned off by the official yellow tape. All morning, vans from the far corners of the Metroplex were arriving to view the scene, since it was now not just the site of a plane crash but the site of a celebrity crash.

At the *Citizen,* I was brewing some espresso coffee in Daddy's old coffeepot when Claude Sanders dropped by to inform me of the latest plane crash activity and to let me know that in case I was thinking of interviewing him, he was saving his story to sell to *Life* or *People* to make up for losing his Swiss chard crop.

"What story are you talking about, Claude? How you and Cissy buried the hatchet?" He was insulted by that and glared at me as if he thought my nose for news was too poor to understand the significance of his role in this media event. Claude was blond, short, and stocky, had been an all-state running back for the Midnight High School Owls and later played for the Texas Tech Red Raiders, but was, unfortunately, not running for anything anymore, so his stockiness had gone to paunch and jowl, giving him a feisty bulldog look. He wore his blond hair in a crew cut, which meant you could look right through to his pinkish scalp when he wasn't wearing his red Midnight Owls shitkicker cap. Claude reported that Paisley Blue had skipped school and donned her Little Miss Heart-o'-Texas Rodeo outfit and was selling Coke Classics and Dr Peppers outside their mobile home and twirling her baton and hoping to sign autographs. Paisley Blue lived for the day when someone would ask for her autograph, Claude said. I thought to myself that Paisley Blue would probably have to make an "X" but I didn't say it.

A phone call from Dorothy Little of the Midnight Cafe informed me that stringers for the national media had been arriving in town since the day before and stopping by the café for coffee and directions to the crash site. Dorothy had selflessly been up all night cooking, making extra lemon cream pies and carrot cakes for the influx of strangers. This she reported to me as if her cooking had been Good Samaritanism, rather than what it seemed to me: simply a case of rampant capitalism.

Dorothy admitted it might turn out to be the biggest bonanza for her since that singing fool George Jones had failed to show at the Star Theatre during Octoberfest the year before. The Star Theatre, Midnight's old failed movie house, was opened up a couple of times a year for special events. It was the kind of theater only young people could patronize because the floors were so sticky from decades of cherry Cokes and Sugar Daddys that it was like a Jane Fonda workout getting to a seat and back.

Once Claude had exited and I'd poured myself a cup of espresso which nevertheless smelled like burned linoleum in Daddy's aged percolator, I went in the back to hide in Daddy's office, which overlooks the Piggly Wiggly parking lot. Every woman and divorced man in Midnight shops at the Piggly Wiggly at least once a week, and approximately half of them stop off at the *Citizen* to tell me their news or ask a question or just visit. They didn't do that to Daddy, but they think that since I'm a female my time is theirs. If I'm up front they come in the front door and talk, and if I'm in the office they come in the back door. But that morning I pulled the shade down, making the office a dusty cell, and stirring up my hay fever, but people like Claude kept catching me when I went to the front, needing coffee as I did. On my second cup Nadine Love caught me and said that she'd known ahead of time that something incredible was going to happen the day before because her right temple had throbbed in the certain way it did prior to a major occurrence.

"You might want to put that in your story," she said. The truth was that Nadine, who worked at the post office and was mother-in-law to my only son, did have special powers. I had

Patricia Browning Griffith

seen them work myself. She removed warts. I, fortunately, never had warts, but Daddy had warts on his hands and I'd watched him go to the post office to see Nadine. Right there in the window she would take a needle and touch it to each wart. Then she'd bury the needle in some secret place and within ten days Daddy's warts would be gone. That's true, I saw it with my own eyes when I was about ten or eleven. Other than that power, Nadine is a rather scrawny, chicken-necked woman with banana-colored skin and overpermed dishwater hair that looks like a scouring pad. She is also a Holy Roller, or charismatic fundamentalist they're called now. I hadn't known until that morning that Nadine could also predict disasters. Oh, yes, she said, she was good at predicting disasters.

"You, for instance," she said, and her small gray eyes, floating on a waxed sea of aquamarine, fixed on my left shoulder. "You are going to have some disturbing news."

I could feel my heart thump. Could Nadine have foreseen the North Dallas toll road breakdown and intervention that was altering my world?

"You are going to have a great change in your life which will make you very sad and then very happy." I managed a half-laugh and she said, "I can also predict fires. Have all my life. There's going to be a big fire around here soon." Then she pulled her eyes away from my shoulder, turned, and walked away in her strange springy, thick-ankle stride that is exactly like Traci Dawn's. I wondered then if her prediction meant I would be forced to torch the *Citizen* to free myself, an act which I was certain Mama would take to be a fairly drastic step.

Around ten-thirty Cissy Sanders appeared, late to open the Pastel Beauty Studio but not too late to give me the up-to-the-minute on the crash site. She said it was just crazy out at her place there was so much going on, and she just couldn't get over a famous person crashing into Claude's Swiss chard.

Cissy has tiny features like a movie star's, and flawless ivory skin, and always wears purple and smells of White Linen cologne because she thinks that both she and Paisley Blue should have certain trademarks. That day she was wearing a purple Indian-print dress with a matching scarf wound around her red hair. I had known Cissy all her life, but she was about five years younger and we hadn't been exactly close growing up. Still, I'd gotten to know her pretty well in the past month, since the Pastel Beauty Studio and Exercise Center was just across the street from the *Midnight Citizen*. Whenever I went out the front door of the paper I had a good view of the Pastel, its windows decorated at that moment with a seasonal display of purple netting with artificial daisies strewn around a pair of sunglasses and an *Interview* magazine opened to show photographs of the latest hairstyles, none of which Cissy ever performed on the heads of her customers. Inside the shop, in addition to the usual, there were two Exercycles below two hair dryers so that customers had the option of working out while their hair dried. Cissy Sanders believed in innovation, and she was a truly talented intelligence source. A steady stream of comment and information bubbled from her purple-painted lips. No Ph.D. could have made a more in-depth study of the living habits of the citizens of Midnight, including both romance and birth control methods. She was the first to warn women about the dangers of the IUD and the first to know when the banker's daughter had switched to vegetarianism and herbal birth control, and the first to patronize Hypermart USA, the giant shopping establishment in Garland that offers forty-eight checkout counters and clerks on roller skates.

"Congratulations on you and Claude making up," I told her. "Now aren't you glad you didn't employ your pearl-handled Saturday-night special?"

Cissy laughed and her ivory face blushed, giving her an eighteen-year-old's first-love glow. I didn't know the reasons for their divorce, and I respected her for having kept the specifics to herself, which was downright rare for Midnight.

"I guess that's about the biggest miracle I ever heard tell of," Cissy said. She leaned on the old wooden counter that separated the customers from the working area of the newspaper, and yawned. She said there was so much coming and going at their place in the night they could hardly sleep. Poor little Paisley Blue had circles under her eyes that morning and she wouldn't even take time to soak them with tea bags, like Jane Fonda recommended, before she was out twirling.

Cissy and Paisley were getting ready to hit the Little Miss

circuit as soon as school was out. "Lord, that business is a full-time job in itself," she said. "I'm away from the Pastel too much as it is, and with summer coming on . . ." She began counting on her fingers: "The Mineola Watermelon Festival, the Athens Black-eyed Pea Jamboree, the Luling Watermelon Thump, Laredo Frontier Days and Rattlesnake Roundup . . ."

"Well, Cissy, why don't you just stay home and curl hair, then?"

She looked at me with her beautiful violet eyes—possibly the only violet eyes in the world besides Elizabeth Taylor's (though who knows for certain about Elizabeth Taylor's, since sometimes, Cissy says, they photograph as simply blue).

"Dinah, I can't do that. It just about breaks Paisley's heart to miss one of those competitions. But I am in a dilemma," she said.

"You want some coffee?" I asked her.

"Is it decaf?"

I told her no. She said thanks anyway, but caffeine gave her lumps in her bosoms.

"You know, I'm not telling anyone else, but I'm saving for Paisley Blue's surgery."

I brought my coffee mug over to Cissy so she could lower her voice. "What surgery? What's wrong with Paisley Blue?" I asked.

"Well." Cissy sighed. "You haven't noticed?" I said no indeed.

Actually I had noticed that Paisley, like her father, tended toward a spare tire around the middle. I asked if maybe she was going to have her swallow one of those diet balloons, which were then blown up in the stomach to suppress the appetite. Cissy threw back her red hair laughing, revealing a flash of gold at the rear of her mouth, the only physical flaw she seemed to have.

"Dinah, haven't you noticed that one of Paisley's eyelids droops a little?"

I said, "Now that you mention it, but I always thought that was one of her charms."

Cissy said, "Dinah, if you are really serious about going all the way with this beauty pageantry, Paisley Blue has to be perfect." I sipped my coffee and fanned my face with my hand. The air conditioner at the *Citizen*, an antique that labors like a threshing machine in a back window, is completely undone by one cup of coffee. I said that I didn't think anyone was perfect.

"Nevertheless you have to try for it," Cissy said. She added that she'd read where the photographer who scouts for *Playboy* Playmates said he'd never really seen a "ten." She was hoping, she said, that Paisley would be the first "ten" he ever saw.

I said, "Surely you wouldn't want Paisley to exploit her body for *Playboy*?"

Cissy turned away thoughtfully. "I don't know, Dinah," she said. "I think it would be up to Paisley. But I don't think she should be ashamed of a beautiful body, if she has a beautiful body. Of course we don't know yet," she added. I started to say that wasn't the point, but I didn't really want to get into philosophy and *Playboy,* so I just let it go. That was one of the frustrations of being in Midnight, a lot of times I wanted to argue about things but I'd think I would be gone soon so I might as well not stir up a hornet's nest even temporarily. I knew from past experience that Midnight was like one square mile of spilled tar, and setting your foot down in one controversy would eventually lead to being as immobilized as Brer Rabbit.

Cissy said she was also saving for Paisley Blue's orthodontics. "Lord knows what her teeth are gonna do. I pray for the Lord to make her teeth straight. You wouldn't think that'd be too much to ask."

"Well," I answered her, "the Lord must be especially busy now. Think of the Baptists praying for help with the economy."

I knew what Cissy was leading up to. She wanted me to become so interested in Paisley Blue's beauty career that I'd make the *Citizen* a sponsor of one of her upcoming competitions. But she was being careful not to carry it too far. So she ran the strap of her purple Le Sportsac onto her shoulder and headed for the ancient exterior door of the *Citizen,* which wore a Midnight Real Estate calendar turned to September 1962 under a scene of the Grand Canyon. That scene, Daddy used to say, kept the world in perspective.

"Cissy," I called. "You still toting that pistol?" She swung me a radiant smile. "No, ma'am!" she said with real feeling. That smile made my heart ache. I knew what it meant—a lot of companionable days and nights and happy mornings climbing out of bed. Cissy kind of fluttered through the door then, tossing her red hair and smiling back at me like some exotic red-and-purple bird.

I turned back to the *Citizen,* where I had to begin laying out the week's issue. The place seemed drearier than ever. Jud, a skinny, thick-wristed old man who always wore khakis and smelled like a wet dog, was already at the Linotype setting in agate type a public notice that we had to run that week. When he sat facing the wall and working the Linotype, he seemed to be in a dark cave with just the small light over his copy and his long arms moving around, like some great gray spider spinning a clanging web. I looked around, thinking how desperately I needed to get the place sold. Had I been able to talk Daddy into modernizing, maybe Mama could have sold the business months before and this never would have happened to me and Dude.

Years earlier, there for a visit, I'd walked through the door of the *Citizen* and realized it was like stepping back a century.

I'd whispered, "Daddy, the new word is 'computers'! Have you ever considered a computer? A Compugraphic typesetter?" He gave me a hug and said, "Dinah, I would no more do that than I'd shoot Jud. Why," he said, "if I worked for a Dallas paper I'd have to regroup. I'd have to be looking over my shoulder all the time." Over his shoulder that minute was the old Linotype and aged Jud, his face like a waxed-over rotten apple that seemed to have caved in, whacking away at it. "Here I am my own emperor," Daddy said. "I don't have to go modern if I don't want to. Why should I? Me and Jud get along just fine."

So on Daddy's tombstone we put: "Emperor of the *Midnight Citizen.* Devoted husband and father. May he rest in Peace." We didn't speak of the night nurse, Mama and I, and I never told Dude. I don't know why. Maybe because he'd think Daddy was like me, basically emotionally undependable. And sometimes I thought that might have been nice for Daddy— falling in love as he lay dying. It wouldn't be a bad way to go.

Around noon Claude Sanders returned to ask me who was going to clean up his field and pay for his Swiss chard crop. I told him I had no idea who cleaned up after a plane crash. He should speak to the FAA about it. And talk to his insurance company about the Swiss chard. It seemed to disgust Claude, as it did a lot of people, when I, as the temporary journalist in charge, didn't have the answer to every question.

"Well, I want that airplane, or what's left of it, out of my Swiss chard," he said. And furthermore he was tired of people plowing into his front yard to gawk at the plane crash and ruining his St. Augustine grass. I could see he was riling himself into a semi-tantrum. I asked if he'd decided which magazine to sell his story to and he said he was still negotiating. "And by the way," he said, leaning close enough for me to see the line of sweat on his slightly distended upper lip, "I hope your mother has told that M. Q. Blankety-blank Whatever-it-is Company to go to hell and stay there!"

"What are you talking about?" I said, but he was already heading out the door.

When he'd left and I'd puzzled a minute, I realized I should start writing the plane crash story for the lead in the paper. I knew how Daddy would have handled it. He'd have taken the story from *The Dallas Morning News,* done a little personal tailoring, and let it go at that. But I thought it would take my mind off other problems to write a decent story, and besides, I hadn't done that in years, maybe since college. And the *Morning News* had missed the fact that the singer had been born in Midnight, not to mention that he was the biggest baby ever born there, although his family had moved away when he was a kid. What an oddity—his plane's crashing where he was born.

So I began by phoning Baylor Hospital in Dallas and inquiring about the survivor. A woman at the reception desk put me on hold, and I had a few minutes of an elevator-style

"Raindrops Keep Falling on My Head." Finally a nurse answered to say the pilot had suffered a broken arm and a concussion. His condition was guarded, and his name was Buddy Branch. Since the Cowboys and others of their ilk play football with concussions, I asked if I could speak with him. She paused a minute and said she didn't think so.

"Why not?" I asked.

"He doesn't speak," she said.

"What do you mean, 'He doesn't speak'!"

She said he hadn't said a word. They were trying to contact his family in California.

"You mean to say the plane was being flown by a dumb man?"

She said I'd have to talk to somebody else and hung up the phone. Well, I thought that was all a bit peculiar. But I knew you couldn't trust anybody to tell you the facts over the phone. You have to investigate in person. That's one of the things wrong with the whole nation, Daddy used to say. Newsmen had grown so lazy that for the most part they took news handouts and didn't bother to go after the truth unless it was some bizarre national scandal. My theory is, if they'd dig around more there'd be a lot more bizarre scandals. It was funny that Daddy never seemed to consider his rewriting the *Morning News* stories as anything at all like writing from handouts.

But this was certainly a new angle to the plane crash story that had escaped the Metroplex news. It would be a coup to scoop the big papers, especially Dude's big paper, I thought. It might just relieve some of the volcanic ache that had been building up moment by moment in the general area of my heart.

So I bought a pack of sugarless gum, which I have to do occasionally since I quit smoking, put gas in my car, and headed for Baylor Hospital. On the radio George Strait was singing "All My Ex's Live in Texas," which isn't true, since George Strait has been married only once.

I knew the trip would give me a chance to think about me and Dude more than I wanted to. But I've learned over the years that that's what you do when someone dies or a relationship ends, you have to sift through the experience and catch up before you can move on, much like having to pay your old parking tickets before getting your license renewed. So I started that afternoon with me and Dude, even though I was still having trouble believing that the evening before wasn't just a vivid nightmare that would soon fade away.

As I entered the hospital I thought it would be just my luck to run into Audrey, Daddy's last love. Of course, I did. I was on the elevator with what seemed like a whole troop of Boy Scouts and turned around and found myself crushed shoulder to shoulder with her, only her shoulder was closer to my elbow. But I thought, Well, she owes me one. Maybe I'll get some real news from her. So I reminded her who I was. A pale pink blush spread from her neck to the brown roots of her butterscotch hair. She said she was on days now and looked away, giving me a chance to observe her closely. She had a sweet round face and wore heavy makeup and bright red lipstick. She was thirtyish, petite, very young for Daddy. She had a thick curvaceous body the Boy Scouts seemed to be appreciating, and full lips, everything exactly opposite from Mama, who was built up kind of tall, wide, and flat. I couldn't imagine how this nurse could have gotten so involved with Daddy, but then, other people's romances are always a mystery.

"Your father was such a sweet man," Audrey said in a backwoods twang that sounded like Loretta Lynn. "I'm sorry about that." I wasn't sure if she was being sorry that Daddy had died or sorry that she'd stolen him away from Mama in those last hours or sorry he was so sweet he'd fallen in love with her.

"Tell me about the plane crash victim," I said to her.

She told me that the pilot was remarkably unharmed for a man who'd been in a fatal plane crash. "He was really lucky," she said.

"I heard he doesn't talk."

"They think he's in shock or the trauma has left him temporarily speechless." The elevator opened and two male orderlies wearing hospital-green pajamas said hi to Audrey and pushed an elderly woman on a gurney into the elevator, separating me from Audrey. The Boy Scouts plastered themselves against the walls of the elevator, groaning and carrying on about being overcrowded. One stomped on my foot and didn't say one word of apology. The poor woman lying on the gurney stared up at the faces of the Boy Scouts, who by this time were making gagging noises. I wanted to suggest to her that she close her eyes and pretend to be unconscious, but the elevator stopped and the Boy Scouts exited.

"Does that happen, not talking?" I asked Audrey across the gurney. She was trying to pull herself around the orderlies and the woman to exit on the next floor.

"I don't know," she said. "His vital signs are normal, so it wasn't like . . ." I didn't hear the last through the opening of the elevator door, and then she was gone.

I rode up another floor, then wandered around the antiseptic halls looking for the room number I'd been given downstairs. A NO VISITORS sign was posted, but I cracked the door enough to see a young man lying pale and motionless against the white pillow, his eyes wide open staring at the acoustical tile on the ceiling. There was a strange concentration about him that for a moment made me think he might be dead. Then he blinked slowly and I realized he seemed only stunned, as if someone had just bopped him on the head. He had longish brown wavy hair that was spread out on the pillow around him like Willie Nelson's in *Honeysuckle Rose.* Then an old-fashioned nurse with a stiff uniform and manner spotted me. "Are you family?" she asked.

"Not exactly . . ."

"No visitors," she said officiously.

"Well, look," I began, "I'm from . . ."

"No visitors," she repeated like a recording, as she herded me back toward the elevator. I began to wonder if maybe I should just plagiarize the *Morning News,* too.

"I'm a reporter and I'd like to talk to his doctor," I said to the nurse. She said his doctor was not there. I asked for the doctor's name and when and where he could be reached. She said she had no idea when he could be reached. She presented a typical Metroplex attitude, as Daddy would have said, unhelpful.

When the elevator opened two floors down, I saw Audrey at the nurses' station. I managed to stop the doors from closing on my leg and pushed myself off the elevator to ask her for a favor.

Audrey said, "If you give me your card, I'll phone you when he starts talking."

"My card?" I wondered what kind of nurse would ask me for a card.

"I don't have a card," I told her. But I wrote the *Citizen*'s number on a page of the old steno book I was carrying around in my straw purse while I played reporter.

When I got back to Mama's in the late afternoon, my son Larry's highway patrol car, with its heavy male antenna, a symbol of authority and communicative power designed to intimidate us normal people, was parked in front of the house. Mama was inside with him. She was crying.

"What in the world . . . ?" I asked.

I hugged Larry sitting there on the big-daddy recliner and wondered at how all the men gravitated to the seat of power.

"What's going on?" I asked. They both looked miserable. Larry's handsome blond head hung forward in a way only livestock and the very young allow themselves. Mama held a pink tissue to her nose.

"Traci's . . . missing," Larry muttered.

I dropped onto the couch. Mama sniffed.

"Since . . . yesterday morning," he said.

He looked so miserable I could hardly stand it. That I had predicted she would make his life unbearable didn't make me feel but a tiny bit better.

"You don't know where she is?"

He shook his head slowly, looking down at Mama's practical sculptured beige-on-beige carpeting. I knew he was half scared and half embarrassed.

"Is the baby with her?"

"Nadine has her at the post office."

I imagined the baby strapped into her little yellow plastic chair with the red-checked ruffled lining being lost among dirty bags of mail.

"And Nadine doesn't know where Traci is?"

Larry shook his head. It was always a miracle to me that

I'd had a blond-haired kid. Dude had been towheaded when he was a boy, too, but I hadn't known that when we married. Larry was as tall as Dude but thinner. He'd gotten the best of both of us. Which means that all he got from me was a friendly smile and a love of Dr Peppers. But whenever he appeared I felt a moment of wonder at what we'd produced.

"She dropped Misty Dawn at her mother's. Hasn't been seen since," Mama inserted.

I winced at the name. It was all right for Indians to have names like that. But we weren't Indians.

"She didn't go to work. She just disappeared, vanished," Larry said.

"My Lord! This is the awfulest thing!" Mama said. "They'll probably put her on a milk carton!"

Larry was drinking a Dr Pepper. He held it up and stared at it, shook it, in the same thoughtful way Dude does a beer.

"Well, have you alerted the authorities?"

"I *am* the authorities," Larry said.

"Well, I know that, honey, but have you told other authorities?"

"No," he said.

"No," Mama echoed.

"Maybe you should call Easy."

Larry took another drink of his Dr Pepper and looked at me with green eyes like his father's. Only where Dude's always seemed to be half smiling at me, Larry's always seemed suspicious, unsure of my trustworthiness. I laid that to the fact that we were male and female and there was for some reason a gap of trust that could never be bridged. It would have been nice, I let myself think now and then, to have a daughter, who might trust me.

"I don't know why all these awful things are happening!" Mama said. I wondered again if she somehow knew about me and Dude, and threw her a warning glance, but Larry was too engaged with his own misery to listen to Mama.

"We had a fight." He shook the Dr Pepper again. "I'm not sure she's been kidnapped," he said quietly.

"You mean you think she's run away?"

He stared down at his well-polished boots. He was vain about his boots and his hair, and he was extremely knowledgeable about football and cars. In other words, he was a fairly average young man, who preferred Midnight to Dallas. Midnight was manageable, he said. Predictable . . .

"It would be . . . What if . . . You know, it would be pretty dumb to have the FBI out looking for her and she's . . ."

"Run away?" I finished for him.

He was quiet behind the can of Dr Pepper.

He talked so slowly since he'd married Traci that I was always finishing his sentences, which I hated myself for doing. Traci Dawn talked like an Uzi. My theory was that in speaking so slowly he was desperately and unconsciously searching for some modicum of order in their lives.

"Well, honey, what are you going to do, then?"

"Look for her."

"Where?"

"Where?" Mama repeated.

"Motels. Movies."

"Oh . . ." Mama said, bringing her hands to the chest of her black-and-white-checked blouse as if the thought of his looking for her in motels and movie houses was giving her a heart attack. I hesitated a moment to see if she was indeed going to fall out of her chair.

"Larry, are you saying that you think Traci ran away?"

"Oh, no!" Mama said.

"I'm not saying anything!" he shouted slowly.

"Well, don't get mad at me. I'm just trying to find out what's going on."

He leaned back in the chair and looked up at the ceiling in a hostile manner, as if I personally had put him in the lineup. He'd been such a sweet, sunny little boy. Then in his early teens he'd become sulky and obstinate and unhappy, and the choices he was making in his life were making him only more unhappy.

"But you've been having trouble?" I continued.

Mama sniffed.

Larry didn't answer, and I knew that, as a matter of fact, it was a silly question, since they'd been having trouble from the first instant he'd set eyes on her miniature body. It was simply a matter of degree.

We sat there in silence for a moment, all of us miserable.

The room was cluttered with knickknacks I and everyone else in the family had given Mama for forty years. Artificial-flower arrangements, plastic fruit in a milk-glass bowl, candlesticks with candles that were never lighted. I hated it all, and she probably did, too, but was too kind to throw them away. Occasionally I would try to break something I particularly disliked. I considered suggesting that every time a disaster like this occurred we could break some horrible knickknack, but I wasn't sure that would help anyone but me. It seemed suddenly that our lives had become as cluttered with problems as the room.

I tried to think of some consoling words to make Larry feel better. Had he been a nineteen-year-old girl, I might have said he looked pretty, a familiar but outdated habit of speech that doesn't mean anything beyond the attempt to comfort someone. It was one of those traps you fall into when you're desperate or vulnerable or both. Since he was a twenty-year-old male I told him he looked nice, and without even looking at me, he pulled his lips into a brief smirk. He thought he wanted only the truth, not having lived enough to suffer under it. But I doubted he'd want to hear that while he looked handsome in his uniform I hated it. I'd expected my only son to live a life of briefcases and expense accounts, not guns and handcuffs. Thank God, I often thought, Traci Dawn hadn't suggested the Texas Rangers.

Since I could think of nothing more to say, I went over and perched on the side of his chair and put an arm around his shoulders. He swallowed the last of the Dr Pepper and set the can down on Mama's mahogany table with the doily and lamp. But my embrace didn't seem to ease his pain. He sat there stiff-backed and sad. He'd never been a very warm physical person, with me anyway. With Traci Dawn he seemed to have been driven insane.

"Well, is there anything I can do?" I asked him.

"Stay here for supper, Little Dude," Mama said.

I looked at her. Of all times for her to fall into the "Little Dude" mode!

"Please don't call me that, Grandmother," he said quietly. Mama sniffed. He was always sweet to Mama. He never missed a year sending her a valentine.

"I've gotta pick up the baby." He stood and lifted his wide-brimmed hat from Mama's coffee table.

"Poor thing," Mama said.

I rose and took his arm. His six feet towered over me.

"Well, honey, Traci is young. Maybe she just wanted a day of independence."

"And a night?"

"Maybe," I said, and he sighed and looked away, rejecting the foolish hope he knew I didn't really believe, either. I was being a Pollyanna, like Mama, tossing out unrealistic hopes. Mama announced she had to go by Happy Acres and see how her mother was doing. Mama checked on Lilly every day.

"You haven't seen her in a week," she said to me. "Why don't we all run by there. That would make her so happy. You know how she loves to see all her family together."

I looked at Larry's suffering face and thought that seeing Lilly might cheer him up. He seemed so young and dreary standing there holding his big hat. Maybe a dose of old people with a variety of suffering would make him feel less sorry for himself. Me, too. That's the way I was raised. If your heart is broken, just be glad your feet aren't amputated.

"You're a good kid," I said to Larry, patting his arm.

"I'm not a kid," he said, holding Mama's front door open for us.

"You're right about that." I sighed.

Larry had always loved riding around in cars, and now he rode around for a living. I tried to think of it that way every time I watched him slide his lanky body inside the patrol car with all the grace and authority of the professional driver. The truth is, of course, he and Traci had been far too young to get married. Now he'd never finish college. He'd spend his life riding up and down the highways and looking in motels and movie houses for the skinny little bit of a girl he'd vowed to spend his life with.

"Come on," Mama called to Larry, her voice unsteady. "It won't hurt you to stop by and see your great-grandmother a minute." It's hard to go against Mama when she's crying, so I drove over to Happy Acres with her, and Larry followed in the patrol car.

Lilly had eaten supper and was in the dining room playing

dominoes. She's a big game player and since she's been there she's gotten people who'd been semi-comatose into dominoes, canasta, and forty-two. That's the way she is: she organizes, admits to being bossy, and is always cheerful and alert. Those old people fight to be her roommate because the others complain all the time. Of course, they have reason to complain— most of them feel bad or hurt and are just propped there waiting to die.

The worst part of going to Happy Acres is the scene as we enter. We walk through the heavy glass doors (the older and weaker you are, the heavier the doors on your abode, is my theory). The lobby opens onto a large reception area, where the inhabitants of Happy Acres sit when they aren't in their rooms or in the dining room. But the assorted couches and wheelchairs all face the front door as though they were a platoon lined up for inspection. Most of the time it is totally silent. I have been thinking of printing up a poster at the *Citizen* saying: CONVERSATIONAL GROUPS ARE FUN. It's a terrible feeling to walk in there and see people all facing the world outside those heavy glass doors, waiting for something to happen, even if it's just for them to die. Well, you never catch Lilly there. She'll be in the dining room playing games or in her room reading a romance or a religious book. She'd been reading Billy Graham's book on angels and giving us brief summaries. Or she might be watching one of her programs. She's been watching *As the World Turns* since it went on the air. She is always occupied and cheerful and happy to see us. One of the few good things about being back in Midnight is getting to see Lilly more often.

Lilly insisted on leaving her game of forty-two, which collapsed when she stopped playing, wheelchairs reversing in every direction. We all gave her a hug and Larry pushed her back down the mauve-colored hall with the railing to her room. The walls were posted with the day's menu and agenda. It started at seven-thirty with Devotion-in-Motion, which is assorted exercises done to hymns, followed by breakfast, then Bible study or arts and crafts, lunch, bingo, and so on. Lilly was in a wheelchair because of her broken hip. Which was an irony, since she is the fastest walker I've ever known. Consequently, Mama and I are fast walkers. A broken hip is the most common ailment of the women in Happy Acres. At age fifty, women's hips begin to melt away until they become fragile as spider webs. Sometimes I look at myself in the mirror and think of that year when my bones will start dissolving inside me. Lilly also has a heart condition, which makes even a cold dangerous for her.

In her room, Larry helped her onto her bed and we distributed ourselves, Mama in the chair, me on the foot of the bed, and Larry standing. Lilly wore a pink—her favorite color—three-piece polyester dress with a triple rope of fake pink pearls, a rhinestone brooch at her neck, and a pop-a-pearl bracelet. In the pocket of her dress was a pink flowered handkerchief Mama had washed and ironed. Her chunky legs were neatly covered with hose held by old-fashioned blue elastic garters just above her dress hem. Her body is loose and soft, and touching her always reminds me of the featherbeds she used to sleep on. Her face is hardly wrinkled and she smells of Jean Naté cologne. She wore plastic-and-rhinestone bifocals and an excess of face powder. I remember when going somewhere with her, Mama or I would always lean toward her and brush away excess powder from her face. She has been widowed twice and has had little money in her life, but she may be the only person I'll ever know who seems to be adored by one hundred percent of the people who have shared her life. She held Larry's hand, and as he smiled at her he looked for a moment just like the photograph beside her bed showing him at four grinning over the handlebars of his tricycle.

She gave us a report on the Billy Graham book. When she talks about angels I can nearly believe in them. She reads with a heavy magnifying glass, so it takes her longer than most. Her room is small and she shares it with another woman, the two areas separated by a curtain neither of them can pull. Each has her own TV and chest of drawers, photographs of her own family, and a few plants. Lilly has the part of the room with the window, so she can look out at the highway. On the ledge are a snake plant, a devil's ivy, and an African violet in bloom. When it quits blooming Mama will bring her another plant in bloom. When Lilly was there two years before, after breaking her leg, she'd had a room in the rear of the building, where Daddy hung a bird feeder outside her window. But after Daddy died and she had to come back, we knew no one else would ever get around to filling her bird feeder regularly, so she moved to the highway side, which she says is fine. She likes watching the cars and trucks pass on the highway and she can see who's coming in and out of Midnight, and who's being carried off by the Dunn Brothers' Funeral Home. She claims to have become an expert on sunsets.

Lilly asked me about the plane crash and remembered that Calvin Troope was the biggest baby ever born in Midnight. At eighty-three, she doesn't forget anything. But her remembrances skip decades, so she might be talking about angels and Billy Graham one minute and suddenly start talking about when she was a girl and used to cut through the wagon yard in Clarksville. She has in her life survived a fire that burned most of the town and threatened her own house until the wind changed, she has survived the deaths of two husbands and a five-year-old daughter, she has been caught in quicksand and rescued at the last minute, and she was once laid out for dead after having scarlet fever, only to be revived when a neighbor sitting up with her body said, *"Why, this child isn't dead!"* She remembers traveling in wagons and buggies, and the first car she ever saw. She still writes thank-you notes for all the gifts she receives. She is the only person I've ever known who likes chocolate-covered cherries. She has seen most of her generation die.

Lilly asked Larry about "what's-her-name and the baby." She is sometimes forgetful of names. I was embarrassed to have to repeat "Traci" and "Misty." I could tell that Lilly would just as soon have forgotten those names, too. Larry said they were fine, and his face clouded over for a moment, but Lilly didn't seem to notice. She started telling us about Anthony Spencer Mainard, the new man who pulled a gun on the staff when they wouldn't give him a room to himself. Lilly said the gun turned out not to be loaded, but he got his single room and had the whole staff marching to his tune. She said he was a wealthy man who had his meals brought in from the

Midnight Cafe, and, "Darlin'," she said to me in her sweet, soft voice, "he's asked me to have supper with him in his room!" Larry laughed. Mama looked shocked. She said she certainly hoped Lilly wouldn't do any such a thing.

"Why not?" Lilly asked her.

Mama said, "Well . . . where is he from?"

"Dallas," Lilly said. Mama nodded as if it had been Sodom and Gomorrah.

"He said I shouldn't send money to Billy Graham," Lilly added.

I said, "Well, Lilly, I don't think you should send money to Billy Graham, either."

"Oh, darlin'," she said, "I just send a little money. It doesn't amount to hardly anything. And he does so much good."

I was afraid to ask her how much it amounted to. Our family was notorious for rotten financial dealings. When Lilly moved from East Texas to Midnight, she gave, free of charge, her nice two-acre lot east of town to a friend because, Lilly explained, she owed five hundred dollars in back taxes and it had a creek running through it, so nobody would want it anyway. Dude always said he'd never seen a family that needed a lawyer in it so badly. That's what we'd hoped for Larry.

"Well, I think it's real nice that Anthony Spencer Mainard is inviting you for dinner in his room," I said to Lilly. Mama gave me a dark, censoring look. "It's something different, Mother," I said. "After all, Lilly, you are a very attractive woman." Which is true. "And how many adventures like that come along?" I asked Mama.

"I think you oughta have a chaperone," Larry teased her. Lilly laughed. The word reminded me of old movies and un-liberated women. At the time I labored under the illusion that I was a liberated woman.

Lilly said it was sure going to be a lot more interesting around Happy Acres with Anthony Spencer Mainard there. When the staff had threatened to kick him out, he'd told them he was the largest stockholder in the corporation that owned the place and they most assuredly couldn't evict him. Actually, he told Lilly, he didn't really own stock in that corporation but it would make them stop and think the next time they were pushy to him. I suggested that maybe Anthony Spencer Mainard would organize conversational groupings in the reception hall. Lilly said that she was positive they wouldn't dress him up like Little Red Riding Hood on Halloween the way they had done Mr. Mann last time she was there.

I was thinking Anthony Spencer Mainard might be a profile for the *Citizen* but then reminded myself not to think that way. What I really wanted to do, after all, was to sell the damn thing and flee to Dallas and feed my cats and do my real job and lick my wounds and maybe change Dude's mind. I looked at poor miserable Larry and told Lilly we must go, thinking we had to go before one of us let slip our various marriage disasters. We tried to not worry Lilly with our problems. And it did seem to me that if I could just get back to Dallas, life wouldn't seem so threatening. In Midnight, because we know what happens to every family, life seems to be coming at you fists up all the time.

We left Lilly and waved as we passed the outward-facing platoon of wheelchair occupants staring vacantly toward the front door. Outside the wind was strong as always, whipping around the corner of the nursing home as if it had come straight down the Panhandle across Fort Worth on its way right there to Happy Acres. It was nearly dark now, and I hated to see Larry go. I clung to his arm and asked him if he knew who'd clean up Claude Sanders's Swiss chard field. He said the FAA would investigate and either the owner of the plane or the insurance company would clean the vicinity. I wondered if I should go ahead and tell him about me and his father, but when I looked up at his face so grim under the silly hat I just couldn't. So I stood watching Larry get into the patrol car in the parking lot of Happy Acres and told him Traci would probably be home when he got there. He looked at me a moment and nearly smiled, knowing as he did that I was only once again saying what I was conditioned to say, always and eternally predicting the best.

"I hate that patrol car," I said to Mama as he drove away.

Mama said, "Just be glad he's not a drug addict." That's Mama's way of looking on the sunny side.

We got into Mama's Chrysler that talks and started to her house. The car told her it needed windshield-wiper fluid. Neither of us responded. I was thinking about Traci. Truthfully, neither of us ever said much about her. Especially after she named the baby Misty Dawn.

"Maybe she is an Indian," Mama had said.

"I wish she were," I'd said to Mama. "But you know what she is, Mama? She's white trash, that's what she is, pure, unadulterated."

"I wish you wouldn't always be talking about white trash," Mama had said. "That's racist."

"Racist? Why is it racist?"

She hadn't answered. A lot of the time she just ignores it when she's wrong about something, and goes on to another topic sentence.

"Wonder where she went." Mama sighed then.

"Well, I don't know, but I doubt somebody would kidnap her."

"She doesn't have the sense the Lord gave a fly," Mama said.

"Maybe she went back to Memphis to worship Elvis."

"I just can't imagine a woman running off when she has a new baby," Mama said.

"She's immature," I said.

"Well, that's no excuse," Mama said.

"I'm not saying that's an excuse, Mama." Then I regretted sounding harsh. It doesn't take much for me and Mama to get into a tussle.

Back at Mama's, I dropped onto the couch, exhausted from all the disasters.

"Well, Lilly seemed in a good mood," I said, looking again for the sunny side.

"She did," Mama said. "That woman is an inspiration. But I feel bad about her being there."

"Mama, you know you can't take care of her. You can't lift her. Besides, she seems happy as can be. She's taught all those people to play forty-two. You know she doesn't want to burden you."

"I know," Mama said. "But it just doesn't seem right." She

always said that, even though she went to see Lilly every day she wasn't in bed with the shingles, took care of her laundry, and saw to everything she wanted. If the oatmeal was lumpy that day, Mama mentioned it to the nurse. Sweetly. In a Christian way.

I tried to imagine what was up with Traci. I wondered if I should phone Dude and tell him. It was as good an excuse to talk to him as I'd have, I decided. I got a strange, hollow feeling when I thought of him. I wondered if I could just pretend it never happened, pretend he was still there in North Dallas, feeding my cats and waiting for me. But he should know about Traci, I thought. It was his son, too, his daughter-in-law. He'd always been more sympathetic to her than I had. So I did phone him. I phoned every hour till the ten-o'clock news. At ten there was an update about the plane crash. I was sitting there cursing Dude and thinking of my poor cats, one probably hanging on the screen and the other sulking in the back kitchen window, when who should appear right there on Mama's living room TV but Bobby Joe Daniels.

"The manager of Calvin Troope, nationally known religious pop singer who died Monday when his plane crashed outside Midnight, arrived this afternoon at DFW. Bob Daniels . . ." Suddenly Bobby Joe Daniels was right there in the room with us in color. If I'd been the type of person to have a past, there it was, right there.

"It's a real tragedy . . ." Bobby Joe said to the reporter. It was a bad shot, showing his face only fleetingly, and then in shadow.

"Lord help us!" Mama said, as if Bobby Joe's appearing was worse than the original plane crash.

By the time she hushed, I'd missed what he'd said next and the TV had gone to another story.

"That boy always means trouble," she said.

"I don't know what you're talking about, Mama, and my goodness, he's forty-something years old! I haven't seen him in thirty years." That was a bit of an exaggeration.

"You'd know what I was talking about if you'd let yourself," she said.

"Well, as a matter of fact, the reason Dude Reynolds came

here last night was to tell me he was interested in another woman!"

That was a touché if there ever was one. But I hadn't meant to shock her like that, it just spilled out of my mouth. Mama's hands flew to her face, as in "see no evil."

"You don't mean that, Dinah?"

"I'm afraid I do."

Mama patted her breast. When she'd pulled herself together, she asked me how Dude had met her and whether she was married. I realized she was probably thinking it was what she'd always expected, but whatever she was thinking she simply said she was sorry and patted me on the knee. If Mama was predictable it was in her unpredictability, though I suspected in a day or two she'd have worked it out in her Baptist way that my sinful nature was responsible for my marriage's failing. Something like, if I'd only listened to the sermons when I was a child instead of passing notes and looking at wallet photos, this would never have happened.

I retreated before the weather and "Here's Johnny." As I brushed my teeth, I realized the one glimpse of Bobby Joe had brought the first flicker of color to the gray terrain of my life since Dude had brought his untimely news. I must confess that all along in a side pocket of my imagination I'd been thinking that maybe his cousin Calvin Troope's death might draw Bobby Joe back to Midnight. But as Calvin Troope's manager!

When Calvin Troope had visited in the summer he'd always been one of those skinny little boys—despite his being the biggest baby born in Midnight, he grew up skinny, with an oily complexion—who picked at the scabs on his knees and then cried when they came off. He was the kind of kid you always wanted to pinch, and sometimes I did, as a matter of fact. When he finished high school he'd gone off to North Texas State to become a high school band director, which would have suited him. That he'd somehow gotten involved with a famous alumnus of North Texas State and become a semi-successful religious pop singer had been a joke to us.

Bobby Joe looked good, I thought, what little I saw of him. I knew he wasn't old and ugly, because Cissy had spotted him in a *People* magazine photograph with Calvin and an earlier fiancée, the one right before the recent and late fiancée. Cissy had given it to Mama to show me. Cissy, besides running the Pastel and managing Paisley Blue's incipient Little Miss campaign, also charts the romances of each citizen of Midnight. She's even interested in romances that go back twenty-odd years. Of course, I'd known Bobby Joe was destined for great things because I'd read his fortune in playing cards probably a hundred times or more over the years when we were kids growing up, and his hands were always full of kings, including, of course, the king of hearts. I had thought, however, that the great things he was headed for would be more significant than managing Calvin Troope and his religious pop career. Which just goes to show again how it's all spin the bottle.

I lay there thinking of Dude and how the appearance of Bobby Joe might be my best chance of revenge, much better than the other retaliatory measures I'd considered, which bordered on simple vandalism. I imagined Dude seeing Bobby Joe on the news and rushing from Marilyn's side straight to Midnight, eighty miles an hour, to ask my forgiveness. I made up a scene where I was witty and made Dude laugh and he broke down and said he'd made a terrible mistake. He was tired of that woman and her car repairs. He'd discovered the thin blonde was a shallow and dull woman. Not robust and unpredictable like me. I mean I will, given some reason, still climb trees, which I think is unusual for a woman my age.

I revised the scene several times in my mind, but I fell asleep before I got it to be truly as wonderful as I was certain it could be.

I'd taken Daddy's coffeepot home the day before and soaked it overnight in soda water. In the morning, even before the espresso had perked and begun once more to smell like burning linoleum, Mary and Martha Fisher appeared at the *Midnight Citizen* on their way to their weekly hair appointments at the Pastel Beauty Studio. Mary and Martha, one wearing a green, the other a blue polyester pants suit, are identical twins, unmarried, and retired piano teachers. They've taught probably half the youth of Midnight over the last forty years the very same piano pieces in the exact same sequence. Every time I see them I start playing "Country Gardens" in my mind, as if I'd been brainwashed like the guy in *The Manchurian Candidate*. Cissy says she plays "The Spinning Song."

Mary and Martha are distinguishable one from the other only because one of them—I can never remember which one it is—had a goiter operation years ago, which left a three-inch stapled-looking scar down her throat, which she always leaves visible so that people can tell them apart. They live in a duplex in the west section of Midnight, next to the water tower, and have standing hair appointments at the Pastel, where Cissy sits them side by side and works on them simultaneously, as if they were Siamese twins. Despite Cissy's displays of the latest hair designs, everyone who comes out of the Pastel Beauty Studio wears one of two styles. Both are short, tightly permed curls, but one has curly bangs and the other has curls brushed back, winglike. Every woman in Midnight—besides me, Cissy, and a few leftover hippie types—has one of those two hairdos. Mama has the brush-back. The Fisher twins have the Mamie Eisenhower curled bangs.

Mary and Martha asked what Mama was thinking about the AMQ Company offer. I told them I didn't know what they were talking about. The one with the stapled neck said maybe they'd heard wrong, but they'd heard that the AMQ Company was interested in buying the *Citizen*.

"What is the AMQ Company?"

"Some investment group from Tucson."

"You're kidding!" I said, stunned to think I was being betrayed not only by my husband but by my own mother as well, who could maybe sell the *Citizen* and thereby save my life and marriage and hadn't even mentioned the possibility to me.

The twins went on to report that they had a major story for the *Citizen*. So I got out my steno pad, which always seemed to reassure people, though I couldn't remember but a couple of strokes of shorthand, and they started their story twenty years back, when they took in a homeless yellow tiger cat with extra toes who simply appeared one morning on their back steps. They thought he'd come all the way from New England, because cats with extra toes were rare in Texas but common in New England.

"A traveler, like in *Lassie Come Home*," I joked.

"Lassie Come Home was a dog in *old* England," they corrected me, then watched me write "Rare in Texas." They then went through several generations of descendants of these extra-toed cats before they reached the climax of their story. All their cats, four descendants, three generations, had suddenly disappeared.

"What color were your cats?" I asked. Yellow and white, they said. "Calico?" They said absolutely not. There was nothing wrong with the reproductive function of their cats. Their cats were yellow-and-white marmalade cats. I said okay and wrote down: "Yellow-and-white marmalade, extra toes." They said that wasn't all—they had talked to several neighbors whose cats were also missing.

"Well, that is certainly a mystery," I said, and took their phone number and told them I'd follow up on it.

They pointed out to me before they left that the plane crash was an event that had already happened. Their cat story was a story unfolding at that very minute. And they were offering a reward for one of their cats.

I said, "You mean you are missing four cats and you're offering a reward for only one?"

Mary or Martha, one of them, forced a feeble smile.

When they'd left, Mama made a rare *Citizen* appearance to say that when she went by to see Lilly that morning she was eating breakfast with Anthony Spencer Mainard.

"Lilly," Mama said, "was in his room with the door closed."

I said, "Really, Mama, what's wrong with that?"

She said, "Dinah, you know how Mama always said she couldn't stand old men."

I said, "Well, let's face it, Mother, she hadn't encountered all old men."

Mother didn't seem happy with that answer; indeed, she groaned as though it made her shingles worse. She also said Larry had called and he was taking a leave from his job to look for Traci. He'd be there later today. He should phone the police, I told her. Then, trying to be calm, I said, "Mama, what's this I hear about some M. Q. Something Company offering to buy the *Citizen*?"

Mama pursed her lips and turned away, and I thought for a minute she was going to completely ignore my question.

"Mother?"

"Oh, nothing," she said.

"Nothing?"

She shushed me. The worst thing in the world that anyone can do to Mama is to cause a scene. She'd prefer to be mugged.

"I'll tell you about it later," she said, arching her narrow natural-brown eyebrows to indicate it was a subject to be broached only in private.

"Well, everybody in town seems to know about it . . . except me, of course."

At that moment Cissy arrived to announce the daily crash site report and Mama was saved from further inquiry. Cissy, too, had seen Bobby Joe on TV and she kept grinning at me as if she'd seen the two of us as teenagers necking on TV. I finally managed to change the subject back to the plane crash and she reported that the investigators had brought out a drug-sniffing dog and walked it around the area, but it had picked up only the scent of Cissy's poodle dog, Pattycake, and lunged at her through the screen door. Cissy said the investigators were finished surveying the site and Paisley Blue had put away her Coca-Colas and gone back to school and Claude was stomping around trying to find out who would clean up the mess. He had gotten in the background of a shot made by a *Fort Worth Star-Telegram* photographer but *People* hadn't returned his calls. It was a shame, I thought looking at her, that Paisley Blue didn't take after her mother instead of her father. Cissy's clear ivory skin was unusual for Texas, where the sun and wind tend to give women's complexions an alligator effect.

Cissy said that because of the crash she'd have to revise Paisley Blue's little résumé. I said fine, and told her to bring it in and we'd print it up after we got that week's paper out.

She paused thoughtfully. "Don't you think, Dinah, that the plane crashing into our field means that there are great things in store for Paisley Blue?"

I said, "Maybe so, Cissy. But I'm not real keen on 'signs' and that kind of thing. Maybe you should talk to Nadine Love."

Cissy said Paisley Blue had never in her life had a wart. The big question now, Cissy moved on, was where would the funeral be held. Would there be a joint funeral in Hollywood for Calvin Troope and his fiancée, or what? She'd tried to get Bobby Joe in Dallas at the hotel, Cissy said. She'd left a message for him to call her. She was talking to Brother Tommy about having a memorial service in Midnight simultaneously with the funeral in Hollywood, and did I know how much it would cost to have a satellite hookup? Once more I failed in my position and said I had no idea how much it would cost to have a satellite hookup from the Baptist church to a funeral parlor in Los Angeles, but why didn't she call Cliff Robertson. For a moment she was quiet.

"Maybe you could help me plan this," she said. "Get your mind off things."

"What things?" I asked, immediately suspicious.

Cissy opened her purple bag and pulled out a roll of mints and offered me one. She pushed two mints into her own mouth with fingernails that perfectly matched her purple lips.

"There are some strange things going on around here," she said thoughtfully.

"What?" I asked her, thinking maybe she knew something about the disappearance of Traci.

"Well," she said, leaning on the counter and sucking her mints. "Both mornings when I've gotten up and looked out the kitchen window at that crash site there's been a rainbow over it."

"Cissy," I said, "a rainbow is simply the refraction of the sun's rays in drops of rain."

"I know that, Dinah, but it hasn't rained."

"That's dew." I shrugged. "What are you trying to tell me?"

"I don't know, Dinah," she said gravely, and turned away.

When Cissy was gone, I phoned the hospital. First I tried Buddy Branch's room, but there was no answer, so I phoned Audrey, who reported that the mystery pilot still hadn't spoken. I asked her if she'd seen the manager there. She said no.

"Does the pilot eat?" I asked. "Yes, ma'am, he eats just

fine," Audrey said. The "ma'am" reverberated in my ears. "He seems to be functioning fine, he just doesn't speak," Audrey went on. "Curious," I said. "Yes, ma'am," Audrey agreed.

I asked her if they'd had a patient come in, and I described Traci—nineteen, five-feet-two, skinny, four holes in each ear, narrow plucked eyebrows, with probably blond hair and dark roots, though it could be red or black hair. A mole, or what Traci called a beauty mark, on her chin. Bad teeth so that she talks with her mouth closed. Audrey said she didn't think so. "If you find someone who fits that description would you give me a call?" I asked her. An amnesia victim perhaps. She said she would. In repayment for her cooperation, I asked her if she'd give me a quote about the mystery pilot. She thought for a moment and then said, "Perhaps the silent mystery pilot is from a strange and foreign land where people don't talk."

I said, Thanks, that's an interesting thought, and hung up.

Larry came in around noon. He'd been to Weatherford to see some of Traci's relatives who run a junk store outside of town specializing in old pinball machines and video games. I don't know why anyone would want such things, since video games are going the way of oil fields, but that's the kind of people they are, the kind who hang out in bus stations and collect old cars, old washing machines and refrigerators, anything tacky and capable of rust.

Larry looked like he hadn't slept since Traci disappeared.

"This is getting serious," I admitted.

He said he'd talked to some of Traci's girlfriends who worked at places like the potato-chip plant in Oak Cliff or the Stop & Shop in Euless. My heart ached for him. Sometimes I could remember the feeling of being that age and wild for someone. It's my opinion that most people are naturally crazy in their teens and it's just luck if you get through those years without marrying a serial killer.

I also thought that he knew something he wasn't telling. Otherwise he'd have phoned the Texas Rangers and the FBI.

"Have you talked to your father?" I asked him.

He looked at me strangely, since he knew that I apprised Dude of my every other waking moment.

He said no, he hadn't.

I said, "Well, if I were you, I'd talk to your father."

I was right about his knowing more than he was saying. About three o'clock that afternoon, when I'd started my plane crash story and begun dummying the week's issue of the *Citizen*, and after Larry had gone to hunt some more of Traci's cheap girlfriends, Traci phoned the *Citizen*, in person.

I said, "Traci, you know Larry is worried to death about you. Where are you? How could you leave that little baby?" She began to cry. "I knew I shouldn't of phoned you!"

I took a deep breath and realized I should find out if she was being tortured and held for ransom before I fussed at her. She said to tell Larry she was all right. She would get in touch again soon. "Well, I hope so," I said. "Where are you?" She said she was safe but she needed some time to herself. Traci talks in soap-operaese. If there's a cliché around she'll grab it.

I said, "You're not stealing cats, are you?"

She said, "Are you crazy, Mama Dinah?"

"Traci, please don't call me 'Mama Dinah'! It makes me sound like a fortune-teller, not to mention a hundred years old." She said she would make a decision soon. A decision about what, I asked. She said she couldn't tell me. Just to tell Larry that she was safe and not to worry about her and she'd get in touch later. She finished with a semi-sob.

I said, "What about your baby? Your six-month-old beautiful baby girl?" She said her mother would take care of her. "Does Nadine know where you are?"

She didn't answer. "Later," she said, which was a pretty fancy sign-off for Traci.

MAYBE you've wondered who those people are who make pilgrimages to Graceland on Elvis Presley's birthday? The throngs who appear briefly on the evening news, tearfully carrying candles to Elvis's grave? Who buy supermarket tabloids supporting the notion that Presley, the King, might still be alive? People who are willing to shell out good green dollars to pay their respects at Elvis museums located throughout the nation in places like Woodbridge, Virginia? Well, meet the Love clan—including Nadine the wart remover, her husband, and other aging Elvis groupies related to my daughter-in-law, Traci Dawn Love.

When I was a kid, mothers said things like, "It's just as easy to fall in love with a rich man as a poor man." That was obviously shallow fantasy spawned by Hollywood, since only one girl in ten thousand ever lays eyes on a rich man outside television.

Dude and I weren't expecting Larry to marry a nuclear physicist, but we did think he'd marry someone with at least a nodding acquaintance with higher education, who had had periodic dental care and had some notion of basic nutrition. Maybe what it boils down to is the fact that the middle class is not so bad when you see the alternatives. As one who's tried to live by the Golden Rule, I have found this whole relationship between Larry and Traci Dawn Love a test, and at numerous points I've realized I was failing badly.

Larry happened upon Traci sitting in her battered red Rabbit at the Dairy Queen one Mother's Day weekend when we'd come to visit Mama. Larry was in his first year at the University of Texas, Arlington. Traci Dawn Love was as slender and straight as a toothbrush and about as bristly. Her only interests in the world, besides how she looked and what new junk fad had come out that week, were money and consumer products with specific brand names. If tested on the earth's scale of acquisitive natures, she would doubtless score close to Rupert Murdoch and Imelda Marcos. Traci had no better sense than to ask people flat out if they were wearing fourteen-carat-gold earrings. She'd been out of high school a year, too, and was launching her career with a job at a video store, a night course in fashion design, as well as peddling a line of cosmetics favored by aspiring vampires. She is industrious, I'll say that for her. And when she saw Larry that night over her french fries and catsup, that was it. She locked onto him like radar and he never had a chance. In two shakes of a sheep's tail Larry had put all his savings from his summer job at the Barcelona Car Wash into a one-carat marquise diamond for her child-size finger. They were engaged. The next thing I knew, he was talking about quitting college after two years to join the highway patrol.

But the engagement seesawed for months. Poor Larry was a wreck. It seemed that at least once a month Traci would meet some failure-to-thrive in the video store and change her mind about the "relationship." She'd call me occasionally to discuss the "relationship." I tried to be nice to her. I knew all it would take would be for me to emit one hostile whimper and she'd be installed in our lives, hot hair-twisters and all. But she seemed so wishy-washy I really thought it would never come off. It would be a period of on-and-off soap-opera drama until she disappeared on the back of some bandito's motorcycle, and eventually Larry would find a sweet, intelligent coed who read books and would let him get a word in edgewise. But that turned out to be wishful thinking. On my side, let me say, I simply hate to see my only, beloved son cut down, emotionally stunted to a life of junior high melodrama before he has a chance to grow up. It seemed only yesterday I was cutting his meat for him, then suddenly he was talking wedding ceremony.

They married, finally, in a ceremony that looked like an outtake from *Gone With the Wind,* only with nineteen-year-olds. Traci Dawn was in a white lace off-the-shoulder dress with a hoopskirt, little lace gloves, her thin, gelled hair curled into ringlets peeking from the sides of her picture hat. Her four bridesmaids wore red taffeta dresses with hoopskirts and matching red picture hats. With their vampire makeup, they looked as though they were all heading for a Las Vegas act where they might tilt their hoops to moon below. They carried blue plastic roses, and the little flower girl, some skinny cousin of Traci's who bore signs of pellagra, dawdled up the aisle dropping blue plastic roses and stopping every two pews to stare and pick her nose so that people in front had to call to her like a cat to keep her going.

Traci had wanted me to wear a hoopskirt. That was our first set-to. Looking at me with her little yellow spitfire eyes, she charged me with trying to ruin her wedding by not conforming to the "theme." Then I lost my temper and told her I would no more wear a hoopskirt than I'd do cartwheels naked down the aisle. At that she stomped to her red Rabbit, screeched out of our driveway, and burned rubber as she headed up the block.

Traci said she'd hoped to marry a man who could sing to her as she walked down the aisle. Larry at that time was a fairly thoughtful young man, capable of changing the oil in our cars and taking out the garbage, who sometimes even remembered my birthday, but he was no singer. She considered having him lip-synch "Love Me Tender," but sensibly he refused to do that. So she set up a boom box behind a bank of flowers to enable the late King Elvis himself to entertain. Her family, the Loves, claim some distant relationship with the Presley family. Their house is a living monument—pictures of Elvis everywhere, dishes with Elvis on them, a platter with eyes that follow you, even a big black velvet job in the dining room over the electric fountain they plug in whenever someone rings the doorbell, which chimes "You Ain't Nothing but a Hound Dog."

So Traci walked down the aisle to "Love Me Tender" and exited to "Shake, Rattle and Roll," and having borrowed my car, she and Larry began their married life with a weekend honeymoon in a motel on beautiful Lake Whitney, near Waco.

Is it any wonder that after Traci's call that afternoon saying she was fine but she needed more time, I felt some modicum of relief that she was safe, but also a mixture of emotions welling up in me.

When I phoned Larry he said, "Tell me every word she said."

You're a fine person, I wanted to say to him, you don't deserve this. But I didn't dare, since he's been known to take even a slight pause in conversation as criticism of Traci. I tried to be as upbeat as possible under the circumstances, but when he said good night, he sounded as if he were signing off from the bowels of the earth.

That evening Mama reported that after prayer meeting several people had mentioned cats missing and the Baptist faithful were praying that Roy Randolph, who had diabetes with complications and had had a leg amputated, would live till Sunday, when it was his and Kitty Randolph's sixtieth anniversary.

I waited patiently through her report, and then I said, "Okay, Mama, what is this about an M and M Company wanting to buy the *Citizen*?"

She said she'd tell me all about it when she'd changed clothes. So I waited, remembering how she'd always insisted we wash the breakfast dishes on Christmas morning before we could open our presents. Passive aggressive, I'd realized years later: a syndrome endemic to her generation.

When she returned in her gown, duster, and hairnet, with metal clips projecting from each temple, she stood rubbing cream in her hands a minute before flipping on the TV. I could smell the old faithful Jergens lotion she'd used all my life, the plain, white kind. Mama was nothing if not faithful. She had her hair washed and set Thursday mornings at nine at the Pastel. She'd had that standing appointment for years, and when she went on vacation or to visit a relative out of town she'd always leave on a Friday and come back the next Wednesday so she'd be there and ready at the appointed hour.

"Ahem . . . Knock, knock . . ." I said when she'd sat down.

"Well," she began, not looking at me. "You know Martin Turner?"

"The realtor I suggested you talk to a while back."

"He phoned me one day and said this MPO Company was interested in buying the *Citizen* building."

I leaned forward waiting while Mama yawned.

"I asked if they were going to run the *Citizen,* and Martin said he didn't know. He had the impression they were interested only in the property. So I asked him to find out if they would continue the newspaper. And I haven't heard from him since."

"When was that, Mama?"

"Oh, a couple of months ago."

"Why haven't you called him?"

She looked down at her fingernails a moment and pushed at a cuticle with a thumbnail.

"Well, Dinah, a lot of people got real upset when they heard somebody wanted to buy the building and might not run the paper."

"You might still find out for certain!"

"I wish you wouldn't get so loud," Mama said.

I leaned back and tried to calm myself. I couldn't exactly tell her my being there was ruining my life. At least I knew it would be unkind to say that.

"Maybe you could talk the M. Q. Whatever into getting someone to run the paper."

"I don't know," Mama said. She shook her head as if it were too much to contemplate. I felt as if biting worms were crawling around in my stomach.

"Do you mind if I phone Martin Turner?" I asked her.

She shrugged as if she didn't care one way or the other, and settled back to watch the television. We sat there a minute in what I'd label an uneasy silence.

"You know your father would turn over in his grave if we sold to someone who wouldn't continue the *Citizen.*"

She was right about that. I sighed and after a minute left for the "guest" bedroom decorated Holiday Inn style. For some reason I've never understood, Mama had thrown out the nice maple furniture I'd grown up with—which included a spindle bedstead—and replaced it with a suite of Swedish modern from a motel removal sale inside the Metroplex. The chest of drawers even held a Gideon Bible. I felt like *Death of a Salesman* every night. Mama and I usually dressed for bed, put on our robes, and then came back to the living room to watch the late news, which more likely than not consisted of what scandals our elected officials were up to and whether or not they'd ever open the cracked nuclear plant in South Texas, and who'd had a wreck on the local highway.

This routine of Mama's and mine was bothering me. Sitting there nightly with Mama in our wash-'n'-wear summer robes, I had begun to feel like one of the Fisher sisters. Since Dude had dropped the bomb on me I'd kept making unvarnished inspections of myself in the mirror. God knows I was no beauty. And I really didn't understand how people could get as old as Lilly and stand to look at themselves. I would have to learn some trick about that before I got older. Mama has said she's always surprised when she sees a picture of herself. Maybe that's it—you think of yourself in your mind as the way you were in the past and you try to ignore the present. That was another reason I needed Dude. We'd known one another forever. When he looked at me he could remember me at seventeen and twenty-three. No new man could ever do that. However, I thought to myself, I'm not so sure it would matter a lot to me whether or not I lived a few more days, like Roy Randolph, until my sixtieth wedding anniversary. What was so wonderful about simply enduring? Surely the quality of endurance should be considered. Everyone in Midnight knew Roy Randolph was tacky to Kitty Randolph as well as cheap.

Mama called that the news was on. I slipped my blue robe on over my yellow gown. I'll say one thing for Traci, her clothes match. I suddenly imagined this new, telecommunicating woman, Marilyn, wearing matching earth-tone silk lingerie. I wondered if a woman who'd steal another woman's husband could be truly liberated. Surely not!

After I'd sat down for the news, Mama told me the Randolphs were hoping I'd come to their open house on Sunday and take a picture of the couple if Roy was still alive. I asked her if she didn't see something macabre about that. Mama laughed. "Well," she said, "they are just facing the facts, Dinah."

There was a news report about nine whales dying along the Cape Cod beaches because of a paralyzing toxin in red tide. I was waiting to hear the accusation that this was somehow the fault of Texas, because half the time when anything suffers a bizarre death or anyone is a victim of violence it's blamed on Texas. An anonymous spokesperson would probably claim the nine whales had lunched off the Texas Gulf before swimming to Cape Cod for help. However, red tide was a terrible thing, even worse than the grasshopper swarm that had swept over office buildings in downtown Houston a year or so back. Mama said this was another sign that the end of the world was near.

The next-to-last news report was that the funeral for Calvin Troope and his fiancée would be held Saturday in Hollywood. I realized Bobby Joe would probably return for the funeral, if he hadn't already. If I was going to see him, I had to act, I decided. I could no longer leave a possible encounter in the hands of fate. I vowed I would get up early the next morning, get the *Citizen* proofed, and drive to Dallas.

I could see Mama breathing a sign of relief, thinking Bobby Joe was getting away without my creating some embarrassing incident. I was completely surprised at what she said to me next.

"Dinah, what are you going to do about Dude?"

I said I didn't know if I could do anything.

"I'm feeling better. Maybe you should go home."

"Just lock the *Citizen* and leave?" I looked at her square ivory face creamed free of color and then smeared with Vaseline. This procedure she shares with Doris Day, according to an article she read in *Ladies' Home Journal.*

"Maybe you should," she said. "I'll manage."

"I appreciate that, Mama," I said. "I'll phone Martin Turner tomorrow."

When I crawled into the motel bed, which now seemed large and lonely, I wondered if there was anything else I could do. I lay there imagining myself celebrating a sixtieth anniversary alone in Happy Acres, my back bent with osteoporosis, senile but still publishing some newsletter full of misspellings, like the organist at the Baptist church who refuses to retire yet keeps pumping out "Tara's Theme" from *Gone With the Wind* because it's the only music she can remember.

The first thing I did at the *Citizen* the next morning was phone Martin Turner and leave my name and number on his answering machine. Then I began proofing and laying out the paper. Jud arrived, alarmed and suspicious at my early appearance.

The lead was, of course, the plane crash. The second story was the missing cats. "Honor Graduates Named at High School" would have been the lead if it hadn't been for the crash and the cat mystery. That, I had to admit, was still unsubstantiated, and let's face it, a lot of people couldn't care less if all the cats in the world were carried off in a UFO. So on second thought I decided to give equal play to the honor graduates and the cats. We had two weddings with photographs and two engagement announcements, one with a picture of the happy couple and one showing only the bride-to-be.

In recent years, Mama says, the trend has been for the prospective bride and bridegroom both to pose for their engagement picture, usually in casual clothes—jeans, and sometimes the man wears a western hat—and leaning against a tree. (Mama said one couple's picture showed both of them wearing western hats, but the girl had been a barrel-racing champion.) The wedding news would go on the inside, of course, because of the photographs of the crash and a stock shot of Calvin Troope at his electric organ on page one. There were, amazingly, two births that week.

In the time I'd been here this was the biggest news week. The week before, I'd had to go with "West 9th Street to Be Repaved." I remember once Daddy led with "School Year Ends," which he agreed was the nadir for the *Midnight Citizen*. Fairly often the lead is a car crash on the highway, with photos, or an award made by the ABWA, the American Business Women's Association. Every woman in Midnight with a position above baby-sitter has won that award, some more than once. Dorothy Little at the Midnight Cafe has been honored three times. Her three bronze plaques line the wall just behind her cash register, beside the photograph of her late husband and his blue marlin catch from the Gulf in 1973. I guess if I had to stay in Midnight for another month or so I would win a plaque, too. That week, besides the plane crash and the cats' disappearing, there was also the grand opening of a shoe store specializing in odd-size shoes. So there was a picture of Mayor Downey and his wife, who is the new proprietor, cutting the ribbon with a lot of relatives in the background, all of whom are known for their oversize feet, including one cousin with twelve toes.

There were three brief obits and four thank-yous from two families who'd lost a loved one and two people who'd been in the hospital, all four thanking friends and neighbors for their cards, flowers, food, and prayers. The school menu for the coming week protected parents from providing chili dogs the same evening the school cafeteria served them for lunch, and this was followed by three community-news columns. Midnight is "city" to a number of communities even more south of the Metroplex—Cedar Hill, Little Springs, Post Oak, et cetera. I could lay the *Citizen* out, all four pages, and write the heads in an hour or two if I weren't interrupted every three minutes and if the community-news items and the local ads were all in on time. But that day, with so much news, I knew we'd have a six-page paper. And just as I got started working, here came Faye Belt wanting me to run a big notice for her gratis.

Faye Belt is a woman of indeterminate age, which is, I suppose, typical of witches. Not that she is a real witch, but she certainly looks like one, with her long, dirty, black hair pulled into a messy knot at the back of her neck. That day she wore an old black crepe dress with a sweetheart neck decorated with a few remaining black bugle beads and the hem pulled out and sagging on the sides. Winter or summer she wears a coat of some sort, that day a faded turquoise Mexican embroidered jacket, and her skin bore the muddy orange aura that the mentally unstable often have. She pulled her ad out of her old, cracked black patent purse and spread it on the counter before me. Then she curled her thin lips that looked like narrow strips of raw liver and studied me a minute as the aroma of garlic reached me from the clove or two she always wears strung around her neck to ward off germs. I turned my head to breathe. Rumor had it that she was starving her bedridden husband. Two women from the Baptist Missionary Society had visited Mr. Belt, bearing a quart of cherry-vanilla ice cream, but Faye Belt wouldn't let them in the house, claiming he could digest only rose hips and yogurt. They'd argued until the ice cream started melting down one lady's arm.

I read the ad.

REWARD
For information concerning the person or persons who stole my ladder outside the bank building this past Tuesday.
John 3:16

"Well, you've got to put your name on it or they won't know whose bank building," I told her. Actually they would, since she's the only one who'd put in an ad like that and everyone knows she owns the bank building. She scrawled "Faye Belt" right below "John 3:16" and shoved the ad back toward me. I told her it was awful late for another ad.

People like Faye Belt flourish in Midnight. If it were absolutely true that she was starving her husband, who would handle it? Easy Malone, the sheriff, is certainly not going to tangle with her. She'd chew him into rose hips if he so much as looked at her. Faye Belt also owns a lot of downtown property, including the rusting tin ceiling over the Pastel Beauty Studio. It is rumored, also, that she has a fortune buried near her house, so generation after generation of kids sneak around her place digging holes and searching her sagging lean-tos. When she catches them, she gets out her well-oiled shotgun and fires, or sics one of her seventeen dogs on them. When the town council voted that she had to install a toilet facility in the bank building, she put in a toilet herself and then locked the door so no one could use it.

66

I said, "Mrs. Belt, John 3:16 is, 'For God so loved the world,' et cetera. Frankly, I don't see the pertinence of that scripture to the situation of your missing ladder."

Faye Belt said, "Well, put in 'Thou shalt not steal,' then."

I said, "Fine. You owe me . . ." and started figuring up the cost of such a notice. Then we had our usual argument about how she thought I should run her notices for free simply because she'd been the victim of a crime. Each week we argued and she'd storm out, and I'd put the notice in, send her a bill, and she'd never pay. That had been going on since Daddy died.

I said, "Mrs. Belt, if you don't pay your bill I'm not going to run any more notices." I punched the counter with my finger once for emphasis.

"Your father was a Christian gentleman," she spat at me. "Praise the Lord that he'd have such a daughter!"

That didn't make sense to me, but I ignored it.

"He was a gentleman, Mrs. Belt, but I'm trying to get out the paper today."

Faye Belt leaned toward me and licked her liver lips and for a moment I thought she might bite me or spit on me, though I knew she and Daddy had had the same argument every week for years and periodically she'd pay something on her bill and then it would start all over again. If she lived in Dallas, I thought, watching her spin on her green shower clogs and exit in her sagging black crepe dress, she'd be carted off to a mental institution. But in Midnight she continues on her merry, odoriferous way, starving her husband, putting her notices in the paper, collecting her rent, locking the bank toilet, making scores of stray dogs into something like werewolves by penning them inside an eight-foot-high wooden compound where they all bark, yowl, and go crazy. Not to mention the series of little shacks around her house that formerly served as toolsheds and chicken houses until she decided to rent them to the growing number of people down on their luck with the current oil gloom. She also has a small mobile-home court at the edge of her property where the homes are sunk into the sandy land dirt as if they'd grown there, no longer mobile unless a tornado rushes by and rolls one over.

As soon as Faye Belt was out the door, I got a call from Ned English, senior editor of Mid-Texian Publishing, Inc., who in normal times smiles kindly upon me five days a week. Now that my two closest friends had recently departed the area—Marianne for a year in France to purify her French accent, because, she claimed, the French she taught students at a local university could be understood only by other Texans; and Shirley, who with her editor husband had just moved to Baltimore—Ned and his lover and companion, Pete, are about my best friends. (Aside from Dude, of course, who was always my best friend until I guess now, that position being *available*.) But Pete can make me laugh and Ned is a wonderful cook; however, he knows nothing about cowboys or Texas, being from Chester, Pennsylvania. Of course I have lots of casual friends, the kind we'd invite to an open house once a year, but I'm talking about the kind of friend you can tell your problems to and count on to commiserate with you on birthdays.

"Dinah, listen here," Ned said cheerfully. "We got a new project for you."

"What kind of project?" I asked.

"Cowboy project," he said, going into a bit of detail about the cowboy turned preacher and now author. I leaned against Daddy's desk and looked toward the Piggly Wiggly lot at the back of the building, where the sun pooled on the roofs of the cars, creating a mirage of tiny sun-baked lakes. I picked up a map of Egypt from a *National Geographic* and fanned myself. I wanted to tell Ned about Dude, but I couldn't do it over the telephone. There are just some things too painful to discuss over the telephone, true personal love disasters being one of them.

"You can't be serious about another book on cowboys! I mean, really, Ned! I think we've about exhausted it with the nostalgia cowboy market and then some, unless you've found reading life on Mars."

"Oh, no, no, no," he said. "Negative thinking."

"I thought we were talking now books, news you can use, how-to, substantive subject matter."

"Yeah, but there are still folks who'll buy a cowboy book,

Dinah," he said. "It's hard times, remember? We've got to stick with the reliable product. Besides, this is cowboys today. No nostalgia. Right-now cowboys, breathing dust around Waco."

"Come on, Ned. There aren't cowboys around Waco. If there were, what they'd be breathing around Waco is the aroma of turkey shit. Have you already contracted this book?"

"Yes, yes, yes," Ned said.

I handed Faye Belt's late ad to Jud for setting, grateful that I was on the phone and didn't have to respond to his dragon-snorting acceptance.

"If you're still interested in nostalgia, you oughta think cowgirls. Now that's a fresh subject. Or oil," I said. "There's something dead and dying. How about some picture books on oil-field roughnecks? Some capped wells? Rusting drilling-rigs?"

"Hey," he said, "we're talking cowboys here. We need you for this book."

"You know my situation."

"There's just so long we can hold the reins, Dinah."

"I know that, Ned." I couldn't believe he could be threatening me when he didn't know beans about cowboys and wouldn't have a job if I hadn't been propping him up for the past five years whispering to him facts like, "East Texas has trees, for God's sakes!" I looked at Daddy's Dr Pepper clock with the painted hands on ten, two, and four. I told Ned I had to go, it was deadline for us. He asked if I'd seen Tina Turner on cable. "Ned," I said, "do you really think anybody's sixty-five-year-old mother is gonna watch Tina Turner?" He said, "Gotcha, Dinah," and was gone.

I phoned the hospital at ten twenty-nine and fifteen seconds on the Dr Pepper clock and asked for Buddy Branch's room. The phone was picked up in the middle of the first ring. "Bob Daniels," he answered, and despite the profound gloom in my soul, hearing his voice was like a sudden sunrise inside the sepia walls of the old *Citizen*.

"Bobby Joe?" I said carefully.

"Dinah," he said, as if he'd been sitting there waiting for

my call, and twenty-something years went winging past me. His voice still had a touch of Texas twang, but it sounded professional, like maybe a radio announcer's.

"Do women editors eat lunch?" he asked. I felt good that he knew something about me. Knew at least I wasn't waiting tables, which for someone from Midnight was always a threat.

"They do if they can get out of Midnight," I said to him.

"Midnight? What are you doing in Midnight, Dinah?"

I wanted him to repeat my name about forty more times. It made me think of licking an ice cream cone after a two-week starvation diet.

"It's a long heartrending story," I told him. He said to come tell him, quick, and in no time at all I was swishing my car through a car wash and speeding toward Dallas at seventy miles an hour, the car still dripping and the whole shiny day, which had been miserable and hot, seeming to improve. As I passed two acres of marked-down Mazdas, the bright plastic flags strung above them waved merrily in the hot wind. I turned onto Highway 67 singing along with Willie Nelson and Julio Iglesias about all the girls they'd loved, which must be one of those numbers nearing infinity, and headed toward Bobby Joe like some guided missile with more explosive power than I knew I had. And I completely forgot to warn myself to be cool since I was, after all, in an unstable condition and headed for dangerous territory, or at least for territory I'd avoided for a very long time and meanwhile the rules of the game had changed. But after hearing his voice, I was amazed that he could have been so close for twenty-four hours without my moving toward him, after all those years when I could have identified him a mile away, maybe the impression of his shoes, the skid marks of his car, which pair of jeans were his hanging on the line, how his chewing gum or a beer can he'd folded looked tossed by the road. Exactly an hour from when I'd phoned I pulled up to the Gaston Street entrance to the hospital, and there he was, waiting in a white Thunderbird rent-a-car, holding a car phone to his ear. That phone might have rung the tiniest bell, I thought later, the most subtle warning, like the earliest gray cloud before a thunderstorm, the thin lemon taste from the smallest leaf of clover. Now I realize that in my emotionally weakened condition I missed several clues anyone but a sick orangutan would have picked up on.

I pulled up behind him and he looked at me in the rearview mirror and raised his hand in what we used to call an Indian salute. I jumped out of the car and ran and threw my arms around him. It wasn't till I pulled back that I realized my legs felt spongy. I have learned that you can know someone for years, or think you do, but you can still learn something with a hug. The body's retort gives so much away. But hugging Bobby Joe just felt familiar and comfortable, though "Can I trust him?" did flicker across my mind for half a second. After all, when we last embraced he was supposedly heading back to Houston to tell someone he was going to marry me.

"Well!" I said, studying him. His hair was still brown and thick, and he wasn't scalped like the men who emerged from the Midnight barbershop. He wore one of those year-round California tans, which blended with the chunky gold non-wedding ring on his right hand and the gold Rolex on his left wrist below the long sleeve of a navy shirt that had smart stitching on it, and a tan kid sports jacket that I'd never buy because I'd be worried about the expense of having it cleaned. His jeans were pressed and new, and he wore black lizard boots that obviously had not come from the Discount Boot Barn on the Grapevine highway inside the Metroplex.

"My God, you look better than you used to," I said.

"You look pretty good yourself," he said, adding, "for a little girl from Midnight." What else could he say, right? "Your neck sags"? But I of course believed it, grabbed and swallowed it like someone dying of thirst who's just been handed an iced tea.

"Don't even mention Midnight, okay?" I said. And the way he looked at me was still with that smile that said he was waiting for dessert and I was it.

I followed him to the parking lot, where he parked the rent-a-car, meanwhile marveling at the way one adjusts to the years. I remember thinking how perfect he looked in fourth grade hanging upside down from a swing set. In my mind's eye he wasn't a kid at all then. At every age he'd seemed to be what I'd wanted, and now he was here with a touch of something slick—the word "Hollywood" came to mind—like someone who could be in *People* magazine and not send photocopies of tearsheets to his relatives.

Immediately backsliding from self-sufficiency and independence, I offered him the keys to my car, and he climbed in, saying, "Let's find some dark rendezvous where we can be incognito." I laughed. That sounded like us when we were kids, the kind of word we'd play with, "incognito." I didn't even wonder why he might not want to be seen with me, or if it ran through my mind I didn't dwell on it.

He said he liked my car, which was a navy-blue Honda Prelude I'd bought when Dude and I discovered there would be no reason to hang onto the rest of the money we'd saved for Larry's education. We got inside and Bobby Joe pushed his bucket seat back and pulled away from the hospital.

"How's Buddy Branch?" I managed to ask as he headed toward town.

"Doing fine," he said casually.

"I heard he didn't talk." Bobby Joe said he was talking all right that morning.

I wanted to ask him why in the world he would work for creepy Calvin Troope, but Lilly always said never to speak ill of the dead, so I just said I was sorry Calvin had to go like that.

Bobby Joe laughed. "Oh, if he'd known how much publicity he'd get he'd probably have planned it himself."

He pushed the gas down and zoomed around a Jeep Cherokee with DON'T MESS WITH TEXAS on the bumper.

"Tell me about yourself," he said.

"Well, right after you left that day . . ." I began twenty-odd years ago, but he didn't smile—just glanced at me, recognizing my charge. Bobby Joe and I had been "in love" for maybe fifteen of our first twenty years, and then we'd left for college and gone our separate ways. While I met resistible football players with excessive glandular activity (what could you expect when they fed them overcooked steaks twice a day?), Bobby Joe ran into another world. I'd thought we'd always live pretty much the same way—drinking coffee around a Formica kitchen table and listening to singers like the Sweethearts of the Rodeo. But Bobby Joe ran into the sweetheart of River Oaks, who offered, in addition to the usual, a free ticket to anywhere on her family's plane, with designer condos awaiting.

The week before their wedding, when silver bowls were arriving from all fifty states and abroad, Bobby Joe appeared in Midnight, where I was home nursing my wounded heart and ego, and claimed he didn't want to live in River Oaks with its accompanying accoutrements, so why didn't we run away to Oklahoma, get married, and live comfortably ever after. He made it sound simple, but of course I said, "That's no way to get married!" I was offended. It wasn't that he wanted me, it was that he didn't want her, and it hadn't seemed right to run off to Oklahoma and hide. I thought he should face her and say forget it. And then we'd consider the next move. After all, I had some pride. So he went back to Houston, but instead of saying no, the next thing I knew, I was reading an account of a wedding that was so special it was mentioned in the "Milestones" of a newsmagazine. Bobby Joe phoned me once and said Merry Christmas. Then about three years later, a boat white-water-rafting on the Colorado River turned over and the bride from River Oaks suffered head injuries and lived brain-dead for nearly a year in a coma. Afterward Bobby Joe disappeared to California, where people from around here commonly disappear to when they start over again. By that time Dude and I were married, and after a while questions arose of what might have been and over the years Dude is known to have pondered those questions. When the wife hit her head in the Colorado River it reverberated all the way to Dallas.

So my major uncertainty on that occasion, as I rode down McKinney Avenue beside Bobby Joe, was, Just when does the statute of limitations begin or end? When is it appropriate not to say anymore, "You behaved like an asshole and I'll never speak to you again"? Just when does "again" end?

Near downtown Dallas, Bobby Joe turned onto a side street and pulled up for valet parking before a small building with neon stripes. Dallas is mad for valet parking. There'll be a space at the curb ten feet away and people will still pull up for valet parking. It seems ridiculous usually, but I hardly noticed when Bobby Joe slammed on the brakes and handed my car keys to a fresh-faced attendant.

Inside, the restaurant was sleek white with a long pastel bar. We were led to a garden with a few round tables, shaded by a grape arbor. Bobby Joe ordered a bottle of wine and I recalled when we were kids how we'd drunk grape soda from jelly glasses, pretending it was wine. The closest to real wine in Midnight when we were growing up was the thimble of Welch's grape juice the Baptists used every few months for communion. Bobby Joe claimed he'd been doomed to hell all his life because when he was five, without the sanctity of baptism, he'd innocently drunk a thimble of the grape juice when it was passed around, which meant he would burn in hell along with Hitler and the heads of drug cartels.

We did a lot of toasting that afternoon, just as we'd done when we were kids, and it was nice to be surrounded by freshly watered beds of red impatiens which gave off a pungent, earthy fragrance. While above us grapes were developing into the possibility of wine, Bobby Joe poured more Chardonnay before our glasses were empty.

I told him about Daddy dying and why I was in Midnight.

"And Dude and I are going our separate ways. His idea, not mine," I added matter-of-factly. I hadn't intended to volunteer that information in the first fifteen minutes, but it just fell out of my mouth and for a moment a cloud passed over my soul. But Bobby Joe didn't seem surprised, so maybe he'd talked to Dude.

"It's been a long time." I sighed. I meant since he'd been in Midnight and I'd seen him, but as soon as I said it I knew I was talking about other things, too. He said, "You're right," and caught my hand, and there was a kind of weighty acknowledgment of the past between us that was so strong we didn't have to say a word but could just sit there breathing it in as though it were as tangible as passing a polecat or new-cut grass or summer rain along a highway. Sitting there, I forgot I was a rejected married woman, a mother of a semi-educated highway patrolman, a mother-in-law with a berserko disappeared daughter-in-law, a woman about to lose her job if she didn't get back to work, a woman unwanted by all but a two-bit publishing company that couldn't get beyond cowboys. As we talked, Midnight and all its strife, struggle, and missing cats drained out of my mind and I felt I could sit there and suck on the past like on the stalks of sugarcane we used to steal from the fields at Halloween. No wonder I wanted so badly to see him, I thought, I've already invested in him so much emotional energy I feel I'm due some back, especially now that I need it.

At one point he said, "Dinah, I don't know what to say. Except that it was the biggest mistake I'll ever make." Leaning toward me, he cocked his head, and I remembered his getting a flat-top haircut once with his head cocked. I'd gone around for a week cocking my head every time I looked at him.

"I don't believe everything I'm told anymore, Bobby Joe," I said.

He looked away and then whispered, "Dinah, just calling me 'Bobby Joe' is maybe enough revenge for a lifetime. I haven't heard that in about twenty years." We laughed.

We ate some kind of stir-fried chicken dish with walnuts and a salad with raspberry vinegar. I was too enthralled with Bobby Joe to taste it. I just remember the walnuts crunching. We drank the wine, ordered coffee and kiwi sorbet, known in Midnight as sherbet. We talked about Dude, about California, about Midnight, about Texas and the economy, about Lilly. I told him about Larry and Traci Dawn Love Reynolds, and for the first time I laughed at the silliness of their Elvis wedding. We recalled things that had fascinated us as kids— Siamese twins, Lena Horne, black widow spiders, what a jerk Calvin Troope was even then. And I drank enough wine that at some point I said, "Don't you think it's peculiar, your showing up just as I'm a semi-free woman?"

"Fate," he said.

"Maybe. A lot of strange things have been happening. My father fell in love as he was dying and my grandmother is having breakfast alone with a new man at the nursing home and then Dude meets someone and now you show up. . . ." I realized I was making romance sound like a communicable disease, which maybe it is.

"You're still my favorite person," he said.

We were alone in the little garden. I leaned back and took a deep breath of wisteria or honeysuckle, one of those Garden of Eden fragrances of early summer that semi-intoxicate the world.

We spent two hours there, and then he looked at his watch and said he had an appointment and suddenly the world was *on* again and I realized I'd forgotten all about the *Midnight Citizen*, "Where Texas Still Is," and its six pages I should have been proofing that minute. So we left the grape arbor and I dropped him by his hotel, where in the shadow of the tallest tower, which my father had sworn never to enter, I kissed Bobby Joe good-bye. Then I watched him walk away, not even looking back before disappearing into the glowing jungle maze of glass and waterfall and thousand-dollar designer plantings that passes for the pastoral experience within the Metroplex.

On the way back to Midnight, I thought of Dude and felt a shred of guilt for having spongy legs after hugging Bobby Joe. For an instant I hoped Marilyn felt that way about Dude, then I took it back quickly before it came true.

That night over supper Mama said she'd heard I'd disappeared from the *Citizen* and the whole issue might be delayed; that had never happened in the history of the *Citizen,* even when Daddy had had the Asian flu. I told her I'd gone to Dallas to have lunch with Bobby Joe and the *Citizen* would be out the next day if I had to hire the National Guard to help.

"You went sailing off with Bobby Joe!"

I could tell that to her the news was the equivalent of my announcing I was shaving my head and joining the Hare Krishnas.

"Mama, I didn't exactly sail anywhere. We had lunch. It was extremely mature and sane," I lied. I could tell she didn't believe me, but she didn't say anything more, she just started vigorously stirring the sweetener into her iced tea as if she might dissolve my erring ways with her long stainless-steel teaspoon.

I added, "And Mama, please don't start praying me and Bobby Joe apart. It's not necessary. You know we've always been good friends."

"I don't know why you'd care what I prayed for, since you don't believe in it anyway," she said. She was washing her spoon. Mama washed everything as soon as it was used. It drove me crazy.

"I just hate to think about the wasted energy, when you could be praying against starvation and AIDS."

"I don't pray about either of those topics," Mama announced.

"I wish somebody would," I said, spearing a tomato chunk.

Dude phoned to say that he'd talked to Larry and he was coming that weekend to help him look for Traci. I said fine. Bring the Royal Canadian Mounted Police, Special Forces, and Rambo if you want to, but what do you do when you find an adult runaway? Give her demerits? It's not like looking for a lost child. "Frankly, Dude, I find it embarrassing." He laughed. It made me feel good to hear Dude laugh.

"I'm glad you can laugh," I said. "I don't think I'll ever laugh again." After I said that I was shocked at my insincerity. Here I'd been laughing my head off that very day with Bobby Joe. I was obviously going crazy and losing any kind of moral fiber I'd ever had.

"You'll laugh again," Dude said. "I'll bet you sixty thousand bucks."

Jud was tight-lipped and glowering the next morning, but I got in early and the paper went to press about the same time it usually did, which meant simply that Jud moved away from the Linotype machine to lock the type and ink the flatbed press. I liked that part of the *Citizen*'s operation. It was concrete and certainly more useful than cowboy photos. Maybe someone actually needed the used GE refrigerator listed in the classifieds, even if the lead news was sometimes beside the point. And there was a timeless smell to the old press. Computers are dully unfragrant. And the process occupied my mind for a while, getting it off my future of lonely decay.

I phoned Martin Turner's real estate office again and left a more informative message. Then I decided I should do some research on the M. P. Something Development Company in Dallas. I looked in Daddy's outdated phone book but couldn't find anything, and I couldn't call information without the actual name. I needed to ask Dude. He'd know the name. Seems like eighteen times a day I needed to ask Dude something.

Mid-morning Cissy appeared with Paisley Blue's new résumé, which mentioned that Paisley Blue had written a song about the late Calvin Troope's crashing into their Swiss chard. Cissy confided that actually she was the one who had written the song, but didn't I think that was a good idea? Wonderful, I said. She knew I wasn't taking Paisley Blue's career too seriously, but she nevertheless gave me a few bars of Paisley's song, which began:

Out behind the rainbows, beyond the golden leaves . . .

"Leaves," she explained, was easier to rhyme than "chard." The tune sounded like "The Yellow Rose of Texas" to me, but I didn't tell her that. She said to just wait till I heard Paisley Blue sing it with proper instrumentation. Cissy paid sizable sums of money to some western-rock band in Fort Worth to make backup tapes for Paisley Blue to sing along with. Paisley Blue had been taking guitar lessons for three of her eight years, but so far she could play only "The Red River Valley" in two chords.

Cissy said she'd like to have a private word with me in my office. I assumed she was going to spring the big question about whether or not I'd be a sponsor for Paisley Blue, though I didn't understand why that should have to be such a private discussion. But we went back to Daddy's little office, decorated with a Marilyn Monroe calendar on the wall.

"She was something else, wasn't she?" Cissy said, admiring Marilyn. I told Cissy I had real problems with that calendar. I certainly didn't want a girlie picture hanging in *my* office, but this wasn't exactly my office. Mama had hung a towel over it when she'd worked there. And after all, that calendar was probably worth something and the *Citizen* needed every inducement for a prospective buyer it could muster, so I'd left it hanging there. The office was hardly big enough for me plus a fly, but I dragged an old folding chair in and kicked a stack of Daddy's old *National Geographic*s under the desk to make a place for Cissy to sit. After she quit sneezing from the dust, Cissy, for the only time I've known her, seemed at a loss for words.

"Dinah . . ." she started. That day her red hair was braided down her back and tied with a purple ribbon that matched the purple plaid blouse she wore with a flared denim skirt.

"This is just between us," she said solemnly.

"Okay," I said.

"Well," she began. "You know some people arrived to clear up the plane wreckage?"

I told her that Claude had failed to inform me of that activity.

She said, "Well, it took them a while. They went over every inch of ground. I couldn't imagine why it took them so long. But then, I've never had a plane crash in my backyard before. But Paisley and I have gotten kind of friendly with some of the investigators."

I returned the wave of somebody loading groceries in the Piggly Wiggly lot.

"And that's not all," Cissy said. I leaned forward to study her makeup. It was always interesting to me to try to figure out how she stayed so meticulously made-up all the time without some Hollywood makeup person at her elbow to powder her face every few minutes. Every eyelash was darkly, individually coated and curled, and every pore was invisible, her skin as clear as a marble statue. Her nails were long and invariably the same length, painted and unchipped. It was beauty care beyond my comprehension.

"After all the men were gone, Paisley Blue went outside and was just kind of looking around. The ground was burned all the way back to the creek. And it just made a mess of those two live oaks and the big pecan tree, too. Well, the ground wasn't burned anymore. The crash didn't show at all. And the trees were normal. You can't tell they've been damaged. And little Swiss chard shoots are coming up again. What do you think of that?"

"Oh, Cissy, the FAA or whoever probably sprayed the

ground green. I've seen them do that around the courthouse in Dallas."

"Well, I tell you what I think," Cissy said. "I think there's really something funny going on. And that's not all!" She drew back and looked around the office as if someone might be eavesdropping.

"Paisley Blue's droopy eye is gone," she whispered.

"Gone?"

"Normal. Just like the other eye."

I had to laugh at that. "Cissy, I never heard of anything so wild! Maybe Paisley's eye is simply swollen some days from your brushing her eyelashes with Vaseline so much."

"Dinah, Vaseline doesn't hurt eyes!"

I said, "Maybe she's allergic to petroleum jelly."

"No one is allergic to petroleum jelly."

"How do you know?"

Cissy tugged her mouth back in disgust, which brought out her dimples, which made me wonder why people seem not to have dimples anymore.

"I thought you'd be somebody sympathetic to talk to about all this. I might as well have told Claude!"

"You think the plane crash has anything to do with the missing cats?" I asked.

Cissy ran the straps of her purple Le Sportsac onto her shoulder and stood up and retucked her plaid blouse into her skirt. The outline of her push-up lace bra showed through the blouse.

"You'll be sorry if this turns out to be some miracle place that might cure people. Like that place in France."

"Lourdes?"

"Lourdes. Right. You'll miss the biggest story of your life."

"Call me when you see a saint standing around out there."

"Dinah, you know I'm Baptist, I wouldn't know a saint if I sat on one."

"In movies they wear long robes and are kind of misty."

She said, "I have seen those rainbows. Of course, if this gets out we'll have every nut in Texas digging out there in the Swiss chard. I don't think we want that. I would guess that holy ground isn't worth much on the real estate market. I mean, you couldn't build anything but a theme park."

"Claude doesn't know about this?"

"Not yet," she said. "I didn't want him to hoot at me like you're doing."

"If it's a new Lourdes, he might make *People*," I said. I added that maybe Paisley Blue should go out there in the Swiss chard patch and open her mouth and maybe she'd get her teeth fixed, too.

I leaned back and looked at the parking lot and the Piggly Wiggly, where someone was taping up the weekend specials— fresh hams and new potatoes.

Cissy stood looking at Marilyn again. "I heard about you and Dude," she said, which just about floored me.

"How in hell did you hear that?" A sick kind of copper-lining feeling invaded my stomach every time I thought of it. And knowing it was public knowledge, I was afraid that feeling might stay night and day. I wasn't sure I could stand it.

"I don't know," Cissy said.

"Yes you do, Cissy!"

"Somebody saw him with someone, Dinah. And somebody else heard it from the girl."

Girl! I was afraid I was going to burst into tears. If other people knew, it seemed even more true and final.

"I'm real sorry, Dinah," Cissy said. She'd sat down again.

"Honest to God," I said, "I hate this town. I really believe that if you tattooed your own thigh at home in a totally dark closet somebody in Midnight would ask to see it the next morning."

"I'd really thought you two would make it the whole haul," she said, shaking her head.

"Sorry to disappoint you." Just then the phone rang.

"I didn't mean it like that," she said.

"Oh, who even wants a whole haul anymore?" I said. "It'd be boring."

"Hello," I said. It was Ned English. I hadn't returned his last two calls. He was not happy. I made a face and waved to Cissy, who started to the door. Then I told Ned that I was Mama and Dinah was out for the day. Ned said, "Dinah, I know that's you talking!"

When I put the phone down and looked at the Marilyn calendar, it suddenly hit me that one reason I'd been so depressed about Dude was that he'd fallen for a woman named Marilyn, and all this time I'd been thinking about her as if she were this perfect Marilyn, world-famous for her beauty, charm, humor, sexuality, and self-destructiveness. How thoughtless of him to fall for a Marilyn. I told myself to start thinking of plain Marilyns I'd known, but I couldn't come up with a one at the moment.

Around eleven the two free-lance ad stuffers arrived to insert the Piggly Wiggly ads into the *Citizen*. They were both older women who talked a lot and listened to a religious radio station out of Fort Worth at a volume that could have covered half the town. Their arrival did mean that the week's issue was finished, except for Jud's hauling the papers to the post office and the drugstore. So, with some relief, I walked to the post office to get the mail. It was there that I noticed something extremely strange. The box below the *Citizen*'s, which was always clean as a whistle, was stuffed and obviously hadn't been emptied in days. I turned to the window where Nadine Love was pushing change with her wart-removal hands toward a short woman with an eyepatch.

"Martin Turner out of town?" I called to her. Nadine glanced at me with her flat banana-colored face.

When she'd finished counting the change, she said, "Looks that way, don't it?"

I sorted through the *Citizen*'s mail, dropping the junk pieces into the basket there instead of saving them for mine, when suddenly it hit me! For a moment I felt paralyzed with my discovery. Of course Traci wouldn't run away alone! She'd run off with Martin Turner! The town realtor! She'd worked for him part-time. He'd suggested she study acting and that had so impressed her she'd revered him ever since. And Nadine probably knew where they were. I felt my face glow like the red light on a computer at work, but Nadine, if she'd noticed, pretended not to. I took a place at Nadine's window behind the woman with the eyepatch, who was then buying a roll of "Love" stamps for a shut-in neighbor, and waited my turn. When I got to the window I looked Nadine right in the eyes, only hers fled to my shoulder.

"What can I do for you this morning, Dinah?"

"Where are they?"

She glanced at my face for a second. Two men came in the door chatting and lined up behind me. They were typical Midnight citizens, heavyset and past sixty.

"I'm standing here till you tell me where Traci and Martin Turner are," I said, leaning in the window toward her.

The chatting behind me stopped. There was a moment of nervous silence.

"Dinah, I can't tell," Nadine whispered.

"Yes, you can," I said.

"This is absolutely crazy."

Behind me, one of the men cleared his throat.

"I cannot tell you," she said through gritted teeth.

"I'm standing here till you tell me!"

"Lady!" one of the men said. I turned to him. He wore a cheap black hairpiece that spread over his head like a toadstool. "This is a stand-in demonstration," I told him. "I'm not moving till I find out the whereabouts of a family member who's been kidnapped!"

"Dinah!" Nadine said furiously.

"Would you give me fifteen stamps?" one of the men called over my shoulder. Nadine pulled open her stamp drawer.

"I'll tear them up," I said to Nadine. "And swallow them."

Nadine glared at me and spit, "At the Western Inn! Euless!" She leaned closer and added slowly, "They got married."

"Married!"

"Yes, ma'am," Nadine said, with some degree of satisfaction.

I moved to the side so the two men could buy their stamps. "Married?"

Nadine rifled in the stamp drawer and pretended not to hear me.

"Thanks, Nadine," I muttered, and strolled out the door and headed for the *Citizen* office. *Married?*

So that's why I hadn't been able to reach Martin Turner. Midnight's prime realtor, Martin Turner was a pillar of the establishment, if there is such a thing in Midnight. Indeed, a married pillar of the establishment. Why would he marry when he already was married and Traci, his partner in sin, was too?

As I walked down the hot street back toward the *Citizen,* I tried to decide what to do. If I told Larry, he might drive to Euless and shoot them with his highway patrol gun. And I certainly couldn't leave it to Dude. I knew what he'd say: "It isn't my business, leave them alone and they'll come home," something like that. And besides, I couldn't depend on him anymore. I had to make my own decisions.

But Martin Turner! He was, as Daddy used to say, a man you could talk to without wasting your time, which you certainly couldn't say about most Midnight citizens. His wife was a woman named Joyce who taught business and statistics at a college in the Metroplex. She wore suits and blouses that tied at the neck. I wondered if having a wife who taught statistics and wore tie-neck blouses had anything to do with his installing himself and Traci in the Western Inn. But as soon as the thought occurred to me, I realized it was wickedly unfeminist.

Inside the *Citizen,* it seemed as hot as the outdoors, and the Statler Brothers were bleating out a soul-jerker. I turned on the two old, rattling oscillating fans we kept to supplement the pitiful air-conditioning, and the two ad stuffers smiled at me gratefully. I hung around awhile and paid a few bills. Finally I told Jud I was leaving for the day, I had an emergency. He harrumphed disapprovingly. By then I'd mentioned so many emergencies to Jud the word had lost its power.

I headed for my car in the Piggly Wiggly parking lot and set out for Euless and the Western Inn, thinking that this gave me an opportunity to prove that I could handle any kind of bizarre circumstance that arose, whether Dude loved me or not. So I lectured myself on being cool and unhysterical. I knew I had several things to be hysterical about and that I could easily unleash the entire hysterical deluge atop Traci Love's tiny head.

It was about one o'clock by the time I got to the Western Inn and parked near Martin Turner's black Buick. (In Midnight everyone not only knows everyone else but knows everyone else's car.) But when I pulled into the motel drive I didn't know what to do. I didn't want to knock at the door and intrude on a moment of illicit love. But I didn't want to sit there till night, either, and wait for them to get hungry and leave. They might be living on love, or with Traci's eating habits, she might have brought a lifetime supply of Cheetos with her.

I decided I'd go across the highway to a pancake restaurant and have coffee. If I sat by the window I could watch the motel and pretend I was one of those advanced female private eyes, which is just what I did. Before I finished my coffee, there was Traci, sneaking out a door and heading my way, dangerously crossing the highway wearing a little yellow sleeveless dress that came to mid-thigh—all told, about four handkerchiefs of material, obviously of her own design. Both hands clung to the straps of an oversize red purse suspended from her left shoulder. She was the kind of girl a mother might call feisty, always tapping a foot or biting a nail or tugging a hangnail or curling a twig of her thin hair. A school counselor might call her hyperactive. She came parading in the front door with her bouncy on-her-toes gait, like her mother's, and asked for change from the cashier for the cigarette machine. She had insisted on smoking during her pregnancy, despite the fact that I sent her articles explaining that smoking could stunt her baby's growth. And with her being so little to begin with, that could have meant, believe me, infinitesimal.

She dropped a quarter on the floor and some beefy young man wearing jeans and a western shirt with snap buttons tugged tightly across his gut instantly dropped to his knees and began crawling around for her. When he found it, she gave him her wide-eyed teeth-hiding smile of thanks, which always had the effect of wrapping Larry yet another notch around her finger. She finally pulled out a pack of Eve cigarettes and started for the door. Then I called to her. She stopped in mid-step and turned. She smiled an instant, as if she had forgotten the circumstances and was glad to see me. Then immediately her face went sulky and for a moment I thought she might dash out the door, but she came toward me, the bounce gone out of her step.

"Sit down a minute," I said.

"How did you find me?"

"I figured it out," I said. "It wasn't too hard. I noticed Martin's mail was stacked up."

She gave a heavy sigh and sank down across from me and began to pull the cellophane from her cigarettes. She was, I noticed, still wearing the outrageously priced marquise diamond my own son had lavished upon her nearly two years before. Her small girl's face seemed to be freshly made and dewy clear, showing no evidence of crime and illicit passion. Her cheekbones were smudged as usual with the bronze rouge she wore, which gave the effect of bruises, and her eyes were lined with black and shadowed carefully like golden sunsets. She wore only two sets of earrings on her ears, little gold bows and some tiny snake rings, all fourteen-carat gold—I knew because I'd bought them for her. Traci claims she breaks out in a rash if she wears less than fourteen-carat gold. Sitting there for a moment looking at her fiddling with the cigarette pack, I was disarmed somewhat by her fresh face, so much less of the fire-breathing dragon than the image of her I carry around in my mind.

"How's Larry?" she asked me in her little whiskey-gravel voice. "Well, I imagine you can figure that out," I said. "He's worried to death. He's taken off work to look for you."

She glanced across the highway toward the Western Inn. "He'll be worried if I'm gone too long," she said.

"*He'll* be worried!" I said too loudly. She looked down at her cigarette pack like a shamed child.

"What are your plans?" I asked. "Are you and Martin planning on setting up house in that motel? Are you selling off your baby or what?"

At that Traci Dawn Love Reynolds Turner (possibly) burst into tears. She laid her forehead against her thin, chalky-white arms and sobbed onto her fourteen-carat bracelets. Her narrow back shook with sobs. Her short thin brown hair, home-highlighted to give her blond streaks and lavished with every known mousse, thickening gel, and spray dedicated to adding "body," lay protected and stiff as varnished wood. The protection of Traci's hairdo had over the years become an involuntary reaction, like a knee jerk. W. C. Fields couldn't have witnessed such profound misery without feeling some sympathy. I felt like a twelve-ton crushing road-grader. When I patted her little fleshless shoulder it was like trying to pat a grasshopper.

"Okay, Traci, I'm glad you're not harmed, that you haven't been in some kind of accident or kidnapped. Things could be worse," I said. "I'm sorry to be so harsh, we've just been worried and upset. Let's try to work this out as best we can so the least possible damage is done."

Of course, by then there was not a sound in the whole restaurant. Everyone had ceased talking and chewing pancake assortments to listen to us. There was outrage in every face and the outrage was directed at me, as though I'd slapped her right there in front of them all. Even a cook from the kitchen had stuck his head through the infrared glow of the food-warming counter to stare at us. I picked up the little printed prayer propped on the table and gave the room a slow and haughty survey to indicate that it was un-Christian of them to gawk at such misery and for all they knew I was an innocent social worker. They mostly turned back to their syrupy plates, and slowly Traci gained some composure and lifted her head off the table and pulled some paper napkins out of the little metal napkin holder to blot her eyes. Then she lit a cigarette with a large yellow Bic lighter she pulled out of her red purse and began turning our pitcher of syrup—one of which adorned each table—on its sticky round plate.

"Why don't you tell me how all this came about," I said to her. "Maybe that would help. I would like to try to understand this situation." I was thinking this affair might go down as one of the inexplicable events in history, like Napoleon's marching his army through Russia in the fall.

"Would you like something to eat?" I asked her, since between puffs she'd licked a syrupy finger. She shook her head and said she'd like a Diet Dr Pepper. She sniffled for a moment and then was stricken by hiccups. I didn't think this was the moment to try to scare her, so I suggested she swallow a tablespoon of sugar and hold her breath. She broke open a little pack of sugar and poured it into her mouth but it didn't help. So when the waitress brought the Dr Pepper, I asked her to bring us a brown paper bag, which she did, and Traci breathed into it awhile and seemed to feel better. Then she began tearing up the damp napkins and rolling pieces into balls, and stacking them on the table between us like a miniature fortress.

"Well," she began after a hiccup, "I always thought Martin Turner was a nice man." I said, "Well, I always did, too, a lot of people do." I managed not to shout, *But we didn't run off with him!* But she knew what I was thinking, I guess. I mean, I guess I knew what she thought. Really, what do people her age think? I read that television has erased their imaginations so that they can't make up images in their minds even reading romances or fairy tales. So I can't be confident about what she and Larry think. She went on.

"He would (hiccup) stop and talk to me sometimes," she said, "like I was real smart (hiccup). You know he asked me if I ever thought about being an actress." She looked at me to see if I was properly affected by this news. "Nobody had ever said anything like that to me before. The way I (hiccup) grew up . . ." and she made one great sucking sob, and tears started streaming down her face again, and she hiccuped loud enough to stop everyone's eating once again. "The way I grew up, nobody ever said I was anything but just a girl to get married and get beat up like Mama and stuff. . . . Nobody ever said I might could ever amount to anything. They made fun of me wanting to get an education. Said I was acting stuck-up. I always wanted nicer things than Mama," she said. "And I wanted to have a better life with someone who would talk to me. And then I met Larry and everything. But I knew one day after the baby came and me and him weren't getting along good that I'd just cut my life off at the root and it wasn't ever gonna grow into anything more than Mama's. And then I started thinking that I'd ruined Larry's life, too. He should have finished school like you wanted him to, and I understood why you hated me. And I always wanted you to like me. You sent me news clippings and expected me to read them, and nobody in my family ever read anything but *TV Guide*." She stopped for a puff of her cigarette, which she'd largely left smoking in her hand. The puff was interrupted by a hiccup, which started a coughing fit. I pushed my water toward her, but of course like all the young she doesn't drink water. She swallowed some Diet Dr Pepper and after a minute regained control.

"I kept thinking about what Mr. Turner said to me, and I

thought maybe he would hire me in his real estate office and I could learn to sell real estate and make some money. So one day I phoned him and asked him if I could come talk to him. And he said okay. So I went down there and he said I could do some filing and typing for him. Part-time. This was when I was in cashiers' school after I quit the K Mart and the computer school, before I went to design school and worked in the video store." She sniffed and lifted the straw in her Dr Pepper and watched the liquid dripping back into her glass.

"I didn't have anybody to talk to. Larry was always mad at me. And me and Mr. Turner would kinda talk while I was filing. And he told me things about himself, too. And one day after me and Larry had an argument I started crying and told him how I thought I'd made a terrible mistake and what should I do. I don't want Misty Dawn growing up in a family where people are always yelling mean things to one another." She looked up at me, appealing to my natural concern for her offspring. And she did look like misery itself.

"And then"—and I could barely hear her—"Mr. Turner touched me and we both just started"—she shrugged her narrow shoulders—"just trembling. I never had felt like that, Dinah," she said. She looked up at me with her little yellow-brown eyes, the whites wide with wonder, and I knew she wanted me to understand something common as corn but basically inexplicable.

"He made me feel like a grown woman. Before, I'd felt like I was a kid. . . ."

Her narrow chin trembled and she turned and gazed out the window toward the motel, where the man she called "Mr. Turner" was waiting for her. By then I was thinking about Bobby Joe and how I'd wondered a million times what life would have been like if I'd run off with him instead of being sane and practical.

"I really hope you won't feel bad toward Mr. Turner," she pleaded.

We were quiet a minute and then I tried to ask as calmly as possible, "You mind telling me why in the world you got married?"

She didn't seem embarrassed. She glanced up at me and

then fiddled with her straw. "Well," she said, "you know, when Little Dude and I got married it was such a production I didn't feel like it was a real holy thing. You know what I mean?" I told her I could certainly conceive of that.

"I was too busy looking at my blue roses and listening to Elvis. I don't think I heard a word the preacher said. And me and Martin wanted to have something right between us, so I said to him, Let's get married. I never felt, you know, married the first time and I thought we could do that . . . and for a little while be really married."

I didn't know what to say to that. I just looked outside the window, where two plump couples who'd finished their pancakes and left were walking to their car and staring at us as they passed the window, obviously reluctant to leave our little drama. One man with a toothpick in his mouth even nodded good-bye toward us.

"Now I don't know what to do," Traci said. "I didn't really mean to hurt Larry."

I said, "Well, what did you plan to do? How did you think this would end?"

"I didn't think about how it would end," she said.

She nervously turned her diamond ring while lifting her arm several times to shake her assortment of bracelets up and down her wrist, the cheap ones having been carefully lacquered with clear nail polish to protect her delicate skin.

The waitress appeared, and I asked for some more coffee.

"What should I do now?" Traci sighed heavily.

"Well, you could come with me. I could take you to your apartment. To see the baby." I still couldn't bring myself to say the baby's name. "You could try to explain to Larry."

By then I was somewhat seduced by her misery, by the sheer craziness of what she'd done. And I could appreciate her wanting something better for herself and her baby. I watched her take a tiny sip of Dr Pepper and thought maybe I could help her. Maybe we could be friends. I'd never even thought that before.

"Well, I think I'll go talk to Martin," she said. "I can't just leave him there alone in that motel." Martin Turner, I was thinking, the calmest, most sensible man in town? How could he have become so taken with this little bit of a girl?

"I guess it's good you came," she said. "It was getting morning. You know what I mean . . . ? And I miss the baby."

She looked up at me a minute and smiled sadly, cupping a hand in front of her jumbled teeth, and then she stood up, took a bracing deep breath, and darted off.

Watching her cross the highway again and enter the motel room, I felt sorry for her. Even sorry for Martin Turner. She was so hungry for something to be good in her life but so ignorant of how to find it. She didn't know the first thing about making herself happy, I realized. I'd grown up with a man who'd had principles. That fact had carried over into my life and even Larry's. At least Larry when I'd asked him why he wanted to go into the highway patrol had said he thought it would be useful. What do you mean, useful, I'd asked him. Well, helpful, he'd said shrugging, uncomfortable with the statement of it. He had, after all, grown up with a father who'd stop for a woman stranded on the North Dallas toll road. Despite the consequences, the gesture had been noble. And noble gestures seemed to be vanishing from the modern world along with fresh air and the ozone layer.

I paid for our drinks and then drove across the highway so Traci wouldn't have to cross it on foot again, and pulled up in front of the motel office, where a man at the reception desk was reading the *Fort Worth Star-Telegram*. I sat there wondering if maybe I could help Traci, maybe I could even have her teeth fixed. I wondered if it was too late for her to learn some other standard of value besides carats and dollars. I honestly didn't know. But after a while, when she emerged from the motel room carrying a gray tote bag along with her red purse, I thought to myself for the first time ever that no matter how I felt about Traci Dawn Love or what she turned out to be, I was bound to be involved in her life forever, whether I wanted to or not, and I should therefore make the best of it.

I dropped Traci at her and Larry's starter apartment and drove back to Mama's. I told her Traci was back home. I didn't mention Martin Turner, figuring the fewer people who knew, the better. I figured in Midnight it would probably get around like skywriting before very long anyway. But I certainly wouldn't contribute any knowledge I didn't have to. I told Mama that Traci had been visiting a friend close to Fort Worth, which wasn't exactly a lie. Mama told me that Dude had phoned to ask about Traci and left a number where he could be reached. It was an unfamiliar number, so I took a deep breath and dialed. A woman answered the phone. She had a professional voice. She might have been a radio announcer, too. But she, unlike Bobby Joe, didn't have one drop of Texas in her voice. I was so profoundly shocked I couldn't speak. That wasn't fair for him to have not only another woman but a non-Texas woman. That was going too far! I pictured Meryl Streep standing beside him, touching his neck with a thin, lovely, manicured finger. I started to hang up, but somehow the phone slipped away from me and clattered against the wall before banging onto the floor. I grabbed it and hung up. I'd probably broken her eardrum. I went to the bedroom and sat down on the bed to try to calm down.

I was often an alarmist, I reminded myself. I often jump to conclusions. Dude had charged me with that a thousand times. I always expect people to die at the end of movies. So I tried to console myself by thinking that maybe he was at the dentist's. That was probably his dental hygienist from out of state. He'd had a late emergency appointment because he lost a filling or something. That could happen to anyone. Now he'll have a deaf dental hygienist.

I counted to a hundred so they wouldn't think I was the one who'd dropped the phone before. Mama was watching a grim TV drama with Marlo Thomas. I finally went back to the phone and dialed again. The same voice answered. It took me a minute to ask for Dude Reynolds, using the voice I generally use for dismissing telephone solicitors. I heard her call him and in half a minute he was on the phone, obviously without stopping to remove dental implements from his mouth. Once again I was shocked. I wondered when I'd cease being shocked by all this, when I would believe there was another real live woman sharing his life.

"Dinah!" he was saying. "Is it you?"

"Dude," I managed to say finally, "your daughter-in-law is back."

He asked where she'd been and I wanted to tell him the truth so he might feel guilty, too. But I couldn't, knowing that Mama was listening. I wished I'd gone to the Midnight Cafe to call him. Or to the *Citizen*.

"With a friend," I lied. "I just wanted you to know."

He thanked me for calling and I felt dismissed.

"She's at home," I added.

"Good," he said.

But I couldn't let go.

"Is that her?"

"Pardon?"

"Is that *her*, Dude? There. Now. With you?"

"Yes."

"She's not even a Texan?"

"No."

"Well, my goodness," I said. There was an awkward silence. I realized that without thinking I had picked up a ballpoint pen and was filling in the Os on the cover of Mama's telephone book, which she hated for me to do.

"Well, good night," I finally muttered, remembering how I'd always hated for either of us to go to sleep before we said good night to one another.

"Good night, Dinah," he said.

The next morning I had a note from Martin Turner waiting for me at the *Citizen*.

"I have contacted the MPO Development Company," the note said, "and one of their representatives will be in town soon to talk to you and your mother." It was signed "M. Turner."

Well, I thought, dumping some coffee into the pot, what this comes down to is, Will I or will I not deal with the devil to sell the *Citizen* and maybe save my marriage at the expense of collaboration with my only son's nemesis? Nothing is easy, I muttered, thinking I had to have some coffee before I could decide. Maybe, I argued with myself, it wouldn't hurt to just hear what they had to say. Maybe somehow I could circumvent Martin Turner should a deal actually materialize. After all, what were my alternatives besides burning the place down? I pondered that awhile, the future appearing in my mind as either an endless dusty trail of newspapers winding 'round and 'round the face of the earth or a cell in the penitentiary accompanied by years of hard labor hoeing cotton under the brutal sun.

Later that day Calvin Troope was buried in Hollywood. There was a brief clip on the late news showing his relatives plus a standard poodle boarding their limousines, everyone but the dog wearing dark glasses like a Mafia family. Bobby Joe wasn't in sight, but then I knew he was still in Dallas or thereabouts, since I'd phoned his hotel earlier to see if he'd checked out. Traci had called that morning to say she and the baby were staying with her mother and would I talk to Larry since he was real special upset. So I phoned Larry, who wouldn't discuss Traci at all.

"Mama. Just don't talk to me about her. I'm getting a divorce as soon as I find out whether you need to divorce a wife who's married somebody else. And I don't want to hear her name for the rest of my life. I hope she goes to prison for bigamy."

"Larry, I can understand you're upset, but . . ."

"That's the way I feel. And I'll never, ever feel any different!"

Unfortunately, she must have told him about everything, including their getting married. Even Dear Abby says to keep your mouth shut about some mistakes. So I just dropped the subject and said, "Honey, we're expecting you to come to church with us tomorrow. It's Mother's Day." He groaned. And before he could argue with me, I said, "Larry, if I can do it, you can do it." Which was true. After all, having grown up in perfectly normal North Dallas, he had opted for Midnight and its madness, even if he had been love-crazy. And actually, he didn't mind going half as much as I did. But Mama thought it was necessary for her mental health and community reputation that her daughter and grandson accompany her on Mother's Day. She took it very seriously, especially since, as she pointed out, her own mother was in Happy Acres for the first Mother's Day of her life. Furthermore, if she had to go alone, she just wouldn't go. She'd stay home and watch the service from Dallas. Of course, I couldn't let Mama stay home on Mother's Day. And when she watched church on TV she always watched a hysterical right-winger, one of those leaders of the encroaching movement who've caused the next thing to a bloodbath in the Baptist Church. It was blackmail, of course, but I thought I could stand it once a year. Larry groaned again, so I didn't have the nerve to ask him please not to wear his highway patrol uniform.

I went through the whole act. I ordered corsages for everyone. The custom is that you wear a white flower if your mother has passed on, so I ordered white for Lilly. Pink if your mother is sick, red if she's okay. I asked Mama if she wanted pink or red and she stared at me in horror.

"Why, Dinah, what would Mama think if I showed up in a pink corsage on Mother's Day?"

"She'd think we thought she was sick. After all, Mama, she is in a nursing home and you prayed for weeks for the Medicare people to proclaim her ill enough to support her." Mama said, "That's different, Dinah. That was only practical."

That's a typical Baptist attitude, let me tell you. So I didn't say anything more. I ordered one white and two red, one for me and one for her. I considered ordering one for Traci, but I didn't know whether she'd have the nerve to show her face. It was, of course, in two days already an old story that she and Larry were separated. I hadn't heard mention of Martin Turner, but I did know his mail had been picked up, so I supposed he'd left the Western Inn.

The Love family attended a rural Holy Roller church—one of those with trances and speaking in tongues. But as soon as Traci fixed on Larry she joined the Baptists. In her family's stratum the Baptists were upscale.

Usually Dude and I both came home for Mother's Day and he'd take flowers to his mother's grave. I had no idea if Dude would come or not, but that morning getting dressed I started to feel nervous thinking about it. How in the world did I let Mama talk me into this when I should be in mourning over my marriage and here I am subjecting myself and my son to public ridicule? I got a runner, which is just what anyone deserves who wears hose in Texas heat, and I'd slept on my hair wrong and it stuck up in back, and then here came Larry in his highway patrol uniform. But he looked so grim I wouldn't have complained if my life had depended on it.

Mama and I got in the patrol car and I tried not to think about how trashy it would look for Bobby Joe if he saw me riding to the Baptist church in a patrol car wearing a red-carnation corsage on the navy knit dress I keep in case of a sudden funeral. Any chance of romance would be as dead as the melting apostles in front of the church.

When we walked into the church, the old organist was play-ing "Tara's Theme." And there, sitting in the front row of the choir, was Traci Dawn in a shiny black suit and black straw hat with a veil pulled tightly around her face. Her costume would have been perfect for the defendant in a forties black-and-white-movie murder trial. She also wore a white home-made corsage, when everyone knew her mother was alive and probably Holy Rolling that very minute. Traci, we all knew, could not carry a tune in a towsack, and in the twinkling of an eye all my new and semi-kind feelings toward her evapo-rated right there in the Baptist church. How she could have the nerve to run off with Martin Turner and then only days later sit in the first row of the choir and sing about Jesus, I'll never know. It about made my blood boil. And poor Larry turned brick-red when he saw her. But it was too late to retreat without causing a big to-do, since the usher had already es-corted Mama to the front and she was standing there waiting for us to slide in beside her and testify to family fealty. So poor Larry took a seat beside me in his uniform, his face hard as granite.

The preacher, Brother Tommy Newkirk, came in looking terrifically burdened. They mostly do—preachers. Men often seem to compete to see how burdened they can appear, all of them cloaking themselves in an air of lonely authority. Preach-ers are the worst.

Brother Tommy, as he was called, was famous in our family because, over my father's outraged objections, he had brought into the town of Midnight one of the tackiest things in Texas. When the wax museum outside of Fort Worth with its larger-than-life-size Twelve Apostles and Jesus at the Last Supper closed, Brother Tommy arranged somehow to have four wax apostles transported to Midnight and set up on a corner of the church near the parking lot. There they stand under a shed, gross, larger than life, with an expression I would describe as leering, illuminated day and night—Peter, John, and another two. On the other corner near the parking lot Brother Tommy set up a wrecked Chevy with bloodstains on the cushions, which is supposed to be a vivid reminder of the dangers of drunk driving. Over the past couple of years, because of the Texas heat the wax figures have melted to the point that the leering has become more of a grimace, and they have been known to give little children nightmares. I assiduously avoid that entire block whenever possible.

During Brother Tommy's long, tortured opening prayer I prayed Dude wouldn't be there. I hadn't looked right or left when I entered the church, just forward to near the front, where Mama always wants to sit, and there I found Traci and that was bad enough. I thought if I saw Dude there, too, I might surely faint, when, as I've said, I've never fainted.

During the last of the prayer there was a wrestling match at the organ, where the younger organist was trying to unseat the older organist so we could hear something besides "Tara's Theme." There was loud whispering and then actual shoving. Finally the younger organist managed to shove the older one off the polished bench into the arms of a third woman, who led the old organist shoeless to a front pew just as the prayer ended. The young organist slid onto the organ bench just in time for the first chords of the doxology.

I knew the best time to look to the left and right was when the collection plate was passed after the second hymn. We sang "Never Alone"—*I've seen the lightning flashing and heard the thunder roll. . . . I've heard the voice of Jesus telling me still to fight on*—and the deacons moved to the front of the church and began passing the collection plates. I opened my purse and found I had only a twenty-dollar bill, which I certainly wasn't going to donate to the Baptist church and its wax apostles, so I whispered to Larry, who pulled out a dollar and handed it to me without ever looking my way. When the plate came to us, I turned left to take it and then right to pass

it, looking with my eyes but not lifting my head, quickly surveying the auditorium as I had done each week from ages five
to seventeen. Sure enough, there was Dude in the new wing,
sitting toward the back with his aunt he'd kindly escorted on
that special day, and he was looking at me, right zero into my
eyes. I looked away quickly, though I'd collected every familiar thing about him in just a second. If there had been a
strange woman beside him I guess I would have turned to
stone, which I suppose is only Bible talk for having a stroke.
Suddenly, it made me furious to have to suffer junior high
emotions at my age. Is he there or isn't he? That kind of silly
stuff. I considered standing up and denouncing him in front
of the whole church, but of course I couldn't because of
Mother and Larry and Daddy and civilization, I suppose. How
ridiculous the whole scene seemed. And I was far too vulnerable to be in church. I never should have come, or forced
my poor son to endure this lunacy.

"Your father is here," I whispered to Larry, knowing he
was going to wonder why we weren't together. Of course the
whole town now would know we're separated. I might as well
have hired someone in a sandwich board to walk up and down
the aisle. And poor Larry still didn't know. Why hadn't I told
him already? I could have kicked myself. I considered writing
him a note there in church, the way we used to when we were
kids, but I decided I couldn't upset him just now. Not when
he was already about destroyed with that wife up there singing
at that moment "O Zion, Haste."

I sat there wondering what experience of the world Larry
had that might have prepared him for all this. I know he saw
awful scenes of wrecks and mayhem in the highway patrol. I
hated that, too. But the only girl he'd ever loved besides me
and Mama and his third-grade teacher was Traci. And what
could he learn from Traci except pain and betrayal? She never
even cooked a balanced meal. I looked at Mama and thought
that her life must have been fairly pleasant till Daddy's midnight romance. Was there a way to prepare for life's betrayals,
without prior suffering? Did life's greatest instructional experiences always have to be the painful ones?

It turned out that Brother Tommy was especially burdened

that morning because he was going to preach about the plane crash. It was the biggest event to hit town in ages, no pun intended. I mean some people would have bet the numbers on that plane crash, and the preacher was looking for ideas, too. He read some verses from one of those new translations of the Bible that make it sound as if it was written by Rod McKuen. I grew up with the King James Version, which is, whatever you believe, beautiful.

He preached on "You never know when your hour will come." In my life I'd heard sermons on that particular verse five hundred times or more. It was as all-purpose as a good barbecue sauce and could be used on Sunday as well as at funerals. If you were a particularly gloomy preacher, you could also use it at weddings. You know, love one another right now while you can. Driving away with shoes hanging from the car, you could have a wreck and die or Jesus could appear out the back window.

After his reading of the verse, everything lightened up a bit while the music minister sang "Faith of Our Mothers," which is sung to "Faith of Our Fathers" and is the only women's-lib thing to hit the Baptist Church. Then Brother Tommy gave out hyacinth plants to the oldest mother there (ninety-three, Mayor Downey's grandmother) and the youngest mother (who turned out to be Traci Dawn Love Reynolds, who came tripping out of the choir loft, in her black patent high-heel granny boots). I could feel poor Larry sitting rigid as a hammer. She picked up her hyacinth and then stood there helping the ninety-three-year-old mother balance her hyacinth plant against her walker till the child who'd come farthest to be with his or her mother was decided upon. That was embarrassing, since it turned out to be a woman who'd come only from Waco, not halfway across the world. Such a meager pilgrimage seemed to add to Brother Tommy's general burden and I wondered for a moment if he might not refuse to give her the hyacinth, but he did finally.

Mother whispered to me that they should choose the oldest mother last so she wouldn't have to stand up there holding her plant so long. Mother is always practical. "And also," she whispered, "last year they gave gardenias."

From what I heard of the sermon, Brother Tommy didn't break any new ground. He discussed the possibility of that fine young Christian Calvin Troope's crashing outside Midnight, where he was born, being part of some divine plan, a warning from God to the Metroplex. He gave the impression that Calvin's religious pop career was based more on missionary zeal than on box-office aggrandizement. When he mentioned "the mysteries of God's will" Cissy (red corsage), sitting with her mother (white corsage), and I exchanged glances that said, *If only he knew it could be a Catholic miracle out there* . . .

After church we had a gloomy drive home in the highway patrol car, and while Mama was making the fruit salad I told Larry about his father and me. I just told him flat out that we were separating for a little while. He kept asking why, and I said, "You'll have to talk to your father about it, I don't think I should say." And that made him mad at me. He claimed I always treated him like a child. Then he stomped out of the house, leaving me and Mama with about three times too much food to eat.

After we ate a mammoth meal and cleaned up, Mama rested a little before we went to Happy Acres to see Lilly. Lilly asked where Larry was and I told her he'd had to work. Mama gave me a censuring look. She doesn't even believe in social lies, though I've seen her tell them, too. Well, Lilly was wearing two corsages on her white three-piece dress: the small white-carnation corsage I'd ordered for her and a white-orchid spray on the other shoulder, sent her by Anthony Spencer Mainard.

"Well!" Mama said, slightly incensed that Lilly had two corsages. Lilly seemed thrilled, and blushed when she told us. I said, "Isn't that sweet!"

Mama said, "Mama, I thought you didn't like old men."

Lilly said, "Well, honey, I didn't know all old men, and he is just as dear a man as I ever met."

When a woman starts talking "dear man," she's a goner. For a minute Mama had a look of sheer panic, so I changed the subject and asked Lilly what page she was on in Billy Graham's angel book. She said that morning at breakfast the nursing home had given out inspirational bookmarks. She'd received one for being a great-great-grandmother. The oldest mother in Happy Acres, Lilly reported, was Willetta Clark, who was 102. Lilly said maybe I should interview her for the *Citizen*. I reminded her that Willetta Clark didn't know who she was anymore, so it would be hard to interview her. Lilly always thinks I can do anything.

She said, "Dinah, darlin', don't you think you could work out some way to talk to her? She was a wing-walker, you know. She'd be tickled to death." I told Lilly I didn't see how she could have been a wing-walker, since it seemed to me she'd have been too old in the thirties when they walked on airplane wings, but I told her I'd think about it.

When we left it was raining, but we drove straight to Roy and Kitty Randolph's sixtieth-wedding-anniversary open house, where, it turned out, old Roy was still alive. He was propped up in bed and I took their picture, Kitty sitting on the bed beside him where his right leg would have been. In the process of their posing, their grandson Jeff Randolph made some crude remarks about having to take their pictures in the bed. But neither of them hears very well, so they probably didn't hear him.

People asked me about the plane crash and I told them I didn't know any more than what was in the *Citizen*. People always think journalists have inside secrets to reveal. There was considerable interest in the missing-cat story, also. Kitty said she'd had a yellow cat once years before that had peed in the toilet just like a man. Roy said they'd never had no yellow cat that peed like a man. "We sure did, Roy," Kitty said good-naturedly, and winked at me.

When Mama and I pulled up to her house the rain had let up and Dude was waiting outside in his navy Mercury Tracer— he insists on buying American cars, even though the Tracer is made in Mexico, a fact he did not know when he bought it. I asked him if he wanted to come in, but he said no, thanks, he just wanted to talk to me a minute. I told him I preferred not to sit in the car like a teenager, but I finally got in so my hair wouldn't frizz and the first thing I saw was some other woman's lipstick on a Styrofoam cup in the Dewey Motors plastic litter bag that hung from the radio dial.

I told Dude, who was wearing a blue sports jacket that I'd

bought him the Easter before last, because he hates to shop, that I was placed in the unpleasant position of telling his son that we were separated, but I'd left it up to him to tell why. I lifted a piece of lint off his blue-striped tie without thinking and then pulled back, not knowing if I should do that or not; so I just flicked the lint, which fell onto the sleeve of his jacket.

"Okay, I'll talk to him," he said quietly, as he brushed the piece of lint off his sleeve.

"And if you were sensitive to my feelings, you wouldn't leave another woman's leavings in your car when you're asking me to sit in it!"

I fished the cup out of the litter bag with my fingernails and held it before him the way TV cops hold evidence at the scene of a crime. I could see he felt bad about it. I wanted to make him feel terrible. Every week of my growing-up life I had felt like a crazed warthog on Sunday afternoons.

"Why didn't you tell Brother Tommy you'd come all the way from Dallas? It would have been sweet to have the entire estranged family lined up there in the front of the church."

"Come on, Dinah, where was Traci?" Dude asked.

"I don't know why Larry is upset! All she did is just run off with Martin Turner and get married. Do you understand that? I found them in the Western Inn and she went back to Larry and now she's at her mother's, with Misty Dawn subjected to trances and speaking in tongues so that she'll probably never learn English."

"Married?"

"Of course."

"Jesus!"

"She fell in love. It was an act of God, like the North Dallas toll road breakdown."

I felt a pang of remorse at making fun of Traci when I'd only just resolved to try to help her straighten out her life. But torturing Dude seemed to override any resolve. Since a person's real character comes out in times of calamity, I was aware as I said all those awful things that mine was dead in the water.

"How's Larry taking it?"

"Dude, why are you asking me? Why aren't you in touch with him? You should be able to take Traci's side and explain just how sensible it is to do such a thing. What can I say except to show him how to be angry?"

"That's outrageous, Dinah, and you know it. And I don't think you want me to point out to him the differences."

"Why not tell *me* the differences, Dude?"

"I'll tell you one difference," he said. "They're kids and they haven't known each other three whole years. I've spent the last twenty-two years living with your best interest in mind as well as my own. That's a long time. . . . And you know that's true, damn it! And I'm not so sure you can say that about yourself."

He was right. Never until that awful night did I have any other thought but that Dude always wished me well and happy and with him.

"And now you're thinking about yourself," I said. "I can understand that." It was getting hot in the car. We both rolled our windows down and I fanned myself with my hand.

"I guess you've seen Bobby Joe," he said.

The question was like a rocket going off inside the car. My turn, I thought, feeling a hot energy race through my veins. I looked at him a minute, pausing, gathering strength before the lob into his court.

"Yes indeed, I've seen Bobby Joe," I said. "And it was absolutely wonderful."

I watched his face becoming the same kind of brick red I'd seen on Larry's a while earlier. He turned away and I felt something that I now know was a self-loathing ricocheting all through the Mercury Tracer.

"I'm sorry, Dude. That was cheap. Actually, we had a nice, friendly lunch. That's all." He looked so relieved I wished I'd not retreated. I'd never win him back if I was going to be such a coward, I thought. Besides, alone one cannot be cowardly. One must have the strength to deal with car repairs and to rebuff Jehovah's Witnesses, not to mention to open jars and kid-proof aspirin bottles.

"If you want to know the truth, the secret sex in my mind is driving me crazy. I spend about fifty percent of my time imagining you and Marilyn Monroe in the bed with her earth-tone lingerie on the floor, to be perfectly frank."

"Do you have to be perfectly frank, Dinah?"

"Yes, if I'm going to live alone and defend my cats, Dude. Or if I'm not going to live alone, let me in on it. Otherwise I'm going to be completely frank."

He made one of his big colossal sighs and I realized he must have had to be crazy in love to put up with what he knew he'd have to endure from me. And how silly I was. After all, from the perspective of a starving woman in Bangladesh, why should I be feeling so miserable anyway? What does one aging woman outside the Metroplex matter? Really?

Suddenly I heard the strains of Frank Sinatra singing "I've Got the World on a String" and Mama's next-door neighbor appeared on her screened porch pretending to water her plants. She not only has the complete Frank Sinatra opus but has seen him in person five times—four times in Las Vegas and once in Miami, Mama says. Besides listening to Frank Sinatra and spying, she gives lingerie parties. She was smoking a cigarette and clogging her plants' pores with smoke.

"I'm sorry," I said. "If a crisis is supposed to bring out the real person, I suppose I'm not so wonderful. What do you want?" I asked him. "I mean, why are you here?"

"I wanted to know where Traci had been," he said, "and I wanted to see if you were okay." Dude tapped his thumbs on the steering wheel. He has double-jointed thumbs that can bend in ways mine can't. They'd always fascinated me. Larry has them, too.

"I just hate that woman. At seven o'clock in the morning she's listening to Frank Sinatra. . . . And as you can see, I'm okay. Super-duper," I said sarcastically.

"Why in the world would she do a thing like that?" He was back to Traci, shaking his head.

"I don't know. That's another thing I haven't understood lately."

He said he'd talk to Larry this week.

"Goody," I said.

We listened to a minute more of Sinatra before the neighbor retreated inside her house and closed the door, just as Frank was coming in behind trumpets for the last verse.

"I hate this, Dude."

"I know," he said.

"Why did you do this? I thought we were happy. I was happy."

"I'm sorry. Really . . ." He turned away and looked outside the car at the damp, familiar world, so dull and dismal that moment. It seemed so painful for him to hurt me. I couldn't figure out how he could do it.

"Any news about the *Citizen*?"

"Let's face it, the *Citizen* wasn't prime real estate when things were great. Now, I guess it's about as desirable as a rattlesnake farm. I've been calling these developers. . . ."

"Good," Dude said. I took his hand off the steering wheel and held it for just a moment. There was a wonderful, familiar texture to it, and I loved the color of his skin against the Indian ring with the strip of turquoise I'd bought him in Santa Fe.

I put his hand back on the steering wheel.

"Not touching anybody really bothers me," I said. "I may have to get a dog. Now I know why teenagers have stuffed animals. But I'm okay. Thanks for asking." I gave him a forced but reassuring grin and got out of the car. The sun had come out and the damp grass was dazzling.

I leaned down to the window. "I still hate this little town," I said. "And I hate Traci Dawn Love most of the time and I feel guilty about it."

He looked at me in a way that made me wonder again how he could be leaving. I pulled my navy funeral dress away from where it had stuck to my back and started up the sidewalk. Mama had red verbenas planted on either side which had been there ever since I could remember, generation after generation of straggling red verbenas. I stopped to pull out a small clump of nut grass then walked on to Mama's porch, where I consciously didn't turn around to wave before going inside.

Mama was watching a Disney program, which was usually a story about some handicapped person, so she could get a really good cry. I sat down across from her and said, "Mama, you don't seem to be the kind of person who'd name her only daughter after Dinah Shore." She said she hadn't planned for me to be her only daughter. She was going to name her next daughter Rosalie.

"Well, that's not a lot better," I said. "But 'Dinah' sounds like a commercial vacuum cleaner."

She didn't even look at me. She knew about Sundays, too.

She was eating some leftover fruit salad. She'd pushed all the miniature marshmallows to the side of her bowl. Our conversations, I'd noticed, were often composed of only two sentences. I looked at the TV long enough to find out the story was about the first seeing-eye dog in America and how he was discriminated against. At the end the dog was dying but he nevertheless dragged himself around an obstacle course so other dogs would be permitted to ride buses.

"Mama, why do you put marshmallows in the fruit salad if you don't like them?" I asked her.

"Your father liked them." She paused, glancing up at me then, and blushed, and quickly looked back at the TV, and I realized her paths were changed, too. I patted her arm, which was surprisingly soft, more like Lilly's than I'd ever noticed.

"I'm going on a diet tomorrow. Don't cook anything for me till next year," I told her.

That night Roy Randolph's crude grandson called to say Roy had died. He said he'd give me an obit the next day and asked if I'd also run a short story about the sixtieth-anniversary celebration but without the picture.

"Dinah, maybe you'd send Grandmother one of the pictures, though," he said.

I said, "Sure, Jeff. I'm sorry." And I had the feeling he was sorry he'd been crude about their having their last photo together taken in the bed.

I'VE made it a point all my life to take stock on Monday mornings. If you are happy with your life on Monday mornings, yours should be a happy one, I believe. This was the eighth Monday I'd been in Midnight. It seemed like the ninety-fourth. Remembering back to a time when I woke somewhere other than in Mama's motel bedroom was like thinking back to childhood, where my memories are vague. For the past two Monday mornings I'd entered the kitchen, where Mama was making toast, singing, "Ninety-nine bottles of beer on the wall . . ." She hadn't seen the humor in that and I suppose it was more protest than comedy. But this Monday morning I woke to the sound of Mama scraping toast and I had to confront the fact that not only was my mission for the week a mustering of yet another issue of the *Midnight Citizen* but the thin filament of life and love between Midnight and North Dallas, where Dude was no doubt playing tennis as he did each Monday morning at seven, was severed or at least notched by another individual, with a non-Texas accent. I could feel my very blood slow with dread of the day ahead of me. I remembered Martin Turner and the MPO Development Company and felt some hope; then I remembered Bobby Joe only a few miles away, and with the possibilities that presented my blood moved onward, might have even splashed a little against the right ventricle of my heart.

But even before I reached the hot sepia world of the *Citizen,* I had to face the hundred-bottle question of what would fill those next four or six pages. Certainly there'd be nothing like the newsworthiness of a plane crash. There was the death of

107

Roy Randolph, but everyone in town including Roy Randolph had been expecting that for some time. There was the cat mystery, but with no new developments there wasn't much I could add. Of course I might start a list of missing cats in agate type, like the lists of pardoned prisoners run by newspapers back in the twenties when Ma Ferguson was governor of Texas and felt it her mission to empty the jails. But a long column of missing cats didn't exactly grab me as a startling news story.

Therefore, when I ran into Easy Malone in front of the post office mid-morning, I asked him if he'd had any leads in the feline search. He squinted and settled leaning to the right while I explained what I meant. He was about to write a fifteen-dollar ticket for not feeding a fifteen-minute penny meter. I said, Hold on, Easy, and slipped a penny into the meter in front of what I knew to be Martin Turner's wife's car. That put Easy off right away. He began making a stripping sound in his throat and twisting the bottoms of his shoes on the pavement, first one foot and then the other, as if he were a skinny bull in washed-out khakis about to charge.

"I'll be dadgum! Why'd you do that?" Easy shouted. "And me standing right here!"

"I thought I'd save her a ticket. Why pay fifteen dollars when you don't have to?"

He turned and expectorated toward a littered RC Cola can at the curb.

"This is the way the city survives." He said it as if I were singlehandedly destroying the economy of the metropolis of Midnight, which he always referred to as a city, which kills me.

"You gonna go around feeding everybody's meter?"

I explained that I certainly wouldn't put a penny in the meter before Faye Belt's visual-pollution '62 pickup three spaces down, in the back end of which she'd tied up a bony brown-and-white bird dog with only half of one ear who lunged and growled at everyone who passed. The bird dog was no doubt protecting the assortment of rusty tools, broken appliances, discarded ironing boards, and no telling what other trash Faye Belt scavenged on garbage days for her weekend yard sales.

I avoided looking closely for fear of finding a severed arm or her poor starved husband back there.

I had not seen Martin Turner's wife, Joyce, since the Western Inn contretemps, but I could certainly feel for what she must be going through, and it seemed the least I could do was put a penny in her meter.

Trying to change the subject, I asked Easy once more if he'd gotten any clues on the cat disappearance. He slapped his ticket book closed, scowled under his straw hat, and scratched his neck where dark brown hair like grandaddy spiders crawled out the collar of his khaki shirt.

"Any clues?" he asked. I looked away from his gray eyes with gunk in the corners. "I don't have any clues 'cause I'm not looking for no dadburn cats! They don't pay me around here to look after dadburn cats."

"I thought they paid you to look after the citizens' welfare, and citizens are concerned about their cats."

"You missing a cat?"

"No, I'm not missing a cat. I don't live here. My cats are safely protected by the Dallas police department."

Easy said he hated cats, good-for-nothing animals 'cept if you have a barn, and he sure wasn't wasting the taxpayers' money looking for any sorry dadburn cats. I said, "Terrific, I'll quote you on that one," and I started off to the *Citizen*, thinking he had about as much backbone as a mushroom.

When I got to the *Citizen* I found the phone off the hook. Jud customarily left people who asked for me waiting till whenever I returned, whether it was the next day or not. But maybe the man hadn't been waiting long, because he was still on the line. He was a Mr. Chapman from Longview, who said he'd read in the Dallas paper about the *Citizen*'s being for sale and he'd like to drive over and take a look at the operation.

I stopped myself from laughing at the term "operation" and saying it would make a wonderful museum. I'd always known I'd never make a salesperson, but I was so desperate—which is probably the secret of salesmanship—I managed to tell him it was a reliable, established business, in a lovely town just outside the Metroplex, with lots of news and a prosperous advertising base. As I spoke, I looked out the window at the building across the street, owned by Faye Belt, formerly the Post Office Cafe. It had been boarded up for the last five years and covered with layer after layer of graffiti. Occasionally derelicts came around and pulled the plywood down and slept there till Easy ran them off and Faye Belt boarded it up again. The more I tried to sell, the more I got the feeling that Mr. Chapman on the other end of the line was getting colder, like that old kid's clapping game. Maybe it was a case of obvious oversale. Nevertheless, we made an appointment for the following afternoon.

I put the phone down and spun around, laughing maniacally until Jud turned from the Linotype and gave me the evil eye. Maybe my luck was changing, I thought. Maybe Bobby Joe will change everything. Then I looked at Jud's collapsed-apple head turned back to the Linotype machine, where he was setting a column of classified ads, and wondered if in the next twenty-four hours there was any legal way of polishing him and the rest of the place up.

Meanwhile, Easy Malone was double-parking his sheriff's car outside, then stomping into the *Citizen* as if he were the late J. Edgar Hoover about to arrest public enemy number one.

He burst in through the front door. "I didn't say nothing about them dadburn cats to be quoted in the *Citizen*!"

After the phone call reviving the flame of hope, I felt more conciliatory. "Well, Easy, I'll be glad not to quote you, but even if people happen to hear your attitude about their beloved pets they might be a little upset. If I were you, I'd take a look around. Maybe you'll find them. It would make a lot of people happy." I knew Easy Malone didn't care if anybody was happy or not and he probably couldn't find a cat unless it jumped into his patrol car and planted itself on his shoulder.

He muttered as he turned away, something about "pushy woman," but he didn't have the guts to face me and say it flat out, just as he didn't have the guts to come right out and curse. Just then, Claude Sanders in his red Midnight Owls baseball hat came roaring in the door with bags under his eyes and a smear of shaving cream under his right ear.

"Don't know why anybody'd want a bunch of good-for-nothin' cats," Easy growled as he passed Claude.

"That's a good idea! Begin the search by considering the motivation," I called.

"Dinah," Claude began grimly. "The city council met last night and we spent half the meetin' talking about you."

"Well, I'm flattered, Claude."

"You shouldn't be," he said. "First of all, it has come to our attention that you are trying to sell the *Citizen* to the MPO Development Company. I was elected to speak to you on behalf of the council. Everybody is real upset."

"Everybody in the city council or everybody in the world?"

Claude paused a minute, turning away and taking a deep breath. I leaned forward and wiped the strip of shaving cream from his neck. The human touch seemed to soothe him.

"The second matter is, you have refused to decorate for the rodeo."

"What is the city council going to do about that? Put me in stocks?"

"That's a thought, Dinah."

"Why is everybody so hot and bothered about the MPO Development Company?"

"We've already been through that with your mother, for God's sakes!"

"Been through what?"

"Don't you know that company just wants to get their hands on as much of this town as they can so they can tear it down and hold the land till the Metroplex gets here? If you sell to that group, not only will we not have a newspaper, one of the principal businesses of this town, they'll raze this entire block. They've already bought half a block from Faye Belt before we knew what was going on. That's MPO's specialty: ruining small communities. And they don't have a whit of conscience about how they do it. If they can't buy what they want, they get some big chain store to relocate right outside the city limits and drive all the downtown merchants out of business."

"I bet anything they're communists, too," I said.

"We don't think this is funny, Dinah. We're talking about a way of life here. A way of life your father loved, I might add."

Claude's roundish brown eyes looked straight into mine. I could understand why the city council chose him to deliver the reprimand. There was a spaniel's earnestness about him.

"Dinah, think of it this way: Do you want a Taco Stop next to your mama's house?"

"Claude, tell the city council I'll certainly give the matter some thought. After all, it is up to Mama. Just because it's ruining my life and driving me crazy, why should I have anything to say about it?"

"It may be hard on you, Dinah. But this is bigger than one person. How's your mama feeling?"

"Not good enough, I'm afraid. And about the second matter, I put a rodeo poster in my window. But I'm not hanging up flags and bunting or dressing up like a pioneer woman. This is still a democracy, isn't it? Tell the city council I'm in mourning."

Claude shook his head, lifted his Midnight Owls cap, and brushed a hand over his crew cut to signal an end to the subject. Then he wrote out a classified ad warning people his place was posted, to stay off his property. As he wrote the ad, I noticed how his blond crew cut stuck through the net ventilation in his cap. First it was sightseers running over his St. Augustine grass, he said angrily. "Now there's people wandering around out there in the night waking us up. Cars coming and going, littering in the woods."

"Littering in the woods? Why would anyone be hanging out there in the woods?" Saints surely wouldn't litter, I thought.

"I don't know," he said, "but I'm getting tired of it. That whole plane crash has become a downright nightmare," he said. I asked him if he'd managed to sell his story to a magazine, but he said he'd decided to hold out for the book. Maybe the movie, he said. He could play himself in the movie, and it might be Paisley Blue's big break. He laughed. He wanted me to think he was only joking, but I knew he was only half joking. Paisley was learning all of Calvin Troope's songs, he said. "She just sings her little heart out."

Claude took off his cap and fanned his face. "Haven't you got air-conditioning in here, Dinah?"

I pointed to the old metal box choking and chugging in a back window. "One of the originals."

Claude continued fanning as he wrote his ad. "If Cissy

wouldn't have a fit I'd take a chair out there for a couple of nights and see if I couldn't discourage a few trespassers with my shotgun." Claude pulled out a pack of Juicy Fruit and offered me a stick.

"I'd forget the shotgun, Claude," I said, shaking my head at the chewing gum.

Claude resettled his hat and doubled the stick of gum into his mouth. "Why don't you come sit with me, Dinah? Might get you a big story," he said, grinning and at the same time chewing hard to break in his gum.

"Well, Claude, I learned a long time ago to stay out of the woods at night with strange men. 'Specially men with red-haired wives."

Claude laughed. He handed me his classified notice. "Course," he muttered, "we'll be dead from lack of sleep 'fore this paper comes out on Friday."

"Soon as you solve that mystery in the woods, why don't you come to town and help Easy look for cats," I suggested.

"Cats!" Claude spit. "You're a lot of help, Dinah." He paid me four quarters and twenty pennies for the ad and was out the door, heading, he said, for the Radio Shack in the Metro-plex.

Cissy stopped by later in the morning with a new super-market tabloid featuring a spread on the late Calvin Troope. She'd spent the morning doing Medicare sets. Cissy says the women in Happy Acres always perk up when they have their hair done. Mama says Cissy does half of them for free. She has a regular nook with a shampoo chair with purple cushions and out-of-date *People* magazines. Cissy says at Happy Acres it doesn't matter whether the magazine is 1978 or 1988.

Just as Bobby Joe said, Calvin Troope had become more celebrated in death than in life. The tabloid featured a long story on the family's grief. There was even an AP photograph of the crash site, with Claude Sanders in the background, though he'd been airbrushed out so that he'd become a small, dark, scarcely noticeable whirlwind at the right of the picture. The story said that Calvin Troope had had a premonition about his death. He had even written a song entitled "Lord, I'm Ready When You Are." Next to the article on Calvin was a story about a man who'd freeze-dried all his animals when they died.

Cissy said she was already tuckered out. She'd given a facial to one of the women who then complained when she still had wrinkles. "Let's face it," Cissy said, "I'm not a miracle worker."

"Any news about the mystery pilot?" she asked, surveying my complexion. I knew what she really wanted to ask. I told her I didn't have any news.

"Claude is really mad. He's fixin' to shoot somebody if they don't quit trespassing in our woods," she said. I told her Claude had already been in to make that report. "Oh," she said. She leaned her chin on her hands with silver-painted nails and smiled her conspiratorial smile.

"Well, what was it like?" she asked.

"What was what like?"

"You know, Bobby Joe?"

"How in the world did you know about that?"

"Honey, you are talking to a network here."

"Okay," I said coolly. "He seemed pretty good, given our advanced years." I calmly sipped the last of my coffee and glanced toward Jud, who'd just pulled proofs of some ads.

"Must have been really something, seeing him after all these years?" She smiled dreamily. "You must have just about died." She raised her brown eyebrows knowingly.

"What are you doing, research about aging love?"

"Dinah, you know I'm gonna be curious. Everyone in town has been wondering for years about Bobby Joe. He and Calvin Troope are the only big names Midnight ever had."

"How could you forget your own daughter?"

"Oh, you know what I mean," she said, and sensing I was trying to edge her off the topic, she came zeroing back. "Where'd y'all go?"

"We went to a prayer meeting in Dallas," I told her.

"Dinah, come on and tell me," she begged. I gave her a sketchy report.

"Poor man," she said. "Is he married?"

"I don't know."

"You didn't find out that basic?"

"No. Sorry."

"Poor Bobby Joe," she said.

"Believe me," I said, "he didn't seem at all pitiful."

"I mean that wife dying and losing you, too. Just like a miniseries," she said, and winked. Only in Midnight, I thought, do people still wink.

Cissy tugged at her purple print scarf wrapped African style around her head. "Hi you, Jud?" she called over my shoulder as he rose from the Linotype. I had noted that Jud harrumphed with more feeling toward Cissy than anyone.

"How are the miracles in the Swiss chard?" I asked Cissy.

"You better be quiet about that," she said. "I don't know what's going on out there but it's something weird, I tell you," she said, and ended the sentence with a yawn. "Listen, Dinah. Claude is supposed to go fishing up at Lake Texoma Saturday, and I was wondering if you'd come out and watch a movie with me. Maybe we could meet at the café, get a bite, and then get a movie?"

Since it sounded like something at least as interesting as watching *The Golden Girls* with Mama, I agreed and asked her what time.

"Oh, about ten," she said.

"Ten? What are you up to, Cissy?"

"And by the way," she said, "you oughta go out to Happy Acres and talk to Lilly."

"Why?"

"Your mama has cut off her tint."

"What do you mean, 'cut off her tint'?"

"Your mama told Lilly to tell me not to put a tint on her hair anymore."

I said I didn't know Lilly got a tint. Cissy opened her mouth in mock wonder.

"I don't know how you could be so innocent of modern beauty procedure," Cissy said. "Your mother doesn't get a tint, so she's decided Lilly doesn't need a tint, and Lilly, bless her heart, is real upset about it. And frankly, I don't blame her. It's just a dollar. I went ahead and did it anyway."

I said, "Well, surely we can afford a dollar. I'll discuss it with Mama."

115

"Well, I wish you'd go see Lilly," Cissy said.

"Cissy, Mama goes to see her every day."

"Sure can't beat around the bush with you. The point is, she wants to talk to you. She has some news." Cissy looked toward the peeling paint on the ceiling and considered. "Your mama is conservative, Dinah. You never noticed?"

"Of course," I said. "But who isn't around here?"

"Sometimes I wonder about you," Cissy said.

"Well, I'll stop by and see Lilly as soon as I can," I said, feeling rather offended.

"Well," Cissy said smugly, eyeing me closely, "it's gonna be real interesting to see what's gonna happen here."

"About the tint?" I asked.

"Oh yeah, Dinah," Cissy said, shifting a shoulder strap as she swished toward the door.

By noon I was still sorting piles of papers and trying to decide what I could do to make the *Citizen* appear more appealing for the prospective buyer. I could sweep the floor, paint the walls, buy some flowers. Hire majorettes to stand around looking halfway alive. But then it would be hard to see them without spotlights. The lighting was pure Abraham Lincoln. Let's face it, I thought to myself, the building needed complete renovation. It was beyond cosmetic attention. Daddy hadn't had any work done on it in thirty years. Not since the roof leaked in front of the Linotype machine and Jud had to work wearing a football helmet for a week.

I tried removing Daddy's assortment of photos from the wall—LBJ and his gallbladder operation scar, Nixon pushing Ron Ziegler, John Nance Garner leering at a Kilgore Rangerette. These were scattered among the more anonymous disaster-and-mayhem pictures of tornadoes and floods and the two men who'd shot each other in the Ti-dy Washateria. I took down several of the photographs, but they left discolorings on the wall that looked as bad as the pictures, not to mention that they revealed a veritable insect kingdom which obviously hadn't been disturbed in decades. I could ruin the ecological system of the community, I figured, as I returned them to the wall, trying to match the spider webs and nests with their proper spots. I looked around at the whole crummy place. Jud was leaving, "Harrumph," out the door to check on the weekly trash ad inserts. I called for him to go on home if he wanted to. I couldn't change much with him looking over my shoulder. I could feel his aggravation every time I sifted through a pile of trash or each time a blackout windowshade from World War II came apart in my hand. I toted a few piles of old papers out the back door. I threw out a box of the Fisher sisters' piano recital programs from 1962.

After a while I sat down to eat my luncheon yogurt and wondered why Daddy had kept the place so messy when he was such a neat man at home. Never dropped his clothes on the floor like a lot of men, never got the typical big-belly award, always kept the yard clean and raked. Finally I had to admit that short of demolition there wasn't much I could do except clean the front windows, and I'd done that. They were no longer opaque.

Mary and Martha Fisher dropped by in the afternoon to make certain I had their phone number in case the cat story in the *Citizen,* not to mention the offer of a reward for the one cat, brought some information.

"They're probably so homesick," Mary or Martha said. I thought it sad that they'd assume all the cats were still alive. But then why would anyone but the demon barber of Fleet Street kill a bunch of cats? I wondered that myself.

On the way to Mama's I stopped by Happy Acres, where to my good fortune most of the inhabitants were in the dining hall having their supper of SpaghettiOs and Jell-O. I went to Lilly's room, where her roommate, Katie, informed me that Lilly was having supper with Anthony Spencer Mainard in his room. She said this in such a way that I got the feeling even Katie had reservations about Lilly's dining alone with Anthony Spencer Mainard. Katie herself had spent thousands of dollars on a lifetime membership in an Arthur Murray dance studio, an investment great enough to lure several lithe young male dance instructors to visit her occasionally. To the delight of several Happy Acres inhabitants, two of the dance instructors had given a tango exhibition one Sunday afternoon, an event that scandalized a lot of Baptists, who didn't believe in dancing, let alone on Sunday. Lilly claimed that one lady who hadn't shuffled a dance foot in fifty years dropped her walker and tried a tango up and down the easy-care vinyl floor of the reception room.

I found Lilly and Anthony drinking what they said was decaf tea from Styrofoam cups, after sharing a piece of Midnight Cafe coconut cream pie for dessert. In contrast to the SpaghettiOs, she and Anthony had had chicken divan with braised carrots and cornbread—cornbread being one of Lilly's favorite things. Anthony wore a tie tucked into his red sweater, and his cornflower-blue eyes smiled whenever he looked at Lilly. He offered me a chair, but Lilly said that if he didn't mind, she thought we should speak privately. So I shook hands with Anthony Spencer Mainard, who was about to light up a cigar, and wheeled Lilly back to her room, alerting the young high school kid outside Anthony's door that Anthony was ready for him to return the dinner dishes to the Midnight Cafe.

Katie was watching *Entertainment Tonight,* which meant that Lilly and I could speak, because, she said, Katie couldn't hear a thing over that TV. "Dinah, come sit there, darlin'," she said. As I helped her settle on the bed with a bright multicolored afghan she'd crocheted herself, I noticed that the photograph of Larry at four on her bedside table had been joined by a new photograph of a handsome young man.

"That's Anthony when he was eighteen," she explained. "Wasn't he the handsomest thing?"

"I hear Mama has cut off your hair tint."

"And honey, it's only a dollar," she said, touching my hand for emphasis. Mama had never been stingy. I couldn't understand it. I told her I thought her hair looked real nice; Lilly got the tight curls with bangs, like all of Happy Acres. Lilly said she'd talked Cissy into tinting it for her anyway and promised to pay her later. I told her to go ahead and do it and I'd pay for the tint. Or I'd fix it with Mama. Lilly said she was so relieved. I'd never even noticed before, but Lilly's hair was a shade darker than Mama's, which was classic gray dishwater.

"How's your angel book?" I asked, just making conversation. She said she hadn't been reading much lately. And then she said she had something very important to tell me. I leaned forward in my chair so she could speak low.

"Oh, darlin'," she said, taking my hand, "Anthony Spencer Mainard is a wonderful man!"

"I'm glad you have a new friend, Lilly," I said.

"And honey, darlin'," she said, leaning closer, "he wants to marry me."

I held her hand, the skin soft and loose over the bones. She wore a narrow gold band from her last marriage, which had ended about thirty years earlier. She couldn't get it off over her knuckles now because, she claimed, she'd foolishly popped her knuckles when she was a young girl. "Don't ever pop your knuckles, Dinah," she'd always advised me.

"Well," I said, "you'll have to get this ring cut off, won't you, Lilly?"

"Oh, you don't think that's an awful idea?" My response seemed to please her.

"No, I don't think it's an awful idea. But I don't exactly understand why you'd want to get married, either."

I realized suddenly that must be the reason Mama was cutting off her tint. She didn't want Lilly to marry.

"Well, honey, darlin', for the same reasons anybody gets married," she said. "Why did you marry that nice man . . . ?"

"Dude," I said. "Well, I loved him. I wanted to share my life with him and have babies." I suddenly remembered waking up in the morning wondering if I was pregnant. Lying in the bed with Dude and talking. How comfortable it was all those years beside him in a bed he'd never wanted to be any wider. I made myself stop remembering. I didn't want to mar her happiness with my messy life.

"Well, I'd like to share the rest of my life with Anthony Spencer Mainard," Lilly said. She glanced at the photograph beside the bed. "I wish I'd met him a long time ago."

I sat back and thought about it a minute. I looked at Lilly and her strand of pink pearls and her frog brooch with one ruby eye missing. There was a velvety pink down on her face. Once when she was sick I'd come in with Mama and found her teeth in a glass of water beside her bed. She'd been embarrassed and annoyed with Mama for letting me see them. I thought how sad it would be if something happened to hurt her.

119

"Where would you live?"

"Darlin', we'd live right here, for now anyway."

"Does Happy Acres allow married couples?"

"They let those two sisters room together till they had a falling-out. Then the older one died. But," Lilly said, "Anthony Spencer Mainard doesn't always abide by the rules."

I said, "Are you sure you want to get married and you're not just wanting that because he does?"

She pulled the bright-colored afghan closer around her.

"I really want to be with him," she said. "He is such a smart man, and as kind as he can be." She said that Anthony had come to Happy Acres rather than stay in his son's house because his son had a Dallas socialite wife he didn't get along with. Indeed, when Lilly mentioned her name I recognized it as that of a woman I'd seen in the "High Profile" section of *The Dallas Morning News* posing in designer dresses beside pools at Dallas society parties. "He doesn't want to be a burden to his son. That's why he came all the way to Midnight, so his son wouldn't feel he had to visit all the time. I'm teaching him to play forty-two," she added.

"You've mentioned this to Mother?"

She nodded.

"But why marry?" I asked. "Couldn't you stay friends without marrying? Marrying causes so many problems in the world."

"Honey, darlin', he wants to marry me. He said that whatever else happened in his life, he would like to put his arms around me at night and wake up in the room with me in the morning. He's only seventy-eight!"

I looked out Lilly's window. A big auto hauler passed carrying a load of Pontiacs. She had thought when she moved into that room all she'd have left besides dying and visiting with us was what passed outside that window—and now this. Somebody wanting her when she was eighty-three.

"Well, if that would make you happy," I said, "I don't see why not. But I imagine he has to talk to his family."

"Why, honey, he's a wealthy man. He'll take care of me. Your mother won't have to worry. And we're certainly old enough to know what we're doing." She laughed. I looked at her Jean Naté cologne and the coordinated talcum on her chest of drawers. The photo of Mama at ten in a school-play angel costume, and me and Dude when we married. Everything in her world seemed so neatly arranged.

"Well, I just don't want anything to happen to hurt you," I said. "I'm sure that's how Mama must feel, too."

"Oh," she said. "He loves me, Dinah. Anthony Spencer Mainard would never, ever hurt me. He is a kind man."

"But what if he dies, Lilly?" I had to say it.

"Well, darlin', we all have to die. I've accepted that. But we could have such a good time for a while. That's all anyone has. A while."

Looking at Lilly, I thought how it seemed that she was having a sweet, slow ending and now this conflagration at the end. Like Daddy. I could see her eyes were getting heavy. She sometimes took a nap after her supper.

I said I'd better leave. I gave her a kiss and told her that was very exciting news. "Let me know the date. I'll help you all I can."

She caught my hand and said, "Dinah, I would like you to be my best woman, but I didn't want to hurt your mother's feelings. I hope you understand."

I told her I understood. What I didn't say was that I had the feeling Mama wasn't going to settle easily into this wedding scheme.

Mama was folding freshly laundered yellow towels we'd used Saturday, Sunday, and that morning. Before she was racked with the shingles, she did laundry and vacuuming on alternate days. Although her sickness had interrupted her routine, she still didn't leave anything tumbled in a dryer for days, the way I did at my house. Even with her sick, you still couldn't get a clean towel broken in before it was washed again.

Right away I asked her how her shingles were. She said, as she always does, that they were still there, right across her back like a streak of brick-colored lightning. Though less prominent now, she said, it still hurt. The doctor had told her the shingles could last for a year.

I started to sit on the bed but remembered she didn't like anyone to do that, so I stood and told her about Claude coming to see me for the city council and then about the phone call from Mr. Chapman in Longview. She said everyone in town had been after her when she'd first heard from the MPO Development Company. That's why she hadn't mentioned it. Instead of being excited about the phone call from Longview, she warned me not to get my hopes up too much. I should have known she was in too negative a mood for me to bring up the possibility of Lilly's getting married, but I've never been good at playing cagey so I stormed ahead.

"Mama, why did you make Lilly quit getting a dark rinse on her little bit of hair?"

She stopped folding and looked at me. "I don't get a dark rinse, why should she get a dark rinse?" Mama said. She lifted another yellow towel and folded it with a karate chop across the middle.

"She *wants* a dark rinse. It's just a dollar."

"Well, I just didn't see any use in it," she said. She opened a yellow daisy-print sheet to fold and I went to help her, and she pulled it away from me and folded it alone. She always accuses me of being sloppy at folding towels and sheets and making beds.

"I'll be glad to pay for it."

She glanced at me sourly over the daisy sheet, holding it like a shield in front of her body, then ironing it with her hands.

"No. If it's so important, I'll pay for it."

I hesitated only a moment. Since I'd made the first incision, I decided I should go ahead and slice all the way.

"What do you think of the approaching marriage?"

She stopped suddenly, clasping the folded sheet against her body. Her face was pinched with disapproval.

"Dinah," she said, "that's perfectly ridiculous."

"Why?"

"Because. It just is." She'd said that to me when I was a kid. It always drove me wild. She plopped the sheet on top of its carefully folded mate, lifted them, and I waited for her to ferry them to the hall linen closet and back. I heard the slight slam of the closet door and then she returned for the towels.

"Mother, she wants to do it," I said.

"I don't care, Dinah."

"Mother, even if she's eighty-three, you can't just dismiss her wanting to get married. She doesn't have to have your permission." Mother lifted the stack of yellow and white towels, propping her chin on the top. "She wants you to be her matron of honor. You've always regretted never being a bridesmaid."

With her chin on the towels, she stopped and stared at me.

"Dinah, that is the silliest thing I ever heard," she said, and turned and exited the room. This time I followed her into the hall, where she lined the towels up perfectly, all yellow together, all white on top. Everything folded into neat, clean squares, darker colors at the bottom of the stack.

"Mama, are you being prejudiced about old age?"

"Dinah, sometimes you really make me mad. You're so know-it-all." She closed the door and I had to follow her to the kitchen.

"Mama, I'm not trying to make you mad. Lilly wants to get married. She has a right to marry if she wants to."

Mama turned on the cold water in the sink and started filling up the kettle for making tea, when I knew good and well she'd made tea that morning and it was sitting there right on the counter in a pitcher.

"There are financial considerations. We don't know a thing about him," Mama said, staring out the window and letting the water overrun the kettle.

She turned off the water and poured some out of the kettle and set it on the stove, without turning on the fire beneath it. She turned and faced me then.

"I would be embarrassed to death, Dinah."

"Why?"

"I just would. You would just love to embarrass me like that, wouldn't you?" I was afraid she was going to cry.

"No, I wouldn't," I said.

"I guess you'd want someone to have a bridal shower for them, too."

"Well, I hadn't thought about that, but I guess it's possible. We could get them bath gel." I laughed.

She looked out the window again, as if she were wishing she could escape.

"Just because I'm not as goofy as you and your father!" she said with real conviction. And with that incomplete denunciation she left the room. I heard her walk down the hall to her bedroom, then go into her bathroom and close the door. I stood in the kitchen looking at the meatloaf she'd already made, which was cooling on top of the oven. I went over and pulled a crusty piece off the edge and ate it. She made wonderful meatloaf. I really couldn't understand why she'd be so mad or upset or whatever. And I'd certainly never thought of my father as "goofy." And then I realized she was referring to the incident in the hospital. His romance with Audrey. She couldn't get over it. Forty-seven years with a faithful husband and one jolt at the end to ruin everything. I started setting the table for supper, pulled out the two freshly washed quilted placemats and two glasses from the cabinet, opened the refrigerator and dropped ice cubes into the glasses until they were filled. Then Mama returned.

"I wish you'd do that without holding the freezer door open the whole time," she said. "It lets the cold out." I could tell she'd been wanting to say that to me for weeks but she'd had to wait till she was angry to get it out. But she wasn't just mad at me. She was mad at Lilly, but even more than that she was mad at Daddy.

I poured iced tea into the glasses and set them on the table.

"You want peas or corn?" she asked me.

"I don't care."

She pulled out a box of frozen peas and I wished I'd said corn. I looked at her untinted gray hair and wondered if she ever considered tinting it. She was an attractive woman but she didn't try to make much of herself. Never had. Maybe it was admirable that she accepted herself so readily. I was always trying to improve myself. If I could have, I'd have erased myself entirely and started all over. We were very different people, and that minute it seemed to me there was something wrong with both of us, but I couldn't figure out what it was.

I watched her drop the peas into some boiling water and

wondered if she'd ever get over being so angry at Daddy. It occurred to me then that it was like my anger with Dude. It was the first time I'd realized we had that in common. But hers, I was afraid, could never be resolved unless in heaven. At least, I thought, I had a chance.

☆

When the phone rang, I was dreaming. Dude and I were driving down a street together. At first I thought it was the office phoning with another cowboy proposition. Finally I woke up and realized I was in Mama's motel bedroom and the phone in the hall was ringing above the roar of the attic fan Mama turned on at night to save on air-conditioning.

"Dinah." The voice was urgent. "I sure hate to wake you up this time of night but . . ."

The voice sounded vaguely familiar.

"Who is this?"

"It's Dorothy Little at the café. And Easy Malone was in here a while ago having some coffee. And he got a call from the night watchman and it seems like Little Dude is parked across from the drugstore and shooting at the red light. And Easy just left, looking mad as a wet hen, like he might feel better if he could arrest somebody tonight."

"Oh, I sure do thank you a lot, Dorothy. I really appreciate your calling me."

"Sure thing, honey," she said, and added, "You sure do seem to be having your share of problems lately. 'Night."

It was a kind sentiment, but it only underscored the fact that everybody in Midnight knew everything.

As we'd talked, Mama had come to her door barefooted, her shoulders scrunched together under her thin gown as if she were cold. It was extremely rare to see Mama barefoot. She switched off the attic fan in the hall and it was suddenly quiet.

"What's wrong?"

"Oh, nothing, Mama. Dorothy Little said Larry was parked downtown and there was some trouble. I'm sorry it woke you up."

I went back to the bedroom and started pulling on my jeans.

Mama followed me, shaking her head, like she was thinking this was just another nail in the coffin of her family's reputation, whatever that was.

"So where're you going?"

"Sounds like he's been drinking, Mama. Supposedly he's been shooting at the red light."

She turned away modestly when I pulled my gown over my head.

"Well, I know he's real upset about Traci," she said. Her voice was soft and girlish, a tone I'd never heard. And I thought about Daddy hearing her like that in the night.

"I guess if anybody has a reason to shoot at the red light, he does," I said, slipping on a T-shirt.

She said nothing. Just stood at the door watching as I stepped into sandals.

"That phone ringing in the night just about scares me to death," she said.

"Why?"

"Mama," she said in her soft voice.

"Well, try to go back to sleep," I said.

"Oh, it doesn't matter," she said, already moving down the hall toward her bedroom.

The sheriff's patrol car with its red turret light circling was indeed pulled up beside Larry's patrol car parked across from the drugstore in front of the red light. I stopped on the other side of Larry's car and hopped out, though I wasn't looking forward to another round with Easy. The night air was soft and velvety and there was a gentle breeze against my face.

"Where'd you come from?" Easy said.

"Mother's instinct," I said. "Like radar."

"I reckon he's about two sheets to the wind," Easy said. "Maybe more. Plum crazy. Been shooting at the red light. Wonder he didn't kill some innocent traveler." He was standing beside the open driver's door. I couldn't even see Larry.

When I got to the car, I saw that he was sleeping in the front seat, lying on his side as if he'd just passed out behind the wheel.

"Hi, darling," I said to Larry. He didn't stir. I leaned inside and patted his arm, but he didn't move.

"Kid is drunk as a skunk," Easy said.

"You know the highway patrol quits working at midnight—I mean twelve o'clock midnight," I said to Easy.

I thought how this could ruin Larry with the highway patrol forever. They wouldn't like their personnel shooting at traffic lights. At first I felt an instant of relief that he might be rid of the highway patrol, but seeing him lying there like a dead man, I was sorry. I might want something else for him, but not because he'd gotten kicked out of the highway patrol, for God's sakes.

"Easy," I said, then remembered that people called him Lemuel to his face, "I'll drive him home." I opened the driver's door and tried to slide onto the seat beside Larry, but there was just an edge, so I leaned against it and put my arm along his and patted his sleeping shoulder.

Easy lifted his straw western hat and scratched his head underneath the few strands of hair. I could tell he was torn. As much as he'd love to arrest my son, Larry did represent some authority and Easy didn't cotton to having to back up such a charge to someone with more clout. He preferred to arrest drunken unemployed strangers.

Easy backed away and shuffled his feet once or twice. I felt like I was waiting for our old press to function.

"Sheriff, he's having some bad times. This boy has never been in any kind of trouble in his life. 'Cept marrying trouble, if you know what I mean. Let him off this time. I promise you this will never happen again. Really." I had unconsciously slipped into my most extreme Texas twang, the twang I tried to hide when I was being professional. I thought how women will do almost anything for their kids, even play for Easy Malone's sympathy.

Easy stepped back and looked toward the dark row of buildings. We both knew that by now the night patrolman would be back asleep in the barbershop. He'd get up in a couple of hours and walk around checking the stores with his flashlight again and then go back for another two hours of sleep. No one was watching, he was thinking. Who would know?

"You were saying some tough things to me 'bout them cats this morning," he said, still gazing at his dark domain.

"Look, I'm not writing a word about you and the cats. I

was simply suggesting you take a look around because some people are really upset and they'd appreciate it."

The red stoplight was flashing yellow now, and a car pulling a horse trailer sped through heading south. Easy shuffled his feet again. I looked above the old marigold-colored railroad depot, which is falling down since trains don't pass through Midnight anymore. In the vast wide sky above it the moon was nearly full, and I watched as it seemed to glide quickly in front of a cloud black as tar and then pass on through the starless sky.

"Well"—he cleared his throat—"you tell him I don't wanna see his face around here anytime soon. You hear?"

"I hear," I said. "I appreciate this, Sheriff."

"No time soon," he repeated. Easy hitched his pants and raked his throat and spit toward a clump of Johnsongrass.

"You all ever thought about making that old train depot into a shelter for the homeless?" I asked Easy. He turned and looked at me and sighed the same way Mama had earlier, and without even answering he walked on to his patrol car. I wondered when he slept. No wonder he has gunk in his eyes, I thought.

I locked up my own car and went back to Larry. Easy turned off the circling turret light and pulled into the highway. I shook Larry, but he didn't stir. So I shoved him with my hip till I could get behind the wheel. He was heavy as lead. I could see his pistol underneath him. He mumbled something but didn't stir. I locked the door so I wouldn't fall out. That's how I happened to be pulling out in the patrol car, when what should come cruising into town at approximately two thirty-two A.M. but that white Thunderbird rent-a-car with none other than Bobby Joe Daniels in the driver's seat. I braked the patrol car, since I didn't want to run into him and with the seat pushed back so far I could hardly touch the brakes it was a distinct possibility. He didn't even look my way, since I'd forgotten to turn on the headlights, but drove right through town, heading toward Dallas.

"My Lord!" I said to myself, and leaned on the steering wheel looking after him until the car was out of sight. Larry took a raspy breath and stirred. I prayed he wouldn't come to and shoot me. I drove slowly back to Mama's, parked in the driveway, and tried to wake him up again. I shook his shoulder, but it didn't do any good. So I carefully and nervously tugged the gun out from under him, thinking all the while of the headline—"Mother Shoots Only Son in Patrol Car Tussle"—and shoved it under the car seat. Then I sighed with relief and brushed his nice but sweaty blond hair back and looked at the side of his unhappy face. "You were such a wonderful kid," I said to him. I touched his cheek. His beard was heavy, like his father's. It's a mystery what you feel for a son. It broke my heart for him to be suffering and maybe ruining his life.

I made a few more attempts to wake him, hoping I could install him inside the house, but finally I gave up. It was like talking to the dead. It wouldn't be the first time a man had slept in a driveway in Midnight as a result of misery and overindulgence. So I just left the car and walked toward the breezeway and the side-door entrance to Mama's house. I knew Mama's neighbor would wake him up with a Frank Sinatra record at about seven o'clock. When I got inside I tiptoed around, but Mama called from her bedroom asking how he was. I swear she could hear a pin drop.

I said, "Actually, Mama, he was drunk and passed out. He's out there in the patrol car. I couldn't wake him up."

I expected her to quote a scripture of condemnation, but she said, "Well, bless his heart." She was always surprising me. But then, too, she was always more sympathetic with men than with women.

"Why is that?" I'd asked her once.

"Men are such kids," she'd said. "A lot of men don't ever grow up the way women do."

I crawled into bed and wondered before I fell asleep if Dude had grown up. And it occurred to me quickly that maybe I couldn't tell because I hadn't grown up, either. But that's just a term, I told myself. What does it mean? I had to admit I wasn't sure. Maybe it meant being willing to settle, compromise. Being willing not to run off and marry someone when you're already married. To accept the delicate balance of individuality and freedom and at the same time making some kind of commitment.

I closed my eyes. In my mind's eye Bobby Joe again drove

through the yellow light, heading for Dallas in his white Thunderbird rent-a-car, presenting a whole new mystery.

The patrol car was gone when I woke up next morning and stepped out the front door. Over the soft cries of the mourning doves, Sinatra was pouring out "A Foggy Day." I closed the door and leaned against it, wishing I'd left Larry a note asking him to phone. I felt like I'd been dragged behind a car for about a mile. I was too old to be rescuing men in the middle of the night. I called the highway patrol dispatcher, who told me Larry was taking leave that day. I didn't want to phone his apartment and wake him up, so I managed to shuffle to town, where I tried to invest my little tad of energy in *Citizen* improvement for the potential buyer from Longview. However, after a brief and discouraging attack on a pile of moldy phone books, I decided to share some of my distress with Dude.

"Dude," I said, "I hate to interfere with your ongoing life and loves . . ." I was heading into profound bitchiness. Vicious words welled up as uncontrollable as overflowing lava. "Our son was drunk last night and shooting at the red light in downtown Midnight. Fortunately, Dorothy Little phoned me and I rescued him from Easy Malone, who was about to send him to Alcatraz."

"Alcatraz is closed," he corrected.

"That's simply a factlet, Dude. You get the picture. Right? Huntsville, how's that?" Worse than Alcatraz. Everyone knows going to jail in Texas is like being imprisoned in Turkey or Syria. "And would you quit editing my conversation!" I told him.

He said to hold on a minute please, and the line went empty. When I got off hold, I was icy, which wasn't the way I wanted to be at all. I felt as if I was standing there watching some strange woman do the opposite of what I would have done. I wanted to be sweet and loving so he'd want me back. Instead, I was being mean as a panther. Any day now, I thought, I might find myself shooting him, like Cissy with Claude.

"Anyway," I continued in ice, "perchance is there a possibility you might drive over and talk to him tomorrow evening or sometime soon when you could fit it into your busy social schedule?"

"Sure," he said nicely. "When should I come?"

"You don't even care enough to be tacky back," I said too loudly, and slammed the door to Daddy's office cell, whereupon the Marilyn Monroe calendar fell face forward to the floor.

"You sound tired, Dinah," Dude said.

"Well, I was up half the night trying to save our son from the clutches of the law!"

"Sorry," he said calmly. "Lucky for him it happened in Midnight. The Dallas police might not have been so thoughtful."

"Thoughtful! Don't say anything nice about Midnight, Dude Reynolds!"

"I mean, Dinah, he didn't get beaten up, right?"

"If he'd never been in this crummy town in the first place, he wouldn't be in this awful situation where he had to get drunk and obliterate his mind. I just hope he doesn't have brain damage. You know that destroys brain cells."

I could hear talk in the background, men's voices, a bell from the news wires calling attention to an important story, a woman's laugh, and I suddenly ached with resentment at his being in the world where life was going on while I was stuck in this backwash with bugs behind every photo and where the news is missing cats.

"Should I come tonight?" he asked.

"No, he'll probably be feeling terrible tonight. Today he took sick leave. Tomorrow?"

"I can't make it tomorrow."

"Well, if you're ever free you might . . ."

"Okay, tomorrow," he interrupted, "if he isn't working."

"I doubt he'll be working," I said. "He'll be lucky if he hasn't been laid off."

I didn't really think he'd be laid off. I was just saying that because I wanted Dude to feel that everyone's life had gone crashing like the plane because he had been a Good Samaritan on the North Dallas toll road. Of course, if I'd been with him and he hadn't stopped on the North Dallas toll road, I'd have charged him with being a callous, heartless male citizen of the Metroplex and no doubt brought up Kitty Genovese.

Listening to the busy sounds of a real newspaper reminded me that it was Tuesday and not only had I not written a lick of the paper that would go to press Thursday, I had no real lead. Since nothing had happened except Roy Randolph's death and cats were still missing, I decided to do a follow-up on the plane crash. I sat down at Daddy's old Royal typewriter with the "d" that sticks and drafted a follow-up lead mentioning the funeral in Los Angeles on Saturday and Calvin Troope's new hit single, "Lord, I'm Ready When You Are." I was hoping to finish the lead before the man from Longview arrived so I could devote my full attention to my sales position. Then he could also witness the lively procedure of getting out our weekly rag, which in my mind was like my singlehandedly pushing an old steam locomotive through the downtown.

But before I had even finished the first draft I phoned Audrey, Daddy's love, and asked how Buddy Branch was doing. She said he'd left the hospital on Friday.

After a pause I said, "Audrey, you're talking about Buddy Branch who was in the plane crash with Calvin Troope?"

"Yes, ma'am," Audrey said. "He left early Friday."

"And what was his condition?" I pulled the "d" away from the typewriter paper and came back with a smear of ink on my fingers.

"He still wasn't talking."

"You're sure?"

"Yes ma'am, that's what I heard." She sounded a bit huffy at my cross-examination.

"Well, I'm sorry, Audrey, somebody just told me wrong. I appreciate the information. You've been a help." *Except for Daddy, of course.* And then I wasn't sure of that, either.

"Anytime your loved ones are in the hospital just let me know," Audrey said.

I was trying to decide whether to remove the 1962 calendar picture of the Grand Canyon from the door, when Roy Randolph's funeral procession wound up Midnight's main street from the Baptist church, ten cars with headlights burning rolling behind the Dunn Brothers' two-tone gray hearse. Like me, all the other citizens and merchants along the main street rushed to their windows, which were being decorated patriotically for the rodeo opening, unlike mine—Cissy across the street, the man at the cleaner's down the block, Dorothy Little at the Midnight Cafe, all of us counting the final measure of tribute to Roy Randolph.

Ten cars, as Cissy would declare later, wasn't bad at all for a man mean as Roy Randolph. We watched, too, to see if all the facing traffic pulled properly to the side of the street and stopped in respect for the passing dead. It was another custom in Midnight that was lost in the Metroplex. Daddy had once suggested that a sign be placed at either end of town demanding that passing vehicles pull over for funeral processions and warning that failure to do so would bring arrest and fines and possibly the sheriff standing in the road shooting at you. I had to smile thinking of the contrast with Calvin Troope and his fiancée and their gospel funeral on Saturday followed by a procession along a California freeway, where people would probably shoot if someone tried to stop.

I waited all afternoon for the man from Longview, leaning out the door occasionally, hoping to find a strange car pausing at the red light. I practiced in my mind the little anecdotes about the warmth and community of a little town. I'd appeal to his vanity. Tell him how Daddy was revered by the community, the very backbone. I even made a few notes for my final story—how after all these years the *Citizen* was passing on to new management, who I'm sure would run it with similar regard and repression, only I wouldn't say the latter, of course. I practiced a big smile and a restrained but effective, I thought, sales pitch. But no Mr. Chapman arrived. I was thinking at the same time about the old truism that if you waited for one guy to phone, another one might. Then I might find out why in the world Bobby Joe was cruising through Midnight in the middle of the night.

However, Martin Turner phoned to say Mr. Hugh Overton of the MPO Development Company would like to meet with me. I told Martin Turner, since after all we were nearly related, his having recently married my daughter-in-law, that

I'd had a visit from a representative of the city council. Martin Turner said the city council had leaned on Mama, too. He said, "Frankly, Ms. Reynolds, there's another side of this situation. If a sale to the MPO Company meant some new industry or business in the area and consequently some new jobs, a lot of people would be thrilled. The city council is, after all, made up mostly of downtown merchants who want to maintain the status quo." I told him I'd talk to Mama and get back to him. Of course, Martin Turner wasn't going to make any commission by maintaining the status quo, either. That's one of the problems of a place like Midnight—everybody and his dog has a vested interest in anything that happens.

I wondered if Daddy would have done business with a man who'd run off and married his daughter-in-law. That seemed to me such a daunting question of business ethics I decided I should discuss it with Dude, he being the only person I knew who'd studied philosophy, and it seemed to me I had every right to call and bother him with just such a problem. So I phoned.

"Reynolds," he answered pleasantly.

"Hi," I said. "Question: Is it immoral to have business dealings with a man who's run away with your daughter-in-law and married her, thereby committing bigamy? And (b), what if he's the only realtor in the area and the only one with the answer to your problem?"

I hung up the phone before Dude could comment and vowed that if the man from Longview didn't materialize I'd sell the *Citizen* to the devil to get away from there, knowing at the same time, of course, that Mama had no truck at all with the devil.

I put in a call to Ned English so I could mention the potential buyers, on the grounds that waiting for a potential buyer was the next best thing to getting back to work. Actually, while I was on my telephone blitz I wanted to tell him I would never look at another cowboy photograph for the rest of my life, but fortunately he was out.

For a while after Jud left at four-thirty I sang to myself in the emptiness of the *Citizen* while I piled trash into plastic garbage bags and pulled them into the back alley. I went from Hank Williams to Emmylou Harris to Jerry Jeff Walker on down to Janis's "Women Is Losers," and the Sweethearts of the Rodeo's "Blue to the Bone."

By six-thirty I was ready to drown my sorrows in some honky-tonk that didn't even exist anymore. Drowning sorrows was a much less casual thing than it used to be, even around Midnight. Obviously the man from Longview had changed his mind or gotten lost or been carried away by a UFO. I went back to Daddy's office to get my purse. Another day lost in Midnight. I mentally crossed off the day on the Dunn Brothers' Funeral Home calendar, which was the only current calendar in the place. It hung between Marilyn and a 1972 cowboy calendar I'd given Daddy that year, never dreaming I'd have to look at it someday.

I sat down in the office a minute wishing I still smoked so I could have a quiet cigarette and work out my life. In that dreary interlude it suddenly occurred to me that my life had gone downhill ever since I quit smoking, which was six years before, but at that moment it seemed only a brief interval. I was capable of connecting every world catastrophe to my quitting smoking if I worked at it awhile. There was only a sprinkle of cars in the Piggly Wiggly parking lot. Most people were already home eating supper and talking about their day to someone else. It was dark on the horizon above the feed store, but on the left a pink-and-scarlet line spilled over from the west, where the sun was going down somewhere around Lubbock. I'd never seen Lubbock, but I always thought of the sun going down just past Lubbock. I'd always heard it was a town with a friendly personality.

Suddenly I saw myself sitting there, like a view from a space capsule, me, a speck with a great question mark above my body. I thought of all the cars that moment streaming along the Woodall Rogers Freeway in Dallas, past the tall lighted buildings glowing in the dusk, past the Texas Commerce Tower with the hole in the middle. I might have been the only person in the world who'd admit to loving Dallas. There was a lot of passion in Dallas, and not just for money. Dallas was also full of people from little towns who'd moved there and been liberated from the constant scrutiny of a place like Midnight, black people and white people who moved there looking for jobs after the cotton economy moved west and little towns began to dry up. People all of a sudden looking at city lights for the first time. I thought of a long-gone rhythm-and-blues piano player out on Lemmon Avenue who used to sing songs like "Cherry, Cherry," beating on the piano until in the middle of the song he'd jump on top of the piano and the whole crummy bar would be rocking and rolling with him. "Cherry, Cherry" and "Honey Love," he'd sing in his lusty, wild, turn-on voice. I wondered what he thought of us white kids. Me and Bobby Joe carrying our brown sacks with the liquor inside, ordering setups and waiting in interminable lines at the toilets. I could remember all the old nightclubs scattered along the outskirts of Dallas and Fort Worth, scattered all over the state at the edge of cities, places where musicians like Willie Nelson paid their dues, nightclubs where you found a honky-tonk life that Hollywood never ever got hold of. Like that skinny piano player out on Lemmon Avenue jumping on top of the piano.

"Come on, Dinah," I said to myself out loud, "snap out of it, girl."

I turned off the old air conditioner and the place was remarkably hushed. For a moment in the old ink-and-dust smell I felt Daddy's presence, as if he were there with me to give me a pat on the back. And suddenly I had a feeling of good possibilities, as if sunshine were flooding my nicotine-free soul. I walked to the front to lock up and prayed the man from Longview would come the next day.

Outside, it was fading dusk, just when the light sinks from gray to navy. Across the street, Cissy was still doing a perm. I saw her talking steadily to the woman in the chair, who was separating tissues for her to wrap under the rollers. Paisley Blue, wearing a white T-shirt with pink pants tucked into white majorette boots, sat in a shampoo chair swinging her feet and blowing pink bubble gum as she bent over her homework, waiting for her mother to finish work and drive her home. It was a peaceful sight. For a moment I considered crossing over to study Paisley Blue's eyelid.

As I walked to my car, I thought of the long evening ahead.

A diet meal highlighted by a rice cake, TV with Mama, then the climax of the evening—the evening news. I was considering driving into the Metroplex for a movie, when I reached the Piggly Wiggly parking lot and saw a skinny black cat with a white line down its right rear leg.

"How come you're still loose, cat?" I called. It ran to me and made a quick, nervous rub against my leg. When I bent to pat it, it jumped and shied away, then scurried into the alley.

"You better watch it, cat," I called. For a minute I considered phoning Easy Malone and suggesting he tail that cat. The idea made me start laughing. By the time I got to the car I fell against it, half laughing and half crying. Midnight could drive me crazy anytime, not just on Sundays.

I was reading Maud Crow's community news of the week when Traci came trotting in the door dressed in a lemon jumpsuit. All eight ear holes were plugged, with a fourteen-carat assortment. She'd had her colors done in Dallas and lemon was supposedly good for her coloring, she said. Actually, I thought it bleached her out. She must have thought so, too, because she had slapped on an extra stroke of green eye shadow and liner. Traci claimed she had green eyes, but they weren't, they were plain old Hershey's brown except when she got mad and they looked yellow, but it made her mad if you said that. Even on her driver's license she'd said green. I thought it was interesting that she used food to describe her colors, when she never cooked. It was as if she'd corrupted the language by taking all the food words—like "strawberry," "vanilla," "butterscotch," "plum," "pumpkin," et cetera— and making them into clothes words. When I saw her I couldn't help but feel a leftover of annoyance after her first-row-of-the-choir performance on Sunday.

"Dinah," she said, "could I talk to you?" Like nothing odd had ever happened. I said, "Listen to this." I read a bit from the Oak Hills community-news column: " 'Brother Joe gave an inspiring sermon on Sunday, based on Luke ten, though he was still having trouble with his new aluminum hip and it was raining cats and dogs. . . .' " I laughed, but Traci just stood there tapping a long, tomato-colored fingernail against the counter. For a skinny person, she was immensely serious. I think if I were that thin I'd laugh and be carefree.

"How's your hyacinth?" I asked her.

"One of Daddy's pit bulls chewed it up."

"Oh, Lord!" I said, thinking not even a puny hyacinth should fall prey to such a fate.

"Have you talked to Larry?" she asked me. Tap, tap, tap.

"Traci, I think I should tell you that nobody was thrilled about your showing yourself off in the first row of the choir on Mother's Day right after news of your separation had gotten around town."

She dropped her head. I could see small white specks like dandruff in the part of her thin hair. Looking at that girl from any angle you found problems, I thought. Then I felt guilty for cursing her out first thing.

"I was trying to make things normal," she said.

"Traci, honey, things aren't normal," I replied. "And I don't think that's the way to get from here to there."

"Did you talk to Larry?" she asked me.

"I tried, but he doesn't want to talk," I said. "I'm afraid what he wants is a period of silence followed by a divorce." She stopped tapping her fingers against the counter and stood still for once, staring at me as if I'd struck her.

"A divorce!" Her small face was suddenly pale, stricken, and unbelieving. I could see a slight twitch under the green line of her right eye.

"Oh, no!" She leaned on the wooden counter, which was so worn there were grooves for arms. She cupped her hand with the marquise diamond over her face but I knew she was crying. I get a low humming burn in my stomach when people start crying in my presence. I sometimes have to leave a supermarket when a baby cries.

"Traci," I said, "surely you expected that?"

She shook her head and sniffed.

"You run off and marry someone else and you don't . . . ?" I let it go. "How would you feel if he'd done that to you?" I asked her.

"What can I do?" she asked.

"Since when did you really want to save this marriage?" I asked, sounding like that *Ladies' Home Journal* column that every English-speaking woman in America, I'll bet, has read at least twice: "Can This Marriage Be Saved?" My mother has read it every month for fifty years.

"About one minute after I got in the room with Martin Turner," she said, "I knew it was a mistake."

"Well, I don't know what you can do," I said. "Wait and give it some time, I suppose." I felt guilty for being so caught up in my own problems that I hadn't focused on the debacle of Larry and Traci.

"He'll calm down," I said.

"Maybe we could have counseling," she said hopefully. There is a marriage counselor on every corner in Texas, just as there used to be mom-and-pop grocery stores. It's the hottest thing going next to valet parking and car phones. Hotter than Texas Trivial Pursuit. It has been a godsend for numbers of down-at-the-heel preachers. One told Mama he'd given up the pulpit in order to allow his patients the opportunity to pay him. It's more important to them that way, he'd said.

"Where's the baby?" I asked.

"She's in the car." Traci sniffed, fumbling for a tissue in her basket purse.

"In the car! Alone?"

She nodded.

"Traci, honey, don't you know you shouldn't leave a baby in the car alone, especially in hot weather? They can smother," I said, trying to be calm. "Even Faye Belt ties her dogs in the back end!"

Traci looked up with green smudges and swept a pink tissue like a windshield wiper under each eye. It reminded me that she'd hinted that what she wanted for Christmas this year was to have her eyelids tattooed so she wouldn't have to wear eyeliner that would run.

"I'm sorry," she said. "I left on the air conditioner."

"She could get carbon monoxide poisoning with the air-conditioning on. Where's the car?"

"In the Piggly Wiggly lot." She sniffed again and raced out the door, leaving it to slam behind her. I hurried to the office and looked out the window at her old, crumpled red Rabbit. It was amazing the air-conditioning worked. I watched Traci rush to the car, open it, lift the baby from her car seat, and hug her. She kissed the baby and then lifted the baby's arm and waved it toward me. I felt guilty then for scaring her. It seemed to me that no matter how I tried to get along with that girl, I always ended up in semi-hysterics.

I watched till Traci had strapped the baby back in her seat and driven off, waving to the passing free-lance ad stuffers who shortly arrived through the front door to fold the ads they would stuff inside the paper on Friday. One wore a crossing-guard uniform. They turned the radio to their religious music station and began folding ads and teasing Jud. It was the only time I ever heard him talk about anything but the weather. He was a serious weather observer. I stared at the crummy office walls and told myself that if I concentrated on writing stories maybe the man from Longview would appear. Maybe he'd be some noble, handsome widower about Mama's age. They'd fall in love and go on a honeymoon and Mama would get a golden tan.

I tried to pull myself away from that daydream to edit the weekly Sunday-school lesson. I had to concentrate on the story since I'd caused a panic the first week I was there by cutting it at the end, thereby leaving sinful Saul on the road to Damascus before he'd had the vision and become St. Paul. I rewrote the plane crash follow-up story and proofed the ads Jud had already set.

About five, Cissy stuck her head in the door to say she'd see me Saturday night about ten.

"Why so late, Cissy?" I asked her.

Cissy said that was Saturday-night hours in Midnight.

"I bet it's a lot more interesting here than in Dallas," she called.

"Well, I wouldn't say that."

"You wouldn't admit it if you thought it. You've always been prejudiced about Midnight," she said, holding the door open and letting what little air-conditioning we had escape into the street.

"There's good reason for prejudice about Midnight," I

called. "It's a crummy little dying town. I feel no guilt at all."

I surprised myself saying that, and I could tell Cissy was offended. Even the free-lance ad stuffers grew silent. But Cissy knew how to get back at me.

"When you going to see Bobby Joe again?" she called. It was like spearing me with a dart. Seeing my pained face, Cissy must have felt bad. She smiled, as if it were all just a joke, and waved her little palm-up wave.

"Well, I better go make someone beautiful. See y'all later," she said, and let the door slam.

I stood there, realizing Cissy had opened the tightly drawn curtain to questions about Bobby Joe that I hadn't let myself ask. Whatever was he doing driving through Midnight at two thirty-two A.M.? Why hadn't he phoned me? Why had he said the mystery pilot was talking? What if he went back to California without another word! Should I phone him? Women phoned men nowadays, I told myself, but I knew I wasn't going to do that. Was there any possible, reasonable way I could park myself in the lobby of his hotel and casually run into him in the elevator? If I were working, I thought, not captured by the *Citizen,* I might take a cowboy writer for a drink there. Of course, that wasn't where we usually took cowboy writers, but maybe I could make an exception.

That day I couldn't get one miserable thought out before another would hit me. "Please, dear Lord, let that man from Longview come today and buy this place!" I must have said it aloud, because when I turned around, the two ad stuffers were staring at me.

That night Dude phoned from the Midnight Cafe, where he and Larry had just finished the Wednesday-night special—all-you-can-eat heated frozen fried clams with rolls that were always damp on the bottom and hard on top and a help-yourself salad bar featuring week-old vegetables and moldy croutons and occasional weevils. (People put up with that kind of meal in order to have the lemon pie.) Larry, Dude reported, had been suspended from the highway patrol. On down the road that Sunday night, a Corona beer distributor was a bit steamed and felt it his civic duty to report to a cop that someone in downtown Midnight in a highway patrol car was shooting at the red light as he'd driven past. After an inquiry, Easy remembered the entire matter quickly.

"Oh, shoot," I said.

"He wants to talk to you, too. He says he's made some important decisions and he wants to tell you at the same time and get it all in the open."

"Another important decision, Dude, and I may have to check into Happy Acres."

But Dude wasn't worrying about my mental health that moment, he was thinking about his son, as obviously I should have been.

"He probably figures what he says to you may get back to Traci. He's saying he never wants to see or hear from her again but . . . who knows . . ."

I wondered if Dude meant that as a secret message for me. I read everything he said in layers, like the French layer cake he claims his mother made him on birthdays as a child—one white, one spice, and one chocolate layer, all with chocolate icing and marbles and charms and one quarter baked inside. How did he keep from swallowing the charms and marbles, not to mention the quarter? I never understood that. Maybe if I'd made him French layer cake on his birthdays, he'd never have fallen in love with Marilyn. And maybe I should ask him if she will make him a French layer cake. If she is a thin woman, it is altogether possible that she might not even discuss a French layer cake, and maybe he's not realized that.

"You're asking if I can be civil for a while and think about Larry's problems and not my own?"

"I didn't say that, Dinah. I'm just asking if we can come over and discuss his problems. There's no hidden agenda that I'm aware of."

"Don't forget I've lived with you long enough to know what you're saying without your saying it." He sighed and I realized maybe it was boring that we knew one another so well and maybe I shouldn't have pointed it out. And for a minute my heart clutched at the thought of him there at the wall phone in the back of the Midnight Cafe, leaning on the little shelf that's supposed to hold the Midnight phone book that's been missing for decades, stationed there between the two restrooms—COWBOY, COWGIRL—and holding his breath every time a door opened.

"Believe me, I don't forget that, Dinah. Not for a second. How could I?"

"I'm sorry. Come on over. Mama can watch her doctor program in the bedroom. But if you want beer, Dude, you'll have to bring some."

"We don't need beer," he said. "Larry's had enough for his whole lifetime."

I went to the bathroom to powder my nose, brush my teeth, and fluff my hair. Mysteriously, my hair seemed to have succumbed to a serious drooping disease the minute Dude dropped the bomb on me. It had gotten worse each day since then. It looked as if it needed a good fertilizer. I tried to make up for it all by putting on generous makeup, which only made me look phony, so I washed it off and started again, and that made my whole face look swollen. At this age, the face becomes like Play-Doh.

Hugging Larry at the door was a bit like hugging a mannequin. Dude touched my arm in passing, the way he might touch a maiden aunt with a mustache.

Mama, who'd just returned from Wednesday-night prayer meeting, announced that on that particular evening the preacher was especially burdened by the nationwide crack epidemic. Crack was spreading into the wilds of East Texas, an area generally considered backward even for Texas. She reported also on three people who were sick and two who'd had their houses broken into, rumors of another teenager succumbing to drugs, and the disappearance of yet another cat. She said that most people were looking to the *Midnight Citizen* to solve the cat mystery and she pointedly looked at me. And at that I noticed even Dude gave me a pitying glance. Before she left to change clothes, which she did each time she left the premises and returned, she pointed out to Larry that there were homemade cookies in the freezer if he wanted them. Then she tactfully retreated to her room. Mama is good about making cookies, but they're never eaten because they're always frozen. After a year she'll throw them out and bake some new ones to freeze, and it goes on and on.

Larry looked pitiful. His forehead, which was usually clear and handsome, was broken out, and his hair was dirty and needed cutting, and when he wasn't inhaling or lighting a cigarette he was biting his nails. His eyes showed the distortions of excessive alcohol indulgence, punishing to the face even at his age. He headed straight for Daddy's recliner, the problem chair. He was back to wearing jeans and a wrinkled shirt. Traci didn't iron and he wouldn't. Mostly she paid a laundry about one-quarter of Larry's salary to iron for them, since she thought ironing had gone out with black-and-white TV and dial phones.

Larry looked so grim I went over and kissed his forehead, pale with unhappiness, and asked how he felt.

"Okay," he mumbled, like someone just awakening from an amputation.

"Macho man," I teased, giving him a love pinch on his arm, and he managed a tiny flicker of a smile just for his mother. I could tell that no one else in the world could have provoked that smile, and I was grateful.

I took a seat across from Dude, not daring to sit beside him on the couch, even though I preferred he not look at me directly, and asked Larry about his job status. He mumbled in the dull monotone of the depressed and homeless that there'd be a hearing and then he might go back to work but be on probation for six months.

"Well, that's not so bad," I said, donning my Pollyanna smile.

"That's the best possibility," he said. "Since every third person in Texas is looking for a job, I reckon that might not happen." He shrugged, lifting his empty hands in an Italian-inspired gesture. He inherited all my bad habits and excesses—exaggerating, biting hangnails, smoking, and cavities. Dude didn't have a single cavity. It was a joy to look in his mouth. But "reckon" came directly from Traci Dawn Love.

"Do you really want that job?" I asked him. I had to bite my tongue to keep from saying, After all, it was Traci who got you into it in the first place. "I mean, this is a time when you might reconsider your options."

I could feel Dude glaring at me, trying to warn me off. Larry didn't need an "I told you so" from me, Dude was indicating.

Larry leaned forward and held his head, his thick blond hair scissoring through his fingers.

"Yeah, I know, Mama, you're probably glad this happened. You think I haven't done anything right." He looked at me and pounded on the arm of the recliner, making it obvious who it was he'd prefer to be pounding—Traci first, me second.

"Larry, we all make mistakes. . . . I'm not saying you did, it's just that now you have the chance to stop and think about what you really want."

He kept his head ducked, and for a minute it looked as if he was going to cover his ears. "You mean what *you* want, don't you?" he charged, without looking at me.

Dude came to my rescue. "I know it's hard to realize it," he cut in, "but you'll get past all this, Larry." For the first time I thought how painful this must be for Dude, too, especially coming on the heels of his dumping me, which even in my state of anger I knew wasn't easy for him. And I felt grateful that we were forever connected, that even though we might all live separately there'd remain something among the three of us that couldn't completely disappear, no matter what new allegiances we made. Like twins separated at birth who forty years later encounter one another wearing identical sneakers. I found that momentarily reassuring.

Larry looked up at us calmly. "I want the baby," he announced, stubbing his cigarette into Daddy's beanbag ashtray, which Mama still kept on the arm of his recliner. "I don't want her raising my baby."

"Maybe that's a possibility," Dude said, "but shouldn't you wait awhile to make a decision like that? That's a drastic step."

I couldn't contain myself. "Oh, Larry, you can't imagine how hard it is to raise a kid nowadays!" I said to him. Of course, it was simultaneously occurring to me that if Larry got the baby we could maybe change her name. But he was glaring at me.

"I don't need any preaching about how I don't know enough to make any decisions," he said slowly. He leaned back in the chair, as if distancing himself from me and at the same time bracing himself to launch an attack. "That's what you always say, Dinah. You've got all the answers 'cause your heart was broken over some guy. You didn't have the guts to do what you wanted to, but you know what everybody else oughta do."

If he'd socked me suddenly I wouldn't have been more stunned. He'd never in his life talked to me like that. And how on earth could he know about Bobby Joe? "That is the wildest thing!" I exclaimed.

"Come on, Larry, don't attack your mother. She's thinking about you, you know that."

I heard Mama's front door open and close, but it took me a few seconds before it registered that Traci had come prancing into the room with her springy walk, wearing black tights and sandals and a long black T-shirt with "*amore*" written all over it. She had a black sash around her head tied with a bow across her forehead, a style I happened to know she stole from Cher because she'd shown me the magazine photo. Her brown gelled hair fell in waves over the bow like a fountain.

"Larry, I've gotta talk to you, please. I've phoned and phoned. . . ." She turned to appeal to Dude and me. "He wouldn't let me in the apartment, even to get my things. . . . And I just must talk to you, Larry. I'm so sorry, you've gotta let me explain and . . ."

I could see her hands trembling as Larry rose from the chair and faced her.

"Get out of my grandmother's house, bitch. You don't belong in here and I don't want to even look at you. . . ."

When I was a teenager we'd cut out little sayings we'd clip from women's magazines and tack them on our bulletin boards. Like: *It's better to have loved and lost than never to have loved at all.* Corny sayings. And seeing him look at her, one of them flashed in my mind: *Hate is the embers of affection.*

"I don't want to look at you, and I'm gonna get my baby. You aren't . . ." he sputtered, "capable of raising a kid decent!"

I guess that's the worst thing you can say to a woman, threatening to take her child. I must have realized it instinctively, because I suddenly moved protectively toward Traci.

"Just get out of my life, you whore!" Larry shouted at her. She seemed stunned by his fury.

"Please listen, Larry . . ." I said.

Traci picked up the box of tissues Mama kept on a lamp table beside the couch, carefully camouflaged by a yellow crocheted cover, and began hitting Larry in the chest and shoulders.

"You'll never take my baby!" she shouted.

I looked to Dude to extinguish the incendiary atmosphere and saw him watching Traci with something like admiration, even fondness, which I certainly didn't understand. Why wasn't he standing up for his own son? And then I realized what he was reacting to was her passion. Obviously he hadn't found enough in me during all those years. I wondered for the first time if I'd squandered that on romantic dreams, and for the first time I had some understanding of Marilyn and why Dude's stop on the North Dallas toll road had changed our lives.

When I saw them standing there shouting at one another I was amazed, too. There I'd been, thinking of them as foolish kids, when actually they were older than Romeo and Juliet. They were lovers with all the agony and the ecstasy being lovers implies. When TV needs dramatic passion they have a shooting or a car wreck or a fire. They couldn't possibly put that kind of passion on the TV, or the screen would ignite.

Suddenly Mama appeared at the door. "Stop this!" she shouted.

Traci dropped the tissue box and began to cry.

"My stars!" Mama said.

I sat down. Larry turned his back to Traci and stood there on Mama's practical sculptured beige-on-beige carpeting. I told myself that I wasn't going to apologize to Mama. This is life, I'd tell her later, even if it is what she'd call goofy.

"Larry, let her speak," Dude said.

"She doesn't have any right to speak to me."

"You can't take my baby!" she said. "You'll never take my baby!"

"Traci is a good mother," I said.

I saw Dude glance at me with some surprise. I was through with trying to control things like Mama. I was going to let things happen.

Mama flipped on the ceiling fan to defuse the anger, and

the pseudo-brass blades slowly began to stir, creating a mosquitolike hum above us. We watched as she moved over to Traci and bent to pick up her tissue box.

"I'm sorry," Traci said to Mama. Then she began afresh with her little rusty-sounding voice, which could be very effective. "I'm sorry, Larry. I did a terrible thing, I realize now. But it's all over. Now I can't imagine why I did such a dumb thing. It's like I was temporarily insane. Crazy. But now I know I love you, Larry," she said softly. "I promise, if you'll just give me another chance I'll prove it. . . ."

I couldn't help but root for her since she was such an incredible underdog, rooting for the underdog being instinctual in my white-trash genes. If only she'd stopped then.

"I wish you'd forgive me. I know it may take a while but I'll wait. I just want you to know that with all my heart I want to live with you and be your wife and raise our daughter. . . ." It was too much, like my oversale to the man from Longview. And it began to sound like a bad speech from a made-for-TV movie. I wondered if Traci had picked it up from the TV or if that kind of thing funneled involuntarily into her little gray matter as if she had a Nielsen hookup to the back of her brain.

"I'm sorry about your job, too," she whispered rather sweetly. "I know that is all my fault, too, and . . ."

Just when I began to wonder if he was maybe responding, Larry turned, his face stripped of all but exhaustion.

"Words are cheap . . ." he began.

That line came from an old boyfriend of Marianne's. We'd thought it pretty clever in high school, and I'd passed it on to Larry years later, warning him of people who promised but never delivered.

". . . and I swear to God," he continued, the muscles in his pale face rigid, "I won't forgive you if I live to be a hundred and forty, and I'm going to divorce your ass and take my baby and see you go to jail. And if that doesn't get you out of my life, I'm gonna kill you."

There was a pause, all of us looking at Larry—Mama and Dude and me and Traci—all of us sick with love or the hurt of it. Then Mama turned around and started toward her room and Larry went out the opposite door, followed by Traci, sobbing. Outside, she screamed something at him I couldn't understand—a loud, hysterical burst of words that rattled the air like an automatic weapon. After a minute we heard him start the old pickup he was driving now that the patrol car was off-limits, and his headlights flashed through Mama's front window across me and Dude. Then he backed out of the drive and started toward town.

I looked around, feeling like a train had gone through the room. I half expected the furniture to be crushed and splintered. I fell back against the couch, exhausted.

"Why is everything so crazy?"

Dude didn't answer for a minute.

"I don't know, Dinah." When he said my name he sounded like a stranger.

"They'll calm down," he said.

"You think they'll get back together?"

"Probably. It hasn't worn out yet."

I thought that was a curious thing to say and realized maybe that's what had happened to us. It had worn out for him, and then suddenly romance had appeared on the scene—the North Dallas toll road, to be exact—rearing its blond head.

"I hope they won't have one of those endlessly battling marriages that goes on and on like a soap opera year after year," I said.

"I do, too."

"We didn't have that."

"No, we didn't," he agreed, not giving me the satisfaction of looking at me.

He walked back into the kitchen and I listened to him pour himself a glass of water out of Mama's water bottle from the fridge. When he came back I said, "Look, Dude, I don't know where he heard about Bobby Joe. Really. I never said a word to him."

He paused, looked at me grimly. "Any one of a hundred or so people could have clued him in, Dinah."

"Well, that's not fair, Dude."

He started for the door and I felt desperate to stop him.

"Have you figured out my ethical problem yet?"

"No," he said. "Frankly, I haven't given it much thought."

Then he raised his hand in a half good-bye and was out the door.

I went into the kitchen and drank some tepid tap water out of his glass, thinking it was really very simple, he just didn't like me anymore.

MARTIN Turner and Hugh Overton were waiting for me the next morning in front of the *Citizen* when I arrived. Hugh Overton was large and florid-faced, and from his manner and bearing, I expected his teeth might be diamond-inlaid.

I said, "Good morning," which seemed to me not too compromising. Martin Turner said, "Ms. Reynolds, this is Hugh Overton." I shook his hand before really looking flat out at Turner. He was a slim, grayish man with shortstop sideburns who was not at all the *homme fatal* one might expect from his hot-pillow incident with Traci.

"You know my phone call about the MPO Development Company was made prior to your recent sojourn in the Western Motel in Euless," I reminded Turner. His ears turned red; then the color spread rapidly across his head and down his neck. I mean, after all, was I going to do business with and thereby give a commission to the architect of my only child's betrayal?

"Ms. Reynolds, I think this concerns primarily your mother and Mr. Overton here. I just want to be of service in any way I can." I rolled my eyes at that one. "And I assure you the arrangement concerning my services will be handled in any way you find satisfactory. But from your calls, I felt you were eager to explore Mr. Overton's proposal."

If Mr. Overton, who'd taken that interval to light a small cigar, was confused or wondering what we were talking about, he gave no indication. I suppose there's so much subterfuge around the average business deal that most people don't figure

151

to understand but a portion of the discussion anyway. This is typical of the kind of sticky situation that happens in Midnight. Maybe the answer to the ethical question Dude hadn't thought about was that in a place like Midnight you couldn't be ethical; it was an impossibility. Maybe that's why Jesus hung around cities like Jerusalem instead of Bethlehem. But I continued doing what I'd promised to do, just letting things happen, spin the bottle.

Hugh Overton had already had a stroll around the building and Turner indicated to me that MPO—O for "Overton"— Development Company would make an even nicer offer than it had made earlier. So I phoned Mama immediately. But Mama wasn't at home. It took me a minute to realize it was Thursday morning and she was having her hair done.

I excused myself and hightailed it across the street to Cissy's, where Mama had just had her shampoo and was sitting with a purple towel wound around her head, waiting for Cissy to perform the usual.

I quickly and quietly explained things to Mama, and she said it would take at least an hour before her hair was set and dried. I said, "Well, maybe I can entertain them or they'll come back in an hour." Then she looked up at me over the *People* magazine she'd been thumbing through all the time I was talking to her and said, "No."

I said, "Mama, what do you mean, 'No'?"

She said, "I told you, Dinah, that you could talk to the MPO Development Company, but I didn't say I'd sell the *Citizen* to them."

By this time Cissy, wearing a purple Mexican dress with embroidered white doves across the bodice, intruded herself into the conversation. "Dinah, surely you can't be serious about selling to them? They ruin every town they've ever had anything to do with. You might as well shoot us all dead in the head as sell out to those speculators. I wouldn't be surprised if they weren't part of the Mafia."

"Am I serious?" I said. "Cissy, I'd sell to Shiite Muslims to get out of this situation."

She commenced to squeeze the purple towel atop Mama's head. "Well, the city council would (a) get an injunction and then (b) sue you," she said. "If that didn't work, we might (c) put out a contract on you."

I turned back to Mama. Cissy spun the chair around so Mama was facing the mirror. Then she pulled the towel off, revealing short, wet kinked hair the color of newsprint. Cissy took a comb out of some kind of cleaning fluid and began the slow, tortuous task of combing and rolling Mama's hair.

"Mama, why would I want to talk to MPO if I weren't going to talk about selling the *Citizen*?"

Mama looked at me in the mirror, careful not to move her head as Cissy combed. "I don't know, Dinah. There are a lot of things you do I don't understand."

In the annals of crime I don't think there are many matricides by daughters, but there was one in my heart that minute, and if I had truly been letting what happened happen, I would have smothered Mama with that damp purple towel right there at that relatively early-morning hour in the Pastel Beauty Studio.

It took every ounce of strength I could muster to walk back to the *Citizen*, take Hugh Overton's card, and lie to him, saying that Mama was toying with another offer and we'd get back to him in a day or two if this didn't work out. He looked at me over his little cigar. He knew I was lying. I knew he knew I was lying. Turner knew I was lying. It was such an anticlimax both of them stared at me a moment, and I could hear Hugh Overton swishing saliva back and forth through his teeth.

I said, "Have a good day," a line I would normally not use even under torture, and turned away and walked into the *Citizen*, where I hid behind the Grand Canyon calendar until I heard them drive away.

As soon as they were gone, I went outside thinking maybe I'd stroll to the water tower, climb to the top, and do a swan dive off it right in front of the Fisher sisters' duplex, except I can't do a swan dive. But I did take a walk up the highway wondering if there were some way I could promise Overton we'd sell the *Citizen* so that Mama would either have to sell it to him or see me go to jail. Of course, given the morning's events, I couldn't be certain which path she'd choose.

When I returned from my walk of fury up the highway, the

ad stuffers had arrived and were still glowering at me because of the unkind comments I'd made about Midnight the day before. Then, before I could pour myself coffee, Traci dragged herself in the door and sagged against the counter. The very sight of her made my right eye start twitching.

"I couldn't sleep a wink last night," she said.

"Daddy used to sing a song that began like that." I sang a few bars for her.

"Dinah," Traci began importantly, "thanks for what you said last night. It's nice . . . how you've been helping me. I'm glad we're friends now. I just hope I can stay in your family. . . ."

It would have been nice if I'd been able to tell her genuinely that I hoped she stayed in my family, too. But I couldn't bring myself to respond in a storybook manner. I simply said that I sincerely hoped things worked out better for her, whatever happened. I knew that wasn't the response she was hoping for. But I watched her in her inimitable fashion take in my lukewarm reaction, then move right along in her choppy, determined way.

"So this morning I just had to talk to him. So I phoned and phoned, but he wouldn't answer. I went by there, he wouldn't let me in. He said the most gross-out things through the door! They would just upset you if I told you what he said. Then he threw beer cans at the door. And all the time he was playing George Jones music like he always does when he's especially destroyed."

She stared at the pictures on the wall behind me a minute, and I felt bad that, instead of Larry's bringing some decency and enlightenment to her life, he seemed to be spiraling down to her family's level of pit bulls and wart removal.

"What if he drinks himself to death, Dinah? You know, I've always wondered if he was unstable."

I stared at her. She wore the same getup she had on the night before. Unusual for Traci not to have a wardrobe change.

"Traci, might I remind you he's not the one who ran off." It was like jabbing a balloon. I could see her deflate as her tears rose, darkening with her plum mascara, first pooling and then welling over and leaving grayish-red tracks down her small face as if I'd run over her with a toy tractor. I wished I'd kept my mouth shut.

"I'm sorry, Traci. Frankly, this hasn't been one of my favorite mornings, not that I'm exactly crazy about mornings to begin with."

"I know it's all my fault!" she cried.

"Traci, to be perfectly frank again, there are several problems on the agenda this morning." I touched her thin, perhaps anorexic, arm. Her diet tended toward sodas, fried pig skins, and Snickers. "But about Larry, you upset him, Traci, but you didn't give him reason to go crazy and shoot at the red light and become a drunk. Don't blame yourself for that. He's supposed to be an adult and adults have to take charge of themselves even in the face of disasters." *Look at me*, I thought, and I might have laughed if Traci hadn't been crying.

"Oh, Dinah, this is the worst disaster of my life."

"Would you like some coffee?" I asked her, as I went to pour some for myself.

"Do you have any grapefruit juice?"

"Traci, I don't have grapefruit juice! Who keeps stuff like grapefruit juice around an office?"

"Mama does," she said. "Mama and the other mail clerks have a refrigerator where Mama keeps grapefruit juice." She shook her head. "What am I gonna do?" she cried.

Behind us, Jud made a scraping sound with his chair, groaned, and hammered on the press with a mallet. He didn't like for women to cry while he worked. He'd managed to convey that message without ever saying a word.

"Well, I'm sorry but I've got to get this paper out. And there's nothing you can do but get your own act together, and then when his head clears maybe you can work something out. If you want to. You can't depend on a man to make your life work, you know."

"I didn't know that," she said, lifting her head. "Nobody ever told me that. Why didn't anybody ever tell me that?" She sniffed and her face brightened. "See, you tell me things, Dinah, that's why I like you."

"Who in the world hasn't heard that, Traci? Why, even the

cloistered nuns of Nepal have probably heard that. I'd think you'd have picked that up on TV if nothing else."

"I only watch *Wheel of Fortune* regularly," she said. "Nobody ever told me nothing."

"Nobody told me '*anything*,' " I corrected.

"You, too?" she asked.

Just then the Fisher sisters drifted in the door, smiling and greeting us cheerily. Traci sniffed, and the Fisher sisters glanced at her sympathetically, then pretended not to notice her streaked face. They handed me an ad for their duplex apartment—"two bedrooms with a view," it said. They asked if there'd been any response to the cat reward. I said there had been none so far. At which point Cissy sashayed in.

"Dinah, stop the press," she shouted.

"Why stop the press?"

"I've been talking to Mayor Downey about Midnight putting up a monument to Calvin Troope," she said, "and we want you to write an editorial for this week while the tragedy is still on everybody's mind."

"An editorial about what?"

"About putting up a memorial monument to Calvin Troope!" she shouted. "Would you stop that press!"

"No," I said. "I can't stop the press and write an editorial now. It's too late. Besides, Cissy, who cares two hoots about a memorial for Calvin Troope? Why Calvin Troope?"

Cissy put her hands on her hips and then slid them off as if she'd remembered they would wrinkle her purple Mexican dress.

"Well," she said, incredulously, "he was a star!"

"Semi," I said.

"Not to mention he was the biggest baby ever born in Midnight!"

The Fisher sisters said that was true. They thought it would be real nice to have a monument. "We have very few monuments in Midnight," one of them said. "There's the First World War memorial and the Second World War memorial and the wax apostles and that's it."

In the background, the old press pounded out the news of the week.

"Where would we put another monument?" I asked.

"Right out there." Cissy pointed in the direction of the red light. "Across from the drugstore, maybe near the Christmas tree."

The Christmas tree was a sycamore that had died years before. But the town had filled the hollow trunk with cement, and each December they shooed away the starlings and strung lights from its sparse, brittle limbs. Every Christmas I expected it to disintegrate, leaving nothing but a lump of cement, but it continued to stand upright against all logic, like the town itself.

"What about in the minimall? Or outside the Ti-dy Washateria? We could also put a plaque on the spot where Ernie and Louie shot one another," I suggested.

"I wish he'd change the name to 'Laundromat,' " Cissy said. "That's so white-trash—'Washateria.' Inside the Metroplex, the word is 'laundromat.' "

With the controversy, Traci had perked up and was no longer sagging against the counter. "In Dallas they have tanning booths you can lie in while your clothes are washing," she chimed.

The Fisher sisters said wasn't that amazing; there were so many wonderful things nowadays.

At the thought of the Fisher sisters lying in tanning booths, I had to turn away. Traci pulled out a compact and began to redress the tracks down her cheeks.

"Well, I gotta go to my exercise class," she said.

"What class?" I asked.

She said she was learning to pump iron so she could help her half uncle when he opened a spa next to the used-video shop in Euless when the economy picked up. I didn't ask her to explain the half-uncle bit.

Cissy interrupted her. "The mayor and I are serious about this monument, Dinah. Will you or will you not write an editorial? Kind of feel out the mood of the populace?"

I shouted over the press that it was too late for this week. "And furthermore, if you want to know the truth, I don't think there is any way you can document that Calvin Troope was the biggest baby ever born in Midnight. For one thing, he probably wasn't. Calvin Troope was maybe the biggest white baby born in Midnight," I said, "but there may have been bigger black babies or Chicano babies. Are you going to put that on the monument? 'Calvin Troope, the Biggest White Baby'? Then somebody would probably bring a lawsuit and we'd have to put up sister monuments for the biggest black baby, biggest Chicano baby, biggest Vietnamese, and biggest Thai baby. Et cetera." By now the free-lance ad stuffers had quit folding and were joining the discussion.

"That's right," one of them, a woman of African-American descent, said. Her cousin had had a baby a month overdue that weighed nearly twelve pounds.

Cissy glanced at the Dr Pepper clock. Her eleven-o'clock was waiting for her.

"Okay. Forget Calvin Troope as a baby," she said. "How about Calvin Troope as a performer?"

"The only significant thing about Calvin Troope that I can see," I said, "is that he was born here and his plane crashed here. How about a monument to Roy Randolph?" Suddenly the fire alarm sounded and I really had to shout. "He was born here, lived here, and died here."

Cissy shouted, "Dinah, you are deliberately making this complicated." She leaned toward me and enunciating carefully said, "You certainly arose on the wrong side of your *empty* bed this morning!" Then she spun on her espadrilles and was out the door.

Somehow we managed to get the issue of the *Citizen* out the next day. As soon as we were finished I drove to a multi-movie at a shopping mall in the Metroplex and saw two movies to avoid facing Mama. When I came home around ten she was waiting for me but pretending she wasn't by raptly watching a TV movie. I suggested we advertise the *Citizen* in some foreign publications, since foreigners seemed to be about the only people buying land in Texas. Mama didn't even turn away from her TV program. She said, "Your father would spin in his grave if I sold to some foreigner."

Escalating our war, I said, "Yeah, but he's gone, Mama. I'm not."

• • •

At midnight the following night, Cissy and I were drinking jug Chablis under the stars, which I must admit were rife across the sky so that it absolutely took my breath away when I first looked up. Daddy had always warned people that to move inside the Metroplex was to lose the stars at night, and he was certainly right about that. What Cissy was really up to, she finally confessed, was wanting to prove to me that there was indeed strange activity in the woods. So after our ten-o'clock dinner at the Midnight Cafe we drove to her house and sat out on her patio, near the aluminum utility shed and beside her big fig tree, and waited for intruders. Claude was fishing on Lake Texoma and Paisley Blue was staying in town with Cissy's mother. Pattycake was inside the mobile home, locked in a bathroom, where supposedly her shrill yelping couldn't upset Cissy's detective work.

"What in the world are you going to do if somebody shows up? Make a citizen's arrest?"

"Lord no, I'd be scared to death to do that," Cissy said. "But it's making me nervous. I tried to get Easy to come out here, but he's so worthless! So at least if you hear them, I'll have a witness."

"Maybe they're looking for treasure lost in the plane crash. Or maybe it's the saints," I said.

"Dinah, you've had too much wine. You know saints don't appear at night."

We laughed. We'd probably both had too much wine.

"You have a Polaroid camera?"

"Sure," she said, "I have to take Polaroid shots of Paisley right and left."

"Well, get your camera, and if we hear anyone we can snap their picture."

Cissy started giggling. "They were here last night. I saw them when they came 'round the house. They had a flashlight. They walked down the road, must have been parked a good ways off. . . . I can't imagine what they're up to."

"Maybe it's the nucleus of the emerging Paisley Blue Fan Club. They're creating a grotto."

"Dinah, don't make fun of poor Paisley, bless her heart."

"Actually, Cissy, I feel kind of silly sitting here."

"You're going to be sorry if your next lead story is that we've all been killed in our beds."

"You won't be killed. Pattycake will protect you."

"Pattycake couldn't protect a gnat," Cissy said.

Occasionally in the soft breeze we would get a whiff of the ripening figs around us and sometimes the clean smell of the woods beyond, but mostly we smelled the Avon oil Cissy had generously sprayed on our arms and legs the moment we stepped outdoors.

Cissy yawned. "Boy, I don't know how spies stay awake," she whispered. She had a loud whisper.

"They have people like Pussy Galore to keep them awake," I said. I wouldn't have even said that name if I hadn't been drinking wine.

"Girl spies, I mean."

"They have Michael Caine."

Cissy giggled again.

We were quiet for a few moments in the midst of the night noise around us. Through the occasional croak of frogs from an old livestock pond and the constant buzz of cicadas, we'd heard an owl's hoot, deep and lonely, from far in the woods. Like us, I said to Cissy, sitting there in the dark waiting for someone.

"This must be the only place in Midnight where you can't hear a highway," I whispered.

"Sometimes you can," Cissy said. "Even planes sometimes." We looked up where a red-eye was coming in high, a small red light among the stars, heading for Dallas/Fort Worth International Airport about fifteen miles away. The airport was dotted with minibars every few hundred feet with signs reading: DO A DAIQUIRI.

"Dinah. I have been through what's happening to you . . . I mean, what is happening with you and Dude. So you might consider listening to my advice."

"You don't have to give me a résumé, Cissy."

Cissy poured more Chablis into our glasses and set the bottle back on the round white metal table between us.

"Well," she whispered, "have you considered that Dude

might be just testing you? Maybe the other woman isn't serious."

"Oh, it's serious. Marilyn is her name. Unfortunate name. I've heard her voice, too. She sounds like the BBC."

"Foreign?"

"No, but she certainly doesn't sound like us."

"I think you should explore the relationship a bit more before you throw yourself on the divorce pyre. But if Dude doesn't change his mind, you can always move back here and run the *Citizen*. I bet you'd have a good time."

"Good time!" I whispered loudly. "I don't belong here, Cissy. It's like trying to wear clothes you've outgrown, shoes too little. I need a certain amount of automobile pollution and cowboy contact to get through the days. I like jousting on the North Dallas toll road. I like the sight of people armed with briefcases marching toward elevators in glass buildings. I like the smell of men's aftershave in crowded elevators in the morning, the back of a man's neck over a shirt and tie. The camaraderie of coffee breaks, the clatter of office machines. I like the possibilities of the day's mail and the reassurance of pink message slips. I hate a one-light town. I like margaritas after work and the safety of flirting with strange men you're unlikely to ever see again."

Cissy was quiet a minute.

"Are you missing Dude or manila envelopes?"

"All of the above," I said.

"Well, you seem to be giving up. It doesn't always last, you know. I mean, I know that for a fact," she confessed.

"I appreciate your sharing, Cissy. You're saying this could be a simple little fling?"

"Something like that."

"Not Dude."

"Why not Dude?"

"He's just not like that."

"He's a man," Cissy said. "See, you're just depressed, which gives you a chemical imbalance and you can't think straight. You should try to believe that he'll change his mind. And I don't know how you can be so certain he's not the type, when he obviously is."

"I am certain, unfortunately."

"Maybe he'll change his mind. How would you feel if he does?"

"I'd feel enormously grateful. It's partly my fault."

"Women always feel guilty. And you shouldn't," Cissy said.

"For twenty years I've been wishy-washy."

"Everyone is."

"Dude wasn't. Until now."

"Oh," she said, and sighed. "Well, that's different."

"That's how I could be wishy-washy for twenty years. Because he wasn't. I feel tricked. Which makes me madder."

"You were really surprised?"

"Oh, yes. I mean it was like the plane crash. That surprising."

"Strange," she said. "I was never surprised. . . ." Her voice kind of wandered off in the night and we were quiet a minute.

"Maybe they had something else to do tonight," I said. "Or maybe they've found what they're looking for. I'm ready for Mama's motel bed." I stretched and yawned and dreaded the drive back. Midnight in the middle of the night was even more depressing than Midnight in the daylight.

"You're trying to change the subject," Cissy charged. "Just let me add one more little note." She leaned forward. "Dinah, I'd go real slow and not press him about what's gonna happen. Has he mentioned divorce?"

I waved off a mosquito buzzing my ear and hit a fig limb. "No."

"See!" she said.

I thought about that as I shifted my legs. I wondered if she could possibly be right. Could the whole thing vanish with an apology? The idea was tantalizing, but like a daydream it had an air of utter fantasy. Dude was not a wishy-washy type. And I knew that Cissy was a romantic. She confused life with the romance novels she reads, wherein the characters end inevitably rich, happy, and wildly in love forever after. Even in high school, just seeing two teachers chatting was enough to convince her there was romance in the air. She claimed the football coach and the typing teacher had sex in the teachers' lounge. When she caught the home economics teacher having her back rubbed by the business science teacher she proclaimed it to be true love. She swore the bank president and his secretary carried on a romance in the vault after banking hours. Especially after her miraculous reconciliation with Claude, she'd never be realistic. Nevertheless, I longed for her to persuade me that Dude's departure was only a temporary glitch.

It was after one o'clock and we'd drunk a lot of wine by the time we heard them heading toward the road, a small light shining in their path. Somehow they'd managed to enter the woods without our hearing.

"They don't have a criminal crouch," I whispered to Cissy. We watched them a moment more.

Then, because the wine had made me bold, I called, "Hey!" shattering the peaceful, starry night.

"Dinah!" Cissy said, and hissed to me.

The circle of light halted. Then the man in the lead turned toward us.

"Who goes there?" Cissy cried in a trembling voice. If I hadn't been so scared, I'd have giggled at her. That is, until I saw that in her lap Cissy was holding her silver-handled Saturday-night special. She lifted the gun and, holding it with both hands, pointed it toward the approaching figure.

"Cissy, put the gun down!" I grabbed for Claude's flashlight on the table, pushed the button, and pointed it at the intruder. He was not twenty feet away when I shone the flashlight in his face.

"Bobby Joe!"

"Well, whatta you know!" Cissy exclaimed.

"If that's the real thing, I surrender," Bobby Joe said, fairly casually, I thought, for someone with a gun pointed in the vicinity of his heart. Cissy lowered the gun.

Behind him his companion hadn't moved.

"Come on, Buddy," Bobby Joe called. Then Bobby Joe walked over and put an arm around me. After the discussion Cissy and I'd just had about Dude and Marilyn, his arm felt something like divine intervention.

"What on earth are you all doing wandering around our woods in the middle of the night?" Cissy demanded. "About driving us crazy!"

Bobby Joe looked back at his companion a minute. And in that moment the night seemed to grow peaceful again.

"It's a long story," Bobby Joe said. "I think it's about time we told them, don't you, Buddy?" Buddy Branch, his arm in a sling, stood in the shadows of a scrub oak. He spoke not a word.

"Tell you what," Bobby Joe said. "Let me talk to him and tomorrow we'll explain the whole business."

Later I would recall his choice of words.

Midnight moves in a series of processions on Sundays, when the populace streams to one or another of its five churches. They begin at nine-thirty with the march to Sunday school. At eleven, there's another procession to the preaching service. After eleven you can drive up and down the streets and hear hymns or sermons ringing out block after block, the next church's sounds fading in before the last ones are gone. It's the same in every small or midsize town in Texas, except around Austin, where, Daddy used to claim, many individuals are educated beyond their intelligence.

So the streets were deserted when Cissy and I met at nine o'clock in front of the Midnight Cafe, where Dorothy Little was just beginning preparations for her Sunday after-church buffet. Through the windows we could see her assembling her stainless-steel trays where later she'd offer one chicken main dish and one beef, the Sunday midday meal being her biggest draw of the week. Cissy left her car in the parking lot and we drove to Dallas to Bobby Joe's hotel.

At a quarter till ten a young woman wearing a pink terry-cloth robe and carrying a baby answered the door of the hotel suite. The baby had round blue eyes, as did the mother, who also had dark, frizzy Cleopatra hair down to her shoulders. She introduced herself as Sarah Branch and said her husband would be there shortly. She offered us coffee and Danish from a hotel serving cart and then excused herself to change the baby.

Soon Bobby Joe sailed in, gave me a quick and friendly kiss, and poured himself some coffee. He wore that nice early-morning, freshly shaved, relaxed look men can have that makes you want to climb back in the bed. Finally Buddy Branch, the mystery pilot from out of the shadows of the previous evening and the puzzlements of the recent past, appeared. In daylight I recognized him as the man I'd seen in the hospital, but he looked no less strange than he had then. His hair had been cut short and he wore white cotton gloves, and between his gloves and his shirtsleeves and across his forehead was an oozing pink rash which could have been a severe case of poison ivy, from rambling in the woods, or maybe eczema. Bobby Joe introduced us, and Buddy only nodded, then poured himself a cup of coffee with his good arm and took a seat in a tan block-shaped chair.

Of course, when you stop to think what it must be like to have survived a fatal plane crash, I suppose it could be as good a cause for the shingles or hives as anything. I mean it's hard to imagine. Indeed, people who do imagine are the ones who won't set foot in airplanes. And to think that Buddy was piloting it, too, and might therefore feel responsible.

Despite the presence of a disciple of Hollywood, Cissy was not distracted from our basic mission. She gathered the reins and took over, reminding Bobby Joe that she was Cissy Sanders, née Elizabeth McMichaels, and mentioned casually that her eight-year-old daughter, Paisley Blue, was in show business.

We all sipped coffee a moment in an awkward silence before Cissy said, "Now please explain why you two men have been tromping around on my property night after night?"

Bobby Joe said then, in a kindly voice, "Well, Buddy?"

So slowly, nervously, Buddy Branch proceeded to tell us about himself. How he was born in Oklahoma and raised around Hot Springs, Arkansas. He'd worked as a crop duster in Arkansas and Louisiana, then piloted small private passenger planes out of New Orleans, then followed his brother-in-law to Los Angeles. Only when Sarah and the baby returned, the baby freshly dressed in diapers and a T-shirt printed with turtles, did Buddy seem to relax momentarily. Occasionally he would pause, as if he'd forgotten what he was doing, and Bobby Joe would tell him to just take his time, and in a minute he'd continue. Something about him made me remember some miners on TV who'd been buried in a cave-in and dug out after days. They had stories of bizarre sightings, and their eyes were something like his, sunken into his head like those of an older man.

"Everything went along normally when we took off from New Orleans," Buddy said, speaking without looking directly at anyone. "It was a clear day. Visibility was good. We ran into a little rain near Baton Rouge, but it didn't last. When we flew into Central Texas it was clear, a little windy. Calvin was looking for the Trinity River 'cause he wanted to show his friend Midnight, Texas, where he was born."

Buddy paused then and took his first sip of coffee. His wrist was what Mama called "weepy." Bobby Joe got up to pour more coffee, and Buddy continued.

"We'd just made radio contact with Love Field, where we were scheduled to land, when all of a sudden the plane lost power." Buddy paused and held his hands together the way children pray. "The engines died. The electrical system failed. The radio went dead. Everything. It was strange. I kept trying to get the engines started again, trying to make some contact with the airfield. Nothing. Then, when we knew we were going down, I thought maybe I could bring it down on a highway. We weren't far from one, but the highway was just one line of cars, both directions." He stopped and I glanced at Bobby Joe, who was watching Buddy as if it were painful for him, too. By then the baby had fallen asleep in his mother's arms and Sarah had begun to cry. Buddy leaned forward and patted her knee.

"Well, I could see there was too much traffic, so I headed toward a farm-to-market road, but I couldn't make it." He leaned back in the chair and held his head a moment. Bobby Joe stood and moved to the window, his arms folded. Cissy and I glanced at one another, and Sarah, wiping away tears, said, "He's had such an awful time. . . ."

Buddy looked at his wife and the sleeping child and continued.

"Calvin saw we weren't going to make it. Course, you keep hoping, you know. Calvin was praying out loud. He was real calm and praying. I don't know what the girl was doing. I couldn't see her. I think he had his arm around her. He was very calm," Buddy repeated.

Bobby Joe moved back and sat down beside me on the couch and took my hand. Buddy said, "I don't remember the crash. Seems like there was a period of time that passed, and then I saw Calvin Troope and his girl walking along, holding hands, into this wide, bright light. I don't know where I was but I saw that. I was below them. It was just as clear as us sitting in this room." He looked up then, and for the first time he looked at me and then Cissy and he was nearly smiling. He seemed to enjoy that memory, as if that experience in itself had been awesome. He looked peaceful for a moment. And then he looked down as if remembering where he was, and what had happened, and the fact that his skin seemed to have picked up a plague from the Book of Job.

"I could see exactly the way they were walking toward the source of that light. And there was a sound, a high ringing sound. Loud. If I ever hear it again, I'll know it. To tell you the truth," he said, turning to me and Cissy again, "I don't think the three of us were there when that plane crashed. I think we were somewhere else."

I looked at Bobby Joe, who was watching me, and I blushed. I don't know why. Because he caught me believing what Buddy Branch said. I don't know. All I know is, Cissy and I looked at one another and she smiled, as if to say, *See, I knew there were saints in that Swiss chard.*

We all sat there awhile longer and Cissy and I asked Buddy a few questions. He told Cissy that he believed he'd find some evidence of his experience in the woods, and he indicated he was looking for something specific, though he never said what that was. He answered all our questions calmly, as Cissy said later, like an honest man facing a grand jury.

When we rose to leave, Bobby Joe held my hand a moment longer, as if he hated for me to leave. I felt a warm bond between us that had something to do with the present as well as the past. Then he asked me to have dinner with him the next night, which distracted me from the miracle at hand.

I admit it wasn't until later that I even stopped to ask myself if Buddy Branch was crazy. For one reason, I knew Bobby Joe wasn't. I knew, too, there are dimensions between crazy and the truth, something to do with skewed perception. But

Buddy was convincingly awestruck, and he seemed a genuine type of person. And fortunately, for him, he was from Oklahoma—that is, not from Texas—which automatically made him a more reliable witness in the eyes of the world.

I'd been around newspaper people all my life. I have an idea when somebody is lying. You can't always be perfectly certain, but there are some experiences, even fantastic experiences, that simply fall truthfully on the air. I confess I've even a time or two wondered about the kidnapped-by-flying-saucer stuff. Scientists don't rule it out, and let's face it, the world is a marvel and we keep finding out more marvels, so it would seem stupidly closed-minded not to accept the possibility of a lot of inexplicable occurrences. So as fantastic as Buddy Branch's story was, it wasn't something either Cissy or I could completely and immediately dismiss.

"Well, are you going to write up his story?" Cissy asked me as we were driving back to Midnight. I said I didn't know yet, what did she think?

"Well, shoot a mile up the Christmas tree," she said, "I don't guess it's much weirder than some other things. You know there's been a mule now that's had two baby mules, the first one they named Blue Moon. I forget the second one's name. But they used to say that wasn't possible, either." She reminded me of the shooting lights in Marfa, which have been seen for so many years people take them for granted. Cissy could go on and on about supernatural occurrences, such as the woman who found Jesus on her tortilla dough, and the church in West Texas where members of the congregation had been receiving messages from the Virgin Mary.

At the café, Cissy asked me to drive through the parking lot so she could see if her mother and Paisley had opted for the buffet and salad bar.

"I'll be out of town part of this week," Cissy said, sliding out of my car. "I'm taking Paisley Blue to Waco."

"What's happening in Waco?" I asked her.

"A Little Miss Christian workshop," Cissy said. "Working the Christian ethic into your career in beauty competition. They also have a baton-twirling clinic. You oughta come with me."

I told her I was still waiting on the man from Longview.

"You might as well forget that man from Longview," Cissy advised. "And I hope you'll write an editorial this week suggesting a memorial for Calvin Troope. After what Buddy Branch said, you certainly should reconsider. I think we might be witnessing some divine plan, Dinah. And," she added, "I don't know why you don't consider staying in Midnight and running the *Citizen* yourself. You seem to be having a pretty good time of it."

Cissy gave me a thumbs-up sign, like an astronaut, and climbed into her custom-painted lilac Camaro and folded the cardboard sunscreen, leaving the door open till her air conditioner started cooling.

On the way to Mama's, I considered the pilot's story and whether I should print it. I knew what Dude would have counseled: caution. He always did. Of course, I thought, maybe since Marilyn he'd thrown caution to the winds, like Bette Davis in *Now, Voyager*. I couldn't be certain of anything anymore. What if I printed the pilot's story, I wondered. Just an interview. I wished I'd had a tape recorder. Maybe I should go back with a tape recorder, I thought, but I knew it wouldn't work as well the second time around. There's always a certain amount of energy that's lost after the first time a person tells a story.

It did occur to me, I must confess, that the story might attract some attention to the *Citizen*. Obviously, my classified ads in the Dallas and Fort Worth newspapers had not been roaringly successful, since I'd heard from only the one person—the no-show from Longview. Therefore, attracting some attention might lead someone to consider buying a small friendly weekly in the town where Texas still is. I couldn't ignore that possibility. Surely even Mother Teresa thought of her own self-interest occasionally.

When I got to Mama's she was home from church and visiting Lilly and was frying chicken. She said it was the first time she'd felt like frying chicken since she got the shingles.

"I hope you're not frying that for me," I said.

She said she was frying it for herself, thank you very much. Fried chicken is something she gets hungry for every now and then.

"Why don't you just go to Church's Chicken down the highway and get carry-out?" I asked her. "Why go to all the trouble to fry three pieces of chicken?"

She said she didn't like anybody's fried chicken but her own.

I sat down at the kitchen table and watched her. She stood before the skillet like a conductor with a baton, only hers was a set of tongs. She'd taken off her church dress and her hose and put on what she called a housedress, which was a shapeless bright blue print that settled softly over the slight widow's hump of her back. She wore an apron over that and some cheap red cloth sandals she claimed were comfortable. She talked a lot about shoes being comfortable or not. Above the red sandals, her legs were white as milk. So far as I know, Mama had never in her life had a tan except for the time she'd ridden in the car to Carlsbad Caverns with her right arm in the window.

"Mama," I said. "What would you say if somebody told you that Calvin Troope's plane crashed because the pilot saw a heavenly vision?"

Mama looked back to the chicken and turned a piece thoughtfully. Then she looked at me to see if I was pulling her leg. When she saw I was serious, she threw her head back and laughed. Seldom had I seen her laugh like that, gold fillings glistening in the back of her mouth. She laughed, slapping her left thigh with her left hand and waving the chicken-turning tongs with her right.

When she could speak, she said, "I didn't know that paper was going to completely drive you crazy," and wiped the tears from her eyes. Then she started laughing again. Seeing her laugh like that, I couldn't help but join her.

Happy Hour in Bobby Joe's hotel featured free hors d'oeuvres and a piano player in an atrium lined with ficus plants and crowded with young office workers. I was grateful to every one of them for proving that some people in Dallas were still gainfully employed. That summer the economy seemed to deteriorate daily. Every week another savings and loan was felled by hard times and scandal. One federal bank regulator said every time he came to Texas it cost the government a billion dollars, which certainly proves that when Texas goes belly-up it does it in a big way.

To go into a bar in Dallas you'd never know it was a hundred degrees outside. People touch the real air only in the quick jog from air-conditioned car to air-conditioned building. It could have been a hotel in Milwaukee or Seattle, the way people were dressed in suits, only here the free hors d'oeuvres were spicy taco chips and the favored drink was a frozen margarita and the voices ordering them were likely to be soft and twangy with a tendency to laugh a lot.

I had a good opportunity to observe the scene over the margarita I drank while waiting for Bobby Joe to show up. He'd told me to phone suite 442 when I arrived and he'd meet me in the cocktail lounge. It gave me another opportunity, too, to ponder what I had been pondering all day: whether or not I'd run the mystery pilot's story in the next week's *Citizen*. Alternative leads were "Cats Still Missing" and "Paisley Blue Sanders Attends Little Miss Christian Workshop in Waco," Cissy's suggestion, of course. Half of my problem was that I couldn't make up my mind, and the other half was that I couldn't concentrate, for my nervousness about having dinner with Bobby Joe. I was reminded of piano recital days when my fingers always turned to marble lumps at the last minute. But there I was, in my navy funeral dress adorned with a Mexican necklace and even properly weighted by hose.

"Dinah," Cissy had counseled me earlier, "what better way to get back into the real world of men and dating than with an easy old love."

"That might be the real world for a sixteen-year-old," I'd told Cissy, "but it's pretty repulsive for a mature woman. And my real world," I'd announced, "is home, family, friends, and cats. Also Texas and cowboys peripherally. And even if Bobby Joe is an 'old' love, it ain't easy."

As I sat there waiting, I began to think the invitation he'd extended had been a figment of my imagination, something

171

like a hysterical pregnancy, only on a smaller scale. It wasn't until after I'd drained my margarita and licked off the salt that he appeared. He didn't even apologize for keeping me waiting. He just said he'd been tied up.

With what, I wondered, but all I said was, "In this age of miracles, nothing surprises me."

By the time he got there a piano player had settled in, and since I have never outgrown my delight for even bad cocktail-bar piano players, I made the mistake of joining Bobby Joe for another margarita, even though my nervousness and the earlier drink had already softened the hard edges of the world around me, and I've never been celebrated for holding my liquor.

"Dinah, you keep looking better," Bobby Joe said, gazing at me in a way that nearly made me believe him. Those old lines went down as easily as the margaritas. I was touched. I guess if he'd said I looked like Marvin Hagler I'd have been touched at that point.

"All I expected was dinner and a couple of drinks, not flattery or sex," I said, getting it all out there before us on the little round table with the pink cloth.

Bobby Joe looked at me steadily over the tinted snow of our margaritas.

"If you're expecting all that, we better drink up." He grinned and his steady gaze set up within me a low buzz like a shorted neon so that throughout the evening beneath all the talk and laughter and reminiscence there was a horizontal subtext at work and waiting. After twenty or so years of memories and, no doubt, fantasy at work, the blood is bound to respond.

Around us, the after-work crowd was dispersing slowly and being replaced by an older group of drinks-before-dinner people. The piano player began a gaudy rendition of "Memories" and was zipping up and down the keyboard with all the flourishes of a prancing poodle.

Dinner consisted of what must have been—at that price—the last two redfish in captivity served in a Dallas nouvelle cuisine restaurant beside a waterfall. The water was loud, but the hours passed as though we were speeding down an

empty Texas highway alone in the world except for the telephone poles we passed. A couple of times I tried to quiz
Bobby Joe about Buddy Branch's mental-health history and
general reliability, but each time Bobby Joe said this evening
was about us alone, and I was not unhappy to go along with
that.

We talked about a lot of things. About how we could possibly catch up on all those years we'd missed. "If only we'd
kept tapes like the Nixon White House," I said.

"We'll manage, I promise," he said, holding my hand.

The central topic was what it would have been like if things
had worked out differently. If he hadn't gone back to Houston
and I hadn't insisted he go; if I hadn't married Dude.

"I don't regret that," I said. "I loved Dude. I still do,"
which of course was true despite the fact that I was sitting
there with Bobby Joe with stars in my eyes. But it was true
that we both wished it had been the other way; at least we
did that night. He made it clear and I believed him. I believed everything that night. I guess, wanting him so much,
if he'd said he was Jack the Ripper returned from the grave,
I'd still have kicked off my shoes and pulled the covers
back.

After dinner we went back to the hotel, and in the glass
elevator we clung to each other as if we were the only two
people ever headed for a three-point landing on the stiff white
sheets of a hotel bed. But there was even more design. In the
hotel room Bobby Joe put on a tape, music we could dance
to, music we *had* danced to all those years before, the funky
rhythm and blues that had been the theme music of our young
lives. Dancing with Bobby Joe was the other thing I'd dreamed
about over the years. And when I stepped into his arms and
danced as we shed our clothes, it was as if all the sad, lonely
nights there had ever been or would ever be had vanished
from the world.

It was with Bobby Joe I'd learned the first, fresh delicious-
ness of sex, in those early years when our bodies were new
and our motors always on idle. We must have spent a thousand
hours on a hundred lovers' lanes making love not war. That
was back when marriage was customary and virgins over

twelve still existed, before sex was as commonplace as five conversational topics, before everybody got bored with it, and began to die of it, even before *Reader's Digest* published articles on it, back when the greatest luxury in the world was an empty bed. Later, in college, there'd been a sweet, funny medical student I'd assisted in a textbook exploration, chapter by chapter, and learned variations of the art. And then there was Dude, who'd been the only one to promise to worship my body, who had indeed loved me with a rare and convincing earnestness I knew I'd likely never find again.

Dude, let me explain, did not dance. "Dinah," he'd say, those early and uneasy years we were first married, "I don't dance. Period." It was as if he were flatly declaring: Bobby Joe dances, I don't. And you married me. And while the habit of sex improves the act over the years, the fires are banked till there's a kind of death. That night with Bobby Joe I felt born again. The chemistry that had inspired those dreams of making love with him periodically for twenty-something years, that would lead me to blush at seven A.M. when I woke beside my husband, that basic animal magnetism that keeps the world rolling and afloat despite nuclear weapons and the so-called death of God, was still alive and wonderful. But afterward, lying there, I thought of how it must have been like that for Dude with that other woman, and I cried. Bobby Joe kissed my tears away, saying he couldn't remember the last time his making love to a woman had made her cry.

When I woke later in the dark room, the clock on the TV read four forty-three A.M. Bobby Joe slept peacefully beside me. For a minute I lay listening to the sweet rhythm of his breathing, thinking how life can be seen as a series of headlines, and how I'd just lived through one of my banner ones. I kissed his shoulder softly and carefully pulled myself out of bed. I tiptoed about the room in search of strewn clothing, which I carried into the bathroom, where the garish fluorescent light was cruel at that hour. I fixed my face, trying to mask the clear evidence of debauchery and the early hour. I drew three X's on the mirror with Bobby Joe's shaving cream, then staggered around in the dark until I found my purse and fished my shoes out from under the bed, but the navy belt to my funeral dress eluded me. Then I let myself quietly out the door into the nighttime glow of the hotel corridor.

On the way home I felt a sobriety no music, not even the Sweethearts of the Rodeo, could dispel. The attendant I'd awakened in the hotel garage was wearing a mustard jumpsuit, a gold ring in one ear, and a wary sneer. Everything I passed looked stark and tacky as a deserted carnival. My mouth was dry as dirt and I felt exactly like a fortyish woman who'd gotten less than three hours of sleep. And there were several things that bothered me about the previous evening, too. Not only how much I'd given myself over to it, but how perfectly effortless it had been after twenty-two years of honorable fidelity to erase that slate. There were questions I had to ask myself. I glanced in the mirror to see if I was truly the same woman who usually looked in that mirror conscience-clear and self-knowing.

By the time I'd reached the EconoLodge six miles from Midnight, where the early-bird commuters were already heading their lights toward the Metroplex, I had to admit to myself that while Bobby Joe may have rekindled a flame, there was something wrong. One thing was that all the time Bobby Joe was making love to me I had thought of Dude. And also, I realized in those early gray moments, probably what we'd been up to as much as anything else in those intemperate hours was making love to our past selves.

When I reached Midnight the first rays of sun lifted over the rounded synagoguelike roof of the First Baptist Church, softly lighting the grimaces of the wax apostles. On Mama's street the paper boy was throwing daily Metroplex newspapers from his jeep, a few TVs glowed inside houses with early news and weather, and Mama's neighbor had yet to begin her day with Sinatra. At Mama's I sneaked in, knowing she'd note the exact moment my car hit the driveway. After a lengthy shower and shampoo I was trying to make coffee, when Mama entered the kitchen, a tissue to her nose.

"Morning, Mama," I greeted her cheerily, a lot more cheerily than I actually felt.

She mumbled into the tissue. It was the kind of greeting an arsonist might receive from someone whose house had just burned. For a week Mama didn't look at me. Occasionally her gaze would brush my shoulder or settle near my waist. It was an escalation of our semi-war.

☆

While Cissy and Paisley Blue were gone to Waco, I wrote a lead story: "Mystery Pilot Claims Vision Caused Crash."

Buddy Branch, the mystery pilot who, according to hospital officials, didn't speak for days following the plane crash outside Midnight on May 12, has stated that at the time of the crash he saw Calvin Troope and his fiancée, who were both killed in the crash, walk hand in hand into a bright, shining light in the sky. At the same time, Buddy Branch, 29 and a native of Stillwater, Oklahoma, says he believes the crash occurred in order for him to testify that the end of the world is near and that another sign will soon appear.

Branch, who states he has not been a religious man since the age of 10, says there was a sudden malfunction of the plane prior to the crash. He heard a strange ringing sound and suddenly the sky was filled with roiling clouds which completely obstructed his view except for the scene of his two passengers walking hand in hand into the heavens. Branch says at the time he was unaware of the crash.

Dr. Rock Leeland of Baylor Hospital says that tests made shortly after the crash revealed no sign of drugs or elevated alcohol level in the pilot's blood. Branch suffered a broken arm, internal injuries, and a concussion in the crash.

Religious pop singer Calvin Troope and his fiancée, Tanya Cooper, died in the accident. Troope was traveling to Love Field in Dallas in his private Cessna for a performance that night. In an odd coincidence, Troope had been born in Midnight, son of the late Edna and Billy Don Troope, although at the time of his death he was living in Los Angeles.

Asked for an explanation for the deaths of Troope and Cooper, Branch says that he believes it is part of a divine plan. He believes, also, that Troope had a premonition of his death. Branch believes that between the time of the crash and his regaining consciousness in the hospital he was taken elsewhere and given this message. He says he was given several signs which will later be proof of his experience, but he refuses to elaborate on what the signs would be, although he says he will do so at a later date.

Branch, who is the father of a three-month-old son, says he will change his son's name to Vision of Heaven, and call him Vision for short.

Maybe I was foolish not to realize what would happen if I printed the story. Maybe I should have consulted with someone else. But I was, after all, only reporting in good faith what I had been told. And, I justified to myself, if, as pollsters say, half the population of the United States believes the world will end and Christ will return to earth—people like Mama, for instance—why should such testimony as Buddy Branch's be shocking or cause for alarm? Only someone with no imagination would deny the possibility. Certainly not I. I liked to think I had an open mind, though I have to admit I did wonder why some greater being would choose a ratty town like Midnight for the event. But then there was the manger in Bethlehem, which, I reminded myself, hadn't exactly been four stars. If, I argued to myself, thousands of people believe that Jerry Falwell can deflect a hurricane, if Billy Graham and Lilly can believe in angels maybe standing there beside the Linotype machine, if . . .

So I stuck the story at the back of Jud's copy as I would any other story and went to the post office, where they'd just cut the window hours to two full days a week and the rest half-days.

"This country," Claude Sanders shouted to me in the post office, "is getting more like Turkey or some third-world locale where they have electricity only two hours a day."

"Don't fuss at me, write your congressman," Nadine Love called to Claude from her window.

"I'm not sure Turkey would be considered third world," I said to Claude, who completely ignored my edit.

"That damn congressman don't even open his mail anymore," Claude said. "What y'all going to do back there with the windows closed half a day, four days a week, Nadine?" Claude hollered.

"Play hearts," Nadine said.

Claude bellowed and exited angrily.

When I returned from the post office, Jud was making those sounds he makes when he's upset. Sounds a lazy dog makes when it doesn't want to sit up and give a full-hearted bark, a kind of back-throat rumbling. Then Jud stomped over and dropped the lead copy on the counter in front of me as if it were radioactive, and stomped out the front door. I was stunned. In all his years with Daddy, I'd never heard of Jud refusing to set a story. It also made me mad. So I just sat down to set it myself. It took me an hour to peck out half of it, and even then I didn't have the spacing right. When Jud came back later, I ignored him and went right on setting it until I got up to answer the phone. He finally took the chair and finished it himself—or I guess I'd still be there.

The second lead was "Cats Still Missing." "Paisley Blue Sanders Attends Little Miss Christian Workshop in Waco" I left to the inside page, which I knew would make Cissy mad. I composed a speech about how if Cissy didn't stop trying to pressure the press she'd find Paisley's various festival appearances of the summer would go unnoted. I also worked in my mind on a speech I'd make to Mama when she asked what the lead was this week, but she was hardly speaking to me, so for once she didn't even ask. When she'd quit laughing that Sunday afternoon, she'd decided what I'd told her was blasphemy.

"You, along with ninety million other Americans, believe the world is going to end, Mama, don't you? You're always talking about it."

She'd said, "I certainly do. The Bible says it clear as day." She quoted, " 'For the Lord himself shall descend from heaven with a shout, with the voice of the archangel, and with the trumpet of God.' "

"So why couldn't that happen in Midnight? It's possible."

She grew more angry each time I said it.

"Dinah, that is no more going to happen in Midnight than a man in the moon."

"Well, that's close," I said, and that made her furious.

She'd told me once that she'd dreamed of Jesus returning to earth via Union Station in Washington through the special entrance President Roosevelt had reserved for Kate Smith during World War II. Jesus had a broad smile and wore a brown suit and brown-and-white spectator shoes and everyone in the world knew at once that Jesus was back. It sounded to me like Colonel Blake's last appearance on *M*A*S*H* but I didn't say it.

That Sunday she'd been cooking her chicken she'd said, "Dinah, I am serious. Now, I would never have let you take over the *Citizen* if I'd thought you would become involved in something like this."

"Let me take over!" I said.

"You know what I mean," she said.

"Mama, I was doing you a favor, a big favor. Remember?"

She didn't answer, just stood there with her self-righteous Baptist face and shingles on her back.

"Remember the shingles!" I added, "Mama, this newspaper may be the reason for my marriage breaking up!"

And then she had the nerve to look me in the face and say, "Dinah, you were on the rebound. Your marriage has been in trouble since the day you married." Which about floored me.

Then I thought, if she had such a low opinion of me, why shouldn't I do whatever was necessary to sell the paper, even to Hugh Overton? If running the story would help my chances of selling, then that's what I should do.

My next rationalization was that if I didn't run the story, somebody else probably would. I doubted that Buddy Branch was going to keep it under his hat much longer. And I wouldn't have been a bit surprised if Bobby Joe wasn't there to prompt him about the whole thing. And I still had a newsperson's sense of responsibility. Some things you don't print, like details about noted people's sex lives, or at least you didn't use to, until the supermarket tabloids came along. (Or *Confidential*. That was the first one. Which would be a good title for an autobiography—*I Remember Confidential*, the autobiography of an older person.) So maybe it would get the *Citizen* some publicity and someone would buy it. That thought was the clincher. One thing for sure, I pledged to myself that day, especially after Mama's acting so tacky, if the *Citizen* didn't sell soon, I was walking out. I was going to make myself a deadline and Mama could either sell or get someone else to run it. She rarely mentioned her shingles anymore. The first of August, I swore to myself and whoever else might be interested, I would be home in North Dallas. I wasn't about to ruin my entire life over the *Midnight Citizen.* I phoned Ned English and left word for him I'd be back at work the last of July, come hell or high water, drought, plague, or plane crash.

On Thursday, Mrs. Willetta Clark, age 102 and a third, former wing-walker, she claimed, and the oldest citizen of Midnight, passed away, having as far as I know never been interviewed. I could have changed the lead, I suppose, since age and mortality are of great interest in Midnight, but I decided to be firm in my decision. Also, I decided, when this week's issue was out I was going to get Jud to set three or four posters saying "Dinah Reynolds, at Home in North Dallas, August 1" for me to display around Mama's house, in the windows of the *Citizen,* and maybe in the Midnight Cafe.

That Friday evening I went home to Dallas for the first time since Dude had dropped the bomb on me. Before that I'd gone home most weekends except when Mama could hardly rise from her bed. Since Dude's news I had dreaded what it would be like, knowing the life I'd had there might be over. But it was one way to avoid Mama's reaction to the *Citizen* story, and besides, I was homesick for my cats and I wanted to see Dude. Bobby Joe had phoned me at Mama's the day after I left him sleeping peacefully in the hotel, and for reasons unclear even to me I hadn't returned the call. I'd phoned Dude instead.

"How is Larry?" he'd asked. I told him I hadn't talked to Larry since the night of a thousand knives in Mama's living room. Of course, I felt guilty.

"How are my cats?" I asked him.

"Lonesome," he said.

I thought his response was interesting. Maybe he was speaking for himself. "Really?"

"They look wan," he said.

"Wan? I never heard you use that word. Are you learning a whole new vocabulary, too?"

"What are you talking about, Dinah?"

"Never mind," I said. "I was thinking I'd come see my cats this weekend. You wouldn't mind, would you?" I said with just a pinch of sarcasm.

"I'll tell them you're coming," he joked before we hung up.

On the way to Dallas, I stopped by to see Lilly. She and Anthony Spencer Mainard had ordered their wedding announcements. The ceremony would be held in the reception room of Happy Acres. Families plus the other residents—never "patients"—would be invited. The administration, however, wasn't much happier than Mama about this wedding but had eventually agreed and set about making it a big social occasion. (The Happy Acres social director was forever looking for events to celebrate. There was even a Rodeo Day during the Fat Stock Show in Fort Worth.)

Mama had gradually gotten into the spirit of things, and that afternoon she'd arrived with three three-piece dresses for Lilly to choose from for the ceremony. My opinion was also to be considered, so I would meet them at Happy Acres at five before driving on to Dallas. I prayed Mama hadn't seen the *Citizen* yet, and I guess she hadn't, because she seemed in a pretty good mood and even gave me a pat on the arm, which was the first sign I'd had from her that she didn't think I should be banished.

When I first came in, I knocked on Anthony Spencer Mainard's door to say hello. I had come to like Anthony Spencer Mainard. There was something about him that reminded me of Daddy and I found myself thinking Daddy would have been able to talk to him without wasting his time. When he answered my knock, I stuck my head in the door. He sat in his wheelchair smoking a cigar with his right hand, lifting a weight with his left, and watching a boxing match on cable TV. He said there was a lot of woman talk going on down the hall. I told him I didn't see how he could do all those things at once, and he smiled at me with his cheery blue eyes and waved with his cigar. I went on down the hall to the deliberations in Lilly's room, where Mama was holding up the three dresses, one by one, before Lilly and Katie.

"Well, the groom is certainly cheerful," I said to Lilly when I kissed her, and she laughed in what even Mama had to admit was a giggle. She had had a new permanent before Cissy left for Waco, and Katie had painted her nails what they called "sweetheart pink."

"Which one, Dinah?" Mama asked me as she held up a blue-and-white print, a blue-and-pink-and-white print, and a pink print. I voted for the pink print, as had Lilly and Katie. It wasn't Mama's choice, I could tell, but she took it fairly well.

Lilly wanted to know if I thought she should wear a hat, and I said no, I thought she should wear flowers in her hair. That's when Mama patted my arm. I kissed them all good-bye then and headed for Dallas.

It was after seven by the time I fought my way through Friday-evening traffic and turned into my own driveway. For a moment I wished I'd waited till the morning and sunshine to arrive. But there was my warm cherry-painted front door. It had taken me months to find just the right inviting color paint, but when I opened the door then, it was like entering a ghost town: inside were the relics of another time. The particular smell of my own life met me, but it was stuffy and reeked of disuse, like a seldom opened closet.

I set down my overnight bag and turned on the air-conditioning. The dear cats had heard the car drive up and the gray one, Jerry Jeff, was on the kitchen window ledge waiting, his gold eyes gleaming at me coolly. The black cat, Bobby McGee, hung reliably from the back screen door. Seeing them so familiar made me feel better. At least they hadn't been kidnapped. Outside on the back deck, there was fresh food in their bowls, so I realized Dude must have hired a neighbor kid to feed them. That would mean he wouldn't have to be home at any certain time, or home at all.

On the dining table, mail had piled up but was sorted into orderly hers and ours stacks, so he must have checked in occasionally. Those segregated stacks reminded me of how separate we had become. I looked around the rooms I liked so much, imagining all the furniture sawed down the middle, even the phones and the cats bisected.

I went through the mail and pulled out the few personal things, including a card from Marianne at Fontainebleau saying the French still wouldn't speak to her in French. Both cats were rubbing against my legs wanting to be held, so I sat holding each for a few minutes, telling them how much I'd missed them and how beautiful they were. I told them in the future they could sleep on the bed with me, something Dude hadn't approved of, not being wild about cats himself. See, there's always a silver lining, I tried to tell myself.

I walked around then from plant to plant to survey their health and care. The fiddle-leaf fig, which had strung itself magnificently across one living room wall, needed dusting. My assorted cactuses in the south window of the dining room were still thriving. That kind of defensive plant with thorns could survive separation. But the gentle oxalises were wilted, each pot wearing a collar of crisp brown leaves, and the small white flowers sagged. I watered them one by one, thinking afterward that I should let them all die and draw an X across the windows to match.

The answering machine contained three inconsequential messages, and a yellow legal pad listed others for the weeks I'd been away. All of them were trivial. Nothing seemed important. How wrong I had been to think the details of my life mattered. I'd been away for more than a month and everyone including Dude and the Lighthouse for the Blind had replaced me.

In the bedroom, I lifted the spread and saw there were sheets on the bed. In the bathroom, his razor was gone. That made everything definite and final, more evidence of loss than a legal document. I considered crawling into the bed and going to sleep like Goldilocks. I hadn't expected the place to hit me so hard. And then I heard Dude's Tracer pull into the driveway and in a minute he was unlocking the front door. I listened to him walk through the house, calling, "Hey, cats," as he passed them.

"Dinah?"

"Here."

"Hi," he said, coming to the bedroom door. He was nearly as tall as the door frame and he looked uneasy. I felt for a moment how much I liked him. My instinct was to walk over and kiss him. Then I stopped myself, remembering I couldn't operate on automatic anymore. It all came zinging back and I remembered I couldn't like him so much anymore, either.

"You got here okay?"

"I'm here."

I hated it that since he'd met that woman he'd begun saying superfluous things like other people. Like me. He didn't use to.

"I don't think there's much to eat," he said. "You want to go out?"

"I know my way around," I said. "I'll make do."

"You doing okay?"

"Sure," I said.

"That's some story you stirred up."

"Yeah."

"I sent a feature writer out."

"Feature writer? That's hard news, I'll have you know."

Dude laughed. "You want some coffee or something? A drink?"

"A drink."

He turned and went toward the bar in the den. I kicked off my shoes and followed him.

"The cats seem okay," I said. They'd both settled like hens on their favorite chairs, and they blinked their eyes at me lovingly when I spoke to them.

"Yeah. I got Darlene next door to feed them," Dude said as he poured me a bourbon. "At an exorbitant rate. She doesn't seem to know there's a recession."

"Don't worry about the plants anymore. I think I'll just let them die. Plants are more responsibility than I want right now. You might want to keep the fiddle-leaf fig alive. It's too big to move out and it would probably add something to the sale of the house."

He glanced at mc as he handed me the drink and sat down. I hated the way he looked at me now, warily, as if I were some aged structure that might collapse under the slightest additional load.

"Cheers," I said, lifting my glass in his direction and trying to overcome the feeling I had that I was approaching quicksand and was uncertain where to step.

"You want to talk?"

"Sure," he said. He was wrinkled a bit, straight from work and Friday-weary. Fridays in our earlier life we'd either eaten out with friends and gone to a movie or ordered in and watched TV in bed. We'd usually made love on Friday nights and slept late on Saturday like ordinary people. That moment it seemed wonderful and all the details of him appealing. A fountain pen protruded from his blue shirt pocket. Over the years he'd continued to use fountain pens when everyone else switched to ballpoint. I loved his neat, inky signature.

"Well, what do you want to do? I told work I'd be back at the end of July, sale of *Citizen* or not."

He didn't answer. He stroked my gray cat sitting by him on the couch and I could hear the cat's purr push up to high.

"Do you want a divorce? A legal separation? Are you just going to live with this woman and ask me to hang around till after the sixty-day trial period? What's on your mind?"

He sighed and hammered the side of his shoe. I knew he would hammer it twice. Then he'd fold his arms, press his thumb to his teeth, and look at me. He did those very things.

"You in a big hurry for any particular reason? I'd rather wait . . . till you come back . . ."

I interrupted. "Oh, I should just sit here and play the quiet game. Wait for you to decide. Or maybe you'll eventually say eeny, meeny, miney, mo?"

"Maybe you want a divorce," he said.

"I do," I replied firmly, as if I really meant it. I said that with such profound conviction, grasping at any path that seemed firm. Being back there had thrown me for another loop when I was already reeling.

Just then, a car pulled into the driveway. We listened to the door slam. I thought, Oh, my God, what if it's Marilyn? What will I do? Maybe for the first time in my life I'll faint. I looked down at my moldy-looking bare feet.

The doorbell rang. It was a nice F-sharp bell. It always seemed to signal someone I wanted to see. That moment another scene from our past life flashed before me. Reading the papers in bed Sunday mornings with coffee and croissants, peeking through the miniblinds when the doorbell rang, and crawling back into bed if it was Jehovah's Witnesses. Those mornings seemed golden, glowing with a contentment I hadn't realized. Why hadn't I been purring, I wondered.

Dude opened the door and greeted someone. I could tell he was surprised. Then Bobby Joe Daniels stepped through the door. For an instant I felt disoriented seeing him in this setting.

"Your mother said you were here. Thought I'd say hello." He gave me a warm smile that held my eyes a minute too long. I could feel myself blush. I introduced my cats.

"Designer cats?" Bobby Joe said, teasing me. They aren't at all. They're cheap alley cats with skimpy fur, plain as dirt.

Dude fixed him a drink as Bobby Joe told us he'd been around the state talent-scouting. "Lost our star," he said. "We've got to dig up a new model." He showed no particle of remorse.

I went to the kitchen and opened a can of peanuts to pass around. Bobby Joe mentioned a singer in Austin and a band or two in Dallas. There followed then a conversation as awkward as I'd ever heard. We talked about the weather. *Hot here. What's it like in California now?* The whiskey. *We don't drink as much hard liquor as we used to.* Restaurants. *Falling like dominoes with the hard times.* Politics. Dude told a joke that wasn't very funny, though I laughed as much as I could. It was the most self-conscious drink I'd had since I was sixteen and first tried a martini with the high school football coach. After the one drink, Bobby Joe said he had to move on. When he stood up he pulled the belt of my navy-blue funeral dress out of his pocket and handed it to me rolled up discreetly. But taking it, I let it unfurl, and it fell like a snake, and Dude, when I glanced at him, looked as though he'd been bitten.

I thanked Bobby Joe and walked him to the door.

When I turned around, Dude was watching me, and I felt bad about it. It was almost as good as one of my daydreams of vengeance, but it didn't make me feel any better.

"I hope you're happy as hell," he said.

"Dude, that wasn't intentional. And I'm not happy. I missed you. I miss you. When I was with him I missed you. I thought how it must have been for you and her."

"Well, isn't that an irony!" He finished his drink and set his glass down in a final, finishing gesture. But I went on.

"I might have had some fantasies over the years, but I never acted on them. They weren't real like this thing you have. This doesn't have anything to do with me and Bobby Joe, Dude. Not really."

"To hell with that! What's love about, Dinah, if it's not about something exclusive? I never had a moment's confidence with you. It's probably a matter of sheer accident you didn't run off with one of those cowboys, or several of them. Who the hell knows, maybe you did. I don't know why you ever married me."

He'd never said that before. "I married you because I loved you. I still do. And there was never ever even one cowboy, Dude. You know that. You're not being fair."

We stood there looking at one another and shortly afterward he left, and I spent the weekend with my cats. I let them sleep on the bed that night and they woke me up at four batting at one another across my body, both agitating to get outside to prowl. That left me two hours before sunrise to lie there and think about my future. About selling my house with the cherry-painted door and living the rest of my life alone. By six A.M., when I went back to sleep, my future was mapped. Immediately upon selling the house, I would become aged and diseased. I would lose my job and soon afterward join the ranks of the homeless.

When I woke up later Saturday morning, I made myself admit that my end might not be exactly like that. That weekend I lay on the deck in the sun and read the papers and their stories about Buddy Branch's vision till it would get too hot to stay outdoors. Several times the phone rang but I let the machine pick it up. It took all the willpower I might have for the rest of my life to pat my cats good-bye, get myself back in my car Sunday evening, and head south.

When I arrived at Mama's, she announced that Anthony Spencer Mainard had decided he and Lilly should move to a retirement apartment in Dallas.

NOW when I think about the day I made the decision to run Buddy Branch's story, it's like looking back on a head-on collision that changed my life.

"It's like the goddamn plane has crashed all over again!" Claude Sanders shouted at me several times in the next few days.

There was so much commotion that week I couldn't get anything done for answering the phone. The story had become a national and then an international event. Stringers from all over the world were interviewing Buddy Branch, his photo was on the front page of all the Metroplex papers, and even more reporters were tromping around in Claude's Swiss chard patch. Carloads of the curious were again trying to peek through the window shutters into Cissy and Claude's mobile home. Of course, I was surprised that my little item had garnered so much attention. Usually no one saw the *Midnight Citizen* but people in Midnight, who by and large weren't in contact with the major media of the Metroplex. Even a group of homeless people appeared with their pitiful belongings, wanting to camp in the woods. Claude might as well have burned his big POSTED sign.

"Dinah," Claude said to me midweek, his face seeming to inflate beneath his red baseball cap, "I'm considering suing you. You and this paper have ruined my crop and I'm gonna see you pay for it."

Behind me I heard a loud I-told-you-so harrumph from Jud.

The only good thing to happen that week was that Larry, with six months' probation, returned to work at the highway

189

patrol. At least *he* felt it was a good thing. He also made an appointment to speak to a lawyer about a divorce or whether he needed one, in view of his wife's recent marriage, the legalities of which seemed daunting. I considered asking him for his lawyer's name, thinking maybe we'd get a break on two divorces in the same family, but I didn't have the heart.

Meanwhile, in West Texas the messages from the Virgin Mary were being more and more touted. It must have looked to the rest of the nation as though the Almighty, seeing Texas in its economic agony, heard the suffering voices of the faithful and responded. Certainly the two stories together created more furor than either one individually.

Paisley Blue, fresh from her Little Miss Christian Workshop, which also seemed providential, according to Cissy, was soon twirling her little heart out in front of assorted minicams.

"See, it's all coming together, Dinah." Cissy's voice lifted breathlessly like a purple balloon sailing into a blue sky.

As a semi-journalist, I am skeptical of polls and statistics, as any right-thinking democratic American has to be, since our politicians have been known to stretch—even alter on occasion—the facts. However, the statistic that says Texas has more religious concern plus number of preachers and churches per square mile than any other part of the nation I believe to be true.

Then along came evangelist Buster Ledbetter in his scripture-painted state-of-the-art TV-equipped Winnebago providing mobile ministry by satellite throughout this far-flung state. Brother Buster parked right across from the Baptist church on Wednesday afternoon and announced that he, too, had received a message from God that the end was at hand and Midnight was the place to be.

After that announcement Buster was afforded nationwide coverage, especially since he had a chisel-faced, cleft-chin attractiveness and his decorated Winnebago created "color," as the TV people call it, while there was little to show in Claude's field but Swiss chard plants, sightseers, and a few twirls by Paisley Blue.

Thursday morning the Fisher twins appeared at the *Citizen* carrying a petition with names of ninety-four people who said they wanted an investigation of the disappearance of the cats.

"At last count, there were within the city limits of Midnight over twenty cats missing," Martha said. "All yellow."

"Yellow?" I said. "So that's why I see that skinny black cat around the Piggly Wiggly. He's the wrong color. Discrimination again."

"All yellow," Mary or Martha Fisher repeated, and shoved the petition at me. They also told me to run their duplex ad again.

I introduced them to a stringer from a newsweekly and suggested they tell him their cat story. Before they left, the twin with the neck scar said they were glad I was running the *Citizen*. "Midnight has never had so much publicity as it's had since you took over," Martha or Mary said.

I looked up at their matching tight perms and round rouged faces and couldn't keep myself from boiling over.

"Listen, Martha and Mary, I'm not running the *Citizen* now. I'm only sitting in till the *Citizen* gets a new owner. And if that doesn't happen soon there won't be a *Midnight Citizen*. I am temporary, short-term, interim, and transient. Soon I'll be getting back to North Dallas and cowboys." As I spoke, Mary and Martha stared at me with round startled eyes, having no idea what cowboys I was talking about and, of course, probably thinking of football players.

Before I could explain, Mama phoned to say that Anthony Spencer Mainard was acting weird and had changed his mind again about where he and Lilly should live. The Fisher twins made a hasty exit as Mama told me that now he wanted them to move to Sweetwater, where his other son lived. Mama said she didn't want Lilly moving way off out there in the middle of West Texas. I told her not to get so upset, but I didn't like the idea of Lilly's moving to Sweetwater, either.

The next issue's lead would be the change in post office hours, with a follow-up on the plane crash and the activity around Claude Sanders's Swiss chard patch with a photograph of Buster Ledbetter in the doorway of his Winnebago.

Traci stopped by not only to report on Brother Buster's crossover crowd but also to announce that she was registering at a local Baptist college that gave credits for "life experiences."

"What kind of life experiences?" I asked her.

"Well, having a baby," she said, "and getting married and taking care of a sick person." I didn't know when she'd taken care of a sick person, but I let it go.

"You write all that down in a notebook and document each experience, like maybe with Polaroid photos, and tell what you learned and how you feel about it, and you get college credit. And I have had a lot of recent experiences," she said earnestly.

"What recent experiences?" I asked her.

"You know, Martin and me running off and my marriage breaking up."

"You can get college credit for that?"

"That's right," she said.

I said I didn't know how she was going to document some of her recent experiences. Traci said, "Dinah, please don't be negative! How's Larry?"

I told her he was back with the highway patrol. Traci said that was wonderful.

"I think I'll write him a little note congratulating him," she said. "You think that's all right?" I told her I thought that would be nice. "I miss him," she said to me.

When Traci had left with her new educational possibilities, Ned English phoned to say he'd been reading about my interview with Buddy Branch and wanted to know if I was on crack.

After that conversation, I felt like running away, but there are some instances when that's impossible. When no one particularly expects you to be anywhere at any certain time, you can hardly run away. I suppose Mama would eventually, after a week or so, have asked Easy Malone to look for my body. I considered driving to the coast, but the red tide was back in the news and I would've been swimming in warm Gulf water with dead fish.

I drove past the Baptist church where Buster Ledbetter's state-of-the-art TV van was parked and past the Midnight Cafe teeming with out-of-town curiosity seekers and journalists, no doubt having the best lemon icebox pie they'd ever tasted. (Though later I would learn that Dorothy's business had become so burgeoning she'd started selling frozen icebox pie trucked in from the Metroplex.) But that moment I felt I had to get away from Midnight and its madness for a while. So I decided I'd drive to Dallas and that glittery hotel and drop in on Bobby Joe and just see what he was up to.

Outside Midnight I turned on the radio and heard something that about stopped me dead. The DJ announced the late, semi-great Calvin Troope's "Lord, I'm Ready When You Are" had risen that week to seventh place on the pop chart, having crossed over from the religious pop chart, where it was number one, and even having made a leap onto the C&W chart at nineteen. With that introduction, he then spun the triple winner. I listened to Calvin whine along with a synthesizer for a few minutes, but then I couldn't stand it any longer, so I found a tape and settled back to sing along with the heartfelt, full-bodied sound of Aretha.

Like a lot of people in this country, I figure that if I'd been the daughter of an African-American Detroit preacher and had had the opportunity to sing in a gospel choir all my life, I too might have become a great singer. Even white, if I'd been as rejected as Janis Joplin—once voted ugliest man on the University of Texas campus—I might have been a rock-and-roll blues singer. Sometimes it does seem that white middle class is so oatmeal-bland that you can't get anywhere from there. Once people become middle class, immediately their kids become whiny dope addicts or tax lawyers.

As soon as I pulled into the hotel garage and saw that same sneering parking attendant in the mustard jumpsuit with the single earring I'd passed the morning I left Bobby Joe, I thought maybe that was a sign this visit wasn't such a good idea. Of course I'd sneer, too, if I worked in a parking garage and breathed auto exhaust all day. But Bobby Joe had phoned me twice since he'd delivered my belt, so I expected to be welcomed, and if he was out or busy, I'd phone Ned English and ask if he and Pete wanted to go to a movie or have dinner. I wouldn't have minded a few of Pete's jokes.

That last encouraging thought propelled me through the garage to the elevator and into the lush hotel lobby. I waited a few minutes for the house phones but they continued to be busy, so I took the glass elevator to the fourth floor.

When I found suite 442 at the end of the hall, I thought I

was in the wrong place. It was a hive of activity, a swank office setup. Through the open door I could see two women typing on computers lickety-split and a third answering a phone. Buddy Branch, no sling in sight, was talking on another line and Bobby Joe was going over some kind of layout with a man. Hanging on the persimmon wall was a giant poster of Calvin Troope—evidently his new album cover—showing his thin white face looking up into the roiling clouds of a brightly lighted path into the heavens. It looked exactly like the scene Buddy Branch had described in explaining the plane crash. In the picture Calvin was obviously singing his new hit, "Lord, I'm Ready When You Are." I stood there a minute stunned at the scene, then stepped inside the door and picked up a press release from one of several stacks on a credenza.

"For Immediate Release": It was all about Calvin Troope's new hit making it to seventh place on the pop chart and had a quotation from a *Billboard* story, "Pop Religious Singer Tops Chart After Crash." Another press release included my very own interview with Buddy Branch from the *Citizen*. About then Bobby Joe spied me and rushed over, conveniently standing between me and his little industry at work. Buddy Branch waved to me but kept talking on the phone. I noticed that he looked a lot more polished and his skin ailment appeared to be remarkably improved. Bobby Joe greeted me cheerfully, as if I were the person he most wanted to see in the world.

"My God! What's going on here?" I demanded. "It looks like the press site for *Gone With the Wind Two*."

"Trying to get some work done while we're here," Bobby Joe said. He started giving me some double-talk about how many details there were to clear up since the crash, but I quit listening. I looked around the room and then at Bobby Joe's mouth and that faint scar on his lower lip from our playful wrestling with a hunting knife when we were fourteen. The scar had always seemed immensely appealing until that moment.

He must have thought I'd been under a stone for the last twenty years. I know a publicity blitz when I see one. This was as twirly as Paisley Blue's baton. I'd seen senatorial campaigns that weren't as smoothly oiled as this.

"How about something to eat?" Bobby Joe said. "I haven't had a thing since this morning." He was trying to make it sound like an invitation for something more than just an over-priced stuffed tomato. But it didn't work. I stared at his California tan, and the truth bore through like a laser.

"So this is what you're doing here in Dallas! That vision in the Swiss chard is drop-kicking Calvin Troope's new single all the way to the top of the charts!"

"Dinah, that's not the whole story, now. . . . Listen . . ."

What I wished that moment was that I could be Samson, the Rambo of the Bible, and could push two of the persimmon-colored walls of suite 442 and bring them down, thereby collapsing the ceiling, which would eventually, in domino fashion, collapse the whole hotel into one great heap of glass, crushed waterfalls, and designer greenery. But I was not Samson, and I obviously wasn't Delilah, either.

"Bobby Joe! You certainly left your conscience, if you have one, in California," I sputtered. Employing my cheerleader voice, I continued. "I'll get even with you for this, if I have to kill you. Only I'll try to work out something more permanently painful than a quick death!"

At which point his come-and-get-it grin melted away and he looked a tad green under his California tan, the same brownish-green disaster color that can happen to dark hair with a home-dye job.

"You bastard!" I tacked on as I spun around and rushed back down the hall just in time to throw myself into the glass elevator that was closing, thereby frightening an older couple, probably on their honeymoon, I thought, because she wore an orchid corsage. When I turned around I caught for one second the sight of Bobby Joe in the middle of the hallway looking after me as if I'd just lobbed a grenade and he was waiting for the explosion.

By the time I reached the parking garage, I was so furious I couldn't hold back the tears. The attendant in the mustard jumpsuit was just returning from parking my car when I shoved my slip through the hole in his glass booth. Tears fell on the ticket as he reached for it.

"Three dollars," he said, and jerked the cash drawer open. Then, sighing heavily, he stepped onto the foot elevator behind him and, glaring over his shoulder at me, descended from sight into some lower depth of the parking garage. A small group gathered to wait for their own cars as I stood crying. From the bowels of the earth I could hear the hurtling sound of a car turning curves on two wheels, and finally my navy Prelude sped around the final turn and skidded to a halt in front of me. If it had been a horse, it would have reared on its hind legs.

"You were driving entirely too fast!" I cried, as the attendant slid out of my car. I scrounged in my purse for a tip. He waited, holding the door ajar, until my compact fell out of my purse onto the pavement and broke into two pieces. I took aim then and kicked each piece across the concrete floor into a darkened greasy area. The attendant then turned back to me and, raising one hand in surrender, said, "That's okay, lady," and pulled the door open wider for me to slide inside.

Leaving the garage, I nearly ran down three normal women. I told myself I had to regain control before I killed somebody else. Me, I wouldn't mind. I was thinking how the whole world from then on was going to be one big laugh track. I would have to relocate to the Fiji Islands or hole up in some cave in Big Bend. For the first time I understood hermits.

It was getting close to rush hour by then, the streets were crowded and the sun blinding, but it was not till the cop pulled up beside me that I realized my car was heading the wrong way on a one-way street. He was young, blond, chewing gum, and wearing those mirrored sunglasses they all do ever since that Paul Newman prison movie. He leaned through his window and pointed out that not only was I going the wrong way down a one-way street but I was blocking a lane of traffic on a two-lane street. He went on chewing when he finished informing me of these facts.

"I'm sorry," I told the cop. I could see he was trying to decide if I was crazy or drunk. I thought of the possibility of being arrested and thrown in jail to be strip-searched and manhandled. It was just that kind of day. I wondered why someone hadn't warned me about what my horoscope must be saying.

I blew my nose and tried to gain control. "I don't know

why we have so many one-way streets," I managed to say to the cop, just to let him know I was a regular citizen and not just a transient lunatic. "My father published the weekly newspaper in Midnight, and he didn't approve of one-way streets."

I guess he thought arresting me might create more of a traffic hazard than I had already, so he waved me on and watched me as I backed around the corner. I gave him an obsequious little wave and took off in the opposite direction from Midnight, and before I knew it I was suddenly on the toll road and heading toward home in North Dallas.

By the time I pulled into our drive, Dude's car was there—that supposedly all-American blue Tracer with the red paint on the dented fenders. It occurred to me that Marilyn could be there, too, lurking behind my own miniblinds. Surely Dude wouldn't do that. Still, in my weakened condition I had to consider all possible disasters. I sat there paralyzed by the thought. And if she weren't, should I tell Dude about this humiliation? What would he think of my being made a national fool? So I backed up. But then I saw weeds around the holly by the door. If the weeds were left, they'd crowd out the chrysanthemums, which were burgundy and matched the cherry-painted front door when they bloomed in September. So I stopped and pulled up again. The holly also needed mulching to control the weeds.

What I wanted was to run through that cherry door and wipe away the past weeks, find it was all a bad dream and Calvin Troope was alive and whining in Hollywood and Bobby Joe was still a painful memory and Dude was still in love with me and our major dispute was over our favorite flavor of Blue Bell ice cream.

Instead I backed up again, but Dude came to the door. He held a newspaper in his hand and he wore cutoffs and a T-shirt. He looked wonderful. He tilted his head quizzically, probably wondering why I was driving back and forth in the driveway. But suddenly I didn't have the courage to face him and admit Bobby Joe's betrayal. At that moment I was too vulnerable to let myself suffer another indignity. So I rolled down the window and called to him, "That holly needs mulching and the weeds pulled!"

He gave me a puzzled smile and a wave as I backed out of the drive.

When I got back to Midnight, Mama was watching a nature program about two juvenile animals who'd been separated from their mothers and were wandering around in the dangerous wilds trying to find them. It dried up my tears immediately. During the commercial Mama told me the list of phone callers was in the hall. She had obviously been aggravated by all the calls, but she acted as if it were against the law to take the phone off the hook, something I do at the drop of a hat.

Bobby Joe had phoned twice. The *Corpus Christi Caller* had phoned, somebody from *People,* a woman from a Fort Worth talk show, and Dude. I called Dude.

"Are you okay?" he asked.

"Yes," I said. "Why do you keep asking me if I'm okay?"

"I just thought it a little weird that you'd drive all the way to North Dallas to tell me to mulch the holly."

"Oh, that," I said. "I hadn't intended to. The car just went that way. I suppose it's tired of Midnight, too."

He said I'd obviously been around Mama's car too long. I thanked him for calling and expressing his concern.

When I put the phone down, Mama called to me, "Oh, that man from Longview phoned about wanting to see the *Citizen.* He apologized for not making it earlier, he said he'd had to take somebody to Temple because they couldn't find out what was wrong with him in East Texas. He's already had a quadruple bypass."

"Sounds like y'all had a good heart-to-heart," I said.

"Well, what's wrong with that?" Mama asked.

I felt so bad I couldn't even get excited about selling the *Citizen.* I went to the door of the living room, where Mama was watching the sad animal program.

"Nothing," I said. "Mama, if he makes any kind of offer at all, I hope you'll consider it."

"Well, of course I'll consider it, Dinah," Mama said. "He said he'd be here sometime this week."

I went into my motel bedroom and lay down. I didn't even want to eat.

Mama called to ask if I was okay, but her program came back on and she didn't seem to notice that I didn't answer. I took my shoes off and went to the kitchen and poured myself a tall glass of iced tea and sat outside on Mama's patio, among her spider plants and snake plants and ferns that were decades old. A group of mourning doves sat in her pecan tree calling sadly. I love the sound of one mourning dove, but a whole slew of mourning doves crying is depressing. I threw a rock at them but hit only the side of Mama's house. I thought to myself, If Mama comes out here and tells me to quit throwing rocks, I'll kill myself. But she didn't. So I just sat there letting it all sink in how I'd been had, mind, body, and soul, about as thoroughly as you could be had. But I couldn't understand how it could all be a hoax. What about Paisley Blue's eye? What about all those rainbows? Maybe Cissy was in on the whole thing. Maybe she was offered a Hollywood contract for Paisley Blue to soften me up for Buddy Branch's story. But when I thought back, it was hard for me to believe that Buddy had made up that entire story unless he was a professional liar, maybe an actor. That's probably what he was, I considered, an actor, or a semi-con man, the kind who steals the life savings of older women.

Slowly and painfully, like digging out a long splinter, I realized the full impact of Bobby Joe's betrayal. The minute the news of Calvin Troope's crash reached Hollywood, he must have sat down with a yellow pad and planned how he could make as many bucks as possible on the disaster. It was too painful to think of alone. I needed to talk to someone. I considered phoning Marianne in France. I thought of phoning Shirley in Baltimore. But I didn't have the energy to go into the whole awful story from the first lie to the latest. I thought of phoning Ned English, even Cissy. I wished I could talk to Mama. I considered phoning the crisis hot line in Dallas, but I knew that with the economic downturn there were so many people in crisis it was hard to get through to a real person. Sometimes people had to wait on hold so long the crisis passed. Besides, I wanted to talk to somebody I could see. A friend.

I walked over to Mama's three Better Boy tomato plants, which keep her in tomatoes most of the summer, and sat down beside them. I'd told Mama she should plant Early Girls instead of Better Boys, but she'd ignored that advice, saying she was satisfied with Better Boys. The smell of even the Better Boys was calming.

The phone rang a couple more times. I called to Mama that I didn't want to talk to anybody.

"What'll I tell them?" she asked.

"Tell them I've died."

"Dinah!"

"Tell them I've left the house," I called, which was true. Mama won't lie about anything.

She came out a moment later to ask why I was sitting on the ground by her tomato plants.

I told her I was thinking.

She said that Jacqueline Kennedy had sat outside after John Kennedy was shot, too.

I thought about that a minute. "Mama, are you trying to tell me Dude's been shot?"

She said, "Don't be silly, Dinah," and went back inside.

I sat there till it got dark and the lightning bugs began to sail through the air. Then the mosquitoes started chewing on me. I nearly wished I could go back to being a kid and chasing lightning bugs. It's funny, I thought, how in retrospect we remember only running through the night chasing lightning bugs, when there must have been mosquitoes chewing on us then, too. And suddenly I remembered Larry's arms when he was about six years old, tanned from playing outside all day. How he'd have mosquito bites and scratch them so there'd be the slightest little trail of blood and I'd take him into the bathroom and wash the bite and doctor it with Campho-Phenique and blow on it a minute in case it burned, the same way Mama had done me, and how eager he'd be to rush back outside to play.

I sat searching my memory for tacky, untrustworthy things Bobby Joe did when we were kids that should have signified the future, but I couldn't remember anything. It seemed to me that Bobby Joe had been a decent person. Even Christian. We'd all joined the Baptist Church when we were ten or eleven, and been baptized. We'd grown up in Sunday schools being indoctrinated in the Ten Commandments. We'd said "Yes, ma'am" and "No, ma'am" till we were grown. We'd sung cowboy songs like Gene Autry's theme song about being back in the saddle again, back where a friend is a friend. How could he have changed so much? Could even Hollywood be that damaging to a person?

When the next phone call came, Mama talked for a few minutes before she cracked the patio door again.

"Dinah, you better come take this. It's Traci and she says Little Dude tried to run her off the road and kill her."

I went inside and slid Mama's patio door closed behind me. She handed me the phone and moved into the kitchen to get a fresh tissue.

"Hello," I said sourly.

"Dinah!" Traci was semi-hysterical. "Larry tried to kill me!"

"I'm sure that's a mistake," I said to her. "Calm down, Traci, so we can talk."

I heard her take a couple of deep breaths.

"I wish you could see my car," she said. "It's about torn up! Would you come get me, and somebody better go and find him before he sure enough kills a bunch of people. He's acting like one of those lunatics who shoots everybody in a Taco Stop or something! A serial murderer!"

I was too tired and disgusted to explain to her the difference between a serial murderer and a lunatic who shoots up a Taco Stop, so I just asked where she was.

"I don't know where I am," she said.

"Well, how am I supposed to find you?"

I heard her ask someone where she was.

"I'm about a mile from Faye Belt's on that road that goes to the Church of Christ preacher's house." I repeated that to Mama. Mama said she was at Brother Hal's house, just past the chicken brooders and right before the hippie girl's cactus shop.

I told Traci I'd be there in a minute and turned back to Mama.

"You mean those two big chicken warehouses past Faye Belt's?"

She said yes. Did I want her to come with me? I said, "Thank you very much, Mama, but you might want to stay here and man the phones, since Larry seems to have gone berserk again."

She said something like "Oh, my Lord!" and gave me a pat on the back as I started off, which I appreciated, given the events of the day.

It was fully dark by the time I reached the highway, a navy-blue summery night, and the Dairy Queen was surrounded with kids in their cars practicing crude language and hoping to make out, just like when I was a kid. The only thing different was the prices. Even some of the same songs were on the jukebox—like "Earth Angel," one of my favorites.

Right before Faye Belt's junky establishment I turned off the highway and started down a gravel road toward the Church of Christ preacher's house and the hippie girl's cactus shop. Frankly, I question whether anyone can make a living selling cactus, especially twenty miles from nowhere, so I suspected maybe the hippie girl might sell some clandestine controlled substance more lucrative than cactus.

The first odd thing that happened was that I began seeing white leghorn hens everywhere. White leghorns are medium-size, undistinguished, often scrawny, white chickens. They were perched on top of the barbed-wire fences beside the road, and chickens were flying around in the road squawking and strolling along beside the road in pairs. I had to slow the car and just roll along to keep from hitting one after another.

When I reached the two large chicken brooders, I found that a highway patrol car had plowed into the side of one of them, leaving an opening like a round tunnel of love and thus liberating several hundred chickens. I had a good hunch whose patrol car it might be, too. I pulled over to the side of the road and waded through chickens till I got close enough to see there was no one in the car. The chickens in the second brooder, still in captivity, seemed extremely upset seeing the other chickens walking around free. I had an impulse to go over and open the door for them, too, but it was locked. Well, too bad, I said to them, and I waded back to the road and shooed a chicken off the hood of my car and scraped the bottom of my sandals carefully on the gravel before getting inside. I then proceeded in the direction of the Church of Christ preacher's house, thinking I might find Larry along the road.

It was only half a mile to the shining porch light at Brother Hal's, a brick bungalow with white shutters around a picture window and white painted tires strewn about the yard and planted with marigolds and other cheap kinds of flowers. I didn't feel a bit like socializing with some Church of Christ preacher and his wife and kids, so I honked, even though Daddy would have considered that rude Metroplex behavior. But I assumed Brother Hal and his family would be just as glad to get rid of Traci if she were half as hysterical as she'd sounded on the phone.

She appeared after a minute, calmly waving good-bye and eating an ice cream sandwich. She was wearing her black suede boots that came up to her thin thighs and another personalized oversize black T-shirt, this one with a large hot dog on the front and raised drops of mustard dripping down. She wore large gold dangling earrings, with smaller ones that looked like snails climbing up her ears, and carried her big red shoulder purse.

"Hi," she said, when she'd climbed into the car. "Thank you so very, very much for coming to pick me up. Whew!"

"Traci, try not to drip ice cream inside my car," I said to her.

"Oh," she said, and pulled a tissue out of her purse and held it under her ice cream.

"Where to?" I asked.

"I don't know!" she said. "The police maybe. He tried to kill me."

"You mentioned that, Traci."

"Why are all these chickens everywhere?"

"Act of God," I said. "I guess they're looking for a rooster. Where's your car? Are you sure you can't drive it?"

"I don't know. Go that way," she said, pointing farther down the road. "I was so scared he was going to shoot me." She shoved the last of the ice cream into her mouth and licked her fingers as I started rolling down the road.

"Has anybody ever tried to kill you, Dinah?"

"No, but I wish they had tried and succeeded," I answered.

"Why? What's wrong?"

"Everything."

"Tell me," she said.

I glanced at her as I swerved away from a chicken. It was the first time I could remember Traci showing concern for my state of mind. I asked her if she knew Dude and I were separated. She said, Of course, everyone does. Nevertheless, I summarized the Bobby Joe–Buddy Branch hoax-disaster.

"Oh, Dinah!" she said. "Maybe you're wrong. Surely he wouldn't do that, having been in love with you and all!"

"How do you know that?" I asked her.

"Everybody knows that," she said.

Another example of a distorted collective unconscious in Midnight, I thought.

"I see it all now plain as day. Bobby Joe must have said, 'Hey, guys, I know this real dumb old broad in Central Texas named Dinah. . . .' "

"Oh, Dinah," Traci said. "I'm sorry about that. I'll bet tomorrow you'll find out it's not like that at all."

I glanced at her, amazed that she was picking up the Pollyanna mode like the rest of the family. But I told her I appreciated her effort to soothe my agony. Then I told her about finding the patrol car plowed into the side of the chicken brooder. I also said I thought it was strange that the chickens weren't roosting, since it was night. Traci asked if I wouldn't wander around, too, if it was the first chance I'd ever had to put my feet on something besides chicken wire. I said I guessed I would.

We reached her red Rabbit about a quarter-mile down the road, and indeed it was in the ditch and tilted sideways like Yoko Ono wearing a beret. In her terror, Traci said, she'd dropped her keys, so I turned my car around to shine my headlights on her car. She took the flashlight that Dude made me carry in my glove compartment back when he cared about me and shone it around the ditch full of Johnsongrass for about thirty seconds before she screamed she was afraid of snakes and fire ants. By then we'd outpaced the chickens, who might have distracted the snakes, had there been snakes, so all we could do was leave her car there till morning light. We headed back to town and after a few minutes met the point white leghorn heading toward Fort Worth, as if it were part of an old-time cattle drive.

"What made you think Larry was trying to kill you, Traci? He seemed quite rational when I spoke to him the other day."

"He drove up beside my car waving his arms!"

"Maybe he just wanted to talk to you."

Traci was quiet a minute. "I hadn't thought of that. I'd just stopped at the Dairy Queen, and he pulled up like he was going to ram the car and then he followed me down this lonesome road and . . ."

We drove to where the patrol car crashed into the chicken brooder, and I had to admit to myself that it did support Traci's theory. But when we reached the highway, who should be standing trying to hitch a ride toward town but my own dear son Larry. I pulled the car over and Traci screamed bloody murder, which scared me so badly I nearly ran over him. I managed to stop finally, and he came to my window smiling.

"Dinah," he said. "I'm so glad it's you. Turn the car around. I've got to show you something."

"We've seen the liberated chickens," I said.

"Don't you get in this car, after trying to kill me!" Traci shrieked.

"I wasn't trying to kill you," he said, "I wanted to talk to you. Why didn't you stop?"

"You pointed a gun at me!"

"I didn't point a gun at you!"

He went around to her side of the car, and Traci screamed again, as though he were going to attack her right there.

"Oh, shut up, Traci," he said, and pulled the door open and told her to slide in back, which she did. He settled in the bucket seat beside mine.

"Go back up the gravel road," he directed. For just a minute I thought maybe he'd had a vision, but I came to my senses and turned the car around. With Traci squashed in the back, we were all close in the small car. In the rearview mirror I could see Traci make a slow tentative movement toward Larry's arm. There was such a sexual tension in that car with them close like that, I could have turned off the ignition and we'd have still rolled along.

"Why did you attack the chicken house?" I asked him.

"Oh, I didn't mean to, I was just so mad at her," he said, " 'cause she wouldn't listen to me. She locked her door and screamed like I was a maniac. And it just made me so mad I ran off the road."

We'd gone no more than a quarter of a mile when he told me to pull off the road. He took the flashlight out of the glove compartment, and warning us to be quiet and follow him, he led us out of the car and through an open field toward a thicket of woods. The glow from the flashlight occasionally caught the purple thistle and bright orange heads of Indian paintbrush. Above us and all around as far as the eye could see stretched such a breathtaking array of stars it was like having a view of the entire universe. It took me a few minutes to realize we were heading back toward Faye Belt's house.

"Are you crazy?" I called to Larry. "You want one of her mad Dobermans to eat us up?"

"Sh-h-h," Larry said.

So Traci and I followed him, creeping toward the patch of woods right before Faye Belt's assorted pens, chicken coops, and outhouses. I figured with my luck that day I'd probably get bitten by a rattlesnake and, knowing Faye Belt, she probably had ground traps. Inside the patch of woods it was so dark I couldn't see a thing. Traci took Larry's hand and I had to hang onto the back of her hot-dog T-shirt.

Finally Larry stopped. We were outside what seemed to be a new stockade fence.

"Listen," he said.

I couldn't hear anything but my heart pumping and the faint sound of chickens cawing and clucking and a thousand and two crickets and cicadas and a dog howling somewhere far off and occasionally the distant sound of a truck on the highway braking before entering the city limits of Midnight, population 3,604 not counting the grimacing apostles.

"Listen," Larry said louder. I still didn't hear anything. "Well, look over this fence," he said.

"I can't, I'm not tall enough!"

He handed me the flashlight and, to my amazement, lifted me up. I held onto the top of the fence, which was covered with chicken wire, and shone the flashlight around inside the pen. Slowly, assorted pairs of eyes opened and I could see cats everywhere—stretched out, curled up, or hunkered down henlike, old cats, young cats, twin cats. Some of them stirred or rose, yawning and stretching, meowing plaintively or hissing. A few nervously scampered away, dozens of cats, fat cats and skinny cats, long-haired and short-haired, all of them of the yellow-striped variety.

"Well, my Lord!" I said.

"Let me see," Traci said. Larry set me down and I passed the flashlight to Traci and Larry lifted her up. He held her a long time. I knew he wasn't as interested in her seeing dozens of yellow-striped cats as he was in holding onto her.

Meanwhile the headline came to me all of a sudden: YELLOW-CAT GULAG DISCOVERED BEHIND FAYE BELT'S.

When Larry let her down, Traci began to giggle. Larry still held onto her arm.

"Well, what are we going to do?" I said.

"Liberate these cats just like the chickens," Larry said.

"No," I said. "We don't want them running around like the chickens. These cats have homes and people signing petitions and offering rewards for them. We can't just go springing them loose."

About then one of Faye Belt's hungry dogs awoke, and the dog pen, which must have been fairly close, came to life with a growing chorus of howling and barking. We started backing out of the woods and then broke running through the Johnsongrass and switchgrass toward the road. I could feel the cockleburs catching onto the bottom of my skirt. We got to the car and all fell against it, out of breath but laughing. It reminded me of high school, when stealing sugarcane was a major sport around Halloween. Traci fell against Larry, and he put his arms around her. I pulled off some cockleburs and dropped them in the sandy shoulder of the road.

"Don't be trying to make up with me," he said, teasing her, "just because I'm about to be the town hero for finding eight hundred missing yellow cats." Traci threw her arms around him and broke into tears.

"Sure are lots of yellow cats," I said, trying not to watch them. "Whatever could she have wanted with all those cats?"

I leaned against the car and looked up at the stars and found the Milky Way and Orion's Belt and the Big Dipper and felt happy Traci and Larry were making up. For about one minute and a half I completely forgot my vision disaster. It made me feel nearly peaceful about being in Midnight.

After a few minutes we all got back in my car and I drove to Larry's patrol car, Traci sitting in back with her arms hugging Larry's neck. A few of the slower chickens were still huddled around the open brooder. With Larry and me pushing, Traci managed to back the patrol car out of the chicken brooder and pull onto the road. On the radio Larry called the highway patrol, the county sheriff, and all manner of law enforcement officers who might be bored on a weeknight.

Shortly afterward the vicinity around Faye Belt's cat pen looked like *Miami Vice*. Red turret lights were swirling and people were emptying out of mobile homes and arriving in cars and pickups and suburbans, assorted animals were barking and meowing and crowing, and Faye Belt herself, who'd been disarmed, was shouting bloody murder. Buster Ledbetter arrived in his state-of-the-art TV van expecting another miracle. Easy Malone stood in the center of the commotion, beside Faye Belt, rocking back and forth on his heels and making pronouncements as if he'd just arrested all ten of the FBI's most-wanted criminals in one fell swoop.

When she had quit shouting about the invasion of her property, Faye—who had been treating me with more respect since I'd broken the vision story—said she'd give me her exclusive story the next morning.

Whereupon I left Larry and Traci smooching in the patrol car and, passing the Dairy Queen, realized I hadn't eaten since breakfast. I stopped and ordered a corny dog and a Dr Pepper, then phoned Mama to tell her everything was okay, not to worry. Larry had found the missing cats and would be a big hero. Mama said Bobby Joe had been there looking for me and she thought he was still outside waiting.

After the corny dog and Dr Pepper I ordered a chocolate sundae, thinking maybe I'd eat so much I'd get gobby fat and be unrecognizable and thereby escape ignominy. The chocolate sundae, I decided, was sweeter than it used to be, probably because it was made with chemicals instead of sugar. I lingered over it anyway, watching the young couple in the pickup beside me as the girl, like a mother bird, hand-fed french fries to her boyfriend. On the opposite side was a suburban full of teenage girls. I remembered when I was their age wondering if people my age ever kissed. I would have laughed remembering that if I hadn't been alone.

That's when there occurred to me a more reasonable way to escape ignominy than fleeing to a cave in Big Bend or having plastic surgery or getting gobby fat. Why not just stay in Midnight. That was a simple way to disappear from the earth. Nobody in Midnight would particularly care about my having been a national joke, except maybe Mama. As long as the local citizenry got their names in the paper occasionally and maybe a statue of Calvin Troope to commemorate the celebrity crash, I could stay right there in Midnight and hide. I could stay there and never again be surprised about anything. The statistical chance of a second plane crash bringing surprise was surely infinitesimal. I could rent the Fishers' vacant duplex and wear running shoes and earth sandals for the rest of my life. Live simply with a minimum of furniture and my cats and eat only yogurt and tomatoes and five-grain bread. Take care of Mama in her old age. Baby-sit Misty Dawn. In Midnight I wouldn't even have to be particularly embarrassed about Misty Dawn's name. I would never again have to face a cowboy photo and I could visit Lilly regularly and when Mama's hips melted away I could put her in Happy Acres and visit her. I could let my hair grow long and braid it around my head and wash it only every two weeks. I could champion environmental causes in the *Citizen* and quit wearing makeup and become an interesting older person who prevents the federal government from burying nuclear waste in Texas. I would lobby the legislature until the speed limit was back to seventy, which is what everyone drives anyway. On vacations I would backpack around third-world countries and write a series that someone else would submit, so that to my total and complete surprise the series would win a Pulitzer Prize and I wouldn't seem like such a fool anymore.

When I started home I decided that in order to avoid Bobby Joe, I'd park around the corner from Mama's, walk through the alley, and climb into the house through the window of the utility room next to the garage. It was a secret entrance I'd used in younger days and happier times. But as soon as I got through the window, the light flashed on to reveal Mama in her bubble haircap, standing with a broom raised, about to bop me on the head as an intruder.

"You nearly scared me to death," she muttered, and drooped against her Maytag washer, clutching her pink duster over her heart and lowering her weapon. Her face was drained of all color. If I hadn't been afraid she was having a heart attack, I might have laughed.

"Mama, I'm sorry," I said. "I didn't mean to scare you." When she was calm enough to speak she said, "Dinah, I have to tell you the truth. . . ." She took a deep gasping breath and pulled herself upright, leaning on the dryer. "I have enjoyed having you around (gasp), but living with you (gasp) is like being in a tornado (gasp). I'll be kind of glad when you get back to Dallas (gasp). I don't think I'll ever get rid of the shingles as long as you're here." She turned around and started out the door, but I stopped her.

I said, "But Mama, guess what?" She turned around. "Larry and Traci have made up. And I've decided to stay here and run the *Midnight Citizen* . . . for the rest of my life."

Mama opened her mouth to speak, but nothing came out. Then she let the broom fall to the ground with a thud and left the room without picking it up.

The yellow-cat roundup the next day turned out to be a large media event, with several stations from the Metroplex covering it with footage on the local evening news. There was talk that it might even make the national news, especially since Midnight was a big media name of late.

Easy Malone explained the crime as a case of free enterprise gone awry. After a recent Neiman-Marcus Christmas catalogue offered a new breed of cat called California Spangled, which sold for fourteen hundred dollars a cat, Faye Belt decided she could breed a cat like that herself.

"They looked like plain yellow cats to me," she said on that evening's local news, "only they had spots instead of stripes. Who'd have thought people would get so upset about missing a few alley cats," Faye, in her black crepe dress with the bugle beads, testified before the camera. She'd decided to go the video route with her exclusive story, as opposed to the print route, she'd told me earlier in the day.

The cat roundup started at five o'clock. At first Easy carried the cats outside the fence one by one, as if it were a cattle auction, but people grew impatient with that, especially since he carried them by the back of the neck, as you would rabbits. Then, after a nervous, skinny cat scratched Easy and escaped under a pickup, he decided to shoo the cats into one side of the pen and let their owners inside. It looked like a calf scramble, all the people running and calling after their yellow cats as the video cameras rolled. Cissy said she'd never noticed how cats resemble nationalities. Some looked Oriental, some Italian, and some like white trash.

Larry, handsome in his uniform, I have to say, and smiling happily as he hadn't since Traci left, was interviewed as the hero of the occasion. He had refused the Fishers' reward for their macho male cat, which had been segregated in a rabbit cage because of his aggressiveness.

I took a few pictures for the *Citizen,* which did solve the ninety-nine-bottles-of-beer question for that week. We ran a big photo of Larry in the foreground with a swarm of cats behind him, then a close-up of the Fisher sisters holding two of their cats. Faye Belt was charged with twenty-two counts of robbery despite the Fisher twins' charge that it should be kidnapping, but by the end of the week Faye had managed to have all charges dropped, after agreeing to restitution to each cat owner.

Mama didn't mention my decision to take over the *Citizen.* It had never occurred to me that she might have some reservations about my plan. But I proceeded anyway. I made an appointment with the Fisher sisters to look at their duplex, and I knew that was as good as an engraved announcement to each citizen either that I was staying on or that Mama and I had had a falling out. But I couldn't worry about that. I knew it was important for me to find some place to hide out. It was simply a matter of time before one of the journalists snooping around would uncover the Calvin Troope publicity blitz and figure out how I'd been the biggest fool since that cola company changed its recipe.

When Mama arrived at Happy Acres the next morning with Lilly's fresh laundry and two pairs of earrings to choose between for her approaching wedding, the director of Happy Acres took Mama aside. Anthony Spencer Mainard had had a stroke the night before. He'd been rushed to the hospital and had died about an hour after arrival. She said she'd offered to phone us, but Lilly hadn't wanted to disturb us in the night. Mama phoned me at the *Citizen*. By the time I reached the scene, Lilly was consoling Mama. Beside Lilly's bed stood a large basket of pink roses delivered that morning from Anthony Spencer Mainard. He'd ordered them two days earlier.

When I walked into Mama's that afternoon, she was on the phone with Bobby Joe.

"Would you please talk to this man," Mama said, not even bothering to cover the receiver. "He's driving me crazy calling all the time. He says he's going to talk to you sometime, if he has to come here with a gun." Mama rolled her eyes.

I picked up the phone and gave Bobby Joe my most deadpan greeting. "I wish you'd give up."

"You ought to know I wouldn't give up that easy."

"No, I don't know that. You gave up for twenty-odd years."

"I've got to talk to you, but I don't want to just talk on the phone."

"Well, I don't want to talk in person, or on the phone, either, Bobby Joe. And what good would it do? You can't say one thing that will change the way I feel about this whole disaster, so you might as well just save your breath for Hollywood. It might do you some good out there."

"Dinah, you're making a mistake jumping to conclusions. . . ."

"Well, it won't be the first one," I said. "It just really kills me, all the years I wasted with such fantasies about you. What a waste of time. I might be happily married in North Dallas. Isn't it funny how things you worry about never occur, but always something worse? Though I don't know how I could have missed that possibility the first time I saw you had your hair blow-dried. I should have known."

I kicked off my shoes, one and then the other, into the motel bedroom.

"Dinah, I'm going to tell you something whether you believe me or not. I'll admit we wanted to make some money out of this tragedy. What's wrong with that?" He could sound so sincere. In sounding sincere he would score one hundred on the Richter scale.

"There are lots of ways you can make money, Bobby Joe. You could be a hit man for the Mafia or those new Jamaican posse gangs. Come to think of it, you are kind of a Hollywood hit man. . . ."

I began singing, "Hitting me in the heart . . ."

"God, I'd about forgotten how crazy you get when you're mad."

"Let me tell you, Bobby Joe, you just don't know the half of it. Now that I'm old, I really get mad. When I was young, I was just testing."

I hung up then. Not easily. I still find it hard to hang up unless it's a machine. It's such an indignity, standing there with a phone in your hand and nothing but the smoke of anger on the other end.

Then, of course, I had to spill the whole disaster to Mama, since she'd heard my conversation with Bobby Joe. So I told her everything and she said, "Dinah, anybody in their right mind would have been suspicious about that story."

I said, "Mama, I was suspicious. But it was news. And I was all shook up, remember?"

Mama studied me and said, "Oh, Dinah, you're so like your father," in a rather mild, patient voice.

And I said, "Mama, I'm sorry, but I don't take that as the insult you intend it to be."

• • •

The next morning Mama and I went to Happy Acres to take Lilly to Anthony Spencer Mainard's funeral. It was just what I was in the mood for, of course, a funeral. But when we got to Happy Acres, Lilly had decided not to go.

Mama sounded as if she were truly disappointed and the thing we really were craving to do that morning was drive to Dallas in rush-hour traffic for a funeral.

Lilly had already dressed for the funeral. She wore her best three-piece black-and-white print dress, with the black piping, white imitation pearls with matching earrings, and her frog brooch with the ruby eyes, only, one eye was missing. She looked beautiful.

"I decided," Lilly said, "that I've already buried two men, and I want to remember Anthony alive and happy. I don't know his family or friends there anyway."

Mama said they'd be expecting her.

"No. I've decided, I'd rather not go," she said firmly.

Mama looked to me for help. She had a hard time shifting gears.

"Why don't we go to the café and have lunch," I said.

"Dinah, it's only eight-thirty," Mama said.

"Well, brunch," I said. I told them I was trying to get fat and disappear. Of course they thought I was joking.

Lilly said she'd like to have a little drive out by Cissy's house, where the miracle occurred. Mama gave me a tight, sick little smile. But we helped Lilly down the hall with her walker, past Devotion-in-Motion in the lobby, and out to Mama's car. We'd settled Lilly and her walker in the back and Mama and me in front, with me driving, and as soon as I turned on the motor, the car told us again it needed windshield-wiper fluid.

"Mama, why on earth don't you buy this car some windshield-wiper fluid?"

She said, "I don't know, Dinah. I guess I kind of like it to keep talking to me," she said. It hadn't occurred to me that Mama could be lonesome.

We drove out the highway to Cissy's mobile home and I pointed out where the plane had crashed in the Swiss chard field. The live oaks were sliced off at the top, but it wouldn't have been noticeable if you hadn't known.

"But you can't see a thing," Lilly said. Someone had put up a sign that said PREPARE TO MEET THY MAKER, and there was a minibusload of Boy Scouts scurrying around the crash area. I wondered why I was so often confronted by Boy Scouts. One of the scouts carried a boom box that was playing a Calvin Troope recording of old hymns that wasn't so bad, given it was Calvin Troope. Between hymns we could hear Pattycake barking her shrill, useless barks inside Cissy's house. There were two sleeping bags with men snoring inside under the fig tree near the utility shed, and a couple of young men with their heads shaved were handing out unintelligible leaflets about UFO sightings and the end of the world. In a window of the mobile home there was a poster advertising the Luling Watermelon Thump, where Paisley Blue would compete in a couple of weeks.

"Isn't that just amazing?" Lilly said, looking out the window.

Neither Mama nor I answered.

"Life is full of miracles, isn't it?" Lilly said. "I felt like it was a miracle meeting Anthony Spencer Mainard. I don't regret a minute of it," she said.

We drove to the café after that, and Lilly and I ordered lemon icebox pie. That was when I discovered Dorothy Little had begun importing her lemon pie from the Metroplex. I could tell as soon as I cut into it with my fork and felt the plastic weightiness of the custard part, unlike the cloud-light custard we were accustomed to slicing so easily. Lilly and I felt like crying. And just when I'd decided I could stuff myself all I wanted.

"Imagine how that would upset your father," Mama said.

"He'd have written a front-page editorial," I said. And that's the moment I began to get the idea of how to handle my problem.

After Mama assured me she could get Lilly back to Happy Acres, I left them there in order to employ my energies at the *Citizen* in helping Jud get the week's issue out. I was also planning my renovation of the *Citizen*'s plant and had even removed Marilyn's calendar and Lyndon's gallbladder photo from the wall. It was my office now, I said to myself. I noticed I was talking to myself a lot, but I assumed I would be for the rest of my life and I might as well get used to it.

That evening I suggested to Mama that she phone Mr. Chapman in Longview and tell him I'd decided to stay and run the *Citizen*. I told her I'd put a deposit down on the Fisher sisters' duplex and phoned Larry that afternoon and told him the news. To say he was flabbergasted would be an exaggeration, because Larry is not the type. I told Mama that the "duplex with a view" the Fisher sisters had been advertising actually had only a view of the feet of the water tower, but I'd managed to laugh at that and suggest that we plant morning glories around them. Mama did not join in my cheerful bantering, indeed did not say anything for a pregnant minute.

"Dinah," she began, "I appreciate your willingness to assume this responsibility. . . ." That was a text she'd been rehearsing, no doubt about it. She proceeded with one of those pronouncements as riddled with subterfuge and innuendo as a politician's. I couldn't stop myself from interrupting.

"Mama, please say flat-out what you mean. I'd appreciate it. Do you not want me to take over the *Citizen*? Is that it? You're afraid I'll embarrass you every week?"

Mama sighed. "No, Dinah. I'm not worried about being embarrassed. I just don't think you'd be happy doing this. I think you're depressed and you're making this decision because you're not sure what else to do. I think you should go back to Dallas to your job there and your friends and try to revive your marriage if that's what you want to do."

"Mama, if you don't want me around, if you don't want me to manage the *Citizen*, I'll find something else to do. Maybe I'll go to the seminary and become a music director. I've always liked to sing hymns. Especially those bloody ones." I laughed. "I could join the Peace Corps or the merchant marines."

Mama stared at me a minute and shook her head.

"Mama, believe me. There is nothing wrong with me."

All right, she said. And later on I heard her put in a call to Mr. Chapman and tell him her situation had changed, and while she appreciated his interest, she'd made other plans.

ON Saturday, Cissy called me to say that a Christian movie company and Buddy Branch were at her house scouting locales for a Christian video about Calvin Troope's life and death and Buddy Branch's vision. She said she'd offered to rent them her mobile home, but they were looking for a mountain with a mansion on top. I said, But Cissy, what does a mountain with a mansion have to do with anything? Cissy said it was hard to get a mess of cameras inside a mobile home. She said she was also discussing the possibility of Paisley Blue's having a costarring role in the production and she'd told them, too, that she'd rent Pattycake for next to nothing, and she and Claude would play themselves for less than union scale.

I couldn't sleep that night for thinking how Buddy Branch was now also betraying the world of Christian video, about which, I'll admit, I knew next to nothing. But I did know that I couldn't let the scam go on any longer. I'd have to commit suicide and leave a note explaining the whole hoax, I thought at three A.M. But I've learned over the years that problems don't always seem as drastic at nine A.M. as they do at three. And sure enough, when I woke up that next morning, Daddy told me what to do. Not literally, but I suddenly remembered his talking about the responsibility of the press and how you couldn't have a democratic system without an informed electorate—an idea that seems to have been totally subverted in national politics recently—in other words, Journalism 101, and I remembered the wonderful and basic idea of the special edition and the front-page editorial.

Monday morning I was at the *Citizen* before Jud. When he arrived I announced that we were putting out a four-page special edition, just like in olden times, before television, like when Franklin Roosevelt died and when World War II ended. Jud looked at me for a moment and harrumphed rather happily, I thought.

I'd already written the banner headline.

MIDNIGHT VISION:
HOAX TO SELL RECORDS?

"Everything possible to be believ'd is an image of the truth."
—WILLIAM BLAKE

Since the crash of the Cessna outside Midnight in May, which took the lives of singer Calvin Troope and his fiancée, Tanya Cooper, and the religious testimony of the pilot, Buddy Branch, who survived the crash, the *Citizen* has uncovered a massive publicity campaign indicating that the so-called religious experience of the pilot could be a hoax to promote a record.

The publicity campaign, under the direction of Bob Daniels, a publicist with Jonathan Landau, Inc., of Beverly Hills, London, and New York, formerly Bobby Joe Daniels of Midnight, has succeeded in catapulting Calvin Troope's last recording, "Lord, I'm Ready When You Are," onto the pop, religious, and country-and-western charts.

Since it was this newspaper that published the initial interview with Buddy Branch, it seemed the responsibility of the *Citizen* to bring the ensuing activity to light.

Etc. etc.

Then there were the sidebars:

Cissy Sanders (the former Elizabeth McMichaels): "The plane crash was the most horrible experience I ever had in my life. However, even though I didn't see any bright light opening up in the heavens, there have been many mysterious blessings that have happened to my family since that event, and I believe that God works in mysterious ways and that we should be willing to believe in what is not always believable."

Brother Tommy Newkirk, on miracles: "Dearly beloved, the word 'miracle' has been weakened today. We are told of 'miracle' detergents, 'miracle' cures, 'miracle' drugs, and the many so-called 'miracles' of science, which we sometimes forget are always a demonstration of the grace of God and of his love for us. That we can communicate with one another in so many ways, that we can travel the earth at supersonic speeds, that we can explore the heavens is evidence that we truly live in a time of miracles. And perhaps the greatest miracle—God's return to this earth—has not yet occurred.

"But is it not true that perhaps these mysteries God has given us are a test of our real faith to trust in Him and to love one another?"

The special edition hit the streets on Wednesday morning. Mama was impressed that I'd gotten Brother Tommy to write for the *Citizen*. However, she said, most people she'd talked to now didn't know what to think, and I'd just gone and mixed up everyone's mind even more than they'd been mixed up before.

I said, "Mama, I have to answer to my own conscience. The people of Midnight can make up their own minds. That's not my problem, and isn't that what Daddy expected them to do?"

Mama stared at me a minute and crossed her arms defensively. Her body language is sometimes louder than words.

Finally she said, "Dinah, a lot of the time I don't know what you're talking about."

That afternoon I had a call from a TV producer in Fort Worth asking if I would appear on a noon talk show the following day. So that night I washed my hair and pressed my navy funeral dress and tried to find my cheekbones.

Had I chosen a medium for a face-off with Bobby Joe I would not have picked a TV talk show, since I was neither a media star nor a professional debater. However, a face-off is what happened on Fort Worth's noontime talk show hosted by Barbara Bailes, commonly referred to as "Bubbles" because of her on-camera manner with celebrities. The producer was already attaching the microphone to the neck of my dress, under the scarf printed with a thousand red and green parrots Mama had insisted I wear so I wouldn't look like a Greek widow, when Bobby Joe and Buddy Branch appeared from where they'd been hiding, I suppose, and took a seat across a table from me under those million amps of light that TV requires and in front of a few million people watching TV while they ate their lunch. And here I'd thought I would have the opportunity to explain to all of those I hadn't reached with the *Citizen* special edition that I was an innocent journalist interested only in truth and the Bill of Rights. That I was certainly not allied in any way with a bunch of Hollywood publicists willing to subvert the press for their own financial gain, like the two now sitting there right before me, both of them wearing clunky gold chains around their Hollywood necks. Furthermore, I'd planned to say, having rehearsed my speech numerous times in front of Mama's motel mirror, my father, in whose stead I happened to be in the position of running the *Citizen* in the first place, would have returned and haunted them to their graves had he known about their tactics.

Well, instead of giving that finely prepared statement in the manner of Barbara Jordan, one of my heroines, I sat there sweating under the lights across from Buddy and Bobby Joe, who looked California cool, as if the lights were no more than the California sun they were accustomed to. Bubbles Bailes turned out to be a bony-faced woman like all TV females, with makeup so thick I thought of the first Queen Elizabeth, who supposedly didn't wash her face for five years. That's the kind of historical fact I can remember. Bubbles blotted her makeup with little squares of eyeglass-cleaning paper until the red light turned her way, whereupon she erupted like a flash bulb and welcomed us one by one, me glowering and Bobby Joe and Buddy smiling sickly as if they were staked only a few feet from a wildcat. She began with Buddy, who told his story again while I sat there playing an imaginary violin. This non-plussed Bubbles so much that she turned to me and said, "Ms.

Reynolds, I believe you're showing less than respect for Mr. Branch's account of his experience. Weren't you the first to publish his story in the *Midnight Citizen*?"

"As a matter of fact," I said, looking directly into that red eye that gives access to the hearts and minds of millions of noontime viewers—shut-ins, the unemployed, housewives, and other prisoners, a large audience, given the state's current economy—"I did not know these two outlaws were going to be here today, or I'd never have agreed to be on this show. I am here only to clear up my own involvement in this, which was as an innocent, law-abiding, truth-seeking journalist. I published Mr. Branch's story because I thought the public would be interested in his version of the events. But since that time I've come to realize that his story is nothing but a tissue of lies, a stunt to publicize a record, which I won't even lower myself to name. And I think it is an outrage for people like these two to take advantage of the goodwill of the press and thereby exploit the public for their own nefarious greed!"

Meanwhile Bobby Joe was growing red in the face and kept clearing his throat and waving his left arm and raising his right hand like a schoolboy volunteering, trying to interrupt me, as if we were on one of those talk shows that end up in fisticuffs.

Bubbles's face beneath the makeup seemed to be slipping out of neutral and she shrugged toward somebody off camera holding a clipboard and I could tell she was about to erase me from the airwaves with a station break. When suddenly there was a strange sound, a great rushing roar of wind. My parrot-print scarf fluttered in the windowless studio and there was a momentary pause as everyone looked around, and then, like a book slammed closed, the room went dark and Bubbles screamed and the producer yelled "Help!" and not even the red lights of the cameras were glowing.

That's how Bobby Joe and I came to be sitting over two glasses of iced tea in a restaurant on Camp Bowie Boulevard about a half-hour later.

"Brother, what a crummy business," I said to him. "I think I'd rather kill hogs than do what you do."

"It's the way the world works nowadays, Dinah. Politicians

hire us, dancers hire us, preachers, Miss Americas. Companies, heads of state, armies, revolutions . . .''

"You're saying there's no innocent person anymore and you'd work for any of them."

"That's right."

"Think of the poor Chinese," I said. "Statistically they have a lot less chance of having their fifteen minutes of fame."

"Oh, we'll get there," Bobby Joe said. "One of these days it will be Landau of Beverly Hills, New York, London, and Beijing."

"I guess you had to come to a backwater like Midnight to find so gullible a press you could catch them off guard."

"No, Dinah. I'm sorry this happened. I didn't plan it this way. I had nothing to do with where Calvin Troope's plane would crash."

"For all I know, Bobby Joe, you may work with the CIA or the KGB and have some electronic means of programming plane crashes."

"Dinah, believe me. Buddy Branch is not lying. It was a situation that we simply took advantage of. . . ."

"Blink, blink," I said. "You think I'm going to sit here and believe that?" I looked at his sky-blue Hollywood eyes, the color I will forever after call "betrayal blue," and knew I would never be so innocent again, not to mention stupid.

"It's truly amazing the amount of innocence I've lost in the last month," I said. "Here I thought you and Dude both were semi-saints. What a joke."

I looked out the window, to where a tree had fallen by the road when the tornado ripped through the area shortly before. Now the sky was washed clear to a vivid Kodak blue, as open as my future life.

"Well," I said, and I grabbed the straps of my purse and pulled them over my shoulder in a gesture that, it occurred to me, was what women do instead of lifting their rifles and moving out.

"Thanks for the iced tea. A perfect symbol. That's what I should have been drinking all along from the first minute I saw your blow-dried hair. You're just the kind of man who'll do a daiquiri when you get to the airport, Bobby Joe."

With that I made my exit.

☆

A week or so after my TV fiasco, which Mama likened to an afternoon of tag-team wrestling, I phoned Dude and told him systems were all go for selling the house and having a yard sale and disposing of our mutual life. "Is that right, 'mutual life' or 'mutual lives'?"

"Come on, Dinah," he said, and to change the subject added that my TV appearance had been unforgettable.

"Oh God, you saw it?"

"I did think some of the accompanying histrionics a little much," he chuckled, which made me mad.

"Thanks a lot," I said, "though you'll be disappointed to hear you're not the first negative review. Mama is going around town in sackcloth and ashes."

"I'm not being negative," Dude said. "You got your point across, that's what's important."

"Dude, you don't have to annotate. So you were embarrassed. I've embarrassed you with the whole, entire thing, so all right already. End paragraph."

I was sitting in the *Citizen* office, MY *Citizen* office now, which was going to become twilight gray or French violet or both, maybe each wall done differently, or the colors melding into one another, I hadn't decided. I would hang posters of Tibet, the remains of the Amazon jungle, other such foreign climes on the wall to distract me from the present setting. Out the window in the Piggly Wiggly lot, some joker who'd driven up in an old, tilting van was setting up rows of fat Mexican ceramic pottery—pinkish pigs a foot and a half tall with sparkles on their faces and long, black painted eyelashes, donkeys with planters on their backs, statues of the Virgin Mary praying, tears sliding down her cheeks, all made of cheap chalkish ceramic that chipped when you looked at it.

"Now," I continued to Dude, "on to the heart of the matter. I've called that real estate man who's a friend of Ned's, who plays jazz piano. Of course, you've never met him because you're too elemental macho to go to Ned's parties. But I like him and his piano technique, and I want him to sell the house, or at least handle the paperwork. I'm the one who'll really sell the house. I want to be there when it's shown and explain everything—about the chrysanthemums coordinating with the door and how I have extra quarts of cherry paint, and where in the backyard there's enough sun to plant tomatoes, and how there's that moisture problem across one wall in Larry's bathroom, things like that."

"Fine," he said.

"Also, I want to have a gigantic yard sale and sell everything that you and . . . Larry and Traci"—I couldn't bring myself to say "you and Marilyn"—"don't want. A lot of wedding presents, all those silver bowls I can't stand to polish, books we'll never read again, things like that. What we can't sell I'll give to the women's shelter. I'm living simply from now on. I want only my quilts, one bed, one table, two chairs, a couch, and a yard lounge so I can lie in that vacant lot and watch the cats play around the water tower. No TV, I'm going to sit around and read the classics."

"Great," Dude said. "And Dinah, I want you to know I think it's a terrific idea that you're staying in Midnight to run the *Citizen*. It will mean continuity for the community, and you'll be close to help your mother and Lilly. You'll probably enjoy having the Fisher twins as neighbors."

"Yeah, just think, maybe I'll learn to tell them apart."

"You'll be able to spend more time with the baby."

"Right," I said.

"And you can carry on your father's campaign to protect Midnight from the modern world, also the postmodern world. And I guess you're kind of tired after all the turmoil of the visions and the publicity. You'll be able to rest up for a few years. Maybe you and your mother can take a trip to the Holy Land. She's always wanted to do that."

I couldn't say anything for a minute. My mouth felt vacuumed dry.

"Well," I said finally, "I haven't heard such enthusiasm from you since you told me about Marilyn. Getting me out of your vicinity, not to mention your hair, obviously makes you ecstatic."

He coughed then so he wouldn't have to answer.

"I can't wait to decorate my apartment," I said. "It'll be

minimalist decoration. I'm buying some wonderful new sculp-
ture."

"Let me know when you want to show the house and have
your yard sale and move the cats," Dude said cheerfully.

"It's not *my* yard sale, Dude. Ours. And remember Bobby
McGee has to have a tranquilizer before making a car trip.
Will you phone the vet and pick up some tranquilizers?"

"Yeah, I'll phone the vet," Dude said. It was a task he
wouldn't normally have assumed.

"And thank you very much for your continuing support,"
I concluded.

A few weeks later Larry and I stood on the sagging porch
of a small, faded white frame bungalow, circa 1950s, with a
picture window, a carport on one side and a screened porch
on the other, with the screens peeled back and hanging like
loose scabs. It was in greater Midnight, meaning outside the
city limits, off the main highway, in the direction of the Metroplex. It stood low, on two acres carved out of scrub-oak woods.
The roof was cheap gray asphalt shingles and the front yard
was a sea of dried ruts from years of assorted parked vehicles.
The closest neighbor was a similar house with a rusted camper
on cement blocks parked beside it.

"So what do you think?" Larry asked me as he was locking
the front door. We stepped off the sagging porch and turned
back toward the house.

"It's better than a mobile home," I said. "But looks like
you might need a new roof."

"Look at that big pecan tree back there," he said proudly
as he pointed to the backyard, where the tree stood just far
enough away not to shade the house. "I think we'll put up a
fence. Maybe get a dog."

Above the pecan tree, the vast sky was gray and low, swollen
with rainclouds.

"Frankly," I said, as we walked toward the patrol car, "I
don't see how Traci is going to make this into a Spanish villa,
but maybe that's my lack of imagination."

Opening the door for me, Larry laughed at the thought of
his wife converting this most modest of structures into a Span-

ish villa. I settled inside the patrol car, thinking how absurd the idea was, but I could see Larry was delighted by the notion, her spirit and energy, the sheer outrageousness of her ideas. Somehow that pleasure outweighed the negatives. That's what it takes, I thought, looking at this handsome man sliding into the car beside me, no longer a boy. He seemed to have grown up over the course of the past painful weeks. In this world of frailty, I thought, it's the balancing act we have to accept, so that despite the seesawing unsteadiness and sometimes the dangerous tilt of betrayal, there's most of the time a tolerable upright balance of respect and affection.

He started the engine. "We get in the house, we want to have another baby," he said, turning to me.

"Oh, that would be wonderful," I said. "That would be great for the baby." Of course, then we'd have to call the baby something else, I thought.

"Larry. Promise me if it's a boy you won't name him Elvis Dawn."

Larry laughed.

"Traci wants to build a deck and put in a hot tub. She's got more schemes than T. Boone Pickens," Larry said. He was right about that, but a hot tub in the state of Texas seemed to me redundant.

"I think you're smart to go ahead and buy a house," I told him. "Now *this* is a 'starter house,' if Traci wants to use the term."

Larry waited for a pickup to pass, then pulled into the farm-to-market road.

Actually we were all buying the house: Mama and Dude and I were lending them money for the down payment.

"It'll be nice to have you around, but are you sure you want to live so close to Midnight?" I asked him. "Don't you sometimes get lonesome for Dallas? After all, that's your home."

"I like Midnight," he said. "I kind of like coming home to some place I really know. I like knowing my neighbors."

"Live and learn." I sighed.

"If I stay here I might run for the school board, something like that."

I studied him a minute to see if he was teasing, but there was no trace of humor when he glanced at me to weigh my reaction. Under the big hat, his face so sober, he made me think of Mama. Maybe it wasn't important to me, since I'd learned over the years to be skeptical of community pillars, but it would matter to Traci, I thought, and therefore to Larry, who was that moment chewing a thick wad of gum in his attempt to quit smoking. And somebody has to believe in the role and assume the responsibility. But I wonder sometimes why everyone has to learn everything on his own without benefit of advice and previous experience. Why does every generation have to start all over again?

Larry stopped at an intersection and turned onto the main highway heading back toward Midnight. Not a mile away was the Sanders home and the Swiss chard field wherein Calvin Troope's plane had crashed weeks before, commencing my saga.

"You look thin," Larry said to me.

"Me?"

"Yeah, you," he said.

I lifted my arms, studying them hopefully.

"I'm eating every minute, trying to disappear into obesity. I've been drinking Dr Peppers and eating pralines and peanut patties like crazy."

Larry smiled. "Well, it ain't working," he said. "Maybe you have worms or something."

"My goodness!"

If I'd ever thought about it, I'd have hoped that I'd never have a conversation with my own son about having worms. But there you are.

We were quiet a minute as a few fat raindrops began to splat against the dusty windows of the patrol car, and I prayed there wouldn't be another tornado anytime soon, since I certainly wasn't ready for any more disasters, natural or otherwise. I thought of Nadine's prediction of an impending fire, and wondered if maybe that had actually come to pass, only in the form of passion. However, I had no idea how literally Nadine's predictions were to be taken.

Larry glanced at me and I could tell he was getting up courage for some communication that maybe I didn't want to hear.

"I don't think you ought to stay in Midnight," he said slowly, making the idea sound strangely ominous, as if someone had put out a contract on me.

"Why?"

He turned into town, passing the population sign and starting toward the Baptist church and the grimacing apostles. I wanted to tell him to go another way but I didn't want to interrupt him, so I just closed my eyes for half a block. Larry turned on the windshield wipers. I listened to them laboring with slow slaps across the dusty glass.

"You don't like Midnight, Mama. You like Dallas. You really love Dallas. You love the skyline. You're the only one in the neighborhood who'll collect for the heart fund. You're the only person over thirty who loves the Hard Rock Cafe. You even like to go downtown."

"That's true." I sighed. "Guilty as charged."

I opened my eyes, and we were past the church and the rain had stopped. Larry turned off the windshield wipers. They stopped leaving gray streaks like a runner sliding to third and back to first.

"Your father thinks it's a wonderful idea for me to stay here."

"No, he doesn't," Larry said, a tad impatiently.

"That's certainly what he told me."

"Well, he didn't mean it. He told me it was an emotionally self-destructive decision."

"He said that?"

"Yeah."

I looked out the window as we passed a deserted house with the roof caved in. Midnight had a number of such houses, occupied by dirt dobbers, scorpions, tarantulas, and other hiding creatures.

"That's when he talked to you," I told Larry. "Later, when he talked to me, he obviously wanted me to stay here and self-destruct."

"He just said that to rile you up. I think he wants to make up with you."

He glanced at me as my heart made what felt like a dancing low dip and held there a second.

"Oh, Larry. Where did you get that idea?"

"Talking." He blushed. There was an awkward silence during which we both wished he could verify his claim. I reached over and lifted his right hand from the steering wheel and kissed it and held it a minute. It smelled like kids' grape bubble gum.

"That's probably wishful thinking, honey. But I appreciate it."

"Whatever . . ." he said.

"I'm glad you've made up with your father," I said.

"I'm still mad at him," Larry said. "For what he's doing . . . He had no right to do that. You don't deserve it."

"Thanks," I said. "I appreciate your vote of support. But unfortunately, we don't always get what we deserve. And I'm not sure what I deserve or who decides what anyone deserves. It doesn't seem to work that way."

"I know," he said. "But you're a sweet woman. It's not fair for you to be hurt. And I told him that."

Suddenly in those dozen or so words my world became a safer place. I realized that if I happened to get drunk and shoot at the red light, I could count on my son to drive me home. The world seemed rosier than it had been a minute before. Indeed, after the brief shower, the sun suddenly broke through the clouds and burrowed through the streaked windshield.

"There's not even a movie in Midnight," Larry added.

"But I can come to the Spanish villa and soak in the hot tub. Right?"

"Right," he said, smiling.

As yard sales go, I suppose mine was semi-successful, thanks to Ned English and his delegation of friends, who bought all the silver bowls, most of the plants, several lamps, the espresso machine, and the wok. Dude helped set up, then didn't show his face till it was all over and he returned to help me move the rejects into the garage.

"Why did you sell the wok?" he asked me then. "You worked for years to get it blackened the way you wanted it."

After weeks of never looking at me directly, he was studying me now, puzzled. It made me proud to be unpredictable.

229

"I don't intend to fool with hot food," I said. "It takes too much time and energy. Remember, I'm simplifying." I set a grocery sack of rejected books on top of Dude's handyman table. A pop-psychology book about how to be friends with your marriage partner lay on top. When I'd bought it I didn't know I needed it. I hadn't even finished reading it. Maybe if I got hungry I could sue the author for poor advice, I thought. I turned around and followed Dude back outside. We carried in a chest of drawers and paused to catch our breath. I looked over a little indoor clothesline where I'd sometimes hung panty hose, which would dry there in forty-five minutes.

"Larry reports you said my moving to Midnight is a self-destructive decision."

He didn't answer me; as I've said, he never said anything simple like "yes" or "no." He pulled his mouth sideways and studied me over the clothesline.

"I find it hard to believe you'll be happy there."

"Happy?"

He looked tired. Maybe he's not sleeping well, I hoped, though not because of fiery sex, I hoped even more.

"Why did you tell me you were glad?"

"I know if I tried to talk you out of it you'd be sure and do it."

I studied him a moment. He had a few more gray hairs and there was a slackness about his face I'd not noticed before. Seeing him this close, I thought he looked different, the way a painting will sometimes be unclear till you move away from it.

"So, reverse psychology! I thought that was out of date. But I guess you think I'm so old-fashioned and perverse I'd fall for it, which I did, of course." I had to let it sink in a minute more before rising to full energy level. "Boy, is that condescending! You think I'm that stupid!"

"You're just upset. That's all."

"That's all! That's condescending, too!"

"See," he said, grinning, trying to dilute my anger with a note of humor.

He started toward the door and the few remaining discards, but I blocked the path. Immediately he stepped back. In olden days, being basically a warm, affectionate person, he would have touched me, caught my arm or my shoulder, or held my hand.

"Why the hell do you care anyway?" I suppose I had to pick at the wounds, after what Larry had said about thinking Dude wanted to make up.

"I hate to see you miserable. That's all."

"Oh, really. How do you know I'm miserable? I may be gloriously happy, for all you know!"

He reached a hand out and this time I thought he was going to touch me, but he only braced himself against the water heater, a sign of patience, however unwilling, in the face of my confrontation. Instead of giving me a soulful discussion, he looked over my shoulder toward the rejected shoe rack, two lawn chairs, and a tortilla press.

"Just quit wasting your mental energy on me!" I said, turning away. "I'll take care of myself. We are, after all, *finito!*" The word was a ribbon we had to cut to pass through, so we moved outside again, passing the twin bridal wreaths we'd planted on either side of the door ten years before.

"I even cut up the last of our charge cards yesterday," I called back to him. "I don't even want to see your name floating around in my purse anymore."

As I lifted a lawn chair, it suddenly occurred to me how vital it was for me to play the wounded wife turned bitch. That gave him the role of supportive though departing husband. I stupidly was playing right into his hands like every abandoned wife since Anne Boleyn, only I wasn't totally losing my head. My other alternative was to smother my anger, which would deny my true feelings. There was no way I could win on this one, I thought. Either way I lose. All of us since Anne lose, unless we consider Cissy's threat of the pearl-handled pistol, but that's not such an appetizing choice, either. Weighted with that thought, I barreled toward the garage with a chair overhead like Tarzan.

The problem comes down to time, I thought. In ten years I'll be able to handle this just fine. But what do I do in the meantime? I can't spend ten years doing Jane Fonda constantly to work off my anger. If only there were a way to fast-forward my life for a couple of years like a video, I thought.

After we got the rejects installed in the garage, we tallied the proceeds and I called the cats. I had only one cat transport, so I shoved the more rambunctious cat, Jerry Jeff, inside the maroon carrier and latched it, nearly catching his right whiskers, and called Bobby McGee.

"Damn, I forgot to get tranquilizers," Dude said.

"That's okay," I said magnanimously. I was aware of being magnanimous and I was sick to death of being aware of every damn nuance. We both knew the cat would yowl all the way to Midnight and probably vomit hairballs a few times for good measure.

"Well," I said as I lifted the cat carrier, "doesn't take long to get rid of a life, does it?"

Never should one transport a loose cat through crowded, belligerent freeway traffic on a late Saturday afternoon. For each and every mile I was subjected to a yowling duet. I tried talking to them, singing along with them, I might even have uttered a prayer.

"Listen, I feel the same way," I said to Bobby McGee as we were approaching Irving. "I'm not happy about this." She was crouching somewhere behind me, but my commiserating provoked a leap onto my shoulder, where she braced herself by digging in her claws, her gold eyes wild with hysteria. I clutched the steering wheel as an auto transport carrying Mazdas whooshed by. When I could next glance at my shoulder there was blood oozing through my Cadillac Ranch T-shirt.

When we finally reached Midnight, I stopped at Mama's for first aid.

"What happened to you?" Mama asked as she trailed me to the bathroom, where I was stripping off my T-shirt. The mirror reflected a long scratch from cheek to chin and assorted holes in my right shoulder.

"Bobby McGee," I said, wetting toilet tissue and pressing it onto my wounds. "If I go to jail, maybe I can get plastic surgery for free," I told Mama.

The state of Texas each year spends thousands of dollars on plastic surgery to improve criminals' appearances in the hope that such rehabilitation will encourage them to forsake their lives of crime.

"Why would you go to jail?"

"The Humane Society could arrest me for leaving those cats out there in the car."

I pulled a bottle of witch hazel from the bathroom cabinet, soaked a cotton ball, and ran it down my face and across my shoulder. In the mirror I saw Mama wince sympathetically.

"Dinah, the Fisher sisters say you've stuck cheap pink ceramic pigs in the windows of the duplex."

I held the cotton to my shoulder and moved to the window, where I looked over Mama's white-painted half-window interior shutters to where Bobby McGee was, fortunately, still conscious and perched like a parrot on the back of the driver's seat. I could see her mouth still making yowls.

"What are the Fisher sisters, Mama? Texas Rangers or CIA?"

We looked at one another in the mirror. When Mama is alarmed, there is a way she lifts her eyebrows that makes her lashless eyes look square.

"Dinah, why in the world would you buy a bunch of cheap ceramic pigs?"

"I thought they were funny. Does the town of Midnight have to approve my window treatments? Furthermore, they are not in every window. . . ."

Mama watched thoughtfully as I stretched Band-Aids across my shoulder. When I finished, she said in a takeover voice I remembered from childhood, "Okay, Dinah, let's move those cats into the utility room before they smother."

The following Monday morning, as I was looking out my office window considering the ninety-nine-bottle question of the week, the Misters Chapman, Junior and Senior, of Longview arrived to survey the *Citizen* at Mama's recently reconsidered behest. The young Mr. Chapman, who was mid-thirties, had a salt-and-pepper beard, a professionally laundered shirt, and a bright gold wedding band. Mr. Chapman, Sr., was a stout man of about sixty with thick silver hair and gold-rimmed bifocals. If his hair had been a little longer, he'd have looked like the perfect southern poet, except for the smell of golden-parachute money about him. He also had that Texas look. Dude says you get on any plane heading for Texas and right off you can tell the native Texans heading home. There is a look. For instance, all the men in Daddy's family resembled Lyndon Johnson when they got to around fifty years old.

As soon as the Chapmans arrived, I phoned Mama. "The usurpers are here," I told her.

"Now Dinah, I'm just going to talk to them. This may come to nothing. I'll be there in a few minutes!"

I was unable to muster a Welcome Wagon manner. But Mr. Chapman, Sr., like most newsmen of his era, was a talker. He explained to me that he'd owned a couple of daily newspapers that had been bought out by a conglomerate, which then sold them to another company, which restructured and sold off part of the property until they became padlocked tax deductions. He said he wasn't ready to retire but he wanted things a little easier and couldn't bear to end his journalism days with such a bad taste in his mouth as he had after dealing with that conglomerate. So he was looking for something like the *Midnight Citizen,* where he could be a hands-on editor again and still be close to other business interests in Dallas and not too far from family in Longview.

I told him the *Citizen* was nothing if not a hands-on operation.

Then, while I was on the phone with a citizen lobbying for a memorial to Calvin Troope, the Chapmans strolled around the *Citizen,* looking inside and out and laughing in front of the air conditioner. I had introduced them to Jud, trying to convey the idea that Jud went with the property as much as the antique Linotype machine on which he was setting ads.

When Mama arrived I managed to pull together four chairs, and as soon as the dust had settled and we stopped sneezing, Mama's first line was, "Oh, Dinah, I can't imagine why you'd put those tacky pink pigs in the windows!"

She exchanged a knowing smile with Mr. Chapman, and I knew then she'd already told him something about me, probably mentioning "personal problems" or something coy like that. However, I was wearing my navy funeral dress, which I hoped might offset the fact that my face looked as if I'd been run over by a combine. Also, I wanted the Chapmans to know I was serious competition and that they should take me seriously, which many men don't do unless you're dressed the way they are.

Mama and Mr. Chapman began their discussion in the old-fashioned way, breaking the ice by speaking politely of medical problems before launching into serious business talk. Mama said how kind I'd been to take over after she developed shingles. Mr. Chapman mentioned having had heart surgery the year before. Then Mama began talking quietly about how Daddy had enjoyed the *Citizen* so much and what a charming community it was, and convenient—right on the southern rim of the Metroplex—yet maintaining rural principles and small-town friendliness. Listening to her would make anyone want to rush to Midnight. It might have been Santa Fe before the tourists discovered it, Aspen before the rich and famous arrived, Paris without the French. It was maybe the greatest Pollyanna performance I'd ever seen. Mama said if Mr. Chapman was seriously interested in the *Citizen* she'd like to introduce him to some of the pillars of the community, like Martin Turner and Claude and Cissy Sanders, the sheriff, Lemuel Malone, and the mayor and his wife, "commonly known as 'Feets,' " I inserted. The Chapmans laughed politely.

As Mama talked, I looked out the door to see if the Chapmans were perhaps driving a gold Rolls-Royce pulled by teenage slaves. After all, how could Mama know if old Mr. Chapman was a cult leader or a child pornographer or not? And, as I said to her later, if he wasn't a cult leader or child pornographer, he might be one of those unprincipled entrepreneurs taking advantage of bad times and lapping up people's homes and businesses and forcing families onto the street. How can you know? I asked her. She said she could tell. That's all.

When Mama had completed her Pollyanna sales pitch, I said in fairness I thought it my obligation to point out some of the disadvantages of Midnight. I said, Frankly, my father practiced a medieval style of journalism, the real news was never exposed. The town itself was too poor to buy new tires for its one police car; everybody was into everybody else's business, and most of the downtown was owned by a female variation on Attila the Hun who'd run, until only the past week, a yellow-cat gulag outside of town. Furthermore, I said, there was no fluoride in the water, so everybody's teeth were rotting, and there was no decent place to eat since the Midnight Cafe began importing plastic pies. At any moment at least half the toilets in the high school didn't flush, so you could smell them as you drove by, and as soon as the town was swallowed by the Metroplex, which was only a matter of fifteen minutes or so, the whole area would be one more junk strip of desolation row on the American landscape.

When I finished, with what I thought was quite a flourish, there was a silence during which the two Mr. Chapmans surveyed the bottoms of their fancy boots. Eventually Mama, who'd been looking out the window over the heads of two pigs into the Piggly Wiggly parking lot, said, "Well, Dinah has been living in Dallas for years. . . ." That was a euphemism for *She's become detached from Christian principles.* "And," she continued, "as my husband used to say, though it is important to know when the Yangtze floods and drowns a hundred thousand Chinese, people are actually more interested in knowing about a neighbor's hip replacement." Thus bringing the level of discussion back to Journalism 101, the Baptist Training Union, and World War II propaganda movies.

I said, "Mama, you're forgetting the global-village concept."

And she said, "When we have troubles, we need friends, neighbors, and family," and with that finale, which didn't necessarily follow, Mama stood up, offering to show them the charms of Midnight, and the three of them started out the door to meet the community pillars and generally make the scene. Then at the last moment Mama turned and walked back. She stopped beside me and put her arm around my shoulder. It is unusual for Mama to show affection in public.

I could smell her White Shoulders cologne, which she's worn ever since I've known her and which Daddy had given her a bottle of every Valentine's Day.

"Dinah . . ." She spoke quietly. "I just want to point out to you that every one of those pigs is facing toward Dallas."

I looked at them, at their pinkish, goldish haunches, where a black curled tail was painted on. She was absolutely right. Each and every one of those cheap pink pigs was straining northeast toward Dallas. How could I have missed it?

I said, Thank you, Mama, for pointing that factlet out to me. Then we stood there a minute and it happened, that awful feeling in my throat like the lining is drawing together and you can't breathe. But I swallowed hard and pinched the bridge of my nose and blinked the semi-tears back. Mama kind of hugged my shoulder and walked away.

I paced around the *Citizen* a few minutes, pulling myself together and deciding that since my tour of duty might end soon I might as well play like *The New York Times* while I had the chance. I would lead with *glasnost,* the beginning of the end of communism in Eastern Europe, with a survey of how the citizenry feels about it all. Question two might be: Should we invite Gorbachev to visit Midnight, since it would make him feel better about Armenia, Lithuania, Estonia, and places like that?

WHEN you step outside the house on a bright Texas morning in late summer, the heat wraps itself around your arms like a hot towel. By midday all living creatures hunker down in a soft swoon against the hard, dry earth or cling to sheltering branches, so that by afternoon it is nearly quiet with only a low hum, while all life, unless disturbed, is waiting for night and cool.

For forty years Daddy came home for lunch and had what he called a siesta after the meal. It's foolish to try to live like Bostonians when it's a hundred degrees in the shade, he used to say. He sometimes entertained the idea that Texas should have stayed a republic so we'd have had sensible siestas, like Mexico or Greece, with a noon rush hour when people go home, pull on pajamas, and dream through the worst of the midday heat like the sensible creatures around them.

Since the cake and the caterer had been ordered and the invitations issued for Lilly and Anthony Spencer Mainard's wedding, Lilly and Traci decided they would proceed with a ceremony and reception. After a brief memorial service for Anthony Spencer Mainard, Traci and Larry would renew their marriage vows. After all, Lilly pointed out, many people at Happy Acres wouldn't remember what was supposed to happen anyway.

By ten o'clock that Saturday morning, it was nearing ninety degrees and climbing. Mama and her neighbors had begun watering their yards early each morning. If I had the misfortune to wake before seven o'clock, I'd look out the window of the motel bedroom, myself safely encased in air-conditioning, to see Mama in one of her shapeless, sleeveless zip-up flowered housedresses tugging her green water hoses, like a giant octopus, around the yard. Over the past couple of weeks, since she'd learned I would be going back to Dallas, Mama's shingles had nearly disappeared. The jagged brick-colored welt across her back was as faded as my last summer's tan. I had reneged on the Fisher sisters' duplex-with-a-view and Mr. Chapman, Sr., would soon be taking over the reins of the *Citizen*.

The day of the ceremony I woke around eight, and already Mama had watered the farthest St. Augustine grass near the road and had pulled her hose to mid-yard, where in the early-morning sun a rainbow rose from the grateful, thirsty earth. Mama stood beside the chain-link fence talking to her Frank Sinatra–fan neighbor while each surveyed her separate domain soaking under the lazy twirls of twin sprinklers. It was a yearly battle to keep the St. Augustine grass green in the flinty hard-scrabble earth of north central Texas, where in open fields tiny cactus only inches tall grew wild. By late summer most years, watering yards would be prohibited for water conservation, and Easy Malone would start patrolling the streets sometime in August, giving out warnings and eventually fines to anyone bold enough to have damp, green grass. Then Mama and her neighbors would give up and there'd gradually be wider and wider bare patches between the ganglia of St. Augustine, until by September there would be the soft rustle of dry leaves underfoot and everywhere the grass would turn a taupe color that would remain until spring rains. Then everything would come alive and there'd be three emerald months before summer.

By nine-thirty Mama and I were dressed and ready for the hybrid ceremony. She and Traci had announced I couldn't leave the house if I insisted on wearing my navy funeral dress, so as thanks for my summer services at the *Citizen* Mama had bought me a yellow linen dress that wrinkled when you looked at it and seemed to have its own temperature of a hundred degrees encased in its seams. However, since I would be leaving Midnight soon, I was trying hard to get on Mama's better side so we could part peacefully.

Inside Mama's Chrysler it was about five hundred degrees, and we sat there like mannequins with the doors open till the air-conditioning began cooling. Then Mama closed her door and backed out of the drive and onto the road, and the car said "A door is ajar, a door is ajar" in its authoritative airline-pilot voice. Mama pulled to the side of the road and I got out and stepped into a dry gully surrounded by whipgrass, where-upon a big green grasshopper popped out of the grass, just missing my head, and soared through the air to some hidden and safer spot. I slammed the rear car door and climbed back in the car beside Mama. As soon as we took off again, she said she sure hoped there wouldn't be a bunch of reporters at Happy Acres. That was approximately the ninety-second time she'd said that in the last three days. I said I didn't know why there'd be a bunch of reporters there.

"You know what I mean," she said. "I just hope you didn't tell anyone."

I said, "Mama, I assure you I didn't tell anyone. I'm not the only person in this town who talks to the press, you know."

Of course, she wouldn't admit that, especially since I'd had my fifteen minutes of fame that week when *People* did a piece on "The Woman Who Brought Light to Midnight." It told the whole story about Calvin Troope, his song, and Buddy Branch and his supposed vision, and had a photograph of me at the *Citizen,* which, Cissy said, wouldn't have been half bad if I'd let her tease my hair. The *People* reporter had also interviewed Buddy Branch, who'd testified that he was re-turning to California to start a miracle support ranch for people with breakthrough spiritual experiences, "or may God strike him dead on an LA freeway"—which was somewhat reassur-ing coming from someone heading back to LA. Therefore, despite Daddy's disdain for that magazine, I have to say, it had done much to restore a modicum of my badly scarred reputation. When last seen, the reporter wrote, Bobby Joe Daniels, formerly of Midnight, was in a VIP lounge at DFW airport, waiting to board a jet (first class) to Los Angeles. And I told the reporter that I hoped never to be seen again on what some of us here in Texas called the Third Coast. I knew, also, that maybe my greatest vengeance came from getting *People* to refer to him as "Bobby Joe" instead of "Bob." That was truly a puncture to the core of his ego, which I pictured in my head as an aluminum organ resembling a water sprinkler located approximately where his heart was supposed to be.

"Mama," I said to her as we waited for the red light to change, "I want you to know that never in his life did Daddy ever say an unkind word about you. He had more respect for you than he had for any person on earth. I think he cared for you very much."

Mama's face flashed about neon red, which I expected, but since we were both strapped down by seat belts she couldn't very well leave the room or leap from the car, which is why I'd waited till then to say anything.

"Well, maybe so," she said, flustered, as she stepped on the gas and the Chrysler leapt off through the green light. It wasn't much response, but it was about as good as I could expect. Then she went on to pat my knee and say, "That's nice of you to say," which about floored me.

Mama pulled up to Happy Acres, where a catering truck from the Metroplex was parked out front. The shoulder-crushing door was decorated with pink crepe paper and silver cardboard wedding bells.

"I feel like I'm going to a prom," I said as we entered. But inside, the illusion quickly vanished. Every mobile member of Happy Acres was wheeled up or propped up staring at the north wall of the reception room, where two baskets of daisies and pink carnations stood at attention. Above the assemblage, more pink crepe-paper streamers and silver bells looped from the corners of the ceiling to the center chandelier. At the piano, the old organist, who was a friend of Lilly's—or had been, back when she could remember people—was playing "Tara's Theme" on the spinet. I told Mama I wasn't sure I was up to seeing her wrestled off the piano bench again, but Mama whispered it had already been decided that if she couldn't remember the wedding march when the time came, they'd let her go on playing "Tara's Theme." At least it's not Elvis Presley, Mama reminded me.

I carried Daddy's old Rolleiflex, which Mama said looked

tacky with my new dress, and as soon as all the wheelchairs were locked and invitees grouped about the room, I took a few pictures. Traci's mother held the baby, who was also in pink, her few little strands of blond hair gathered atop her head and wound with a little pink bow. Mama and I went over to take turns with Nadine holding the baby during the ceremony. Paisley Blue had volunteered to twirl for the wedding, but Hazel Jo, the Happy Acres director, had said absolutely not, what if the baton got away from her and hit one of the nursing home clients in the head? Happy Acres might be sued off the face of the earth.

Since then, however, Paisley's life had altered. Cissy had come into the *Citizen* one morning in tears saying that Paisley hadn't wanted to compete in the Luling Watermelon Thump, she was tired of the Little Miss circuit, and she wanted a horse. When I stopped laughing, I congratulated Cissy and suggested that maybe Paisley would become an intellectual instead of a beauty queen. Cissy said she didn't understand how I got from horse to intellectual so quickly, but the idea intrigued her enough that she'd left to phone Claude and tell him he had to cancel his girlie magazines, since Paisley might become an intellectual. But Cissy and Paisley Blue were both in attendance, standing against the wall in matching lavender print dresses, Paisley's miracle eye still bright and round as she held her baton at attention over her heart, just as she did when the Midnight Owl band passed with the flag.

I had over the past weeks further pursued the topic of Paisley's miracle eye with Cissy and forced her to admit that it might have been something other than a miracle that had altered Paisley's eye. Something simple like, say, the end of ragweed season. However, Cissy insisted, she preferred to think of it as a miracle, and she saw no reason for me to insist on scientific validation when we both had experienced Nadine Love's wart-removal magic, so I left it at that.

The procession began as soon as Brother Tommy arrived. It seems Baptists now have ceremonies for every eventuality, I guess including the Luling Watermelon Thump. So Brother Tommy stood between the two baskets of daisies, looking solemnly burdened as usual, in his all-purpose oxblood Florsheims, shiny as new cars. It occurred to me that he must get awfully tired of listening to "Tara's Theme." However, I could imagine how happy he was that Buster Ledbetter and his state-of-the-art video van had packed up and left for Wichita Falls to investigate another possible miracle.

The procession began with Larry pushing Lilly in her wheelchair, the wheels wound with pink crepe paper. She'd decided at the last minute that she'd be more comfortable sitting in her wheelchair than leaning on her walker throughout the ceremony. She looked beautiful in the pink three-piece print dress with brooch, pearls, and matching earrings. Her hair was still tinted a soft brown and she carried a bouquet of pink roses. The rhinestones in her glasses frames caught the light from the overhead chandelier and twinkled warmly, and Larry looked happy and handsome in his highway patrol uniform. Traci, in pink backless spike-heel sandals and an ankle-length pink-flowered kimono, pink roses in her hair and around her ankles, looked like a blonde geisha. Frankly, I didn't understand the philosophy behind the Oriental motif, but I kept that to myself. Traci also carried pink roses and held Larry's arm just above his gun. I for one thought the whole affair would have looked better if he hadn't worn his gun, but then they didn't ask me. The procession slowly made its way to the north wall of the reception room. There was a shushing sound and "Tara's Theme" stopped mid-bar.

I whispered to Mama that I'd bet anything Brother Tommy would use as his text "You know not when the hour will come."

Just at that moment, Dude walked in the door.

"I thought he wasn't coming," I whispered to Mama.

Mama shrugged. "I imagine Larry talked him into it," she whispered. But I guessed that wasn't it, because of the way she pursed her lips into drawstring defensiveness and looked away guiltily. She's a terrible liar on the rare occasions she tries it. I swung Dude what I hoped was an enigmatic glance and turned back to the ceremony. I could imagine that Mama had thought it would be a scene like the one in *Giant* when Elizabeth Taylor and Rock Hudson made cow eyes at one another during her sister's wedding and afterward clinched and went back to the ranch to live rich and happily ever after, not to mention gorgeous.

For Anthony Spencer Mainard's memorial service Brother Tommy said a few words about wisdom and age, and then I was to read a poem Lilly said was her and Anthony's favorite. Brother Tommy gave me an asexual nod and I moved to the central station between the two baskets of daisies and carnations and read:

> *"When Earth's last picture is painted and the tubes are*
> *twisted and dried,*
> *When the oldest colours have faded, and the youngest*
> *critic has died,*
> *We shall rest, and, faith, we shall need it—lie down for*
> *an aeon or two,*
> *Till the master of All Good Workmen shall put us to*
> *work anew. . . ."*

As I read, it came streaming back to me from the time we'd memorized it in the seventh grade at Midnight Junior High four hundred years ago. I could suddenly remember mouthing the words to Bobby Joe when he got up before the class to recite. I remembered, too, that for the four years we were in high school he'd copied my homework nightly, so often I didn't think anything about it. Then I thought how sincerely glad I was that he'd done his daiquiri and gone back to Hollywood. How glad I was that it was all over, except for the dollars pouring into Calvin Troope's coffers and the closely watched Swiss chard crop north of town.

When I finished the poem, Brother Tommy said a long and dreary prayer which blessed this gathering of loved ones, during which Mr. Mann shouted, "What's going on here?" Then the service moved on to the second stage.

For a few minutes there was some loud whispering at the piano as Hazel Jo propped the wedding march in front of the organist. We held our breaths waiting and finally she managed the first few repetitive notes of Mendelssohn, then rather nicely segued back to "Tara's Theme."

"Dearly beloved," Brother Tommy began, and Mama reached for her tissue and I nearly joined her when I thought of my own wedding and how Dude and I had held hands during the ceremony.

Brother Tommy didn't use "You know not when the hour will come" but that wonderful chapter in Corinthians about "though I speak with the tongues of men and of angels and have not love, I am become as sounding brass or a tinkling cymbal" for now we see through a glass darkly, but then face to face. With the new translation Brother Tommy used, it sounded like a psychology textbook, but I translated it into the old King James Version as he went along. Then Brother Tommy said a few words about the true miracle of lasting love, not breaking any new ground. However, I would be the last to criticize, since on many occasions I've wished I'd been more grateful for what I'd had when I lived in North Dallas with Dude and my cats in love and affection, rather than dreaming of something that might have been perfect or endless or romantic in some glossy Hollywood way. For that seemed to be all that remained of those few hot hours with Bobby Joe that had at first seemed so sweet, a brief memory, an instant of time, quick as a flash bulb and then the gray aftermath which left me sadder and wiser and more vulnerable than I'd known I could be.

During the ceremony there were several who cried, including Traci. There were also several in the audience who fell asleep in their wheelchairs, and Mr. Mann, who again shouted out, "What's going on here?" but all in all it was a nice ceremony. No one vomited or peed, Mama pointed out later. At the end Traci and Larry kissed one another and Lilly.

After the ceremony we all shuffled and rolled down to the dining hall for wedding cake, punch, and flat champagne, flat because it had had to be concealed in large, family-size, 7-Up bottles because Brother Tommy won't marry anyone or even renew anyone who's about to consume alcohol. The caterers had set up a lovely spread with a real damask tablecloth—not paper disposable—with a pink-punch fountain, which was especially popular and always had a line of wheelchairs in front of it. There were assorted sandwiches cut in dainty shapes with the crusts removed and assorted soft candies. Thoughtfully, nothing was served that required strong teeth, and Hazel Jo policed the 7-Up bottles so that anyone who shouldn't have alcohol was given real 7-Up.

I took pictures of Traci and Larry cutting the cake and holding the baby. I took pictures of them with Lilly and Mama and the baby, then with Nadine and her pit bull husband and the baby and several other combinations of friends and relatives—always trying to shoot above Larry's gun level, but not always managing that, since most of Traci's relatives were short.

The surprise entertainment was Mr. Mann, in his stained white dinner jacket and maroon tie, who hadn't spoken a coherent word in years. When he finished his wedding cake, he sailed his paper plate across the room, rolled himself into a corner, turned, and burst forth singing in a fine bass voice, "Bye Bye Blackbird."

Everyone turned to listen to him singing there in his wheelchair, stretching out his long arms, his old craggy face glowing at the idea of communicating for maybe the first time in a decade.

At the end of his song, there was much applause and hardly a dry eye in the house, except mine, of course, even though I do love that song. After that a quartet of ladies in blue dresses who sing together regularly, when they aren't having a falling-out, harmonized on "In the Garden." The finale was Paisley Blue, who had changed into a classic white satin majorette outfit and twirled her baton safely outdoors while we watched her through the windows of the dining room.

After taking the obligatory photographs, I took the baby from Nadine, and Dude came over and patted her hand and talked to her and lifted her up, making her laugh gloriously. He was wearing a blue suit and a blue-and-white-striped shirt with a yellow and blue flowery tie. He had dried shaving cream behind one ear, and it was strange to realize I no longer had the right to wipe it off. I could wipe it off some semi-stranger like Claude Sanders, but I no longer had the right to touch Dude's ear or face unless he had a heart attack, God forbid, and I gave him CPR.

I fed the baby the pink rose from my piece of wedding cake and she gave me her most brilliant smile with her three new teeth shining and patted her little hands together and made us laugh.

"Oh, no," I said, "she's going to have a sweet tooth like me!" Dude said all that proved was that she was going to have a passion for vanilla like me. Just hearing the word "passion" hurt my heart. But even so, I took the opportunity to ask him for a ride to Mama's, since I knew she would stay at the reception till the last possible tear and crumb.

Watching Dude carrying the baby around, I considered going to a voodoo woman in South Dallas who cast spells, but I knew it would never work, because I didn't believe in it. You have to honestly believe in those things for them to work, is my theory, and I suppose I have to admit my faith in miracles at that point was weak. But by then I'd drunk three plastic glasses of champagne from the 7-Up bottles and was feeling semi-emotional myself.

So I went over and kissed Lilly and congratulated Traci and Larry and gave them each a hug. Traci was still earning college credit with life experiences and claimed that renewing her marriage vows might just push her over the top for her first six credits. Then, she'd told me, she was going into a human-relations course to get a life-experience degree which would be, she said, the gateway to her becoming a family counselor. I hadn't known what to say to that news, so I'd simply smiled.

Earlier I had told Mama I would stay there and try to help her and the nursing home people clean up, but I could see Anthony Spencer Mainard had hired fine caterers who would clean up themselves. Mama was accustomed to Baptist weddings where the receptions are held in the dank church basement, something like the tomb of Dracula, and the family has to scrape leftovers into Tupperware and wash the dishes and sweep the floors so the little Sunbeams, ages three to four, won't lick up the cake crumbs when they come in for their weekly Bible story.

Inside Dude's Tracer, he cleaned his sunshades with, I noticed, an unironed handkerchief, and I told him that for my last *Citizen* issue I was going to do a retrospective of Daddy's forty years.

We drove up the road for a minute in uneasy silence. Dude

247

had moved his belongings to an intermediate staging area a week or so before, a short-term leased condo off East Lovers Lane. I had remarked, unfortunately, on the extremely fitting name of the area, which is actually an ordinary though major Dallas thoroughfare. I had already agreed to stay in our house until the real estate market came back, or for at least a reasonable period of time in the event the market stayed depressed for the next thousand years. I had asked him earlier if he'd done anything about a divorce and he'd said no, a little too emphatically, I thought, and quickly changed the subject. I'd volunteered that I myself had been so caught up in visions and media and missing cats that I hadn't had time for self-destructive legal activity.

As we headed toward Mama's I noticed a sign on a corner announcing new housing to be built. Already the land adjacent to the Ti-dy Washateria was being cleared and the Ti-dy was boarded up. On the sign was an architectural rendering of one of the prospective houses, designed to resemble an early Texas-style low-slung farmhouse with a narrow gallery running the length of the front. It was the first new housing in Midnight in years. Martin Turner's name was across the bottom of the sign, which led me to theorize to Dude that perhaps his brief interlude with Traci had miraculously led him into new dimensions of profit and community improvement. That would be worthy of a story in the *Citizen*, I thought, and then remembered I didn't have to worry about that anymore.

"Well, I'm glad Traci and Larry have worked it out. Didn't they look happy? There was a kind of radiance about them."

Dude said, "Um . . . ," sounding skeptical. "I thought you were pulling for divorce and a new career?" He seemed genuinely surprised.

I sighed at how out of touch we'd been for him to think that. "Oh, that was ages ago. I'm a changed woman. I'm for love eternal and even the highway patrol if it makes him happy."

Dude turned a corner and then glanced at me through his sexy aviator sunshades. I pulled my new compact from my purse, recalling as I powdered my nose the last one broken and lost on the greasy floor of that Dallas hotel garage. Then I pulled out a Tic Tac and offered one to Dude.

"You didn't think even war and pestilence could change me, huh?" I asked lightly, surprising myself that I sounded like the predisaster person I used to be.

While we stopped at a red light, I felt myself tilting toward my recent bitchy mode. "I'm glad things are going well for everyone," I said, sarcastically, but suddenly I wanted to change. After all, I was a woman who'd been proclaimed a sort of hero in the national press. I should be serene and gracious. I wore an expensive yellow linen dress that hadn't even been on sale, thus proclaiming that the days of mourning in my navy funeral dress were over. I should be proud of my good fortune. This man isn't my life, and after all, I'm not starving in Africa or hooked on crack, and my cats are back in Dallas, returned to their normal state of mental health.

Dude pulled up before Mama's and stopped. Then he squinched his eyes the way some people do when they're about to make an admission.

"You didn't need to change," he said. "There wasn't anything wrong with the way you were," he said.

I looked at him to see if he was kidding. He wasn't. Below the sunshades, his face was glum and sincere. Well, a bone from out of the blue, I thought, a confession of ill faith. But if he was going to be honest, I'd have to be, too.

"Yes, there was," I said, glancing out the window. "I'm not saying you were in any way justified, understand, not by a long shot. But I was as bad as Daddy, always looking back when what could have made me happy was right there in the present. I'll never make that mistake again."

He was grasping the steering wheel with both hands, which was unlike him.

"Just don't blame yourself. That wouldn't be fair."

"That certainly wasn't the drift I picked up first time around," I said, studying him.

He was silent a minute.

"That was . . . defensive," he said. "The truth is, I should have made it clear that I resented your detachment. You were always, in a certain way, at arm's length. I should have insisted we work it out. But I let it go. . . . I guess I hoped it would work itself out. It didn't."

"Oh," I said, as if he'd pinched me. Suddenly a lot of cards fell into place. I had understood it all along, I just hadn't believed my breeziness was that important. Obviously, I was wrong. It had to do with pride as much as anything else. Only that was too simple, another instance of my wanting to simplify.

"Well, I appreciate a tad of truth now and then. But if all of a sudden we're being honest," I said, "I should state that despite all statements to the contrary, I am not anxious or eager for a divorce." The words seemed to hang there between us, thick and concrete and permanent like a Metroplex overpass. Then, being basically the good man he is, he lowered his opaque aviator sunshades and let me see his pained response as I went on: "What I really wanted for a long time was to go to sleep and wake up, and it wouldn't have happened. But of course, that's impossible. Now I realize we're both changed, we would be different whatever happened. So I don't know where that leaves us. . . ."

I longed for him to pass on more good news, but we sat there a minute looking at one another and suddenly I felt something had changed, was changing, there was the slightest alteration in atmospheric pressure. Maybe the admission of truths had somehow altered the air around us and begun some process that would change everything, that would unravel and create an entirely new configuration.

I opened the car door and Mama's neighbor adjusted a vertical blind and surveyed us as Sinatra sang "There's a Small Hotel." Already the St. Augustine grass looked wilted, as though it hadn't been watered first thing that morning. I pulled my sticky new dress out in front, fanned my lonely bosom, and on this special day of harmony, new beginnings, and pardon, I laid down my anger. I took a deep breath and surveyed the mesquite tree beside Mama's house. When everything for miles around is dead as a doornail from the heat and drought, the indomitable mesquite tree survives because its roots burrow down till it finds water. It will survive fire and brimstone and all manner of debilitating civilization. In parts of West Texas they've been trying to rid the land of mesquite for decades, burning it and hacking it, but still it hangs in there, tough like the land and the people around it.

I looked back at Dude and wondered for the millionth time in my life why men wore jackets in the Texas heat. I thought also how surprised and doubtless grateful he'd be if I left without any kind of set-to.

"Thanks for the ride," I said. I gave him a brief, energy-saver smile and got out of the car, whereupon the sun hit me like a sledgehammer. But I straightened up, caught myself, pausing a second before I slammed the door. Then I sucked in my stomach and straightened my shoulders and walked around the front of the car, and gave him a brief wave as he drove away.

Above the mesquite, the vast sky was a pearly blue with a low line of pink clouds strung like Lilly's pink pearl necklace across the horizon. On the porch I sat in one of Mama's old white metal lawn chairs that have been repainted probably twenty times. Sitting there, I saw myself back in square one. Square one? I'd never before wondered what exactly that meant—"square one." Maybe the bottle when it's just set on the floor before the spin. Or maybe it's that place of origin you must pull yourself away from to see yourself clearly, and not through a glass darkly. Midnight, then. Surely Midnight was square one for me. But I was leaving. Within days I'd be out of there, back to those tall glass towers, back to navigating the Pearl Expressway, the woman in the navy Prelude snickering at all the car phones, not exactly starting over again, but carrying considerably more baggage than before, the woman with the one-margarita limit determined to be in control of her life. Then I felt a power suddenly, like when NASA control says, "Three, two, one, liftoff," and the rocket engines ignite, and the rocket hovers there uncertainly for just an instant before it rises, as if it were briefly reluctant to leave the earth for the unknown.

By September, when my burgundy chrysanthemums were blooming beside the front door, I was back in North Dallas, my life on go again. After my multiple media experiences I'd said adieu to cowboy photos and wrangled a job at that other

Dallas newspaper—not Dude's—interpreting the life-styles of those on the outskirts of the Metroplex for those button-down types in the tall glass buildings who don't always understand what the natives are talking about. I'd marketed myself as something of an expert on urban expansion and on those citizens still bound up in traditions of the past, those who hadn't escaped the cultural midnight of belonging to neither the old day nor the new.

In Midnight, Lilly left Happy Acres and moved in with Mama. Cissy talked Mama into putting a soft copper tint on her hair. Frequently I make the trek to Midnight and join Mama, Lilly, and Katie for a fast game of forty-two. Occasionally, I take them to a swing dance in Irving where *all* of us dance. The Spanish villa is slowly, though not obviously, materializing, and several times Mama, Traci, and I have prepared meals together with no one's being stabbed. Larry and Traci are expecting another baby and Traci, too, has promised me if it's a boy she won't name him Elvis. The latest possibility I heard was Hunter.

The *Citizen* has continued in pretty much its time-honored fashion with Jud still clanging away and Mr. Chapman, Sr., making no tumultuous waves. In a follow-up to the yellow-cat gulag, the *Citizen* reported that cats in general live for an average of twelve years.

Once in a while I receive a newsletter published by Buddy Branch at his miracle support ranch somewhere in California.

Back in Dallas, with two cats and a half-empty house, I confess, there were times when I considered breaking down on the North Dallas toll road myself. However, despite Dude's experience, I knew that would be, after all, the ultimate in spin the bottle, and despite the Marfa lights and even if there is some element of life that's unavoidably random, I realize that most of us have to make our own miracles.

One Saturday afternoon just before Thanksgiving, Larry came careening into the driveway on two patrol car wheels to report that his father was going to ask me to dinner on my birthday.

"So?" I did not grasp the enormity of this news immediately.

"I think they've broken up."

"Dude and Marilyn?"

Larry nodded, grinning, reveling in his new role as counselor to the older generation. He seemed to be taking some credit for this miracle of change.

"I think so," he said.

"Well, that doesn't necessarily mean a thing," I said, turning away, though my immediate instinct was to zip over to Dude's short-lease condo and circle the block honking like a teenager. But what could I do really but vow to do my workout video regularly and wait.

A week later I received a phone call from Dude Reynolds asking me to have dinner with him on Friday night.

"Why?" I asked bluntly.

He said my cultural insights into the bizarre clashes of the expanding Metroplex were something he'd like to discuss with me.

"My consulting rate is a hundred dollars an hour," I informed him.

"Come on, Dinah," he said. "I'm paying for dinner," and he mentioned my very favorite restaurant.

Friday night there was a nice ring of that F-sharp doorbell, and behind the cherry door stood Dude with a box of tea roses, which I adore, and a new wok. That instant in the doorway seems a glowing suspended moment, something like a sudden roiling path of light opening into a heavenly future. This was followed by another instant, when my grateful, loving soul was flooded with the vivid memory of pain and suffering from the North Dallas toll road breakdown and its aftermath, indicating an appropriate response might be a moment of mayhem with roses and wok.

"Shall I ring again?" Dude asked me.

I stepped back for him to enter what had been our nice living room, now empty except for that magnificent fiddle-leaf fig plant stretching itself across a bare wall toward a skylight.

"Second thoughts?" he inquired.

I faced him. "Emotional overload in a state of sensory deprivation," I answered. We looked at one another, unsure of the next move.

Will such honesty win the day? I'm not sure. It is still unclear if I will ever lean casually across a car and wipe a speck of shaving cream from Dude's ear. Certainly I will never again be so dispassionate about such loving intimacy or so casual about the welfare of my own sad heart. Larry keeps assuring me that it ain't over till the fat lady sings, whatever that means. And with Cissy and Traci phoning regularly to offer counseling, how can I go wrong, whatever happens?

Meanwhile, should Buddy Branch ever ask me to write an editorial for his newsletter, I'll mention the miracle of love surviving fantasy, not to mention bigamy. I will also mention the minor miracle of sitting across the breakfast table from someone for twenty or so years, with the ever-present threat of egg-on-the-face, and still maybe being loved.

So, believing in that kind of miracle, I am here in Dallas, looking to rise again, like the State itself.

As Mama would say, thank you very much.